THE RUINS OF EARTH

THE RUINS

An Anthology of Stories

Edited b

OF EARTH

f the Immediate Future

THOMAS M. DISCH

G. P. PUTNAM'S SONS, New York

This book is for my niece Caroline
and my nephew Daniel.
May they enjoy the year 2000
as much as I enjoyed 1970.

CONTENTS

Introduction:
ON SAVING THE WORLD
by Thomas M. Disch

In 1953 when I entered high school there was a feeling in Roseville, the suburb we'd just moved to, that the world was very rich. The high school itself, if only by the magnificence of its parking lot, expressed an almost fanatic faith in the growth of the GNP. Each year the marshlands surrounding Roseville yielded larger and lovelier supermarkets. Each year wider highways glittered with longer cars—and their chrome, their colors!

So long ago. The very names of those colors have been forgotten. It was a beautiful world, and it was impossible, living in it, not to believe that it existed.

1953 was also the golden age of a certain kind of science fiction. The best works of Arthur Clarke, Alfred Bester, Kornbluth and Pohl had just come out or were just about to. Whatever their differences the writers of that golden age shared the basic dream of the fifties (though they were ready sometimes to hint that it might be a nightmare), the faith that had built Roseville, its high school and highways, as surely as the Christian faith built Chartres—a faith in Technology.

This is how Fred Pohl expressed it in his classic tale from 1954, "The Midas Plague":

> Malthus was right—for a civilization without machines, automatic factories, hydroponics and food synthesis, nuclear breeder plants, ocean mining for metals and minerals. . . .
> And a vastly increased supply of labor. . . .
> And architecture that rose high in the air and dug deep in the ground and floated far out on the water on piers and pontoons . . . architecture that could be poured one day and lived in the next. . . .
> And robots.
> Above all, robots . . . robots to burrow and haul and smelt and fabricate, to build and farm and weave and sew.

What the land lacked in wealth, the sea was made to yield, and the laboratory invented the rest . . . and the factories became a pipeline of plenty, churning out enough to feed and clothe and house a dozen worlds.

Limitless discovery, infinite power in the atom, tireless labor of humanity and robots, mechanization that drove jungle and swamp and ice off the Earth, and put up office buildings and manufacturing centers and rocket ports in their place. . . .

The pipeline of production spewed out riches that no king in the time of Malthus could have known.

"The Midas Plague" is, of course, a satire on the affluent society, a broad exaggeration of suburban realities, and yet I hear in the lines I've quoted the accents of a true believer. Pohl, while he deplores the effluvia of consumer goods that were drowning us, accepted the technology that produced those goods as a fact of existence, something standing outside the realm of choice, a universal law.

2001, the Kubrick/Clarke collaboration, represents the apotheosis of 1953, with respect both to its technology and its science fiction. This accounts for the beauty and the terror of that movie. It accounts, too, for its hostile reception in some of the s-f circles best equipped to appreciate its excellences. For with devastating clarity it showed that the physical grandeur of the Space Program can only be achieved at ruinous spiritual cost. Technology was equated with the curse of Cain.

The fifties were also the age of the Bomb. Nuclear catastrophe and its aftermath was then, for most of us, the worst nightmare we could imagine. It was unequivocally awful and (unlike today's horrors) *direct*. The bombs themselves were measured in units of how many millions of us they would kill—in "megadeaths."

One learned to live with the bombs largely by looking the other way, by concentrating on the daytime, suburban side of existence. And here we are, a quarter century after Hiroshima, and the bombs still haven't dropped. Looking the other way seems to have worked.

Now, in 1971, it isn't possible to look the other way. It is the daytime, suburban side of existence that has become our nightmare. In effect the bombs are already dropping—as more carbon monoxide pollutes the air of Roseville, as mercury poisons our waters, our fish, and ourselves, and as one by one our technology extinguishes the forms of life upon which our own life on this planet depends. These are not catastrophes of the imagination—they are what's happening.

What is happening? No string of horror stories from the New York *Times* can properly convey what the ecological crisis means, since it's in the nature of news stories to be about somebody else's disasters. Let me instead cite some of the ways the crisis has affected me, personally.

In January of 1966, living on the southern coast of Spain and loving it, I came down with a bad case of hepatitis. I never understood why, except that it was going around. Presently there is an epidemic of hepatitis in Naples thanks to the pollution of the blue waters of the bay. Neapolitans are great seafood eaters. So was I on the Costa del Sol.

I've lived nine of the last thirteen years in Manhattan. There's no city in America I'm happier in, but during the last so often I've come to the reluctant decision that it isn't safe here any more. There are fifty good reasons I could name, and probably as many more I don't know of. My best friend agrees and is taking his family to the country. Too much I get the feeling that I'm playing Russian roulette: each passing month that the Worst hasn't happened is an empty chamber of the revolver. But one of them, sure as hell, *is* loaded.

The question, then, is where to go. Everyone I know is asking himself that question, and there aren't any really good answers.

Not *another* poisoned city, surely.

For a while I'd considered Milford, Pennsylvania. I lived there a year, and I had friends there. It's a beautiful small town, especially in the fall, and it's within striking distance of New York. However —the Army engineers are putting in a dam across the Delaware. Everyone, except the real estate speculators, are against it. It promises to be an ecological and social disaster, since the artificial lake that will be formed will be turned into a mammoth recreation area for vacationers from the city. The woods already are being subdivided. In any case, my friends will be flooded out of their home.

Minnesota? Early in 1970 I revisited the scenes of my childhood nearby Mille Lacs Lake. The old path through the woods was gone. In its place the tracks of snowmobiles had bulldozed wide swaths through the brush. I struck off in another direction and found a junked car. Nowhere in those woods (it was nearly midnight) was it possible to escape the constant whirr of traffic on the throughway that now encircles the lake.

Clearly, I'll have to look farther afield. Canada, where my brother lives now? Well, they've outlawed hunting this fall in one of the provinces. Game fowl have dangerous concentrations of . . . I forget whether it was mercury or DDT. Similarly 300 miles of the Wisconsin River can't be fished.

The mountains? The father of another friend of mine just bought *one* of the Rockies and is converting it to a ski resort. But I suppose there are still a few mountains left.

Finally I decided on France. The classic French cuisine can't survive the end of this decade, and I'd like to think I've had a taste of it before it becomes mere legend. I have a similar sense of urgency about seeing Italy, Venice especially.

Anxiety? Yes, of course. What did *you* do in the blitz?

1953 was also the beginning of the age of large-scale "social engineering." The two big pioneers in this endeavor, IBM and Rand Corporation, developed a new image of man, man as a biologic computer, a being infinitely manipulable. (This task of image-making is one that has traditionally been assumed by religion. In this light IBM and Rand can be seen as rival churches of the new technological faith.) To illustrate the relation between this image and our changing environment, I quote from an essay* by one of the most eloquent critics of the Technocracy, Theodore Roszak:

> What we have here is a transformation of the environment that breaks with the human past as dramatically and violently as our astronauts in their space rockets break from the gravitational grip of earth. And the destination toward which we move is already clearly before us in the image of the astronaut. For here we have a man encapsulated in a *wholly* man-made environment, sealed up and surviving securely in a plastic womb that leaves nothing to chance or natural process. Nothing "irrational"—meaning nothing man has not made, or made allowance for—can intrude upon the astronaut's life-space. . . . As for the astronaut himself, he is almost invariably a military man. And how significant it is that so much of our future, *both as it appears in science fiction and as it emerges in science fact,* should be dominated by the modern soldier—the most machine-tooled and psychically regi-

* "The Artificial Environment," in *New American Review* 9, April, 1970. For a more developed excoriation of technology's effects on a fragile humanity, Roszak's *The Making of a Counter-Culture* is a delight of single-mindedness.

mented breed of human being: a man programmed and under control from within as from without.

I feel there is justice in Roszak's accusation (the italics in the passage I quoted are mine) that too often science fiction has given its implicit moral sanction to this double transformation of man and his environment. Roszak notes the prevalence of military-type heroes; earlier I pointed out the faith, usually unquestioning, in a future in which Technology provides, unstintingly and without visible difficulty, for man's needs. The very form of the so-called "hard-core" s-f saga, in which a single quasi-technical problem is presented and then solved, encourages that peculiar tunnel vision and singleness of focus that is the antithesis of an "ecological" consciousness in which cause-and-effect would be regarded as a web rather than as a single-strand chain. The heroes of these earlier tales often behave in ways uncannily reminiscent of psychotics' case histories; personal relationships (as between the crew members of a spaceship) can be chillingly lacking in affect. These human robots inhabited landscapes that mirrored their own alienation. This is, in fact, the special beauty of the best of older science fiction—of van Vogt, say, or darkest Burroughs. As later writers began to be conscious of the social and psychological ramifications of their imagery, a tension developed in many of them (Bradbury is a good example) between the sheer power of their naïve invention and a desire to bring the "secret subject" of their fictions up to the level of consciousness, their own and their readers'. Predictably these stories often suffered, either from stifled inventiveness or from the off-putting self-absorption of a beginning analysand.

In the best contemporary s-f, however, a new harmony is sometimes achieved, a coming-together of invention and awareness. Not only are the figures and the landscapes of the dream resonantly congruent with each other, but now there is also a sense that the dreamer has come to understand the *meaning* of his dream without outside assistance.

Philip K. Dick and J. G. Ballard are the two writers who have achieved this new synthesis most consistently. Is it coincidental that they should also be the two whose work bears most immediately and directly upon the present ecological crisis? In book after book they have warned us of how we are destroying our world and prophesied of how that world, wounded, will take its revenge.

Ballard's *The Burning World* is probably the single best fictional account of an ecological disaster: its rationale is plausible, its images are crystalline, its allegory is deliberate, precise, and always modest. In the ideal ten-volume version of this anthology *The Burning World* would be Volume I.

It's difficult to find a single work to represent Dick. His novels are more impressive collectively than each by each. Though he's made no attempt to create a consistent, chronological "future-history" of his own, his novels form a unified sequence of mounting intensity and of a kind of eyewitness credibility unmatched in the field. He confronts the horrors of the near-future with a coolness and steadiness of gaze that makes Herman Kahn seem sentimental, with a sense of humor blacker than an Ethiop's ear, and with the quiet compassions one expects only from someone who has survived every disaster known to man.

All this press-agentry because I feel that these two writers—along with Harrison, Leiber, Vonnegut and others in this book—have played a significant part in the very urgent business of saving the world. Not just because they have illuminated, in their stories here and there, central aspects of the crisis now upon us, but because for two decades, while most of us listened, enraptured, to the siren-songs of Technology, they have never ceased to warn of the reefs awaiting us on the other side of the song.

Concerning the stories:

The theme of this book is ecological catastrophe, and the uncomfortable truth is that several of these catastrophes don't require prophecy, only simple observation. Accordingly the first three stories aren't s-f at all, unless one allows the *s* in that abbreviation to stand for "speculative." They show our world—*The Way It Is.*

The other three divisions of the book are rather more arbitrary. Harry Harrison's "Roommates" is an unbeatable example of *How It Could Get Worse,* but it is included in the previous section, *Why It Is the Way It Is.* For its length, or for any length, I know of no more persuasive analysis of the *inevitable* decline of American society as a direct consequence of overpopulation. Most other writers seem to regard the population explosion in somewhat the same light as time travel or ESP—a traditional theme upon which to embroider their own whimsical variations. Harrison clearly believes in the dismal world he describes.

There has never been a more terrifying picture of nature gone awry than Daphne du Maurier's classic tale, "The Birds." Evan Hunter's screenplay for Hitchcock's film was a vast injustice to a good story. Though the birds' awful doings are never explained in a proper science-fictional sense, the story can be read as a parable of our whole environmental crisis: Nature, abused, will take her revenge.

It is also possible by ingenious reasoning and casuistry to show how both Kenward Elmslie's "Accident Vertigo" and R. A. Lafferty's "Groaning Hinges of the World" describe ecological catastrophes, but mostly they are present to offer a moment or two of playfulness (albeit, rather dark) in the midst of what is otherwise a grim lot.

Finally, by way of self-advertisement (which is the purpose, at root, of any introduction), it should be pointed out that of the sixteen stories assembled here, six are original to this volume (those by Wolfe, Harrison, Lafferty, Effinger, Mundis, and Kagan). A moiety of the remainder were published far off the beaten s-f track, in magazines ranging from *Esquire* to *Paris Review*. It is my hope that even the three or four stories that may be familiar to the dedicated fan will take on new shades of meaning in their new context.

I happen to be very optimistic about this new decade—*and* the decades to come—but I keep bumping into people who do not share my enthusiasm. They seem gloomy and disheartened, and I think I know why.

In recent years, several acorns have fallen on the citizens of the United States—in the form of inflation and the war in Vietnam and racial and campus unrest—and suddenly all of the bird-brained Chicken Lickens from coast to coast have come waddling out of their henhouses to cackle about impending disaster. This could have its amusing aspect but, unfortunately, some of us are beginning to listen to these crapehangers and to have doubts about ourselves and this great nation of ours.

. . . . Perhaps if we get to know them better, we can laugh them out of existence—or at least off the airwaves and out of the pages of our newspapers and magazines.

—from a talk delivered July 21, 1970, at the 71st Congress of the National Retail Hardware Association, by Thomas R. Shepard, Jr., the publisher of *Look* magazine.

DEER IN THE WORKS

by Kurt Vonnegut, Jr.

The big black stacks of the Ilium Works of the Federal Apparatus Corporation spewed acid fumes and soot over the hundreds of men and women who were lined up before the red-brick employment office. It was summer. The Ilium Works, already the second-largest industrial plant in America, was increasing its staff by one third in order to meet armament contracts. Every ten minutes or so, a company policeman opened the employment-office door, letting out a chilly gust from the air-conditioned interior and admitting three more applicants.

"Next three," said the policeman.

A middle-sized man in his late twenties, his young face camouflaged with a mustache and spectacles, was admitted after a four-hour wait. His spirits and the new suit he'd bought for the occasion were wilted by the fumes and the August sun, and he'd given up lunch in order to keep his place in line. But his bearing remained jaunty. He was the last, in his group of three, to face the receptionist.

"Screw-machine operator, ma'am," said the first man.

"See Mr. Cormody in booth seven," said the receptionist.

"Plastic extrusion, miss," said the next man.

"See Mr. Hoyt in booth two," she said. "Skill?" she asked the urbane young man in the wilted suit. "Milling machine? Jig borer?"

"Writing," he said. "Any kind of writing."

"You mean advertising and sales promotion?"

"Yes—that's what I mean."

She looked doubtful. "Well, I don't know. We didn't put out a call for that sort of people. You can't run a machine, can you?"

"Typewriter," he said jokingly.

The receptionist was a sober young woman. "The company does not use male stenographers," she said. "See Mr. Dilling in booth twenty-six. He just might know of some advertising-and-sales-promotion-type job."

He straightened his tie and coat, forced a smile that implied he was looking into jobs at the Works as sort of a lark. He walked into booth twenty-six and extended his hand to Mr. Dilling, a man of his own age. "Mr. Dilling, my name is David Potter. I was curious to know what openings you might have in advertising and sales promotion, and thought I'd drop in for a talk."

Mr. Dilling, an old hand at facing young men who tried to hide their eagerness for a job, was polite but outwardly unimpressed. "Well, you came at a bad time, I'm afraid, Mr. Potter. The competition for that kind of job is pretty stiff, as you perhaps know, and there isn't much of anything open just now."

David nodded. "I see." He had had no experience in asking for a job with a big organization, and Mr. Dilling was making him aware of what a fine art it was—if you couldn't run a machine. A duel was under way.

"But have a seat anyway, Mr. Potter."

"Thank you." He looked at his watch. "I really ought to be getting back to my paper soon."

"You work on a paper around here?"

"Yes. I own a weekly paper in Dorset, about ten miles from Ilium."

"Oh—you don't say. Lovely little village. Thinking of giving up the paper, are you?"

"Well, no—not exactly. It's a possibility. I bought the paper soon after the war, so I've been with it for eight years, and I don't want to go stale. I might be wise to move on. It all depends on what opens up."

"You have a family?" said Mr. Dilling pleasantly.

"Yes. My wife, and two boys and two girls."

"A nice, big, well-balanced family," said Mr. Dilling. "And you're so young, too."

"Twenty-nine," said David. He smiled. "We didn't plan it to be quite that big. It's run to twins. The boys are twins, and then, several days ago, the girls came."

"You don't say!" said Mr. Dilling. He winked. "That would certainly start a young man thinking about getting a little security, eh, with a family like that?"

Both of them treated the remark casually, as though it were no more than a pleasantry between two family men. "It's what we wanted, actually, two boys, two girls," said David. "We didn't expect to get them this quickly, but we're glad now. As far as security goes—well, maybe I flatter myself, but I think the administrative and writing experience I've had running the paper would be worth a good bit to the right people, if something happened to the paper."

"One of the big shortages in this country," said Dilling philosophically, concentrating on lighting a cigarette, "is men who know how to do things, and know how to take responsibility and get things done. I only wish there were better openings in advertising and sales promotion than the ones we've got. They're important, interesting jobs, understand, but I don't know how you'd feel about the starting salary."

"Well, I'm just trying to get the lay of the land, now—to see how things are. I have no idea what salary industry might pay a man like me, with my experience."

"The question experienced men like yourself usually ask is: How high can I go and how fast? And the answer to that is that the sky is the limit for a man with drive and creative ambition. And he can go up fast or slow, depending on what he's willing to do and capable of putting into the job. We might start out a man like you at, oh, say, a hundred dollars a week, but that isn't to say you'd be stuck at that level for two years or even two months."

"I suppose a man could keep a family on that until he got rolling," said David.

"You'd find the work in the publicity end just about the same as what you're doing now. Our publicity people have high standards for writing and editing and reporting, and our publicity releases don't wind up in newspaper editors' wastebaskets. Our people do a professional job, and are well-respected as journalists." He stood. "I've got a little matter to attend to—take me about ten minutes. Could you possibly stick around? I'm enjoying our talk."

David looked at his watch. "Oh—guess I could spare another ten or fifteen minutes."

Dilling was back in his booth in three minutes, chuckling over some private joke. "Just talking on the phone with Lou Flammer, the publicity supervisor. Needs a new stenographer. Lou's a card. Everybody here is crazy about Lou. Old weekly man himself, and I guess that's where he learned to be so easy to get along with. Just to feel him out for the hell of it, I told him about you. I didn't commit you to anything —just said what you told me, that you were keeping your eyes open. And guess what Lou said?"

"Guess what, Nan," said David Potter to his wife on the telephone. He was wearing only his shorts, and was phoning from the company hospital. "When you come home from the hospital tomorrow, you'll be coming home to a solid citizen who pulls down a hundred and ten dollars a week, *every* week. I just got my badge and passed my physical!"

"Oh?" said Nan, startled. "It happened awfully fast, didn't it? I didn't think you were going to plunge right in."

"What's there to wait for?"

"Well—I don't know. I mean, how do you know what you're getting into? You've never worked for anybody but yourself, and don't know anything about getting along in a huge organization. I knew you were going to talk to the Ilium people about a job, but I thought you planned to stick with the paper another year, anyway."

"In another year I'll be thirty, Nan."

"Well?"

"That's pretty old to be starting a career in industry. There are guys my age here who've been working their way up for ten years. That's pretty stiff competition, and it'll be that much stiffer a year from now. And how do we know Jason will still want to buy the paper a year from now?" Ed Jason was David's assistant, a recent college graduate whose father wanted to buy the paper for him. "And this job that opened up today in publicity won't be open a year from now, Nan. Now was the time to switch—this afternoon!"

Nan sighed. "I suppose. But it doesn't seem like you. The Works are fine for some people; they seem to thrive on that life. But you've always been so free. And you love the paper—you know you do."

"I do," said David, "and it'll break my heart to let it go. It was a swell thing to do when we had no kids, but it's a shaky living now— with the kids to educate and all."

"But, hon," said Nan, "the paper is making money."

"It could fold like that," said David, snapping his fingers. "A daily could come in with a one-page insert of Dorset news, or—"

"Dorset likes its little paper too much to let that happen. They like you and the job you're doing too much."

David nodded. "What about ten years from now?"

"What about ten years from now in the Works? What about ten years from now anywhere?"

"It's a better bet that the Works will still be here. I haven't got the right to take long chances any more, Nan, not with a big family counting on me."

"It won't be a very happy big family, darling, if you're not doing what you want to do. I want you to go on being happy the way you have been—driving around the countryside, getting news and talking and selling ads; coming home and writing what you want to write, what you believe in. You in the Works!"

"It's what I've got to do."

"All right, if you say so. I've had my say."

"It's still journalism, high-grade journalism," said David.

"Just don't sell the paper to Jason right away. Put him in charge, but let's wait a month or so, please?"

"No sense in waiting, but if you really want to, all right." David held up a brochure he'd been handed after his physical examination was completed. "Listen to this, Nan: under the company Security Package, I get ten dollars a day for hospital expenses in case of illness, full pay for twenty-six weeks, a hundred dollars for special hospital expenses. I get life insurance for about half what it would cost on the outside. For whatever I put into government bonds under the payroll-savings plan, the company will give me a five per cent bonus in company stock—twelve years from now. I get two weeks' vacation with pay each year, and, after fifteen years, I get three weeks. Get free membership in the company country club. After twenty-five years, I'll be eligible for a pension of at least a hundred and twenty-five dollars a month, and much more if I rise in the organization and stick with it for more than twenty-five years!"

"Good heavens!" said Nan.

"I'd be a damn fool to pass that up, Nan."

"I still wish you'd waited until the little girls and I were home and settled, and you got used to them. I feel you were panicked into this."

"No, no—this is it, Nan. Give the little girls a kiss apiece for me. I've got to go now, and report to my new supervisor."

"Your what?"

"Supervisor."

"Oh. I thought that's what you said, but I couldn't be sure."

"Good-by, Nan."

"Good-by, David."

David clipped his badge to his lapel, and stepped out of the hospital and onto the hot asphalt floor of the world within the fences of the Works. Dull thunder came from the buildings around him, a truck honked at him, and a cinder blew in his eye. He dabbed at the cinder with a corner of his handkerchief and finally got it out. When his vision was restored, he looked about himself for Building 31, where his new office and supervisor were. Four busy streets fanned out from where he stood, and each stretched seemingly to infinity.

He stopped a passerby who was in less of a desperate hurry than the rest. "Could you tell me, please, how to find Building 31, Mr. Flammer's office?"

The man he asked was old and bright-eyed, apparently getting as much pleasure from the clangor and smells and nervous activity of the Works as David would have gotten from April in Paris. He squinted at David's badge and then at his face. "Just starting out, are you?"

"Yes sir. My first day."

"What do you know about that?" The old man shook his head wonderingly, and winked. "Just starting out. Building 31? Well, sir, when I first came to work here in 1899, you could see Building 31 from here, with nothing between us and it but mud. Now it's all built up. See that water tank up there, about a quarter of a mile? Well, Avenue 17 branches off there, and you follow that almost to the end, then cut across the tracks, and— Just starting out, eh? Well, I'd better walk you up there. Came here for just a minute to talk to the pension folks, but that can wait. I'd enjoy the walk."

"Thank you."

"Fifty-year man, I was," he said proudly, and he led David up avenues and alleys, across tracks, over ramps and through tunnels, through buildings filled with spitting, whining, grumbling machinery, and down corridors with green walls and numbered black doors.

"Can't be a fifty-year man no more," said the old man pityingly. "Can't come to work until you're eighteen nowadays, and you got to retire when you're sixty-five." He poked his thumb under his lapel to make a small gold button protrude. On it was the number "50" superimposed on the company trademark. "Something none of you youngsters can look forward to wearing some day, no matter how much you want one."

"Very nice button," said David.

The old man pointed out a door. "Here's Flammer's office. Keep your mouth shut till you find out who's who and what *they* think. Good luck."

Lou Flammer's secretary was not at her desk, so David walked to the door of the inner office and knocked.

"Yes?" said a man's voice sweetly. "Please come in."

David opened the door. "Mr. Flammer?"

Lou Flammer was a short, fat man in his early thirties. He beamed at David. "What can I do to help you?"

"I'm David Potter, Mr. Flammer."

Flammer's Santa-Claus-like demeanor decayed. He leaned back, propped his feet on his desk top, and stuffed a cigar, which he'd concealed in his cupped hand, into his large mouth. "Hell—thought you were a scoutmaster." He looked at his desk clock, which was mounted in a miniature of the company's newest automatic dishwasher. "Boy scouts touring the Works. Supposed to stop in here fifteen minutes ago for me to give 'em a talk on scouting and industry. Fifty-six per cent of Federal Apparatus' executives were eagle scouts."

David started to laugh, but found himself doing it all alone, and he stopped. "Amazing figure," he said.

"It *is*," said Flammer judiciously. "Says something for scouting and something for industry. Now, before I tell you where your desk is, I'm supposed to explain the rating-sheet system. That's what the Manuals say. Dilling tell you about that?"

"Not that I recall. There was an awful lot of information all at once."

"Well, there's nothing much to it," said Flammer. "Every six months a rating sheet is made out on you, to let you and to let us know just where you stand, and what sort of progress you've been making. Three people who've been close to your work make out independent ratings of you, and then all the information is brought together on a master copy—with carbons for you, me, and Personnel, and the original for the head of the Advertising and Sales Promotion Division. It's very helpful for everybody, you most of all, if you take it the right way." He waved a rating sheet before David. "See? Blanks for appearance, loyalty, promptness, initiative, cooperativeness—things like that. You'll make out rating sheets on other people, too, and whoever does the rating is anonymous."

"I see." David felt himself reddening with resentment. He fought the emotion, telling himself his reaction was a small-town man's—and that it would do him good to learn to think as a member of a great, efficient team.

"Now about pay, Potter," said Flammer, "there'll never be any point in coming in to ask me for a raise. That's all done on the basis of the rating sheets and the salary curve." He rummaged through his drawers and found a graph, which he spread out on his desk. "Here—now you see this curve? Well, it's the average salary curve for men with college educations in the company. See—you can follow it on up. At thirty, the average man makes this much; at forty, this much—and so on. Now, this curve above it shows what men with real growth potential can make. See? It's a little higher and curves upward a little faster. You're how old?"

"Twenty-nine," said David, trying to see what the salary figures were that ran along one side of the graph. Flammer saw him doing it, and pointedly kept them hidden with his forearm.

"Uh-huh." Flammer wet the tip of a pencil with his tongue, and drew a small "x" on the graph, squarely astride the average man's curve. "There *you* are!"

David looked at the mark, and then followed the curve with his eyes across the paper, over little bumps, up gentle slopes, along desolate plateaus, until it died abruptly at the margin which represented age sixty-five. The graph left no questions to be asked and was deaf to argument. David looked from it to the human being he would also be dealing with. "You had a weekly once, did you, Mr. Flammer?"

Flammer laughed. "In my naïve, idealistic youth, Potter, I sold ads to feed stores, gathered gossip, set type, and wrote editorials that were going to save the world, by God."

David smiled admiringly. "What a circus, eh?"

"Circus?" said Flammer. "Freak show, maybe. It's a good way to grow up fast. Took me about six months to find out I was killing myself for peanuts, that a little guy couldn't even save a village three blocks long, and that the world wasn't worth saving anyway. So I started looking out for Number One. Sold out to a chain, came down here, and here I am."

The telephone rang. "Yes?" said Flammer sweetly. "Puh-*bliss*-itee." His benign smile faded. "No. You're kidding, aren't you? Where? Really—this is no gag? All right, all right. Lord! What a time for this to happen. I haven't got anybody here, and I can't get away on account of the goddam boy scouts." He hung up. "Potter—you've got your first assignment. There's a deer loose in the Works!"

"Deer?"

"Don't know how he got in, but he's in. Plumber went to fix a drinking fountain out at the softball diamond across from Building 217, and flushed a deer out from under the bleachers. Now they got him cornered up around the metallurgy lab." He stood and hammered on his desk. "Murder! The story will go all over the country, Potter. Talk about human interest. Front page! Of all the times for Al Tappin to be out at the Ashtabula Works, taking pictures of a new viscometer they cooked up out there! All right—I'll call up a hack photographer downtown, Potter, and get him to meet you out by the metallurgy lab. You get the story and see that he gets the right shots. Okay?"

He led David into the hallway. "Just go back the way you came, turn left instead of right at fractional horsepower motors, cut through hydraulic engineering, catch bus eleven on Avenue 9, and it'll take you right there. After you get the story and pictures, we'll get them cleared by the law division, the plant security officer, our department head and buildings and grounds, and shoot them right out. Now get going. That deer isn't on the payroll—he isn't going to wait for you. Come to work today—tomorrow your work will be on every front page in the country, if we can get it approved. The name of the photographer you're going to meet is McGarvey. Got it? You're in the big time now, Potter. We'll all be watching." He shut the door behind David.

David found himself trotting down the hall, down a stairway, and into an alley, brushing roughly past persons in a race against time. Many turned to watch the purposeful young man with admiration.

On and on he strode, his mind seething with information: *Flammer, Building 31; deer, metallurgy lab; photographer. Al Tappin. No. Al Tappin in Ashtabula.* Flenny *the hack photographer. No.* McCammer. *No. McCammer is new supervisor. Fifty-six per cent eagle scouts. Deer by viscometer laboratory. No. Viscometer in Ashtabula. Call Danner, new supervisor, and get instructions right. Three weeks' vacation after fifteen years. Danner not new supervisor. Anyway, new supervisor in Building 319. No. Fanner in Building 39981983319.*

David stopped, blocked by a grimy window at the end of a blind alley. All he knew was that he'd never been there before, that his memory had blown a gasket, and that the deer was not on the payroll. The air in the alley was thick with tango music and the stench of scorched insulation. David scrubbed away some of the crust on the window with his handkerchief, praying for a glimpse of something that made sense.

Inside were ranks of women at benches, rocking their heads in time to the music, and dipping soldering irons into great nests of colored wires that crept past them on endless belts. One of them looked up and saw David, and winked in tango rhythm. David fled.

At the mouth of the alley, he stopped a man and asked him if he'd heard anything about a deer in the Works. The man shook his head and looked at David oddly, making David aware of how frantic he must look. "I heard it was out by the lab," David said more calmly.

"Which lab?" said the man.

"That's what I'm not sure of," said David. "There's more than one?"

"Chemical lab?" said the man. "Materials testing lab? Paint lab? Insulation lab?"

"No—I don't think it's any of those," said David.

"Well, I could stand here all afternoon naming labs, and probably not hit the right one. Sorry, I've got to go. You don't know what building they've got the differential analyzer in, do you?"

"Sorry," said David. He stopped several other people, none of whom knew anything about the deer, and he tried to retrace his steps to the office of his supervisor, whatever his name was. He was swept this way and that by the currents of the Works, stranded in backwaters, sucked back into the main stream, and his mind was more and more numbed, and the mere reflexes of self-preservation were more and more in charge.

He chose a building at random, and walked inside for a momentary respite from the summer heat, and was deafened by the clangor of steel sheets being cut and punched, being smashed into strange shapes by great hammers that dropped out of the smoke and dust overhead. A hairy, heavily muscled man was seated near the door on a wooden stool, watching a giant lathe turn a bar of steel the size of a silo.

David now had the idea of going through a company phone directory until he recognized his supervisor's name. He called to the machinist from a few feet away, but his voice was lost in the din. He tapped the man's shoulder. "Telephone around here?"

The man nodded. He cupped his hands around David's ear, and shouted. "Up that, and through the—" Down crashed a hammer. "Turn left and keep going until you—" An overhead crane dropped a stack of steel plates. "Four doors down from there is it. Can't miss it."

David, his ears ringing and his head aching, walked into the street again and chose another door. Here was peace and air conditioning. He was in the lobby of an auditorium, where a group of men were examining a box studded with dials and switches that was spotlighted and mounted on a revolving platform.

"Please, miss," he said to a receptionist by the door, "could you tell me where I could find a telephone?"

"It's right around the corner, sir," she said. "But I'm afraid no one is permitted here today but the crystallographers. Are you with them?"

"Yes," said David.

"Oh—well, come right in. Name?"

He told her, and a man sitting next to her lettered it on a badge. The badge was hung on his chest, and David headed for the telephone. A grinning, bald, big-toothed man, wearing a badge that said, "Stan Dunkel, Sales," caught him and steered him to the display.

"Dr. Potter," said Dunkel, "I ask you: is that the way to build an X-ray spectrogoniometer, or is that the way to build an X-ray spectrogoniometer?"

"Yes," said David. "That's the way, all right."

"Martini, Dr. Potter?" said a maid, offering a tray.

David emptied a Martini in one gloriously hot, stinging gulp.

"What features do you want in an X-ray spectrogoniometer, Doctor?" said Dunkel.

"It should be sturdy, Mr. Dunkel," said David, and he left Dunkel there, pledging his reputation that there wasn't a sturdier one on earth.

In the phone booth, David had barely got through the telephone directory's A's before the name of the supervisor miraculously returned to his consciousness: *Flammer!* He found the number and dialed.

"Mr. Flammer's office," said a woman.

"Could I speak to him, please? This is David Potter."

"Oh—Mr. Potter. Well, Mr. Flammer is somewhere out in the Works now, but he left a message for you. He said there's an added twist on the deer story. When they catch the deer, the venison is going to be used at the Quarter-Century Club picnic."

"Quarter-Century Club?" said David.

"Oh, that's really something, Mr. Potter. It's for people who've been with the company twenty-five years or more. Free drinks and cigars, and just the best of everything. They have a wonderful time."

"Anything else about the deer?"

"Nothing he hasn't already told you," she said, and she hung up.

David Potter, with a third Martini in his otherwise empty stomach, stood in front of the auditorium and looked both ways for a deer.

"But our X-ray spectrogoniometer *is* sturdy, Dr. Potter," Stan Dunkel called to him from the auditorium steps.

Across the street was a patch of green, bordered by hedges. David pushed through the hedges into the outfield of a softball diamond. He crossed it and went behind the bleachers, where there was cool shade, and he sat down with his back to a wiremesh fence which separated one end of the Works from a deep pine woods. There were two gates in the fence, but both were wired shut.

David was going to sit there for just a moment, long enough to get his nerve back, to take bearings. Maybe he could leave a message for Flammer, saying he'd suddenly fallen ill, which was essentially true, or—

"There he goes!" cried somebody from the other side of the diamond. There were gleeful cries, shouted orders, the sounds of men running.

A deer with broken antlers dashed under the bleachers, saw David, and ran frantically into the open again along the fence. He ran with a limp, and his reddish-brown coat was streaked with soot and grease.

"Easy now! Don't rush him! Just keep him there. Shoot into the woods, not the Works."

David came out from under the bleachers to see a great semicircle of men, several ranks deep, closing in slowly on the corner of fence in which the deer was at bay. In the front rank were a dozen company policemen with drawn pistols. Other members of the posse carried sticks and rocks and lariats hastily fashioned from wire.

The deer pawed the grass, and bucked, and jerked its broken antlers in the direction of the crowd.

"Hold it!" shouted a familiar voice. A company limousine rumbled across the diamond to the back of the crowd. Leaning out of a window was Lou Flammer, David's supervisor. "Don't shoot until we get a picture of him alive," commanded Flammer. He pulled a photographer out of the limousine, and pushed him into the front rank.

Flammer saw David standing alone by the fence, his back to a gate. "Good boy, Potter," called Flammer. "Right on the ball! Photographer got lost, and I had to bring him here myself."

The photographer fired his flash bulbs. The deer bucked and sprinted along the fence toward David. David unwired the gate, opened it wide. A second later the deer's white tail was flashing through the woods and gone.

The profound silence was broken first by the whistling of a switch engine and then by the click of a latch as David stepped into the woods and closed the gate behind him. He didn't look back.

We are spreading out over the landscape at a phenomenal rate. Highways now cover with concrete an area the size of Massachusetts, Connecticut, Vermont, Rhode Island, and Delaware. William Vogt has recorded the fact that the National Golf Foundation desires to cover an area the size of New Hampshire and Rhode Island with new golf courses. In downtown L.A. 66% of the space is taken up with parking lots or streets; in the whole L.A. area one third of the land is paved. The trend is toward the creation of Los Angeles everywhere.

—David Lyle, in *Esquire*

THREE MILLION SQUARE MILES

by Gene Wolfe

"Hey," Richard Marquer said to his wife Betty one August afternoon. "Hey, ninety percent of the United States is uninhabited." They were reading the Sunday paper.

"That's right," Betty said, "it's parking lots."

"No, really. It says so right here: 'At least ninety percent of the land area of the United States is employed neither in agriculture nor as sites for roads and buildings.'"

"I didn't know Texas was that big."

"Listen, this is serious. Where the hell is it all?"

"Dick, you don't really believe that junk."

"It says so."

"It says the department store is selling percale sheets twenty percent under cost too."

Richard put down his part of the paper and went to the bookcase. After five minutes work with pencil and paper he said, "Bet?"

"What?"

"I've been making some calculations. According to the almanac—"

"That's an old one. Nineteen sixty-eight."

"It still ought to be pretty accurate, and it says there are—get this —two hundred and ninety-six million eight hundred and thirty-six thousand harvested acres in the United States. Now there's six hundred and forty acres in a square mile, so that means about four hundred and sixty-three thousand harvested square miles. Only the gross area of the United States is three *million* six hundred and twenty-eight thousand one hundred and fifty square miles."

"So it isn't ninety percent. You just proved it yourself."

"I'm not arguing about the exact figure, but look at the size of the thing. Say that half as much is taken up for buildings and backyards as for all the farms. That still leaves over three million square miles unaccounted for. More than three quarters of the country."

"Richard?"

"Yes?"

"Richard, do you really think that's really there? That everybody wouldn't go out and grab it?"

"The facts—"

"Dick, those are talking facts—they're not real. It's like what you were telling me when we bought the car, about the miles on the little thing—"

"Odometer."

"You remember? You said they didn't mean anything. It said thirteen thousand but you said it might be fifteen or twenty thousand really. Anything. Or like when they raised the city income tax. They said it was inflation, but if it was inflation everybody's pay would go up too so the city'd get more—only they took another half percent anyway, remember? You could prove they didn't need it, but it didn't mean anything."

"But it has to be somewhere."

"You really think it's out there? With deer on it, and bears? Dick, it's silly."

"Three *million* square miles."

"When we drove to Baltimore last summer to see my mother, did you see any of it?"

Richard shook his head.

"When you flew to Cleveland for the company—"

"It was too foggy. Everything was socked in, and you couldn't see anything but haze."

"From factories! See?" Betty went back to her paper.

That night *The Wizard of Oz* was shown on television for the two hundredth time. July Garland sang "Over the Rainbow."

Richard took to going on drives. He drove, sometimes for two or three or four hours, before coming home from work. He drove weekends, and once when Betty spent a weekend with her mother he drove from six a.m. Saturday until twelve p.m. Sunday and put sixteen hundred miles on the car. He knew all the best ways into and out of the city, and the best places for food and coffee. Once he was the first person to report an accident to the state highway patrol; once he helped college girls change a tire.

At a roadside zoo he made friends with three deer in a pen—a buck with fine antlers nuzzled his hand for popcorn, and Richard said softly, "I bet if they'd let you out you'd find some of them." Later he asked the operator of the zoo if any animals ever escaped.

"Don't worry about that." (He was a desiccated man of fifty who wore checked sports shirts.) "We keep everything secure here. Look at it from my angle—those animals are valuable to me. You think I'd let them get out where they could hurt people?"

Richard said, "I'm not trying to accuse you of anything. I just wondered if any of them ever got loose."

"Not long as I've had the place, and I been here eight years."

Later Richard asked the boy who pitched hay into the deer's pen, and he said, "Last year. The little buck. I guess the big one was giving him a rough time, and he jumped the fence."

"What happened to him?"

"He got out on the highway and got hit by a car."

Richard began measuring the farm woodlots he passed, and the little acres of waste ground. He carried a hundred-foot tape in the car and picked up hitchhikers—mostly college boys with beaded headbands and fringed buckskin shirts—who would help him, holding one end of the tape while Richard trotted past five or six trees to put the other at the margin of a county road.

He stopped more and more often to examine the bodies of dead animals. Betty asked for a trial separation, and he agreed.

He bought four new tires and had his wheel bearings repacked.

At a roadhouse he paid a three-dollar cover and seventy-five cents for beer to watch a dark-haired, dark-eyed girl with a feather in her hair being undressed by a trained raccoon. The girl was called Princess Running Bare, and after Richard had given the waitress five dollars more she sat at his table and sipped coffee royal for half an hour. "All us Indians are alcoholics," Princess Running Bare said, and she said she was half French Canadian and half Cree, and had been born in a Montreal slum. Richard tried to call Betty's mother's from a telephone booth next to the bar, but no one answered. He left the roadhouse and drove all night.

Outside a steel-making town he took the wrong lane of a three-pronged freeway fork and found himself rushing, with a hundred other cars, in a direction in which he had no wish to go. He pulled off at a service park and asked the attendant.

"Lots of them does that," the attendant said, pulling at the bill of his green cap. "You want to go—" and he waved in the direction from which Richard had come.

"Yes," Richard said. He named the Interstate he wished to use, which was not the one he was on. "Southeast." For some reason he added, "I want to go home." It was about nine o'clock.

"Yeah," the attendant said. He looked around conspiratorially. "Tell you what. Out that way 'bout three-quarters of a mile is the eastbound lanes." He waved an arm toward the back of the service park, where uneven, down-sloping ground was thick with dead grass. "Know what I mean? See, this here is four lanes goin' west and over there is where they come back. Now if you keep going the way you are it's seventeen miles until you can get off and cross over. But sometimes people just jump their tires over that little curb at the back of the station and drive across."

"I see," Richard said.

"Only when you come in you come into the fast lane, naturally. Course it's against the law."

"I'll be careful."

"And if I was you I'd walk out a little way first to make sure it isn't too swampy. Usually dry enough, but you wouldn't want to get stuck."

It felt soft under his feet, but not dangerously so. The eastbound lanes, presumably a thousand yards or so ahead, were not visible, and as he walked the gentle slope buried the westbound lanes behind him, and at last even the red roof of the service park. The distant noises of traffic mingled with the sound of the wind. "Here," he said to himself. "Here."

His shoes crushed the soft tunnels of moles. He looked up and saw a bird that might have been a hawk circling. An old, rusted hubcap lying on its face held a cup of water, and mosquito larvae, and he thought of it springing from the wheel of its car and rolling, rolling all this distance across the empty ground. It seemed a long way.

At the top of the next rise he could see the eastbound lanes, and that the rest of the ground was dry enough to drive over. He turned and went back, but found he had somehow lost his way, and that he was a quarter mile at least from the service park where he had left his car. He began walking back to it along the shoulder of the Interstate, but the traffic passing only a few feet to his right at ninety miles an hour frightened him. He moved away from it, and the ground became really swampy, the mud sticking to his shoes and insects buzzing up with each step he took; so that he went back to the shoulder of the highway, still afraid.

Humboldt has written an interesting chapter on the primitive forest, but no one has yet described for me the difference between that wild forest which once occupied our oldest townships and the tame one which I find there today. . . . The civilized man not only clears the land permanently to a great extent, and cultivates open fields, but he tames and cultivates to a certain extent the forest itself. By his mere presence, almost, he changes the nature of the trees as no other creature does. . . .

. . . Maine perhaps will soon be where Massachusetts is. A good part of her territory is already as bare and commonplace as much of our neighborhood, and her villages generally are not so well shaded as ours. . . . The very willow rows lopped every three years for fuel or power, and every sizable pine and oak, or other forest tree, cut down within the memory of man! As if individual speculators were to be allowed to export the clouds out of the sky, or the stars out of the firmament, one by one. We shall be reduced to gnaw the very crust of the earth for nutriment.

—Henry David Thoreau, in *The Maine Woods*

CLOSING WITH NATURE
by Norman Rush

1.

During the cold, featureless spring of 1967, dryness in physical surfaces began to obsess Jill Beal. She connected the obsession with an earlier, persisting feeling of drifting away from Nature just when, at thirty-three, she might be materially requiring its benefits for the first time. As the spring advanced she considered her feelings but was unable to refine them. She felt herself drifting in some way different from the trivial and normal process of becoming absorbed in the superficies of city life. Her skin, particularly the skin of her hands, felt offensively dry to her; she was affected by the dryness of upholsteries and atmospheres; she found herself wanting to experience, at uncomfortably short intervals, the action or sound of water.

On weekends in April she tried to make use of the public parks, with poor results: apparently the parks had become primarily places where urban man went to wreak his hatred of growing things. Her last park experience had ended in an effort to separate two Negro boys preparing to duel with burnt-out fluorescent light tubes across a plot of reseeded lawn. Sex was the other major enterprise going on in the parks. She had expected to have to see a certain amount of solicitation. But she had encountered something worse: mimic sex, prolonged sporadic exchanges of sexual glances and suppressed gestures of gratification, between obvious strangers who would leave singly afterward, apparently satisfied, never to meet again so far as she could tell. All her sympathy for solitary avid men and unprotected women in the parks had fallen away. Sexual negotiations in the parks struck her as an abuse of the system.

She determined to stop thinking about her problem. She attempted to conclude by thinking, This will be my last thought on the subject: Modern man has a problem about Nature, but what it is exactly is also a problem: unfortunately part of the problem is that the ones supposed to expound Nature to us already possess and enjoy it, they live in the country year round, when they write all they do basically is incite envy over what they have, they can't help it, the last thing they do is elucidate anything: so reading is no help: So we should enjoy whatever of Nature comes our way but meantime get out of the area of this problem mentally, if we can.

But her complaint continued, and she decided to force herself to think deeply about its possible personal origins. She felt no real discontent. She had invested her youth in securely escaping an industrial-Great Lakes background, traversing various clerical employments in pursuit of the one situation—which she had visualized as she went—in which her particular talents would be so clearly displayed that she could expect rapid promotion. She had succeeded. She was in a gratifying period of her life, managing a branch office of a technical-book publisher and earning a good salary. Moreover she felt she was succeeding at self-culture: she had developed a range of intellectual interests that she considered unusual for someone who had had only a high school education and had come from a cultureless home. Her parents' minds and lives were closely confined to the caterers' supply company they owned.

She was single, but saw herself as unconcerned about it. She felt she was in her prime. As her career had progressed there had been progress in the duration and strength of her love-attachments (which she thought of as "love-likings," after a line of D. H. Lawrence). She sensed herself entering a zone of final seriousness in her love life. Her current lover, a divorced free-lance architectural photographer in his early forties, was her most presentable so far. He was Jewish but atypical, being blond, ruddy, with pale eyes and thick noticeable fair eyelashes and eyebrows. He dressed and spoke meticulously: he was sometimes taken for a European. His name was Rolf Stein. They got along well. In two years, their only serious argument had been over his contempt for Jews who anglicized their names. He was forthcoming with examples of inept anglicizations: one branch of his family had exchanged Fleishman for Fleshman. She judged her feeling for Rolf to be almost what it would have to be for her to enter into an impulsive marriage. To Rolf she owed her political education. She could describe herself now as a liberal, without hesitation. She was grateful for the combination of backwardness and goodwill that had made her politically attractive to Rolf in the first place.

She was satisfied with her appearance. She felt that she was aging slowly, losing less to age than she was gaining in other ways. She felt herself to be at a point in life at which she could freely stop, withdraw from her usual concerns, and deal with her special problem. She concluded that her complaint was what it appeared to be, and that it could be cured through a sudden and intense immersion in Nature.

2.

She was en route by bus to a resort offering cheap preseason weekend accommodations. The place was a center for labor and liberal conferences and retreats; it was advertised regularly in *The Nation;*

Rolf had gone there once and had liked it; the resort was convenient to the city, lying only ninety miles to the north. She had expressly not registered for the optional program of lectures.

In early evening, satisfied that the bus was travelling in definite country at last, she thought, Now for my final city-tainted thought: What did I have in mind?: Oh, yes, just to remind myself to keep in mind pity for married women, how they can never normally get out and change their condition except in the one pathetic way of infidelity, having to turn what might easily be only a need for Nature into something sexual: They can never approach Nature singly the way a freak unmarried woman can, oh, except possibly through gardening. She occupied herself with images of women frenziedly gardening.

After leaving the toll road the bus began to make local stops. Night arrived. They were in high, wooded foothills. She gave up trying to follow the stops listed in the timetable. At eight the bus halted at the roadside under a sign identifying her resort. A sparsely-lit entry road led uphill through trees toward a form of buildings. Two men sitting near the front rose and preceded her from the bus. She was slow to debark. Outside the bus she paused to watch the insect-turbulence in the illumination around the sign. The two men had continued ahead, walking just rapidly enough to suggest a desire to arrive separately from her.

She thought, I pray God this place isn't faggot, God forbid any fag conceiving of carrying your suitcase: I only see one suitcase between the two of them.

She walked slowly, showing interest in floodlit trees along the way. She thought, I take it these trees are unusual or old, they seem to be, most of them could be either: This must be their main tree: I hate Rolf, what did he say? "Look, Churchill is showing his crotch again" when Churchill was making the vee for victory during the last documentary I promise I will ever attend in this life: This tree amuses me: Also he said Nature was "clean trash": Also his greatest line against Nature was "Contemplating Nature is like staring at the back of someone's head": Rolf thinks he's smart.

On the bus she had made herself lightly nauseous by deep-breathing the metallic atmosphere, in order to stimulate her need for natural relief.

The night was warm. She thought, This is real warmth, I welcome it: heat would be even better.

3.

She thought, Oh, good, another male face constructed perfectly for aging beautifully, one neat deep vertical groove in each cheek going from his cheekbone down to his jawbone, they make perfect age-drains, time runs down them with the least damage to the skin: you see them in faces basically not worth preserving.

"Is this the office?" she asked.

"Yes."

"Well, thank God. You're hard to find, it's amazing I found you."

"Oh, I'm sorry."

"There seems to be a very enthusiastic crowd for your speaker. Judging by the noise."

"Oh, he's fantastic, he always is. Oh, if you miss one of the talks we . . ."

"No, I'm not on that plan."

"Oh, then. Your name is—"

"Beal."

"Oh, yes you wrote us two or so weeks ago, if I recall, about?"

"Right. No, I'm here strictly for relaxation, for the outdoors part."

"Well, you can always change your mind."

"I hope I won't want to."

"Oh, so do we. Have you had your dinner?"

"No, I'm not hungry though."

"When we leave I'll show you the canteen. We stay open until ten thirty."

The clerk picked up her suitcase and led her to her cabin. She followed silently, postponing any active appreciation of the grounds until morning, deliberately remaining dead to her surroundings.

When the clerk had gone she casually inspected the cabin. There were two rooms and a bath. The sitting room was furnished with rattan chairs, a couch, a dropleaf table, cast-iron floorlamps with orange parchment shades. The bedroom contained a narrow bed, a gas space-heater, a matched blond dresser and wardrobe on whose surfaces ancient scars were preserved under thicknesses of shellac. There were tan straw rugs on the floors. The woodwork was painted gray-green. The rafters were exposed: one was a new unpainted beam along which beads of pitch glistened. She found a hectographed map of the grounds on her nightstand. She was pleased: she had hoped for taste-less accommodations, on the theory that she would then be likelier to stay outdoors.

She thought, Everything natural I've experienced here so far has been forced on me.

4.

At breakfast it was evident that most of the guests were grouped in organized parties. She sat at a table that seemed intended for strays. Her tablemates were women, all of them in middle age or older.

Blocks of cold air jutted in from the open windows. Everyone was squinting. She thought, This place is hideously overlit: I forgot to inhale correctly coming over. She began to inhale forcefully, trying to discriminate the perfume of the trees through the rising odors of break-fast. The dining room was large, with a low ceiling and unpainted beaverboard panelling on the walls. Except for some flourishes in blue enamel along the margins of the swing doors opening into the kitchen, there was no decoration. The floors were of oiled softwood plank. A dense grade of screen had been used on the windows. There were six long rows of trestle-tables, of which only four rows were in use. The lights were off above the vacant tables. Jill was seated at the head of her table, with no one on her left.

She had tried to repress her own fragmentary theories about what Nature would be doing for her. She was reserving judgment on the idea that men were capable of some exclusive relation to Nature. She thought, Possibly you can never know Nature intimately unless at some point you go and live in it in an attempt to make it yield to you in the form of profit: unless you farm, in short, except that every farm-related name you can name hates Nature utterly: So how do we do this?

An old woman seated on her right asked, "How do we do what?"

"Oh, did I say that? I must be getting old. I mean no, I was only thinking how do we, how do we get along without getting out into the country more often? How do we survive in the city, how do we stand it?"

The old woman was harshly made up. She seemed to want to pre-sent herself in profile only. She cringed suddenly, in a way that drew attention to the wilted state of the flesh of her cheeks and neck, and said, "I'm so cold here I can't tell you."

"It is cool, it is, now that you mention it."

"How do you like the Reverend?"

"I'm not signed up for that I'm afraid."

"Ah you should. Ah what a shame. They said two buses were coming tomorrow just for the seminar in the morning."

"Really? When on Sunday is that?"

"Oh, I don't know."

The old woman alternated between an erect sitting posture and disconcerting brief cringing reactions to the cold. She said, "South Africa."

"What did you say?"

"He was in South Africa. They say."

"Ah."

She turned her attention from the old woman, and thought, I could limit my thought to a description of what I'm sensing if I have to: If I can't stop the thinking aspect altogether.

She offered the old woman—who had eaten conspicuously rapidly—her untouched portion of homefried potatoes.

"Could you eat some of these? I can't."

"Oh, you need that, eat it!"

"No, really I haven't touched this. I can't. Your first day in the country you don't have your normal appetite. My egg seemed enormous. They must use gigantic eggs."

"Real butter, they use: they say."

"Please have these."

"Oh, all right."

The old woman resumed eating. While she finished again she held up a finger to check the waiter, who stood over her. He was short, blond, about twenty, with a radically developed body. Waiting, he leaned on the heel of one hand, turning out the face of his forearm: veins showed in heavy relief. His neck was broad, his neck cords were imposing. He was dressed tightly in a white polo shirt and worn but immaculate bluejeans. His head seemed small for his body. There were wads of muscle at his temples. He wore his hair cropped across the crown of his head, and at the sides in wings that drooped from his temples, covered the tops of his ears, and met at his nape.

Presently he was able to clear their plates. For some reason Jill had been included in the old woman's delay.

Jill whispered, "Good God, who was that?"

"Who?" the old woman asked.

"No, I was only exclaiming about the waiter, about our waiter."

"Oh, his name is *Lare*. Lare for short. Wait, I don't know his last name I don't think: if I do I forget it. Wait, I think I do know . . . Lare! Lare, come here! Lare, if you please! Lare!"

"Now please don't do that! Please! Please be quiet!"

But the old woman had already signalled to a woman seated farther down the table. "Tell Lare to come here a second. I can't shout like this."

The waiter ran back to them.

"This young woman wants to know your name and Lare I know you told me last year."

Speaking deeply, he said, "Lawrence Haupt."

As he spoke his last name, the old woman cried, "Haupt! Haupt! I knew it." She closed her eyes in satisfaction.

Impassively, the waiter left them, strongly attending to his work.

"Haupt," the old woman repeated softly, opening her eyes.

5.

Following breakfast, Jill went back to her cabin.

She prepared to begin again. She had sustained her deadness to Nature on the way back. She thought, I can almost say truthfully I have no idea what sort of day it is.

Her cabin faced unoccupied identical cabins. At the rear ran a neglected path grossly overhung and penetrated by bushes and tree limbs. Etiolated leaves pressed against the screen of her bathroom window.

She rinsed her hands. With her nails she scraped at tongue-shaped rust stains under the taps in the washbasin. She lowered the toilet lid and sat on it. She thought, These elderly boors infest places like this, you have to get over it, they love to humiliate: I love this kind of odorless wind: if I took the screen down I could have those dead leaves extending into the room itself: Probably Nature calms you by repetition if you can stand it: think of the sea, the seasons repeating.

In the sitting room, she pushed the couch up to a window, arranged pillows at the head of the couch. Now I can go again, she thought.

Standing outside, she imagined herself proceeding frankly toward the door-mirror in the bedroom, pulling her robe open to reveal herself naked. She would describe herself as small, small-boned, evenly fleshed, on the edge of being thin, high-waisted, having a lined abdomen but taut thighs, an intense face, good color, bright black hair kept very short, excellent hazel eyes. She thought, As to my stomach, from the side something is slightly wrong with the line of it which a minority might actually like: Also there is the one deep age-slash I have across my throat which I prefer to the usual battery of shallow wrinkles you see normally: age is cutting my throat neatly at least. As she walked away from the cabin she pursued her approach to the mirror. She thought, In sex why does a man have to take a breast which is so patently merely modest and hold it in such a way or turn you and place you in such a way it makes you feel secondary, like you hang from your breast instead of the opposite?: They want fullness regardless of your feelings: they seem to.

6.

The day was warm and overcast. She walked at random, hoping to feel impelled in a particular direction. The resort, built on perceptibly slanting terraces cut into a steep hill, occupied no more than twenty-five or thirty acres. The largest terrace held the main buildings: a Victorian manor house where the lectures were given, an apartment-annex, the dining hall. On the lesser terraces were tennis courts, a stable, meager playing fields, a tract of separate cabins. The whole property was enclosed in advanced second-growth. The neighboring hills were blank with woods, empty of settlement. A tier of higher, weakly wooded hills began just above the resort: the ridge line was stony and plucked-looking. Below the resort, westward, the hills relaxed into flat yellow farmland. The resort walks were intermittently defined by struggling plantings. The cabins, at the rear of the highest terrace, lay within a stand of virgin evergreens which she thought might be fir. Except for the plots immediate to the main buildings, the lawns of the resort were in disrepair, alive with sprouting onion grass.

Sounds of moving water attracted her. She followed them across and out of the central grounds, down a fieldstone ramp, to a swimming pool in a separate lower terrace. Water was feeding noisily into the pool; swimming diagonally across the pool was the waiter. He swam rigorously, using a heavy, mauling crawl stroke, turning his face up at intervals as though to complain and then burying it desperately again in the water. She had always found something comical in a rigidly performed Australian crawl.

She stepped up onto the pool curb. She felt self-conscious about her clothes: she was wearing a dark full canvas skirt, a thin rose cardigan sweater over a white blouse with long sleeves, thick-soled walking shoes. She stepped down from the curb. She thought, I gravitate to water.

"Could I ask you something?" she called.

The swimmer relaxed in midcourse, sank, rose, and, treading water, looked inquiringly around.

She said, "I wanted to ask you if you knew of some pond or water around here, a creek or brook."

The waiter swam toward her. Reaching the edge, he raised himself with a practiced movement to a sitting position at her feet. He remained sitting, pressing water out of his hair with his palms.

She thought, The pool is in keeping with everything else here, the edge is chipped: I take it the chair on the diving board means no diving.

"I didn't mean to interrupt," she said, "I'll wait till you get your breath. (Is this actually deep enough for diving?)"

"We need to fix the board."

"No, but is it even when the board is in working order? It looks shallow somehow."

"It's fine."

"Well, do you know of a lake or creek or anything of that kind I could walk to? There's nothing on that little map."

"This is where you swim. This is it for swimming."

"But can't I walk somewhere, hike, and find a natural creek or pond? A creek would do."

"This is the swimming."

"I grasp that. How can I explain this? All right, where does the pool water come from, is it from a creek, is it spring-fed or is it from a stream or something in the area?"

"From our well."

"You mean totally from a well? You mean this is the only water in the whole area? In other words this is a desert of some kind."

"There isn't anything like you want. Not that I know of."

"Not even for an especially determined person, nothing? Really? There must be. Try and think."

He got slowly to his feet, striking remnants of water from his arms and shoulders. His chest was hairless. He ran a hand across his stomach, under the waistband of his black latex trunks. He shook water from his fingers.

She thought, Why swim if you hate water so much you can't wait to rid yourself of it?: I want water moving by gravity not by pump: You end up asking directions from someone who hates water.

"Do you really not know?" she said.

"Up in the Park there might be. All that on the right is State Park, also straight up there is Park, mostly."

"This is a mountain. There have to be streams and pools and so forth."

"Ever hear the word 'drought'?"

"Oh, in other words are you saying all the water has stopped running down to the rivers? Where did the rivers I saw on the bus get their water, I wonder? They seem to be functioning."

He shrugged, crouched, turned, and lowered himself back into the pool.

She left. She thought, My idea of Nature is not exhausted in lawns and crappily made swimming pools, far from it: I wish it could be, I could stay home.

7.

By following her map she found a promising hiking trail leading into the woods above the resort. A park bench stood at the mouth of the trail. Looking back at the main lawn, she made out in it an indistinct current of blemishes, a flow of half-exposed small coral stones. Her perceptiveness encouraged her.

The trees were barely in leaf; the wind at work in the trees produced an abrasive sound. The sun was a mild inflammation in the overcast.

She went up the trail for a hundred yards or so, halted, cleared her mind, and then struck into the undergrowth. The footing was bad. She picked her way over soft beds of leaf mold, gutters and outcrops of stone, mats of vine and sticks, drifts of dead leaves. She pressed between bushes and under low branches, but before she could find a clear route she came to a complex barrier of fallen trees that seemed too rotten to step on. Fins and shelves of fungus grew profusely on the trunks. As she moved to go around the barrier she heard new sounds. Each step she took seemed to arouse agitation in the brush. There was no sign of a clearing.

She thought, I'm disturbing something that lives here.

She began to listen fearfully for the result of each footstep. She turned back from the barrier, retreating idly and circuitously. She let her hands trail through the feeble foliage, then began taking handfuls of leaves and buds which she pulped and squeezed: as she squeezed she closed her eyes and grunted weakly. The experiment embarrassed her. She held her hands to her face and smelled her fingers. Her embarrassment increased. She broke off twigs and smelled their torn bases. She wound a length of dry creeper around her wrist. She thought of opening her mouth and allowing the wind to blow directly into it. In the branches of a tree she noticed a trapped balsa glider, all its insignia bleached away. A bird, a jay with a throbbing, distended throat, settled on a branch above the glider. She broke spiderwebs in her path with a ritual languid movement of her elbows.

She thought, This apparently condemns me to the manmade: things live and have their being in there: what I need is a meadow: I swore not to be afraid, though: When you say meadow you mean something mowed so you can see it isn't inhabited: It would still be Nature: a novice might need something clearly uninhabited to start out with.

She was in the trail, picking spines and burrs from her sleeves. She returned to the bench. The walks were active with guests.

She thought, I love that arrangement of flat rocks in the trail: it helps.

8.

Standing on second base in the deserted baseball diamond, she was startled to see the waiter, now dressed for work, emerge from behind the backstop and come purposefully toward her. She thought, Speak first.

"Hello again," she said.

He came very close to her before speaking: "Let me know if you want to see a fire."

"What fire is that?"

"In the Park. A brushfire. Don't say I told you."

"Who would I tell? Also I hate fire."

"Good for you. This might turn out fairly big."

"Oh. This fire is roughly where?"

"In the Park in a really nice part."

"Oh, too bad. Well, are we in any danger down here?"

He shook his head, but by subtly bracing himself indicated that he was being deliberately reassuring.

She asked, "Where in the Park is it?"

"I couldn't describe it. I know where it is, though."

She thought, Fire is part of Nature: in the city all you get is man-made things burning down all your life.

He said, "They don't want me to say anything about it."

"I gather. You mean the owners."

"The owners."

"The only thing is, I hate fire: (I think). I always have."

"You can see smoke. Look where I'm looking, don't make me point."

In the north, at the ridge line, she saw a few dark strands of smoke.

"Aha. Now how long would it take to get where you could see it. Safely."

"Not too long. Forty minutes. I have to be back here before dinner."

"Dinner! I should hope. What about lunch or are you off?"

"No, I'm off."

She hesitated. He said, "It's whatever you say. I'm going myself anyway."

She said, "Well, I might as well. Why I don't know. I think I will. Also I hold you personally responsible if it goes out before we get there. I'm relying on you."

She agreed to wait while he attended to some small duties. She would meet him at the bench.

9.

He led so rapidly that she wanted to protest. But she reminded herself that he had work to get back to and that she had no right to impose her need for leisured attention to Nature upon him. They had taken the trail she had used earlier, and were now leaving it for a dry streambed running more acutely north.

The streambed intersected a streak of cleared land, a firebreak. The waiter proceeded through it in a crouch, trying, she decided, to keep his head below the level of the banks. One end of the line of cabins was visible from the upper reach of the streambed, where it reentered the trees.

She thought: This is the same undifferentiated thing I seem doomed to: various kinds of trees rip by, life is a blur: We have to go slower than this.

"Can we go any slower than this?" she asked.

She thought, For all he knows I might very much like to handle some of these fuck-aing rocks you nearly break your neck on: or those ferns: if we run like this this whole thing is useless, I might as well go back. She winced at herself: she was obviously reverting to the habit of converting curse words into more innocuous forms by deforming their pronunciation.

"Can we go any slower than this?" she asked again.

She thought, Above all this is the exact tone of sky I hate most: He must be a Balt with that complexion, they all have those fattish white firm faces like his, exactly.

They came to a severe pathless shale slope. Ascending, she had to rest twice on all fours. At the top they both rested before sliding down into the seam between their hill and the next.

She said lightly, "So far this is brutal, may I say that?"

A trail, mottled with black wet spots, followed the seam. At points, meshed tree limbs formed a solid canopy above the trail.

She said, "I love shade. I love this. I wish we could stay in this thing. I wish we could stay in this."

She thought, I wish we had something besides this cheap off-white between the trees: but I love these stains, this thing is a perfect tube almost in some places.

Her tentative complaining sounds failed to attract his attention. She thought, "Cries worked when words failed": I'll be sweating if this keeps up: the main feature of Nature I have to look at is the back of the shirt of a man covered with sweat and terrified by the amount of time this is taking, *terrified:* oblongs of sweat in his shirt.

She said: "This shade is great for a change, don't you think so?"

She thought, I hate this running so much that I have to take some action, I have no choice.

The trail settled into rude switchbacks on a new slope. She waited to speak to him again until they were apposed: "How far are we from the fire at this point? Will you answer that at least?"

"Not far."

"Well, approximately, in hours, days: approximately."

At the next apposition she asked, "Did you say how far it was? I think I missed it if you did."

"We're pretty near."

She thought, If you love me get me out of this at this exact point: Ah, you don't love me, I knew it: What time is it?

10.

Gaining the final ridge, they entered close dimness: the anticipated fresh view to the far side of the ridge was obscured by steadily flowing creamy smoke. She stooped variously in order to see through the smoke, and caught glimpses of lower hills, a precipitous wooded valley. The familiar view on the other side, back toward the resort, was not improved much by their elevation: she could see more of the inland plain, more roads.

The smoke racing at their right made their progress along the ridge toward the fire seem uncannily rapid.

Her eyes burned. She thought, There is an insane lack of color up here.

They came to a gap in the ridge, went down an incline of shifting rock, threaded through a labyrinth of brush, and climbed the opposite incline. The ridge continued at a higher level, rising and swelling out into the smoke, toward the fire.

She thought, Watch for hysteria. The fire was below, burning toward them up the flank of the ridge. Works of pale smoke rose, buckled in the air above them, were swept away. The fire itself showed fitfully as a bright wedge. Isolate colonies of fire burned ahead of the fire front.

"This is close enough," she said.

"It's a whole mile away. I thought you said you wanted to see this."

"I am seeing it. My eyes hurt. This is bad."

"Why don't you wait here a minute?"

"Ah, no, I want to watch you burn to death. That *is* your plan?"

"Why don't you go wait over in those rocks for me?"

"No, your imminent death interests me."

A seething sound, the complaint of green wood yielding to fire, reached them.

"I'll take you to the rock. I'll go with you."

"Oh, thanks."

They fell back to an eminence of rock at the center of the ridge, a stele scantily defaced with Greek letters, monograms, dates and names.

She said, "I felt actual heat once or twice over there. This is hideous on the eyes."

"You couldn't've." As he spoke, a current of smoke washed over them and then quickly swung off.

She was rigid with surprise. When she had recovered herself, she said, "Oh, this is insane! Smoke like that blinds you! I was blind. I can't breathe. Oh, that's enough. We have to go now."

The waiter's smile was condescending.

"Also this gets you filthy. I'm filthy," she said.

The waiter moved toward the fire.

"Wait, you won't leave me here, will you? You can't. You look like you plan to. Also what's that smell? Don't go!"

"What smell?"

"That rotten smell, like something rotten on fire. Look how filthy this gets you. That strong smell."

She thought, Wait, what am I seeing?: you tend to think of forest fires as floral, flowers or beds of flowers of fire, but when you see it the actual center is stringy, a stringy structure, white and not yellow: No, but you should be seeing the fire as a whole instead of trying to look through the smoke at the fire proper all the time: You should absorb the whole structure of fire and smoke as one single picture.

"Listen to it go," he said. He reset his shirttails inside the waist of his pants, blotted his forehead with the backs of his hands.

"I'm going," she said.

He was reluctant, but did follow, resuming the lead shortly. Without explanation he chose a new route for the return.

She thought, There might be some preferred distance you should be vis-à-vis Nature in order to get the right feeling out of it, not too close not too far: I have to laugh at the wildlife so-called: insects: the one bird in the area was deformed: really it was only stout, be fair.

It hurt to breathe. A mineral taste had established itself in her mouth. She wished that women were free to spit in public.

11.

On the return, passing a hollow, she caught sight of a salient of water. She entered the hollow and found a small, forked pond. She comtemplated the grain of the wind in the brown surface.

She shouted over her shoulder, "Why did you say there was no water before?"

The waiter had joined her. "You call that water?"

"Yes, I call it a pond."

"This is private. It's not even in the Park."

"But you did know about it. What if it is private, I wasn't planning to remove it. Besides no one is around. And you did know about it."

"You know how far this is from the hotel?"

"No, but I said when I asked you, *'in walking distance.'* We walked here."

"Guess how deep this is."

"If you know tell me."

"About one foot."

"So you did know about it."

"You couldn't swim in it if you tried. I've seen horses walk across it."

"Now I said nothing whatever about swimming. I made clear I cared nothing whatever about swimming, I never used the word."

"This is a horsepond. Next time I'll know."

"This yellow around the edge is—what?" She pointed to a sulphur-colored collar of scum around the pond.

"Pine pollen."

"Oh. Well. For the record I said nothing about being able to swim. I tried to be clear about that, I thought."

12.

She sought to sleep through the last of the afternoon. Several things escape me, she thought, For example my own physical pains were one thing I thought would be of interest, you never strain your body enough in the city to produce any. Leg pains were keeping her awake: she had lost interest in trying to visualize the shapes of her pains.

At intervals she felt compelled to sit up and look for change in the weather. The sky remained livid.

She thought, Is this *fluorescence* what I had to leave town for, the worst light in the world for your skin?: The best pain out of the three I have is the one due to skipping lunch which I can accomplish any time I want at home: I think I thought of the pain I'd get out of exertion as something to prove I was crossing a line in my life: apparently not, apparently it tells you nothing: This is my first hunger pang in my life: I'm lightheaded: pain by itself apparently tells you nothing, you need your interpreter the male mind, they are so direct: *At any rate:* Not eating could give you simple gas as well as the true stitch of hunger but which is which? What woman could you ask, I ask you?: Should I go in and eat or should I lie here through dinner and go into my pains such as they are?: I know this is hunger acting on me.

She went into the bathroom. Red water bled from the Hot tap when she opened it. She held her hands under the occasional drops. The plumbing crooned. The Cold tap ran normally.

She thought, The perfect thing would be if the fire somehow did this to me, denied me even the elementary pleasure of warm water running out of a faucet in the country in my own basin: Anyway I accuse the fire: I hate fire: They have gauze towels, a new product: This much cheapness lowers you, you come in from outside into something so cheap in which everything in it is cheap, the chairs, cheap mirrors full of *frottage* it looks like inside them: it destroys your appetite.

The dinner gong rang.

She thought, Thank God, the bell: I'm fainting.

13.

At dinner she thought, I could be wronging myself my whole project by eating at all: In the state of Nature you assume man was always usually hungry or starving, so am I right in eating?: I doubt it: On the other hand if you have to drag yourself out into the forest in a fainting state in order to get to appreciate Nature then how often can you go, not often: unless with training.

With her fork she halved the bites of veal chop she had cut.

She thought, Eating could easily be part of this if you could mentally reconstruct the history of each thing as you ate it, they do that in some kindergartens or did at one time, "now I am eating a little sliced-up sex ornament of a peach tree," that sort of thing can be done easily, it bores an adult to tears unfortunately except that *if you recall,* boredom you agreed was something we bring with us to the country, not something we find there, you bring it: you brought it: You have to exclude it when you arrive.

She had singled out a face two tables away on which to concentrate while she ate. She thought, A face in the act of eating is a face at its truest, if you have to deal with faces like these en masse you need help, in some way they all seem extreme: if he drives his glasses back once more pressing on the nosepiece with his knuckle I can't stand it.

She had finished her salad and vegetable. She thought, Look how I resist meat, it's unlike me: Meat is all I have left, I have to cross it to reach my dessert: Unless you could meet someone who knew enough about Nature to earn his living from it what you're doing is probably fruitless: the average man relates to Nature by eating it, unfortunately. She pushed her plate away, brought forward a dish of ragged halves of canned clingstone peach.

She thought, But on the other hand, what about the very real fascination of lost cities, a cliff that looks like primitive man could've had caves and homes in it?: And if you watch clouds you watch the ones that look the most like houses or fortifications, always: you stare into coals in order to see cities and houses. . . .

14.

She thought, In the country it seems insane to smoke indoors, why?

She had driven a wicker armchair through the front door of the cabin and onto the narrow stoop, which, she now saw, the chair would almost completely occupy. She was forced to climb over the back of the chair in order to sit down in it.

She thought, Arms within arms, the chair arms, the porch rails, my own arms. She put her feet up on the front half-rail, pressed the lap of her skirt well down between her thighs. She lit a cigarette.

Laughter came and went in the lecture hall. The lights along the central walks were switched on. Stars manifested, as the clouds in the evening sky thinned. She put her head over the porch rail and looked into the petty growth of fern, mint, and hepatica beside the porch.

She thought, The "beauty" of Nature is a male idea meaning the wish to use Nature: I have a male streak according to Rolf but why do I think Nature is *moving,* then?: Moving means wanting to get people to leave Nature alone, you want to conserve Nature: Which is the opposite of the male concept.

The waiter, strolling and smoking, approached down the lane between the cabins.

I am *crying out,* she thought.

The waiter was a virtuoso smoker: he was enjoying less than an inch of cigarette, nipping the fragment between thumb and forefinger almost at the coal.

She thought, I'll lose my mind if I have to smell pomade again, I saw it leak down his neck out of his hair in little rails, grease-rails.

"Well, well," she said.

He said, "They put you way out here."

"I like it. I prefer it."

"Isn't anyone else out here?"

"Yes, but they're all at the lecture. How's the lecture going?"

He mumbled an unintelligible reply.

She thought, He's mincing his words: I resent that inert facial expression they give you they think is sexy.

She lowered her feet to the stoop deck, sat forward and ground out her cigarette on a nailhead in the railing. She thought, The thing I seem most unable to adjust to about Nature is the idea of re-use, everything being a case or form of something produced infinitely earlier in the history of the planet: I could advance if I could keep that in mind: I might.

She rose. She thought, Now what about my *chair?:* if I try to bring it in he'll try to help me: Also I can't crawl over it the way I did, I have to force around it. She said, "Are your duties all over for the day now?"

I had to do that, she thought.

The waiter nodded, swilling smoke.

"Well, good night. I have to go in. Your hike ruined me," she said. She worked her way through the space between an arm of the chair and the side railing. She thought, This is going to mark me, it hurts.

The screen door was open, caught by the chair. She opened the front door, turned in the doorway, and smiled. She thought, Half the trees around are still in that ugly interstage.

The waiter inhaled raggedly through the smoke of his cigarette, spat the butt away, and kicked dust over it.

She thought, He may mean well.

There was substantial laughter in the lecture hall. She thought, Divide Nature up into compartments, you could do color alone one day, or sound: He won't leave.

She said, "I'm leaving the chair here, I love to sit out. Don't report me."

He could easily be from the slums and just working here, he's no country devil, she thought. She began to close the door.

Raising his voice, he asked, "Have you got a smoke you could spare?"

"I'm all out. I'm sorry. I'm trying to quit."

Hurriedly he said, "Did you get that cold?"

"What cold?"

"You were coughing before."

"I cough when I get exhausted. Good night."

She thought, You may go.

He said, "Good, I was afraid you were getting sick."

She said, "You may go," but added in a louder and more courteous tone, "Good night."

She closed the door and waited by the window. She pinched the curtain off the glass. She thought, Go while I watch.

15.

She sensed foreign matter in her breakfast coffee, and drank through pursed lips until she stopped a fiber—a shred of bark. She had eaten the center of her french toast, leaving the crusts and the batter-lace.

She left the table, compressing her attention, drying her lips as she walked. She thought anxiously, I'm sure that was bark, it was black: the food is foul: wellwater is always full of flecks of matter, organic matter.

She had taken a plum from a bowl on the table. She studied its etched surface, returned it to her sweater pocket. She thought, I might need it: I ate fairly blindly this time but still not up to the animal level of eating devouring everything and only stopping when you're sated.

The tree line rolled evenly in light wind. She thought, if only your mind or senses could be present in the treetops and move around there: They could have a thing like a vessel or canoe you could ride around in: One, it would always be cool, Two, you wouldn't necessarily be doing anything really adverse to birdlife: They could have restaurants, they could have wooden runways leading to decks in the hearts of the crowns of large trees, the larger ones, where you could eat: They won't in this life: The whole thing could be made out of wood to be in keeping, they already have various concessions underwater where you can sit down and eat: Oh, when it's too late probably the first one will open, like cures they discover too late: If you were young you could go up by ladder if you had to: not if you were old: The prototypes would all have ladders or long flights of stairs.

She hurried across the lawn. The waiter had come out onto the dining hall steps.

She went to her cabin, passed behind it to the disused trail that ran there. She walked northward.

The sky was clearing. The trail touched the firebreak she had passed through the day before; she turned off the trail and went up into the firebreak. She began to sweat: she took off her cardigan, tied it around her waist, unbuttoned the neck and cuffs of her blouse.

Ah, my dead stream, my dear friend, she thought. Above the familiar dry streambed the firebreak broadened.

She thought, Who's responsible for the mystique about being the first one to go over a particular part of the earth?: it makes no sense: you like doing it for some reason but are you ever the first one really?: you think you are but are you?: Oh, of course, it's male, another fine product of the friendly male mind for our use.

The first sure sun of the weekend struck her. The grade sharpened. She narrowed her eyes and looked at her surroundings for their color alone. She thought, You have a long bar of light green, humps of gray rock in it, gray lines and straps of tree trunks on the sides with varying light-yellow-green mist higher up depending on the density of the leaves, a marbled blue and white ceiling.

She caught herself thinking of the distance to the top of the firebreak in units of city blocks. She thought, I'm tiring again, that sting in my throat is back, the top of my throat, I love that: At the top of this I should have again my beloved view of electric towers, fine specimens: What keeps this from growing over?: Somewhere I have to pee, in the shade preferably please.

She had reached a flat place in the firebreak. She looked up into a soft empty normal noon spring sky. To her right a body of dark foliage stood out, a compact grove of cedars. She thought, Whatever it is it looks like gigantic parsley, forgive me. The smashed end of a stone wall projected from the cedar grove. Man-made, I bet: It leads into it: I love this dark green, she thought.

The grove was surprisingly open. The cedars made a solid curve out from and back to the firebreak. Except for a dome-shaped boulder the size of a hassock, with a bleached stripped fallen tree trunk on either side of it, the center of the grove was clear. The stone wall, the pivot on which she had turned to enter, ran out of sight into the brush beyond the grove. A thick resilient mold underfoot struck her as clean: she began to walk tenderly. Seedlings and saplings grew thickly along the near end of the wall. She thought, How miniature! But she grimaced at her thought, rejecting it.

You could call this "flask-shaped" since the center is so open and the way in is so small, fairly small, she thought. She encountered several stumps cut so low that they were hidden in the mold. She saw that all had been sawed at the same flat angle. She thought, Aha.

Her need to urinate receded. She thought, The point of exhausting myself before was that I would exhaust myself into something some zone of silence and softness like this.

She felt a sudden contempt for the victims of fantasies of soaring. She thought, My idea of gondolas going through the treetops on ropes is the exact opposite of soaring, mine could be arranged physically, they could have either my system of vessels or their own substitute or simply have walkways at a uniform level forty feet off the ground: It would differ from a tree house you have to build low down in the fork of a tree and not out in the leaves where you want to be: They already have the means for mine, is the point.

She filled her lungs. She thought, I love leaves, these aren't exactly needles, are they?: If I could just once blank out in Nature while I was going from place to place, arrive someplace and look around and not know where you were, I would be happy: But we may need real leaves rather than this type of leaf needle, I don't know: If you want mainly silence out of Nature I pity you, go to the ice cap where nothing is going on, that would be silence, you'd faint except if you were adapted to it: Every tree is a hell of noise inside don't forget, if we could hear it, we thank God we can't hear it: I was washed into this place by accident, into this *cove*.

She could see that the stone wall disappeared into an engulfed stand of flowering fruit trees. She thought, This smells like a closet, this would be *ideal* for a child or for myself as a child, "myself when young," a real paradise except for the lack of a fountain or little play-presence of water of some kind.

I'm drained in some way, she thought, You could easily take the rock object in the middle for furniture: Why do we get this smell in this one case seemingly from wood alone when we usually depend on buds and little cones and so on?: This smell is in the matter of the wood itself: The spaces between the trees uphill could easily be windows: Pine is a male scent in the culture, probably only an expert could pick up the smell stone has, really, unless you heated it, say: the sun is heating it but only an expert could get it, metals differ from trees, they could sell rock scent for men probably, they buy anything: It could be done: The clouds broke like that thin ice, floe ice, as I got here: I think it was then.

She squatted, setting her back against the smoothest face of the central boulder. She set the fingers of her right hand into the clean grooves of the ironwood trunk on that side. She extended her legs fully, sat back, slumped, let her head rest on the brow of the rock. Her arm hairs came erect. She said aloud, "Now what?" She thought, I need more sun than this.

The treetops splayed steadily. Nothing moved within the grove. She thought, This thing my hand is on is the cleanest thing in my life, human attempts to be clean are only copying getting things this clean: the groove for my thumb is larger than the others, it seems to be, inexplicably.

A moth alighted near her hand; it clasped its wings. She thought, He obviously has no fear of me.

She exposed her gums to the sun. She thought of her mother's theory about the good effect of sunlight on the gums. In mind she saw her mother's excellent full dentition, her mother smiling insensately into the sun.

A derelict cloud passed over. She thought, Whatever the thing in Nature is that has eluded the experts it is obviously the same thing I'm after: *Teeth seem insane* in humans, insane we should have them, insane things for a sapient being to have in his mouth, we were the opposite of teeth supposedly I thought.

She got up. She thought, I reject the idea of everything in Nature having to have a root of some sort. She walked along the line of cedars. She thought, I reject the idea it would be ecstatic to pee in here.

In a cavity between the stone wall and the cedars she discovered a fresh midden of bottle lids and empty beer cans. *No,* she thought. Close by she found a semicircle of charred log butts.

She thought coldly, In fact this is a room, not an apparent room but a real room *in use:* I went to the one place they chose to make into a room they still use: I walked into this the same as you go into a motel.

She reentered the firebreak. Turning to descend, she saw a glinting figure dodge clumsily into the brush near the foot of the firebreak. It was the waiter.

Rage overcame her. She began to trot downhill, thinking, For *once* leave me alone!

She began to run, which was hazardous on the uneven ground. She thought, For *once* leave me alone!: ah, you won't!: I pity you when I get there, hide as long as you want, I see you, I used your little waterless house: Oh, I pity you.

She ran recklessly. She thought repeatedly, I pity you!

She kept to the track of flattened weed that marked her upward progress.

She thought, as she ran, Nothing interests me.

Why It Is the Way It Is
Reason #1:
The Nature of Human Intelligence

The astronautical image of man amounts to a spiritual revolution. This is man as he has never lived before; it draws a line through human history that almost assumes the dimensions of an evolutionary turning point. . . . Technology, by giving man, "almost infinite power to change his world and to change himself," has ushered in what Ferkiss calls an "existential revolution." . . . The Greek tragedians would have regarded such a declaration as *hubris*. But the technological mind lacks the tragic dimensions and blinds itself to the terrible possibility that a society wielding such Frankenstein power is subject to reactive forces at work within the human soul, as well as within the repressed natural environment, which may prevent it from surviving for fifty or one hundred more years to exploit its capabilities.

—Theodore Roszak, in *New American Review* No. 9

THE PLOT TO SAVE THE WORLD
by Michael Brownstein

Not too long ago in the hills of our fatherland, on hill 311 to be exact, there lived a young girl divided into three parts: one part rock candy, one part fervent hope, and one part creative seclusion.

This girl spent the final years of her childhood perfecting a foolproof and at the same time fair system for the national lottery. She also developed a cheaper way to stamp coins and was the first person to reject microfilm storage of information using laser beams in favor of simple reliance upon memory banks honed to maximum flow in and minimum flow out. Through discoveries in the field of biochemistry so brilliant as to seem obvious she translated the metaphor of human-life-as-movie into actual biological fact, thereby opening the way to organ and gland transplant by means of the relatively simple and easily learned techniques of film editing. Acting on a hunch, she was able in one short day to revolutionize the scope of human sexual and creative energy through an elementary "sidetrack" process, whereby the *time* any particular act consumed, if thought of in terms of *space,* was reduced drastically, since most of these acts involved very little movement—such as sitting down, lying down, spreading out, and so on.

Although certainly not the first girl to visit France, she was perhaps the first to put into workable algebraic function the girlish realization that France "really is unique," that although this uniqueness was on the wane it could be preserved once changed into an immutable mathematical formula—and that what held true for France would also hold true for any nation or cultural bloc. So that, finally, each national identity could disappear in one sense (something which, she realized, was inevitable anyway) only to pop up again in another more permanent one, in a form obviously requiring no politicians, human blood sacrifice, or waste of time . . .

She astonished the world by her observations on trees as regulators of electricity, as possible media for electrical communications, and on the worldwide disasters which the clearing off of forests to make paper is likely to occasion . . . Her solitary walks in the Black Forest and the Blue Ridge Mountains opened to her new and original views on the harmonies of creation.

During the one or two hours before her bedtime set aside for leisure she painted, composed and played electronic music, and revolutionized the field of night photography . . . And two nights before her eleventh birthday she finally trapped and killed what had been her most elusive *bête noire,* namely sleep: not to avoid it, of course, but how could it be activated, how could sleep in its own way be made to stand up and contribute? Discarding the possibility of somehow "using" her body while it slept, she realized with sudden intuition as she woke up shouting that night from what had been only the third nightmare of her life that, through firm and patient training, two very striking things could be accomplished. One, the virtual elimination of subsidiary dream figures, and also nonhuman dream figures except for those coming under the heading of "landscape" or general atmosphere. Two, the selection and training of *principal* dream figures to the point where, as highly accomplished laboratory assistants, research scholars, typists, lathe operators, etc., they could be given increasingly complex problems and tasks related to those the girl herself was working on . . . So that after only a few months' time she was able to wake up every morning several days ahead of herself, with solutions to problems she had only just formulated the night before.

She was in addition an excessively good-looking and of course widely read young lady, and, anticipating before she was twelve the loss of time and sour moods resulting from body repression, she initiated a fine relationship with a boy from one of the nearby hills, a publisher's son. Usually, when leaving to go home after sharing her love, he would take with him the manuscript for her next technical paper or book, also relaying any pressing messages to the outside world and generally acting as her go-between and all-purpose factotum.

To gain the necessary psychological perspective on the world in which she lived, she participated in or observed one orgy, one coup d'état, one manic depression, one sunny day, one rest home, one sheep slaughter, one anonymous phone call, one transvestite, one sales pitch, one workers' commune, one sleeping village, one alpine meadow, one computer analyst, one wind tunnel, one savage domestic squabble, one happy family, one bigot and one small favor . . .

Since her uncle, moreover, was President of the Fatherland, she luckily avoided that stubborn resistance to fundamental change—to new ideas—which has been the proverbial stumbling block and torment of so many highly original minds throughout human history. She merely had to formulate an idea to have it thoroughly and objectively tested and, more often than not, speedily adopted. Her unbearable fame spread far and wide, very fast, while at the same time she managed to keep it from spreading to her head in the form of exaggerated self-importance. Contrary to what was expected, the rate of her discoveries and their uncontested value and profundity sharply increased rather than leveling off or dropping, so that by the time she was fourteen innovations of the first order were being explained, tested, and put into practice at the rate of three a week . . .

A persistent high-pitched hum could be heard in the valleys and meadows surrounding hill 311. That peculiar light and heat denoting exceptional psychic activity began to dominate the landscape, radiating out from the domed roofs of her compound like the gradual unfolding of some staggering cosmic theory. Neighbors who resisted falling under her influence for a short period of time talked of leaving the area and resettling elsewhere. They complained that their children were losing interest in toys and the mindless games of childhood and were spending more and more time alone in their rooms, or off wandering the hills at all hours of the day and night, filling notebook after notebook with "pointless gibberish" and organizing spontaneous talk fests, lasting hours, from which all adults were excluded . . . A concerned mother would force her way into one of these sessions only to be greeted by a stony silence, followed by the restless scraping of tiny chairs. Eventually the children would leave, or sometimes one of them would produce a baseball or monopoly set and they would begin to play, quietly looking over their shoulders at the mother until she felt she was intruding on nothing, as it were, and subsequently left, swiping at the tears as they formed on her cheeks with the back of a trembling hand.

But those neighbors who on the contrary didn't feel threatened by the power emanating from the top of the hill, never felt better. The wives found that perhaps for the first time since girlhood they were happily occupied, spending their afternoons hoeing earth and improvising the complicated flower gardens that began to appear throughout the neighborhood, spilling down the slopes before their homes . . . Some of these women got carried away to the point of converting every square inch of their lawns to a succession of enormous words spelled out by various flowers that bloomed from early spring to late autumn. Words like FASCINATION, INSPIRATION, and LUCK, or phrases such as LOVE ME, I AM GOD, and TOUCH MY TRIGGER began appearing everywhere, composed of tulip beds, hyacinths and roses—of carnations, zinnias, and sunflowers—running in large suffocating clumps from the front porch to the street below. The words were programmed to change as new flowers came into bloom. LOVE ME after a period of several weeks would become LOVE MY SHORTCOMINGS TOO, although for the most part these gardens were given over to huge single words—BEAUTY, for example, was a great favorite—spelled out in different colors as the summer progressed . . . Soon every house within a radius of two or three miles of where the young girl lived was surrounded by these obsessive, charming patterns. The wives would finish a day of strenuous labor with their bodies hardened and their spirits ready for the humble chores of dinner and the delirious chores of love.

But they also had to learn the virtue of patience, because their husbands, upon returning home from work, found themselves retiring to their workrooms or tool sheds as soon as dinner was over. There, surrounded by a clutter of tools and technical manuals, these middle-aged men experienced a resurgence of the blinding enthusiasm of early youth. Before the young girl's psychic energy affected them they had spent their evenings staring into television screens and darkly guzzling endless cans of beer. Now they suddenly began planning additions to the house, working on a new patio or even teaching themselves a little mechanical engineering in order to implement the unprecedented rush of "bright ideas" they had for some new labor-saving contrivance. As time went on they found themselves working in electronics, microbiology or structural design. One man, for example, invented a new and much sleeker miniature hull for ocean-going yachts, allowing yachtsmen to use the space formerly taken up by a ship's hull to carry more supplies, servants, and young orphan girls with their rucksacks and diaries, happy for a free chance to see the world. Another, a bus driver by trade, found a way to combine television, phonograph, telephone and refrigerator into a single master appliance that pointed the way to a sort of transistorized domestic unit promising a revolution in the technology of everyday life.

Others, more ambitious, brought their newfound lucidity to bear upon problems of psychology and the bewildering gamut of human emotions. They began to tackle such lumbering enigmas as—what, precisely, is the nature of ambition? what, if any, is the relationship between an individual's facial structure and his capacity for mental concentration? why do "perfectly healthy" people the world over find themselves just sitting around? etc.

Meanwhile, on hill 311, the young girl's dizzying rate of activity continued nonstop. She knew the precise extent of her own mental and physical energy and was careful to stop work as soon as it was totally depleted. Those neighbors, however, who were especially advanced in their work found themselves irresistibly drawn to her side as if in a trance, to collaborate and to learn, and she couldn't refuse them. She knew they were an extension of her own vital energy . . .

The hum from the hill grew louder as increasing numbers of these men spent more and more time on hill 311 with the girl, skipping supper and sometimes not even returning home at night. They would appear the next day at the breakfast table, haggard and shaking from exhaustion, but determined to drink some coffee and go off to their regular jobs. Their wives, by the way, thought all this was "just marvelous," and some of them spent the long evenings making sandwiches which they would take up the hill at one or two o'clock in the morning, only to find the girl and her followers collapsed around the work tables in her cavernous laboratory . . .

Suddenly the hum became unbearably painful to hear, as it turned into the sirenlike wail of what amounted to a small town, all of whose inhabitants were expending their last shred of mental energy, at work upon a single task. This in turn spread its magnetism further and further across the countryside, until people numbering in the tens of thousands began planting gardens and working in their tool sheds, only to abandon these projects at a certain point and migrate to hill 311. The girl's last report to the outside world came just before the sound became deafening and her hill was wracked and destroyed by a catastrophic series of earth-shaking tremors. She enthusiastically announced a plan, which she said was "at this moment being successfully implemented," to mobilize the fragmented mental energy of the countless individuals wandering the globe into one mighty, disciplined outburst of scientific achievement, with which the whole world could be instantaneously and completely transformed.

Why It Is the Way It Is
Reason #2:
The Logic of Industrialism

It was a town of red brick, or of brick that would have been red if the smoke and ashes had allowed it; but, as matters stood, it was a town of unnatural red and black, like the painted face of a savage. It was a town of machinery and tall chimneys, out of which interminable serpents of smoke trailed themselves for ever and ever, and never got uncoiled. It had a black canal in it, and a river that ran purple with ill-smelling dye, and vast piles of buildings full of windows where there was a rattling and a trembling all day long, and where the piston of the steam engine worked monotonously up and down, like the head of an elephant in a state of melancholy madness.

—Charles Dickens, in *Hard Times*

AUTOFAC
by Philip K. Dick

Tension hung over the three waiting men. They smoked, paced back and forth, kicked aimlessly at weeds growing by the side of the road. A hot noonday sun glared down on brown fields, rows of neat plastic houses, the distant line of mountains to the west.

"Almost time," Earl Perine said, knotting his skinny hands together. "It varies according to the load, a half-second for every additional pound."

Bitterly, Morrison answered. "You've got it plotted? You're as bad as it is. Let's pretend it just *happens* to be late."

The third man said nothing. O'Neill was visiting from another settlement; he didn't know Perine and Morrison well enough to argue with them. Instead, he crouched down and arranged the papers clipped to his aluminum check board. In the blazing sun, O'Neill's arms were tanned, furry, glistening with sweat. Wiry, with tangled gray hair, horn-rimmed glasses, he was older than the other two. He wore slacks, a sports shirt and crepe-soled shoes. Between his fingers, his fountain pen glittered, metallic and efficient.

"What're you writing?" Perine grumbled.

"I'm laying out the procedure we're going to employ," O'Neill said mildly. "Better to systemize it now, instead of trying at random. We want to know what we tried and what didn't work. Otherwise we'll go around in a circle. The problem we have here is one of communication; that's how I see it."

"Communication," Morrison agreed in his deep, chesty voice. "Yes, we can't get in touch with the damn thing. It comes, leaves off its load and goes on—there's no contact between us and it."

"It's a machine," Perine said excitedly. "It's dead—blind and deaf."

"But it's in contact with the outside world." O'Neill pointed out. "There has to be some way to get to it. Specific semantic signals are meaningful to it; all we have to do is find those signals. Rediscover, actually. Maybe half a dozen out of a billion possibilities."

A low rumble interrupted the three men. They glanced up, wary and alert. The time had come.

"Here it is," Perine said. "Okay, wise guy, let's see you make one single change in its routine."

The truck was massive, rumbling under its tightly packed load. In many ways, it resembled conventional human-operated transportation vehicles, but with one exception—there was no driver's cabin. The horizontal surface was a loading stage, and the part that would normally be the headlights and radiator grill was a fibrous spongelike mass of receptors, the limited sensory apparatus of this mobile utility extension.

Aware of the three men, the truck slowed to a halt, shifted gears and pulled on its emergency brake. A moment passed as relays moved into action; then a portion of the loading surface tilted and a cascade of heavy cartons spilled down onto the roadway. With the objects fluttered a detailed inventory sheet.

"You know what to do," O'Neill said rapidly. "Hurry up, before it gets out of here."

Expertly, grimly, the three men grabbed up the deposited cartons and ripped the protective wrappers from them. Objects gleamed: a binocular microscope, a portable radio, heaps of plastic dishes, medical supplies, razor blades, clothing, food. Most of the shipment, as usual, was food. The three men systematically began smashing the objects. In a few minutes, there was nothing but a chaos of debris littered around them.

"That's that," O'Neill panted, stepping back. He fumbled for his check sheet. "Now let's see what it does."

The truck had begun to move away; abruptly it stopped and backed toward them. Its receptors had taken in the fact that the three men had demolished the dropped-off portion of the load. It spun in a grinding half-circle and came around to face its receptor bank in their direction. Up went its antenna; it had begun communicating with the factory. Instructions were on the way.

A second, identical load was tilted and shoved off the truck.

"We failed," Perine groaned as a duplicate inventory sheet fluttered after the new load. "We destroyed all that stuff for nothing."

"What now?" Morrison asked O'Neill. "What's the next stratagem on your board?"

"Give me a hand." O'Neill grabbed up a carton and lugged it back to the truck. Sliding the carton onto the platform, he turned for another. The other two men followed clumsily after him. They put the load back onto the truck. As the truck started forward, the last square box was again in place.

The truck hesitated. Its receptors registered the return of its load. From within its works came a low sustained buzzing.

"This may drive it crazy," O'Neill commented, sweating. "It went through its operation and accomplished nothing."

The truck made a short, abortive move toward going on. Then it swung purposefully around and, in a blur of speed, again dumped the load onto the road.

"Get them!" O'Neill yelled. The three men grabbed up the cartons and feverishly reloaded them. But as fast as the cartons were shoved back on the horizontal stage, the truck's grapples tilted them down its far-side ramps and onto the road.

"No use," Morrison said, breathing hard. "Water through a sieve."

"We're licked," Perine gasped in wretched agreement, "like always. We humans lose every time."

The truck regarded them calmly, its receptors blank and impassive.

It was doing its job. The planetwide network of automatic factories was smoothly performing the task imposed on it five years before, in the early days of the Total Global Conflict.

"There it goes," Morrison observed dismally. The truck's antenna had come down; it shifted into low gear and released its parking brake.

"One last try," O'Neill said. He swept up one of the cartons and ripped it open. From it he dragged a ten-gallon milk tank and unscrewed the lid. "Silly as it seems."

"This is absurd," Perine protested. Reluctantly, he found a cup among the littered debris and dipped it into the milk. "A kid's game!"

The truck had paused to observe them.

"Do it," O'Neill ordered sharply. "Exactly the way we practiced it."

The three of them drank quickly from the milk tank, visibly allowing the milk to spill down their chins; there had to be no mistaking what they were doing.

As planned, O'Neill was the first. His face twisting in revulsion, he hurled the cup away and violently spat the milk into the road. "God's sake!" he choked.

The other two did the same; stamping and loudly cursing, they kicked over the milk tank and glared accusingly at the truck.

"It's no good!" Morrison roared.

Curious, the truck came slowly back. Electronic synapses clicked and whirred, responding to the situation; its antenna shot up like a flagpole.

"I think this is it," O'Neill said, trembling. As the truck watched, he dragged out a second milk tank, unscrewed its lid and tasted the contents. "The same!" he shouted at the truck. "It's just as bad!"

From the truck popped a metal cylinder. The cylinder dropped at Morrison's feet; he quickly snatched it up and tore it open.

STATE NATURE OF DEFECT

The instruction sheets listed rows of possible defects, with neat boxes by each; a punch stick was included to indicate the particular deficiency of the product.

"What'll I check?" Morrison asked. "Contaminated? Bacterial? Sour? Rancid? Incorrectly labeled? Broken? Crushed? Cracked? Bent? Soiled?"

Thinking rapidly, O'Neill said, "Don't check any of them. The factory's undoubtedly ready to test and resample. It'll make its own analysis and then ignore us." His face glowed as frantic inspiration came. "Write in that blank at the bottom. It's an open space for further data."

"Write what?"

O'Neill said, "Write: *the product is thoroughly pizzled.*"

"What's that?" Perine demanded, baffled.

"Write it! It's a semantic garble—the factory won't be able to understand it. Maybe we can jam the works."

With O'Neill's pen, Morrison carefully wrote that the milk was pizzled. Shaking his head, he resealed the cylinder and returned it to the truck. The truck swept up the milk tanks and slammed its railing tidily into place. With a shriek of tires, it hurtled off. From its slot, a final cylinder bounced; the truck hurriedly departed, leaving the cylinder lying in the dust.

O'Neill got it open and held up the paper for the others to see.

A FACTORY REPRESENTATIVE WILL BE SENT OUT. BE PREPARED TO SUPPLY COMPLETE DATA ON PRODUCT DEFICIENCY.

For a moment, the three men were silent. Then Perine began to giggle. "We did it. We contacted it. We got across."

"We sure did," O'Neill agreed. "It never heard of a product being pizzled."

Cut into the base of the mountains lay the vast metallic cube of the Kansas City factory. Its surface was corroded, pitted with radiation pox, cracked and scarred from the five years of war that had swept over it. Most of the factory was buried subsurface, only its entrance stages visible. The truck was a speck rumbling at high speed toward the expanse of black metal. Presently an opening formed in the uniform surface; the truck plunged into it and disappeared inside. The entrance snapped shut.

"Now the big job remains," O'Neill said. "Now we have to persuade it to close down operations—to shut itself off."

Judith O'Neill served hot black coffee to the people sitting around the living room. Her husband talked while the others listened. O'Neill was as close to being an authority on the autofac system as could still be found.

In his own area, the Chicago region, he had shorted out the protective fence of the local factory long enough to get away with data tapes stored in its posterior brain. The factory, of course, had immediately reconstructed a better type of fence. But he had shown that the factories were not infallible.

"The Institute of Applied Cybernetics," O'Neill explained, "had complete control over the network. Blame the war. Blame the big noise along the lines of communication that wiped out the knowledge we need. In any case, the Institute failed to transmit its information to us, so we can't transmit our information to the factories—the news that the war is over and we're ready to resume control of industrial operations."

"And meanwhile," Morrison added sourly, "the damn network expands and consumes more of our natural resources all the time."

"I get the feeling," Judith said, "that if I stamped hard enough, I'd fall right down into a factory tunnel. They must have mines everywhere by now."

"Isn't there some limiting injunction?" Perine asked nervously. "Were they set up to expand indefinitely?"

"Each factory is limited to its own operational area," O'Neill said, "but the network itself is unbounded. It can go on scooping up our resources forever. The Institute decided it gets top priority; we mere people come second."

"Will there be *anything* left for us?" Morrison wanted to know.

"Not unless we can stop the network's operations. It's already used up half a dozen basic minerals. Its search teams are out all the time, from every factory, looking everywhere for some last scrap to drag home."

"What would happen if tunnels from two factories crossed each other?"

O'Neill shrugged. "Normally, that won't happen. Each factory has its own special section of our planet, its own private cut of the pie for its exclusive use."

"But it *could* happen."

"Well, they're raw-material-tropic; as long as there's anything left, they'll hunt it down." O'Neill pondered the idea with growing interest. "It's something to consider. I suppose as things get scarcer—"

He stopped talking. A figure had come into the room; it stood silently by the door, surveying them all.

In the dull shadows, the figure looked almost human. For a brief moment, O'Neill thought it was a settlement latecomer. Then, as it moved forward, he realized that it was only quasi-human: a functional upright biped chassis, with data receptors mounted at the top, effectors and proprioceptors mounted in a downward worm that ended in floor grippers. Its resemblance to a human being was testimony to nature's efficiency; no sentimental imitation was intended.

The factory representative had arrived.

It began without preamble. "This is a data-collecting machine capable of communicating on an oral basis. It contains both broadcasting and receiving apparatus and can integrate facts relevant to its line of inquiry."

The voice was pleasant, confident. Obviously it was a tape, recorded by some Institute technician before the war. Coming from the quasi-human shape, it sounded grotesque; O'Neill could vividly imagine the dead young man whose cheerful voice now issued from the mechanical mouth of this upright construction of steel and wiring.

"One word of caution," the pleasant voice continued. "It is fruitless to consider this receptor human and to engage it in discussions for which it is not equipped. Although purposeful, it is not capable of conceptual thought; it can only reassemble material already available to it."

The optimistic voice clicked out and a second voice came on. It resembled the first, but now there were no intonations or personal mannerisms. The machine was utilizing the dead man's phonetic speech pattern for its own communication.

"Analysis of the rejected product," it stated, "shows no foreign elements or noticeable deterioration. The product meets the continual testing standards employed throughout the network. Rejection is therefore on a basis outside the test area; standards not available to the network are being employed."

"That's right," O'Neill agreed. Weighing his words with care, he continued, "We found the milk substandard. We want nothing to do with it. We insist on more careful output."

The machine responded presently. "The semantic content of the term *pizzled* is unfamiliar to the network. It does not exist in the taped vocabulary. Can you present a factual analysis of the milk in terms of specific elements present or absent?"

"No," O'Neill said warily; the game he was playing was intricate and dangerous. "Pizzled is an overall term. It can't be reduced to chemical constituents."

"What does pizzled signify?" the machine asked. "Can you define it in terms of alternate semantic symbols?"

O'Neill hesitated. The representative had to be steered from its special inquiry to more general regions, to the ultimate problem of closing down the network. If he could pry it open at any point, get the theoretical discussion started . . .

"Pizzled," he stated, "means the condition of a product that is manufactured when no need exists. It indicates the rejection of objects on the grounds that they are no longer wanted."

The representative said, "Network analysis shows a need of high-grade pasturized milk-substitute in this area. There is no alternate source; the network controls all the synthetic mammary-type equipment in existence." It added, "Original taped instructions describe milk as an essential to human diet."

O'Neill was being outwitted; the machine was returning the discussion to the specific. "We've decided," he said desperately, "that we don't *want* any more milk. We'd prefer to go without it, at least until we can locate cows."

"That is contrary to the network tapes," the representative objected. "There are no cows. All milk is produced synthetically."

"Then we'll produce it synthetically ourselves," Morrison broke in impatiently. "Why can't we take over the machines? My God, we're not children! We can run our own lives!"

The factory representative moved toward the door. "Until such time as your community finds other sources of milk supply, the network will continue to supply you. Analytical and evaluating apparatus will remain in this area, conducting the customary random sampling."

Perine shouted futilely, "How can we find other sources? You have the whole setup! You're running the whole show!" Following after it, he bellowed, "You say we're not ready to run things—you claim we're not capable. How do you know? You don't give us a chance! We'll never have a chance!"

O'Neill was petrified. The machine was leaving; its one-track mind had completely triumphed.

"Look," he said hoarsely, blocking its way. "We want you to shut down, understand. We want to take over your equipment and run it ourselves. The war's over with. Damn it, you're not needed any more!"

The factory representative paused briefly at the door. "The inoperative cycle," it said, "is not geared to begin until network production merely duplicates outside production. There is at this time, according to our continual sampling, no outside production. Therefore network production continues."

Without warning, Morrison swung the steel pipe in his hand. It slashed against the machine's shoulder and burst through the elaborate network of sensory apparatus that made up its chest. The tank of receptors shattered; bits of glass, wiring and minute parts showered everywhere.

"It's a paradox!" Morrison yelled. "A word game—a semantic game they're pulling on us. The Cyberneticists have it rigged." He raised the pipe and again brought it down savagely on the unprotesting machine. "They've got us hamstrung. We're completely helpless."

The room was in uproar. "It's the only way," Perine gasped as he pushed past O'Neill. "We'll have to destroy them—it's the network or us." Grabbing down a lamp, he hurled it in the "face" of the factory representative. The lamp and the intricate surface of plastic burst; Perine waded in, groping blindly for the machine. Now all the people in the room were closing furiously around the upright cylinder, their impotent resentment boiling over. The machine sank down and disappeared as they dragged it to the floor.

Trembling, O'Neill turned away. His wife caught hold of his arm and led him to the side of the room.

"The idiots," he said dejectedly. "They can't destroy it; they'll only teach it to build more defenses. They're making the whole problem worse."

Into the living room rolled a network repair team. Expertly, the mechanical units detached themselves from the half-track motherbug and scurried toward the mound of struggling humans. They slid between people and rapidly burrowed. A moment later, the inert carcass of the factory representative was dragged into the hopper of the mother-bug. Parts were collected, torn remnants gathered up and carried off. The plastic strut and gear was located. Then the units restationed themselves on the bug and the team departed.

Through the open door came a second factory representative, an exact duplicate of the first. And outside in the hall stood two more upright machines. The settlement had been combed at random by a corps of representatives. Like a horde of ants, the mobile data-collecting machines had filtered through the town until, by chance, one of them had come across O'Neill.

"Destruction of network mobile data-gathering equipment is detrimental to best human interests," the factory representative informed the roomful of people. "Raw material intake is at a dangerously low ebb; what basic materials still exist should be utilized in the manufacture of consumer commodities."

O'Neill and the machine stood facing each other.

"Oh?" O'Neill said softly. "That's interesting. I wonder what you're lowest on—and what you'd really be willing to fight for."

Helicopter rotors whined tinnily above O'Neill's head; he ignored them and peered through the cabin window at the ground not far below.

Slag and ruins stretched everywhere. Weeds poked their way up, sickly stalks among which insects scuttled. Here and there, rat colonies were visible: matted hovels constructed of bone and rubble. Radiation had mutated the rats, along with most insects and animals. A little farther, O'Neill identified a squadron of birds pursuing a ground squirrel. The squirrel dived into a carefully prepared crack in the surface of slag and the birds turned, thwarted.

"You think we'll ever have it rebuilt?" Morrison asked. "It makes me sick to look at it."

"In time," O'Neill answered. "Assuming, of course, that we get industrial control back. And assuming that anything remains to work with. At best, it'll be slow. We'll have to inch out from the settlements."

To the right was a human colony, tattered scarecrows, gaunt and emaciated, living among the ruins of what had once been a town. A few acres of barren soil had been cleared; drooping vegetables wilted in the sun, chickens wandered listlessly here and there, and a fly-bothered horse lay panting in the shade of a crude shed.

"Ruins-squatters," O'Neill said gloomily. "Too far from the network—not tangent to any of the factories."

"It's their own fault," Morrison told him angrily. "They could come into one of the settlements."

"That was their town. They're trying to do what *we're* trying to do

—build up things again on their own. But they're starting now, without tools or machines, with their bare hands, nailing together bits of rubble. And it won't work. We need machines. We can't repair ruins; we've got to start industrial production."

Ahead lay a series of broken hills, chipped remains that had once been a ridge. Beyond stretched out the titanic ugly sore of an H-bomb crater, half-filled with stagnant water and slime, a disease-ridden inland sea.

And beyond that—a glitter of busy motion.

"There," O'Neill said tensely. He lowered the helicopter rapidly. "Can you tell which factory they're from?"

"They all look alike to me," Morrison muttered, leaning over to see. "We'll have to wait and follow them back, when they get a load."

"*If* they get a load," O'Neill corrected.

The autofac exploring crew ignored the helicopter buzzing overhead and concentrated on its job. Ahead of the main truck scuttled two tractors; they made their way up mounds of rubble, probes burgeoning like quills, shot down the far slope and disappeared into a blanket of ash that lay spread over the slag. The two scouts burrowed until only their antennae were visible. They burst up to the surface and scuttled on, their treads whirring and clanking.

"What are they after?" Morrison asked.

"God knows." O'Neill leafed intently through the papers on his clipboard. "We'll have to analyze all our back-order slips."

Below them, the autofac exploring crew disappeared behind. The helicopter passed over a deserted stretch of sand and slag on which nothing moved. A grove of scrub-brush appeared and then, far to the right, a series of tiny moving dots.

A procession of automatic ore carts was racing over the bleak slag, a string of rapidly moving metal trucks that followed one another nose to tail. O'Neill turned the helicopter toward them and a few minutes later it hovered above the mine itself.

Masses of squat mining equipment had made their way to the operations. Shafts had been sunk; empty carts waited in patient rows. A steady stream of loaded carts hurried toward the horizon, dribbling ore after them. Activity and the noise of machines hung over the area, an abrupt center of industry in the bleak wastes of slag.

"Here comes that exploring crew," Morrison observed, peering back the way they had come. "You think maybe they'll tangle?" He grinned. "No, I guess it's too much to hope for."

"It is this time," O'Neill answered. "They're looking for different substances, probably. And they're normally conditioned to ignore each other."

The first of the exploring bugs reached the line of ore carts. It veered slightly and continued its search; the carts traveled in their inexorable line as if nothing had happened.

Disappointed, Morrison turned away from the window and swore. "No use. It's like each doesn't exist for the other."

Gradually the exploring crew moved away from the line of carts, past the mining operations and over a ridge beyond. There was no special hurry; they departed without having reacted to the ore-gathering syndrome.

"Maybe they're from the same factory," Morrison said hopefully.

O'Neill pointed to the antennae visible on the major mining equipment. "Their vanes are turned at a different vector, so these represent two factories. It's going to be hard; we'll have to get it exactly right or there won't be any reaction." He clicked on the radio and got hold of the monitor at the settlement. "Any results on the consolidated back-order sheets?"

The operator put him through to the settlement governing offices.

"They're starting to come in," Perine told him. "As soon as we get sufficient samplings, we'll try to determine which raw materials which factories lack. It's going to be risky, trying to extrapolate from complex products. There may be a number of basic elements common to the various sublots."

"What happens when we've identified the missing element?" Morrison asked O'Neill. "What happens when we've got two tangent factories short on the same material?"

"Then," O'Neill said grimly, "we start collecting the material ourselves—even if we have to melt down every object in the settlements."

In the moth-ridden darkness of night, a dim wind stirred, chill and faint. Dense underbrush rattled metallically. Here and there a nocturnal rodent prowled, its senses hyper-alert, peering, planning, seeking food.

The area was wild. No human settlements existed for miles; the entire region had been seared flat, cauterized by repeated H-bomb blasts. Somewhere in the murky darkness, a sluggish trickle of water made its way among slag and weeds, dripping thickly into what had once been an elaborate labyrinth of sewer mains. The pipes lay cracked and broken, jutting up into the night darkness, overgrown with creeping vegetation. The wind raised clouds of black ash that swirled and danced among the weeds. Once an enormous mutant wren stirred sleepily, pulled its crude protective night coat of rags around it and dozed off.

For a time, there was no movement. A streak of stars showed in the sky overhead, glowing starkly, remotely. Earl Perine shivered, peered up and huddled closer to the pulsing heat element placed on the ground between the three men.

"Well?" Morrison challenged, teeth chattering.

O'Neill didn't answer. He finished his cigarette, crushed it against a mound of decaying slag and, getting out his lighter, lit another. The mass of tungsten—the bait—lay a hundred yards directly ahead of them.

During the last few days, both the Detroit and Pittsburgh factories had run short of tungsten. And in at least one sector, their apparatus overlapped. This sluggish heap represented precision cutting tools, parts ripped from electrical switches, high-quality surgical equipment, sections of permanent magnets, measuring devices . . . tungsten from every possible source, gathered feverishly from all the settlements.

Dark mist lay spread over the tungsten mound. Occasionally, a night moth fluttered down, attracted by the glow of reflected starlight. The moth hung momentarily, beat its elongated wings futilely against the interwoven tangle of metal and then drifted off, into the shadows of the thick-packed vines that rose up from the stumps of sewer pipes.

"Not a very damn pretty spot," Perine said wryly.

"Don't kid yourself," O'Neill retorted. "This is the prettiest spot on Earth. This is the spot that marks the grave of the autofac network. People are going to come around here looking for it someday. There's going to be a plaque here a mile high."

"You're trying to keep your morale up," Morrison snorted. "You don't believe they're going to slaughter themselves over a heap of surgical tools and light-bulb filaments. They've probably got a machine down in the bottom level that sucks tungsten out of rock."

"Maybe," O'Neill said, slapping at a mosquito. The insect dodged cannily and then buzzed over to annoy Perine. Perine swung viciously at it and squatted sullenly down against the damp vegetation.

And there was what they had come to see.

O'Neill realized with a start that he had been looking at it for several minutes without recognizing it. The search-bug lay absolutely still. It rested at the crest of a small rise of slag, its anterior end slightly raised, receptors fully extended. It might have been an abandoned hulk; there was no activity of any kind, no sign of life or consciousness. The search-bug fitted perfectly into the wasted, fire-drenched landscape. A vague tub of metal sheets and gears and flat treads, it rested and waited. And watched.

It was examining the heap of tungsten. The bait had drawn its first bite.

"Fish," Perine said thickly. "The line moved. I think the sinker dropped."

"What the hell are you mumbling about?" Morrison grunted. And then he, too, saw the search-bug. "Jesus," he whispered. He half-rose to his feet, massive body arched forward. "Well, there's *one* of them. Now all we need is a unit from the other factory. Which do you suppose it is?"

O'Neill located the communication vane and traced its angle. "Pittsburgh, so pray for Detroit . . . pray like mad."

Satisfied, the search-bug detached itself and rolled forward. Cautiously approaching the mound, it began a series of intricate maneuvers, rolling first one way and then another. The three watching men were mystified—until they glimpsed the first probing stalks of other search-bugs.

"Communication," O'Neill said softly. "Like bees."

Now five Pittsburgh search-bugs were approaching the mound of tungsten products. Receptors waving excitedly, they increased their pace, scurrying in a sudden burst of discovery up the side of the mound to the top. A bug burrowed and rapidly disappeared. The whole mound shuddered; the bug was down inside, exploring the extent of the find.

Ten minutes later, the first Pittsburgh ore carts appeared and began industriously hurrying off with their haul.

"Damn it!" O'Neill said, agonized. "They'll have it all before Detroit shows up."

"Can't we do anything to slow them down?" Perine demanded

helplessly. Leaping to his feet, he grabbed up a rock and heaved it at the nearest cart. The rock bounced off and the cart continued its work, unperturbed.

O'Neill got to his feet and prowled around, body rigid with impotent fury. Where were they? The autofacs were equal in all respects and the spot was the exact same linear distance from each center. Theoretically, the parties should have arrived simultaneously. Yet there was no sign of Detroit—and the final pieces of tungsten were being loaded before his eyes.

But then something streaked past him.

He didn't recognize it, for the object moved too quickly. It shot like a bullet among the tangled vines, raced up the side of the hill crest, poised for an instant to aim itself and hurtled down the far side. It smashed directly into the lead cart. Projectile and victim shattered in an abrupt burst of sound.

Morrison leaped up. "What the hell?"

"That's it!" Perine screamed, dancing around and waving his skinny arms. "It's Detroit!"

A second Detroit search-bug appeared, hesitated as it took in the situation, and then flung itself furiously at the retreating Pittsburgh carts. Fragments of tungsten scattered everywhere—parts, wiring, broken plates, gears and springs and bolts of the two antagonists flew in all directions. The remaining carts wheeled screechingly; one of them dumped its load and rattled off at top speed. A second followed, still weighed down with tungsten. A Detroit search-bug caught up with it, spun directly in its path and neatly overturned it. Bug and cart rolled down a shallow trench, into a stagnant pool of water. Dripping and glistening, the two of them struggled, half-submerged.

"Well," O'Neill said unsteadily, "we did it. We can start back home." His legs felt weak. "Where's our vehicle?"

As he gunned the truck motor, something flashed a long way off, something large and metallic, moving over the dead slag and ash. It was a dense clot of carts, a solid expanse of heavy-duty ore carriers racing to the scene. Which factory were they from?

It didn't matter, for out of the thick tangle of black dripping vines, a web of counter-extensions was creeping to meet them. Both factories were assembling their mobile units. From all directions, bugs slithered and crept, closing in around the remaining heap of tungsten. Neither factory was going to let needed raw material get away; neither was going to give up its find. Blindly, mechanically, in the grip of inflexible directives, the two opponents labored to assemble superior forces.

"Come on," Morrison said urgently. "Let's get out of here. All hell is bursting loose."

O'Neill hastily turned the truck in the direction of the settlement. They began rumbling through the darkness on their way back. Every now and then, a metallic shape shot by them, going in the opposite direction.

"Did you see the load in that last cart?" Perine asked, worried. "It wasn't empty."

Neither were the carts that followed it, a whole procession of bulging supply carriers directed by an elaborate high-level surveying unit.

"Guns," Morrison said, eyes wide with apprehension. "They're taking in weapons. But who's going to use them?"

"They are," O'Neill answered. He indicated a movement to their right. "Look over there. This is something we hadn't expected."

They were seeing the first factory representative move into action.

As the truck pulled into the Kansas City settlement, Judith hurried breathlessly toward them. Fluttering in her hand was a strip of metal-foil paper.

"What is it?" O'Neill demanded, grabbing it from her.

"Just come." His wife struggled to catch her breath. "A mobile car—raced up, dropped it off—and left. Big excitement. Golly, the factory's—a blaze of lights. You can see it for miles."

O'Neill scanned the paper. It was a factory certification for the last group of settlement-placed orders, a total tabulation of requested and factory-analyzed needs. Stamped across the list in heavy black type were six foreboding words:

ALL SHIPMENTS SUSPENDED UNTIL FURTHER NOTICE

Letting out his breath harshly, O'Neill handed the paper over to Perine. "No more consumer goods," he said ironically, a nervous grin twitching across his face. "The network's going on a wartime footing."

"Then we did it?" Morrison asked haltingly.

"That's right," O'Neill said. Now that the conflict had been sparked, he felt a growing, frigid terror. "Pittsburgh and Detroit are in it to the finish. It's too late for us to change our minds, now—they're lining up allies."

Cool morning sunlight lay across the ruined plain of black metallic ash. The ash smouldered a dull, unhealthy red; it was still warm.

"Watch your step," O'Neill cautioned. Grabbing hold of his wife's arm, he led her from the rusty, sagging truck, up onto the top of a pile of strewn concrete blocks, the scattered remains of a pillbox installation. Earl Perine followed, making his way carefully, hesitantly.

Behind them, the dilapidated settlement lay spread out, a disorderly checkerboard of houses, buildings and streets. Since the autofac network had closed down its supply and maintenance, the human settlements had fallen into semibarbarism. The commodities that remained were broken and only partly usable. It had been over a year since the last mobile factory truck had appeared, loaded with food, tools, clothing and repair parts. From the flat expanse of dark concrete and metal at the foot of the mountains, nothing had emerged in their direction.

Their wish had been granted—they were cut off, detached from the network.

On their own.

Around the settlement grew ragged fields of wheat and tattered stalks of sun-baked vegetables. Crude handmade tools had been distributed, primitive artifacts hammered out with great labor by the various settlements. The settlements were linked only by horse-drawn cart and by the slow stutter of the telegraph key.

They had managed to keep their organization, though. Goods and services were exchanged on a slow, steady basis. Basic commodities were produced and distributed. The clothing that O'Neill and his wife and Earl Perine wore was coarse and unbleached, but sturdy. And they had managed to convert a few of the trucks from gasoline to wood.

"Here we are," O'Neill said. "We can see from here."

"Is it worth it?" Judith asked, exhausted. Bending down, she plucked aimlessly at her shoe, trying to dig a pebble from the soft hide hole. "It's a long way to come, to see something we've seen every day for thirteen months."

"True," O'Neill admitted, his hand briefly resting on his wife's slim shoulder. "But this may be the last. And that's what we want to see."

In the gray sky above them, a swift circling dot of opaque black moved. High, remote, the dot spun and darted, following an intricate and wary course. Gradually, its gyrations moved it toward the mountains and the bleak expanse of bomb-rubbled structure sunk in their base.

"San Francisco," O'Neill explained. "One of those long-range hawk projectiles, all the way from the West Coast."

"And you think it's the last?" Perine asked.

"It's the only one we've seen this month." O'Neill seated himself and began sprinkling dried bits of tobacco into a trench of brown paper. "And we used to see hundreds."

"Maybe they have something better," Judith suggested. She found a smooth rock and tiredly seated herself. "Could it be?"

Her husband smiled ironically. "No. They don't have anything better."

The three of them were tensely silent. Above them, the circling dot of black drew closer. There was no sign of activity from the flat surface of metal and concrete; the Kansas City factory remained inert, totally unresponsive. A few billows of warm ash drifted across it and one end was partly submerged in rubble. The factory had taken numerous direct hits. Across the plain, the furrows of its subsurface tunnels lay exposed, clogged with debris and the dark, water-seeking tendrils of tough vines.

"Those damn vines," Perine grumbled, picking at an old sore on his unshaven chin. "They're taking over the world."

Here and there around the factory, the demolished ruin of a mobile extension rusted in the morning dew. Carts, trucks, search-bugs, factory representatives, weapons carriers, guns, supply trains, subsurface projectiles, indiscriminate parts of machinery mixed and fused together in shapeless piles. Some had been destroyed returning to the factory; others had been contacted as they emerged, fully loaded, heavy with equipment. The factory itself—what remained of it—seemed to have settled more deeply into the earth. Its upper surface was barely visible, almost lost in drifting ash.

In four days, there had been no known activity, no visible movement of any sort.

"It's dead," Perine said. "You can see it's dead."

O'Neill didn't answer. Squatting down, he made himself comfortable and prepared to wait. In his own mind, he was sure that some fragment of automation remained in the eroded factory. Time would tell. He examined his wristwatch; it was eight thirty. In the old days, the factory would be starting its daily routine. Processions of trucks and varied mobile units would be coming to the surface, loaded with supplies, to begin their expeditions to the human settlement.

Off to the right, something stirred. He quickly turned his attention to it.

A single battered ore-gathering cart was creeping clumsily toward the factory. One last damaged mobile unit trying to complete its task. The cart was virtually empty; a few meager scraps of metal lay strewn in its hold. A scavenger . . . the metal was sections ripped from destroyed equipment encountered on the way. Feebly, like a blind metallic insect, the cart approached the factory. Its progress was incredibly jerky. Every now and then, it halted, bucked and quivered, and wandered aimlessly off the path.

"Control is bad," Judith said, with a touch of horror in her voice. "The factory's having trouble guiding it back."

Yes, he had seen that. Around New York, the factory had lost its high-frequency transmitter completely. Its mobile units had floundered in crazy gyrations, racing in random circles, crashing against rocks and trees, sliding into gullies, overturning, finally unwinding and becoming reluctantly inanimate.

The ore cart reached the edge of the ruined plain and halted briefly. Above it, the dot of blacks still circled the sky. For a time, the cart remained frozen.

"The factory's trying to decide," Perine said. "It needs the material, but it's afraid of that hawk up there."

The factory debated and nothing stirred. Then the ore cart again resumed its unsteady crawl. It left the tangle of vines and started out across the blasted open plain. Painfully, with infinite caution, it headed toward the slab of dark concrete and metal at the base of the mountains.

The hawk stopped circling.

"Get down!" O'Neill said sharply. "They've got those rigged with the new bombs."

His wife and Perine crouched down beside him and the three of them peered warily at the plain and the metal insect crawling laboriously across it. In the sky, the hawk swept in a straight line until it hung directly over the cart. Then, without sound or warning, it came down in a straight dive.

Hands to her face, Judith shrieked, "I can't watch! It's awful! Like wild animals!"

"It's not after the cart," O'Neill grated.

As the airborne projectile dropped, the cart put on a burst of desperate speed. It raced noisily toward the factory, clanking and rattling, trying in a last futile attempt to reach safety. Forgetting the menace above, the frantically eager factory opened up and guided its mobile unit directly inside. And the hawk had what it wanted.

Before the barrier could close, the hawk swooped down in a long glide parallel with the ground. As the cart disappeared into the depths of the factory, the hawk shot after it, a swift shimmer of metal that hurtled past the clanking cart. Suddenly aware, the factory snapped the barrier shut. Grotesquely, the cart struggled; it was caught fast in the half-closed entrance.

But whether it freed itself didn't matter. There was a dull rumbling stir. The ground moved, billowed, then settled back. A deep shock wave passed beneath the three watching human beings. From the factory rose a single column of black smoke. The surface of concrete split like a dried pod, it shriveled and broke, and dribbled shattered bits of itself in a shower of ruin. The smoke hung for a while, drifting aimlessly away with the morning wind.

The factory was a fused, gutted wreck. It had been penetrated and destroyed.

O'Neill got stiffly to his feet. "That's that. All over with. We've got what we set out after—we've destroyed the autofac network." He glanced at Perine. "Or was that what we were after?"

They looked toward the settlement that lay behind them. Little remained of the orderly rows of houses and streets of the previous year. Without the network, the settlement had rapidly decayed. The original prosperous neatness had dissipated; the settlement was shabby, ill-kept.

"Of course," Perine said haltingly. "Once we get into the factories and start setting up our assembly lines. . . ."

"Is there anything left?" Judith inquired.

"There must be something left. My God, there were levels going down miles!"

"Some of those bombs they developed toward the end were awfully big," Judith pointed out. "Better than anything we had in our war."

"Remember that camp we saw? The ruins-squatters?"

"I wasn't along," Perine said.

"They were like wild animals. Eating roots and larvae. Sharpening rocks, tanning hides. Savagery. Bestiality."

"But that's what people like that want," Perine answered defensively.

"Do they? Do we want this?" O'Neill indicated the straggling settlement. "Is this what we set out looking for, that day we collected the tungsten? Or that day we told the factory truck its milk was—" He couldn't remember the word.

"Pizzled," Judith supplied.

"Come on," O'Neill said. "Let's get started. Let's see what's left of that factory—left for us."

They approached the ruined factory late in the afternoon. Four trucks rumbled shakily up to the rim of the gutted pit and halted, motors steaming, tail-pipes dripping. Wary and alert, workmen scrambled down and stepped gingerly across the hot ash.

"Maybe it's too soon," one of them objected.

O'Neill had no intention of waiting. "Come on," he ordered. Grabbing up a flashlight, he stepped down into the crater.

The sheltered hull of the Kansas City factory lay directly ahead. In its gutted mouth, the ore cart still hung caught, but it was no longer struggling. Beyond the cart was an ominous pool of gloom. O'Neill flashed his light through the entrance; the tangled, jagged remains of upright supports were visible.

"We want to get down deep," he said to Morrison, who prowled cautiously beside him. "If there's anything left, it's at the bottom."

Morrison grunted. "Those boring moles from Atlanta got most of the deep layers."

"Until the others got their mines sunk." O'Neill stepped carefully through the sagging entrance, climbed a heap of debris that had been tossed against the slit from inside, and found himself within the factory—an expanse of confused wreckage, without pattern or meaning.

"Entropy," Morrison breathed, oppressed. "The thing it always hated. The thing it was built to fight. Random particles everywhere. No purpose to it."

"Down underneath," O'Neill said stubbornly, "we may find some sealed enclaves. I know they got so they were dividing up into autonomous sections, trying to preserve repair units intact, to re-form the composite factory."

"The moles got most of them, too," Morrison observed, but he lumbered after O'Neill.

Behind them, the workmen came slowly. A section of wreckage shifted ominously and a shower of hot fragments cascaded down. "You men get back to the trucks," O'Neill said. "No sense endangering any more of us than we have to. If Morrison and I don't come back, forget us—don't risk sending a rescue party." As they left, he pointed out to Morrison a descending ramp still partially intact. "Let's get below."

Silently, the two men passed one dead level after another. Endless miles of dark ruin stretched out, without sound or activity. The vague shapes of darkened machinery, unmoving belts and conveyor equipment were partially visible, and the partially completed husks of war projectiles, bent and twisted by the final blast.

"We can salvage some of that," O'Neill said, but he didn't actually believe it. The machinery was fused, shapeless. Everything in the factory had run together, molten slag without form or use. "Once we get it to the surface. . . ."

"We can't," Morrison contradicted bitterly. "We don't have hoists or winches." He kicked at a heap of charred supplies that had stopped along its broken belt and spilled halfway across the ramp.

"It seemed like a good idea at the time," O'Neill said as the two of them continued past the vacant levels of inert machines. "But now that I look back, I'm not so sure."

They had penetrated a long way into the factory. The final level lap spread out ahead of them. O'Neill flashed the light here and there, trying to locate undestroyed sections, portions of the assembly process still intact.

It was Morrison who felt it first. He suddenly dropped to his hands and knees; heavy body pressed against the floor, he lay listening, face hard, eyes wide. "For God's sake—"

"What is it?" O'Neill cried. Then he, too, felt it. Beneath them, a faint, insistent vibration hummed through the floor, a steady hum of activity. They had been wrong; the hawk had not been totally successful. Below, in a deeper level, the factory was still alive. Closed, limited operations still went on.

"On its own," O'Neill muttered, searching for an extension of the descent lift. "Autonomous activity, set to continue after the rest is gone. How do we get down?"

The descent lift was broken off, sealed by a thick section of metal.

The still-living layer beneath their feet was completely cut off; there was no entrance.

Racing back the way they had come, O'Neill reached the surface and hailed the first truck. "Where'n the hell's the torch? Give it here!"

The precious blowtorch was passed to him and he hurried back, puffing, into the depths of the ruined factory where Morrison waited. Together, the two of them began frantically cutting through the warped metal flooring, burning apart the sealed layers of protective mesh.

"It's coming," Morrison gasped, squinting in the glare of the torch. The plate fell with a clang, disappearing into the level below. A blaze of white light burst up around them and the two men leaped back.

In the sealed chamber, furious activity boomed and echoed, a steady process of moving belts, whirring machine tools, fast-moving mechanical supervisors. At one end, a steady flow of raw materials entered the line; at the far end, the final product was whipped off, inspected and crammed into a conveyor tube.

All this was visible for a split second; then the intrusion was discovered. Robot relays came into play. The blaze of lights flickered and dimmed. The assembly line froze to a halt, stopped in its furious activity.

The machines clicked off and became silent.

At one end, a mobile unit detached itself and sped up the wall toward the hole O'Neill and Morrison had cut. It slammed an emergency seal in place and expertly welded it tight. The scene below was gone. A moment later the floor shivered as activity resumed.

Morrison, white-faced and shaking, turned to O'Neill. "What are they doing? What are they making?"

"Not weapons," O'Neill said.

"That stuff is being sent up"— Morrison gestured convulsively— "to the surface."

Shakily, O'Neill climbed to his feet. "Can we locate the spot?"

"I—think so."

"We better." O'Neill swept up the flashlight and started toward the ascent ramp. "We're going to have to see what those pellets are that they're shooting up."

The exit valve of the conveyor tube was concealed in a tangle of vines and ruins a quarter of a mile beyond the factory. In a slot of rock at the base of the mountains, the valve poked up like a nozzle. From ten yards away, it was invisible; the two men were almost on top of it before they noticed it.

Every few moments, a pellet burst from the valve and shot up into the sky. The nozzle revolved and altered its angle of deflection; each pellet was launched in a slightly varied trajectory.

"How far are they going?" Morrison wondered.

"Probably varies. It's distributing them at random." O'Neill advanced cautiously, but the mechanism took no notice of him. Plastered against the towering wall of rock was a crumpled pellet; by accident, the nozzle had released it directly at the mountainside. O'Neill climbed up, got it and jumped down.

The pellet was a smashed container of machinery, tiny metallic elements too minute to be analyzed without a microscope.

"Not a weapon," O'Neill said.

The cylinder had split. At first he couldn't tell if it had been the impact or deliberate internal mechanisms at work. From the rent, an ooze of metal bits was sliding. Squatting down, O'Neill examined them.

The bits were in motion. Microscopic machinery, smaller than ants, smaller than pins, working energetically, purposefully—constructing something that looked like a tiny rectangle of steel.

"They're building," O'Neill said, awed. He got up and prowled on. Off to the side, at the far edge of the gully, he came across a downed pellet far advanced on its construction. Apparently it had been released some time ago.

This one had made great enough progress to be identified. Minute as it was, the structure was familiar. The machinery was building a miniature replica of the demolished factory.

"Well," O'Neill said thoughtfully, "we're back where we started from. For better or worse . . . I don't know."

"I guess they must be all over Earth by now," Morrison said. "Landing everywhere and going to work."

A thought struck O'Neill. "Maybe some of them are geared to escape velocity. That would be neat——autofac networks throughout the whole universe."

Behind him, the nozzle continued to spurt out its torrent of metal seeds.

Why It Is the Way It Is
Reason #3:
Overpopulation

Paul R. Ehrlich (author of the famous ecological *cri de coeur The Population Bomb*) has written of Harry Harrison's novel *Make Room! Make Room!*:

"I read it last year and thought it about the most effective fictional treatment of the consequences of the population explosion that I have ever come across (the only contender is Anthony Burgess' *The Wanting Seed*)."

In the ideal multivolume version of this anthology, both those novels would have to be included. I'm glad that in the present finite edition I am able to print (for the first time) the story that was the seed from which *Make Room! Make Room!* eventually grew.

ROOMMATES

by Harry Harrison

Summer

The August sun struck in through the open window and burned on Andrew Rusch's bare legs until discomfort dragged him awake from the depths of heavy sleep. Only slowly did he become aware of the heat and the damp and gritty sheet beneath his body. He rubbed at his gummed-shut eyelids, then lay there, staring up at the cracked and stained plaster of the ceiling, only half awake and experiencing a feeling of dislocation, not knowing in those first waking moments just where he was, although he had lived in this room for over seven years. He yawned and the odd sensation slipped away while he groped for the watch that he always put on the chair next to the bed,

then he yawned again as he blinked at the hands mistily seen behind
the scratched crystal. Seven . . . seven o'clock in the morning, and
there was a little number 9 in the middle of the square window. Mon-
day the ninth of August, 1999—and hot as a furnace already, with the
city still imbedded in the heat wave that had baked and suffocated
New York for the past ten days. Andy scratched at a trickle of perspiration on his side, then moved his legs out of the patch of sunlight
and bunched the pillow up under his neck. From the other side of the
thin partition that divided the room in half there came a clanking
whir that quickly rose to a high-pitched drone.

"Morning . . ." he shouted over the sound, then began coughing.
Still coughing he reluctantly stood and crossed the room to draw a
glass of water from the wall tank; it came out in a thin, brownish
trickle. He swallowed it, then rapped the dial on the tank with his
knuckles and the needle bobbed up and down close to the *Empty*
mark. It needed filling, he would have to see to that before he signed
in at four o'clock at the precinct. The day had begun.

A full-length mirror with a crack running down it was fixed to the
front of the hulking wardrobe and he poked his face close to it, rubbing at his bristly jaw. He would have to shave before he went in. No
one should ever look at himself in the morning, naked and revealed,
he decided with distaste, frowning at the dead white of his skin and
the slight bow to his legs that was usually concealed by his pants. And
how did he manage to have ribs that stuck out like those of a starved
horse, as well as a growing potbelly—both at the same time? He
kneaded the soft flesh and thought that it must be the starchy diet,
that and sitting around on his chunk most of the time. But at least
the fat wasn't showing on his face. His forehead was a little higher
each year, but wasn't too obvious as long as his hair was cropped
short. You have just turned thirty, he thought to himself, and the
wrinkles are already starting around your eyes. And your nose is too
big—wasn't it Uncle Brian who always said that was because there was
Welsh blood in the family? And your canine teeth are a little too
obvious so when you smile you look a bit like a hyena. You're a handsome devil, Andy Rusch, and it's a wonder a girl like Shirl will even
look at you, much less kiss you. He scowled at himself, then went to
look for a handkerchief to blow his impressive Welsh nose.

There was just a single pair of clean undershorts in the drawer
and he pulled them on; that was another thing he had to remember
today, to get some washing done. The squealing whine was still com-

ing from the other side of the partition as he pushed through the connecting door.

"You're going to give yourself a coronary, Sol," he told the gray-bearded man who was perched on the wheelless bicycle, pedaling so industriously that perspiration ran down his chest and soaked into the bath towel that he wore tied around his waist.

"Never a coronary," Solomon Kahn gasped out, pumping steadily. "I been doing this every day for so long that my ticker would miss it if I stopped. And no cholesterol in my arteries either since regular flushing with alcohol takes care of that. And no lung cancer since I couldn't afford to smoke even if I wanted to, which I don't. And at the age of seventy-five no prostatitis because . . ."

"Sol, please—spare me the horrible details on an empty stomach. Do you have an ice cube to spare?"

"Take two—it's a hot day. And don't leave the door open too long."

Andy opened the small refrigerator that squatted against the wall and quickly took out the plastic container of margarine, then squeezed two ice cubes from the tray into a glass and slammed the door. He filled the glass with water from the wall tank and put it on the table next to the margarine. "Have you eaten yet?" he asked.

"I'll join you, these things should be charged by now."

Sol stopped pedaling and the whine died away to a moan, then vanished. He disconnected the wires from the electrical generator that was geared to the rear axle of the bike, and carefully coiled them up next to the four black automobile storage batteries that were racked on top of the refrigerator. Then, after wiping his hands on his soiled towel sarong, he pulled out one of the bucket seats, salvaged from an ancient 1975 Ford, and sat down across the table from Andy.

"I heard the six o'clock news," he said. "The Eldsters are organizing another protest march today on relief headquarters. *That's* where you'll see coronaries!"

"I won't, thank God, I'm not on until four and Union Square isn't in our precinct." He opened the breadbox and took out one of the six-inch-square red crackers, then pushed the box over to Sol. He spread margarine thinly on it and took a bite, wrinkling his nose as he chewed. "I think this margarine has turned."

"How can you tell?" Sol grunted, biting into one of the dry crackers. "Anything made from motor oil and whale blubber is turned to begin with."

"Now you begin to sound like a naturist," Andy said, washing his cracker down with cold water. "There's hardly any flavor at all to the fats made from petrochemicals and you know there aren't any whales left so they can't use blubber—it's just good chlorella oil."

"Whales, plankton, herring oil, it's all the same. Tastes fishy. I'll take mine dry so I don't grow no fins." There was a sudden staccato rapping on the door and he groaned. "Not yet eight o'clock and already they are after you."

"It could be anything," Andy said, starting for the door.

"It could be but it's not, that's the callboy's knock and you know it as well as I do and I bet you dollars to doughnuts that's just who it is. See?" He nodded with gloomy satisfaction when Andy unlocked the door and they saw the skinny, bare-legged messenger standing in the dark hall.

"What do you want, Woody?" Andy asked.

"I don' wan' no-fin," Woody lisped over his bare gums. Though he was in his early twenties he didn't have a tooth in his head. "Lieu-tenan' says bring, I bring." He handed Andy the message board with his name written on the outside.

Andy turned toward the light and opened it, reading the lieutenant's spiky scrawl on the slate, then took the chalk and scribbled his initials after it and returned it to the messenger. He closed the door behind him and went back to finish his breakfast, frowning in thought.

"Don't look at me that way," Sol said, "I didn't send the message. Am I wrong in guessing it's not the most pleasant of news?"

"It's the Eldsters, they're jamming the Square already and the precinct needs reinforcements."

"But why you? This sounds like a job for the harness bulls."

"Harness bulls! Where do you get that medieval slang? Of course they need patrolmen for the crowd, but there have to be detectives there to spot known agitators, pickpockets, purse-grabbers and the rest. It'll be murder in that park today. I have to check in by nine, so I have enough time to bring up some water first."

Andy dressed slowly in slacks and a loose sport shirt, then put a pan of water on the windowsill to warm in the sun. He took the two five-gallon plastic jerry cans, and when he went out Sol looked up from the TV set, glancing over the top of his old-fashioned glasses.

"When you bring back the water I'll fix you a drink—or do you think it is too early?"

"Not the way I feel today, it's not."

The hall was ink black once the door had closed behind him and he felt his way carefully along the wall to the stairs, cursing and almost falling when he stumbled over a heap of refuse someone had thrown there. Two flights down a window had been knocked through the wall and enough light came in to show him the way down the last two flights to the street. After the damp hallway the heat of Twenty-fifth Street hit him in a musty wave, a stifling miasma compounded of decay, dirt and unwashed humanity. He had to make his way through the women who already filled the steps of the building, walking carefully so that he didn't step on the children who were playing below. The sidewalk was still in shadow but so jammed with people that he walked in the street, well away from the curb to avoid the rubbish and litter banked high there. Days of heat had softened the tar so that it gave underfoot, then clutched at the soles of his shoes. There was the usual line leading to the columnar red water point on the corner of Seventh Avenue, but it broke up with angry shouts and some waved fists just as he reached it. Still muttering, the crowd dispersed and Andy saw that the duty patrolman was locking the steel door.

"What's going on?" Andy asked. "I thought this point was open until noon?"

The policeman turned, his hand automatically staying close to his gun until he recognized the detective from his own precinct. He tilted back his uniform cap and wiped the sweat from his forehead with the back of his hand.

"Just had the orders from the sergeant, all points closed for twenty-four hours. The reservoir level is low because of the drought, they gotta save water."

"That's a hell of a note," Andy said, looking at the key still in the lock. "I'm going on duty now and this means I'm not going to be drinking for a couple of days. . . ."

After a careful look around, the policeman unlocked the door and took one of the jerry cans from Andy. "One of these ought to hold you." He held it under the faucet while it filled, then lowered his voice. "Don't let it out, but the word is that there was another dynamiting job on the aqueduct upstate."

"Those farmers again?"

"It must be. I was on guard duty up there before I came to this precinct and it's rough, they just as soon blow you up with the aqueduct at the same time. Claim the city's stealing their water."

"They've got enough," Andy said, taking the full container. "More than they need. And there are thirty-five million people here in the city who get damn thirsty."

"Who's arguing?" the cop asked, slamming the door shut again and locking it tight.

Andy pushed his way back through the crowd around the steps and went through to the backyard first. All of the toilets were in use and he had to wait, and when he finally got into one of the cubicles he took the jerry cans with him; one of the kids playing in the pile of rubbish against the fence would be sure to steal them if he left them unguarded.

When he had climbed the dark flights once more and opened the door to the room he heard the clear sound of ice cubes rattling against glass.

"That's Beethoven's Fifth Symphony that you're playing," he said, dropping the containers and falling into a chair.

"It's my favorite tune," Sol said, taking two chilled glasses from the refrigerator and, with the solemnity of a religious ritual, dropped a tiny pearl onion into each. He passed one to Andy, who sipped carefully at the chilled liquid.

"It's when I taste one of these, Sol, that I almost believe you're not crazy after all. Why do they call them gibsons?"

"A secret lost behind the mists of time. Why is a stinger a stinger or a pink lady a pink lady?"

"I don't know—why? I never tasted any of them."

"I don't know either, but that's the name. Like those green things they serve in the knockjoints, Panamas. Doesn't mean anything, just a name."

"Thanks," Andy said, draining his glass. "The day looks better already."

He went into his room and took his gun and holster from the drawer and clipped it inside the waistband of his pants. His shield was on his key ring where he always kept it and he slipped his notepad in on top of it, then hesitated a moment. It was going to be a long and rough day and anything might happen. He dug his nippers out from under his shirts, then the soft plastic tube filled with shot. It might be needed in the crowd, safer than a gun with all those old people milling about. Not only that, but with the new austerity regulations you had to have a damn good reason for using up any ammunition. He washed as well as he could with the pint of water that had been warming in the sun on the windowsill, then scrubbed his face with the small shard of gray and gritty soap until his whiskers softened a bit. His razor blade was beginning to show obvious nicks along both edges and, as he honed it against the inside of his drinking glass, he thought that it was time to think about getting a new one. Maybe in the fall.

Sol was watering his window box when Andy came out, carefully irrigating the rows of herbs and tiny onions. "Don't take any wooden nickels," he said without looking up from his work. Sol had a million of them, all old. What in the world was a wooden nickel?

The sun was higher now and the heat was mounting in the sealed tar and concrete valley of the street. The band of shade was smaller and the steps were so packed with humanity that he couldn't leave the doorway. He carefully pushed by a tiny, runny-nosed girl dressed only in ragged gray underwear and descended a step. The gaunt women moved aside reluctantly, ignoring him, but the men stared at him with a cold look of hatred stamped across their features that gave them a strangely alike appearance, as though they were all members of the same angry family. Andy threaded his way through the last of them and when he reached the sidewalk he had to step over the outstretched leg of an old man who sprawled there. He looked dead, not asleep, and he might be for all that anyone cared. His foot was bare and filthy and a string tied about his ankle led to a naked baby that was sitting vacantly on the sidewalk chewing on a bent plastic dish. The baby was as dirty as the man and the string was tied about its chest under the pipestem arms because its stomach was swollen and heavy. Was the old man dead? Not that it mattered, the only work he had to do in the world was to act as an anchor for the baby and he could do that job just as well alive or dead.

Out of the room now, well away and unable to talk to Sol until he returned, he realized that once again he had not managed to mention Shirl. It would have been a simple enough thing to do, but he kept forgetting it, avoiding it. Sol was always talking about how horny he always was and how often he used to get laid when he was in the Army. He would understand.

They were roommates, that was all. There was nothing else between them. Friends, sure. But bringing a girl in to live wouldn't change that.

So why hadn't he told him?

Fall

"Everyone says this is the coldest October ever, I never seen a colder one. And the rain too, never hard enough to fill the reservoy or anything, but just enough to make you wet so you feel colder. Ain't that right?"

Shirl nodded, hardly listening to the words, but aware by the rising intonation of the woman's voice that a question had been asked. The line moved forward and she shuffled a few steps behind the woman who had been speaking—a shapeless bundle of heavy clothing covered with a torn plastic raincoat, with a cord tied about her middle so that she resembled a lumpy sack. Not that I look much better, Shirl thought, tugging the fold of blanket farther over her head to keep out the persistent drizzle. It wouldn't be much longer now, there were only a few dozen people ahead, but it had taken a lot more time than she thought it would; it was almost dark. A light came on over the tank car, glinting off its black sides and lighting up the slowly falling curtain of rain. The line moved again and the woman ahead of Shirl waddled forward, pulling the child after her, a bundle as wrapped and shapeless as its mother, its face hidden by a knotted scarf, that produced an almost constant whimpering.

"Stop that," the woman said. She turned to Shirl, her puffy face a red lumpiness around the dark opening of her almost toothless mouth. "He's crying because he's been to see the doc, thinks he's sick but it's only the kwash." She held up the child's swollen, ballooning hand. "You can tell when they swell up and get the black spots on the knees. Had to sit two weeks in the Bellevue clinic to see a doc who told me what I knew already. But that's the only way you get him to sign the slip. Got a peanut-butter ration that way. My old man loves the stuff. You live on my block, don't you? I think I seen you there?"

"Twenty-sixth Street," Shirl said, taking the cap off the jerry can and putting it into her coat pocket. She felt chilled through and was sure she was catching a cold.

"That's right, I knew it was you. Stick around and wait for me, we'll walk back together. It's getting late and plenty of punks would like to grab the water, they can always sell it. Mrs. Ramirez in my building, she's a spic but she's all right, you know, her family been in the building since the World War Two, she got a black eye so swole up she can't see through it and two teeth knocked out. Some punk got her with a club and took her water away."

"Yes, I'll wait for you, that's a good idea," Shirl said, suddenly feeling very alone.

"Cards," the patrolman said and she handed him the three Welfare cards, hers, Andy's and Sol's. He held them to the light, then handed them back to her. "Six quarts," he called out to the valve man.

"That's not right," Shirl said.

"Reduced ration today, lady, keep moving, there's a lot of people waiting."

She held out the jerry can and the valve man slipped the end of a large funnel into it and ran in the water. "Next," he called out.

The jerry can gurgled when she walked and was tragically light. She went and stood near the policeman until the woman came up, pulling the child with one hand and in the other carrying a five-gallon kerosene can that seemed almost full. She must have a big family.

"Let's go," the woman said and the child trailed, mewling faintly, at the end of her arm.

As they left the Twelfth Avenue railroad siding it grew darker, the rain soaking up all the failing light. The buildings here were mostly old warehouses and factories with blank solid walls concealing the tenants hidden away inside, the sidewalks wet and empty. The nearest streetlight was a block away. "My husband will give me hell coming home this late," the woman said as they turned the corner. Two figures blocked the sidewalk in front of them.

"Let's have the water," the nearest one said, and the distant light reflected from the knife he held before him.

"No, don't! Please don't!" the woman begged and swung her can of water out behind her, away from them. Shirl huddled against the wall and saw, when they walked forward, that they were just young boys, teen-agers. But they still had a knife.

"The water!" the first one said, jabbing his knife at the woman.

"Take it," she screeched, swinging the can like a weight on the end of her arm. Before the boy could dodge it caught him full in the side of the head, knocking him howling to the ground, the knife flying from his fingers. "You want some too?" she shouted, advancing on the second boy. He was unarmed.

"No, I don't want no trouble," he begged, pulling at the first one's arm, then retreating when she approached. When she bent to pick up the fallen knife, he managed to drag the other boy to his feet and half carry him around the corner. It had only taken a few seconds and all the time Shirl had stood with her back to the wall, trembling with fear.

"They got some surprise," the woman crowed, holding the worn carving knife up to admire it. "I can use this better than they can. Just punks, kids." She was excited and happy. During the entire time she had never released her grip on the child's hand; it was sobbing louder.

There was no more trouble and the woman went with Shirl as far as her door. "Thank you very much," Shirl said. "I don't know what I would have done . . ."

"That's no trouble," the woman beamed. "You saw what I did to him—and who got the knife now!" She stamped away, hauling the heavy can in one hand, the child in the other. Shirl went in.

"Where have you been?" Andy asked when she pushed open the door. "I was beginning to wonder what had happened to you." It was warm in the room, with a faint odor of fishy smoke, and he and Sol were sitting at the table with drinks in their hands.

"It was the water, the line must have been a block long. They only gave me six quarts, the ration has been cut again." She saw his black look and decided not to tell him about the trouble on the way back. He would be twice as angry then and she didn't want this meal to be spoiled.

"That's really wonderful," Andy said sarcastically. "The ration was already too small—so now they lower it even more. Better get out of those wet things, Shirl, and Sol will pour you a gibson. His homemade vermouth has ripened and I bought some vodka."

"Drink up," Sol said, handing her the chilled glass. "I made some soup with that ener-G junk, it's the only way it's edible, and it should be just about ready. We'll have that for the first course, before—" He finished the sentence by jerking his head in the direction of the refrigerator.

"What's up?" Andy asked. "A secret?"

"No secret," Shirl said, opening the refrigerator, "just a surprise. I got these today in the market, one for each of us." She took out a plate with three small soylent burgers on it. "They're the new ones, they had them on TV, with the smoky-barbecue flavor."

"They must have cost a fortune," Andy said. "We won't eat for the rest of the month."

"They're not as expensive as all that. Anyway, it was my own money, not the budget money, I used."

"It doesn't make any difference, money is money. We could probably live for a week on what these things cost."

"Soup's on," Sol said, sliding the plates onto the table. Shirl had a lump in her throat so she couldn't say anything; she sat and looked at her plate and tried not to cry.

"I'm sorry," Andy said. "But you know how prices are going up— we have to look ahead. City income tax is higher, eighty percent now, because of the raised Welfare payment, so it's going to be rough going this winter. Don't think I don't appreciate it. . . ."

"If you do, so why don't you shut up right there and eat your soup?" Sol said.

"Keep out of this, Sol," Andy said.

"I'll keep out of it when you keep the fight out of my room. Now come on, a nice meal like this, it shouldn't be spoiled."

Andy started to answer him, then changed his mind. He reached over and took Shirl's hand. "It is going to be a good dinner," he said. "Let's all enjoy it."

"Not that good," Sol said, puckering his mouth over a spoonful of soup. "Wait until you try this stuff. But the burgers will take the taste out of our mouths."

There was silence after that while they spooned up the soup, until Sol started on one of his Army stories about New Orleans and it was so impossible they had to laugh, and after that things were better. Sol shared out the rest of the gibsons while Shirl served the burgers.

"If I was drunk enough this would almost taste like meat," Sol announced, chewing happily.

"They are good," Shirl said. Andy nodded agreement. She finished the burger quickly and soaked up the juice with a scrap of weed-cracker, then sipped at her drink. The trouble on the way home with the water already seemed far distant. What was it the woman had said was wrong with the child?

"Do you know what 'kwash' is?" she asked.

Andy shrugged. "Some kind of disease, that's all I know. Why do you ask?"

"There was a woman next to me in line for the water, I was talking to her. She had a little boy with her who was sick with this kwash. I don't think she should have had him out in the rain, sick like that. And I was wondering if it was catching."

"That you can forget about," Sol said. " 'Kwash' is short for 'kwashiorkor.' If, in the interest of good health, you watched the medical programs like I do, or opened a book, you would know all about it. You can't catch it because it's a deficiency disease like beriberi."

"I never heard of that either," Shirl said.

"There's not so much of that, but there's plenty of kwash. It comes from not eating enough protein. They used to have it only in Africa but now they got it right across the whole U.S. Isn't that great? There's no meat around, lentils and soybeans cost too much, so the mamas stuff the kids with weedcrackers and candy, whatever is cheap. . . ."

The light bulb flickered, then went out. Sol felt his way across the room and found a switch in the maze of wiring on top of the refrigerator. A dim bulb lit up, connected to his batteries. "Needs a charge," he said, "but it can wait until morning. You shouldn't exercise after eating, bad for the circulation and digestion."

"I'm sure glad you're here, doctor," Andy said. "I need some medical advice. I've got this trouble. You see—everything I eat goes to my stomach. . . ."

"Very funny, Mr. Wiseguy. Shirl, I don't see how you put up with this joker."

They all felt better after the meal and they talked for a while, until Sol announced he was turning off the light to save the juice in the batteries. The small bricks of sea coal had burned to ash and the room was growing cold. They said good night and Andy went in first to get his flashlight; their room was even colder than the other.

"I'm going to bed," Shirl said. "I'm not really tired, but it's the only way to keep warm."

Andy flicked the overhead light switch uselessly. "The current is still off and there are some things I have to do. What is it—a week now since we had any electricity in the evening?"

"Let me get into bed and I'll work the flash for you—will that be all right?"

"It'll have to do."

He opened his notepad on top of the dresser, laid one of the re-usable forms next to it, then began copying information into the report. With his left hand he kept a slow and regular squeezing on the flashlight that produced steady illumination. The city was quiet tonight with the people driven from the streets by the cold and the rain; the whir of the tiny generator and the occasional squeak of the stylo on plastic sounded unnaturally loud. There was enough light from the flash for Shirl to get undressed by. She shivered when she took off her outer clothes and quickly pulled on heavy winter pajamas, a much-darned pair of socks she used for sleeping in, then put her heavy sweater on top. The sheets were cold and damp, they hadn't been changed since the water shortage, though she did try to air them out as often as she could. Her cheeks were damp, as damp as the sheets were when she put her fingertips up to touch them, and she realized that she was crying. She tried not to sniffle and bother Andy. He was doing his best, wasn't he? everything that it was possible to do. Yes, it had been a lot different before she came here, an easy life, good food and a warm room, and her own bodyguard, Tab, when she went out. And all she had to do was sleep with him a couple of times a week. She had hated it, even the touch of his hands, but at least it had been quick. Having Andy in bed was different and good and she wished that he were there right now. She shivered again and wished she could stop crying.

Winter

New York City trembled on the brink of disaster. Every locked warehouse was a nucleus of dissent, surrounded by crowds who were hungry and afraid and searching for someone to blame. Their anger incited them to riot, and the food riots turned to water riots and then to looting, wherever this was possible. The police fought back, only the thinnest of barriers between angry protest and bloody chaos.

At first nightsticks and weighted clubs stopped the trouble, and when this failed gas dispersed the crowds. The tension grew, since the people who fled only reassembled again in a different place. The solid jets of water from the riot trucks stopped them easily when they tried to break into the Welfare stations, but there were not enough trucks, nor was there more water to be had once they had pumped dry their tanks. The Health Department had forbidden the use of river water: it would have been like spraying poison. The little water that was available was badly needed for the fires that were springing up throughout the city. With the streets blocked in many places the fire-fighting equipment could not get through and the trucks were forced to make long detours. Some of the fires were spreading and by noon all of the equipment had been committed and was in use.

The first gun was fired a few minutes past twelve, on the morning of December 21st, by a Welfare Department guard who killed a man who had broken open a window of the Tompkins Square food depot and had tried to climb in. This was the first but not the last shot fired —nor was it the last person to be killed.

Flying wire sealed off some of the trouble areas, but there was only a limited supply of it. When it ran out the copters fluttered helplessly over the surging streets and acted as aerial observation posts for the police, finding the places where reserves were sorely needed. It was a fruitless labor because there were no reserves, everyone was in the front line.

After the first conflict nothing else made a strong impression on Andy. For the rest of the day and most of the night, he along with every other policeman in the city was braving violence and giving violence to restore law and order to a city torn by battle. The only rest he had was after he had fallen victim to his own gas and had managed to make his way to the Department of Hospitals ambulance for treatment. An orderly washed out his eyes and gave him a tablet to counteract the gut-tearing nausea. He lay on one of the stretchers inside, clutching his helmet, bombs and club to his chest, while he recovered. The ambulance driver sat on another stretcher by the door, armed with a .30-caliber carbine, to discourage anyone from too great an interest in the ambulance or its valuable surgical contents. Andy would like to have lain there longer, but the cold mist was rolling in through the open doorway, and he began to shiver so hard that his teeth shook together. It was difficult to drag to his feet and climb to the ground, yet once he was moving he felt a little better—and warmer. The attack had been broken up and he moved slowly to join the nearest cluster of blue-coated figures, wrinkling his nose at the foul odor of his clothes.

From this point on, the fatigue never left him and he had memories only of shouting faces, running feet, the sound of shots, screams, the thud of gas grenades, of something unseen that had been thrown at him and hit the back of his hand and raised an immense bruise.

By nightfall it was raining, a cold downpour mixed with sleet, and it was this and exhaustion that drove the people from the streets, not the police. Yet when the crowds were gone the police found that their work was just beginning. Gaping windows and broken doorways had to be guarded until they could be repaired, the injured had to be found and brought in for treatment, while the Fire Department needed aid in halting the countless fires. This went on through the night and at dawn Andy found himself slumped on a bench in the precinct, hearing his name being called off from a list by Lieutenant Grassioli.

"And that's all that can be spared," the lieutenant added. "You men draw rations before you leave and turn in your riot equipment. I want you all back here at eighteen-hundred and I don't want excuses. Our troubles aren't over yet."

Sometime during the night the rain had stopped. The rising sun cast long shadows down the crosstown streets, putting a golden sheen on the wet, black pavement. A burned-out brownstone was still smoking and Andy picked his way through the charred wreckage that littered the street in front of it. On the corner of Seventh Avenue were the crushed wrecks of two pedicabs, already stripped of any usable parts, and a few feet farther on, the huddled body of a man. He might be asleep, but when Andy passed, the upturned face gave violent evidence that the man was dead. He walked on, ignoring it. The Department of Sanitation would be collecting only corpses today.

The first cavemen were coming out of the subway entrance, blinking at the light. During the summer everyone laughed at the cavemen —the people whom Welfare had assigned to living quarters in the stations of the now-silent subways—but as the cold weather approached, the laughter was replaced by envy. Perhaps it was filthy down there, dusty, dark, but there were always a few electric heaters turned on. They weren't living in luxury, but at least Welfare didn't let them freeze. Andy turned into his own block.

Going up the stairs in his building, he trod heavily on some of the sleepers but was too fatigued to care—or even notice. He had trouble fumbling his key into the lock and Sol heard him and came to open it.

"I just made some soup," Sol said. "You timed it perfectly."

Andy pulled the broken remains of some weedcrackers from his coat pocket and spilled them onto the table.

"Been stealing food?" Sol asked, picking up a piece and nibbling on it. "I thought no grub was being given out for two more days?"

"Police ration."

"Only fair. You can't beat up the citizenry on an empty stomach. I'll throw some of these into the soup, give it some body. I guess you didn't see TV yesterday so you wouldn't know about all the fun and games in Congress. Things are really jumping. . . ."

"Is Shirl awake yet?" Andy asked, shucking out of his coat and dropping heavily into a chair.

Sol was silent a moment, then he said slowly, "She's not here."

Andy yawned. "It's pretty early to go out. Why?"

"Not today, Andy." Sol stirred the soup with his back turned. "She went out yesterday, a couple of hours after you did. She's not back yet—"

"You mean she was out all the time during the riots—and last night too? What did you do?" He sat upright, his bone-weariness forgotten.

"What could I do? Go out and get myself trampled to death like the rest of the old fogies? I bet she's all right, she probably saw all the trouble and decided to stay with friends instead of coming back here."

"What friends? What are you talking about? I have to go find her."

"Sit!" Sol ordered. "What can you do out there? Have some soup and get some sleep, that's the best thing you can do. She'll be okay. I know it," he added reluctantly.

"What do you know, Sol?" Andy took him by the shoulders, half turning him from the stove.

"Don't handle the merchandise!" Sol shouted, pushing the hand away. Then, in a quieter voice: "All I know is she just didn't go out of here for nothing, she had a reason. She had her old coat on, but I could see what looked like a real nifty dress underneath. And nylon stockings. A fortune on her legs. And when she said so long I saw she had lots of makeup on."

"Sol—what are you trying to say?"

"I'm not trying—I'm saying. She was dressed for visiting, not for shopping, like she was on the way out to see someone. Her old man, maybe, she could be visiting him."

"Why should she want to see him?"

"You tell me? You two had a fight, didn't you? Maybe she went away for a while to cool off."

"A fight . . . I guess so." Andy dropped back into the chair, squeezing his forehead between his palms. Had it only been last night? No, the night before last. It seemed a hundred years since they had had that stupid argument. But they were bickering so much these days. One more fight shouldn't make any difference. He looked up with sudden fear. "She didn't take her things—anything with her?" he asked.

"Just a little bag," Sol said, and put a steaming bowl on the table in front of Andy. "Eat up. I'll pour one for myself." Then, "She'll be back."

Andy was almost too tired to argue—and what could be said? He spooned the soup automatically, then realized as he tasted it that he was very hungry. He ate with his elbow on the table, his free hand supporting his head.

"You should have heard the speeches in the Senate yesterday," Sol said. "Funniest show on earth. They're trying to push this Emergency Bill through—some emergency, it's only been a hundred years in the making—and you should hear them talking all around the little points and not mentioning the big ones." His voice settled into a rich Southern accent. "Faced by dire straits, we propose a survey of all the ee-mense riches of this the greatest ee-luvial basin, the delta, suh, of the mightiest of rivers, the Mississippi. Dikes and drains, suh, science, suh, and you will have here the richest farmlands in the Western World!" Sol blew on his soup angrily. " 'Dikes' is right—another finger in the dike. They've been over this ground a thousand times before. But does anyone mention out loud the sole and only reason for the Emergency Bill? They do not. After all these years they're too chicken to come right out and tell the truth, so they got it hidden away in one of the little riders tacked onto the bottom."

"What are you talking about?" Andy asked, only half listening, still worrying about Shirl.

"Birth control, that's what. They are finally getting around to legalizing clinics that will be open to anyone—married or not—and making it a law that all mothers *must* be supplied with birth-control information. Boy, are we going to hear some howling when the bluenoses find out about that—and the Pope will really plotz!"

"Not now, Sol, I'm tired. Did Shirl say anything about when she would be back?"

"Just what I told you . . ." He stopped and listened to the sound of footsteps coming down the hall. They stopped—and there was a light knocking on the door.

Andy was there first, twisting at the knob, tearing the door open. "Shirl!" he said. "Are you all right?"

"Yes, sure—I'm fine."

He held her to him, tightly, almost cutting off her breath. "With the riots—I didn't know what to think," he said. "I just came in a little while ago myself. Where have you been? What happened?"

"I just wanted to get out for a while, that's all." She wrinkled her nose. "What's that funny smell?"

He stepped away from her, anger welling up through the fatigue. "I caught some of my own puke gas and heaved up. It's hard to get off. What do you mean that you wanted to get out for a while?"

"Let me get my coat off."

Andy followed her into the other room and closed the door behind them. She was taking a pair of high-heeled shoes out of the bag she carried and putting them into the closet. "Well?" he said.

"Just that, it's not complicated. I was feeling trapped in here, with the shortages and the cold and everything, and never seeing you, and I felt bad about the fight we had. Nothing seemed to be going right. So I thought if I dressed up and went to one of the restaurants where I used to go, just have a cup of kofee or something, I might feel better. A morale booster, you know." She looked up at his cold face, then glanced quickly away.

"Then what happened?" he asked.

"I'm not in the witness box, Andy. Why the accusing tone?"

He turned his back and looked out the window. "I'm not accusing you of anything, but—you were out all night. How do you expect me to feel?"

"Well, you know how bad it was yesterday, I was afraid to come back. I was up at Curley's—"

"The meateasy?"

"Yes, but if you don't eat anything it's not expensive. It's just the food that costs. I met some people I knew and we talked, they were going to a party and invited me and I went along. We were watching the news about the riots on TV and no one wanted to go out, so the party just went on and on." She paused. "That's all."

"All?" An angry question, a dark suspicion.

"That's all," she said, and her voice was now as cold as his.

She turned her back to him and began to pull off her dress, and their words lay like a cold barrier between them. Andy dropped onto the bed and turned his back on her as well so that they were like strangers, even in the tiny room.

Spring

The funeral drew them together as nothing else had during the cold depths of winter. It was a raw day, gusting wind and rain, but there was still a feeling that winter was on the way out. But it had been too long a winter for Sol and his cough had turned into a cold, the cold into pneumonia, and what can an old man do in a cold room without drugs in a winter that does not seem to end? Die, that was all, so he had died. They had forgotten their differences during his illness and Shirl had nursed him as best she could, but careful nursing does not cure pneumonia. The funeral had been as brief and cold as the day and in the early darkness they went back to the room. They had not been back a half an hour before there was a quick rapping on the door. Shirl gasped.

"The callboy. They can't. You don't have to work today."

"Don't worry. Even Grassy wouldn't go back on his word about a thing like this. And besides, that's not the callboy's knock."

"Maybe a friend of Sol's who couldn't get to the funeral."

She went to unlock the door and had to blink into the darkness of the hall for a moment before she recognized the man standing there.

"Tab! It is you, isn't it? Come in, don't stand there. Andy, I told you about Tab my bodyguard . . ."

"Afternoon, Miss Shirl," Tab said stolidly, staying in the hall. "I'm sorry, but this is no social call. I'm on the job now."

"What is it?" Andy asked, walking over next to Shirl.

"You have to realize I take the work that is offered to me," Tab said. He was unsmiling and gloomy. "I've been in the bodyguard pool since September, just the odd jobs, no regular assignment, we take whatever work we can get. A man turns down a job he goes right back to the end of the list. I have a family to feed. . . ."

"What are you trying to say?" Andy asked. He was aware that someone was standing in the darkness behind Tab and he could tell by the shuffle of feet that there were others out of sight down the hall.

"Don't take no stuff," the man in back of Tab said in an unpleasant nasal voice. He stayed behind the bodyguard where he could not be seen. "I got the law on my side. I paid you. Show him the order!"

"I think I understand now," Andy said. "Get away from the door, Shirl. Come inside, Tab, so we can talk to you."

Tab started forward and the man in the hall tried to follow him. "You don't go in there without me—" he shrilled. His voice was cut off as Andy slammed the door in his face.

"I wish you hadn't done that," Tab said. He was wearing his spike-studded iron knucks, his fist clenched tight around them.

"Relax," Andy said. "I just wanted to talk to you alone first, find out what was going on. He has a squat-order, doesn't he?"

Tab nodded, looking unhappily down at the floor.

"What on earth are you two talking about?" Shirl asked, worriedly glancing back and forth at their set expressions.

Andy didn't answer and Tab turned to her. "A squat-order is issued by the court to anyone who can prove they are really in need of a place to live. They only give so many out, and usually just to people with big families that have had to get out of some other place. With a squat-order you can look around and find a vacant apartment or room or anything like that, and the order is a sort of search warrant. There can be trouble, people don't want to have strangers walking in on them, that kind of thing, so anyone with a squat-order takes along a bodyguard. That's where I come in, the party out there in the hall, name of Belicher, hired me."

"But what are you doing here?" Shirl asked, still not understanding.

"Because Belicher is a ghoul, that's why," Andy said bitterly. "He hangs around the morgue looking for bodies."

"That's one way of saying it," Tab answered, holding on to his temper. "He's also a guy with a wife and kids and no place to live, that's another way of looking at it."

There was a sudden hammering on the door and Belicher's complaining voice could be heard outside. Shirl finally realized the significance of Tab's presence, and she gasped. "You've here because you're helping them," she said. "They found out that Sol is dead and they want this room."

Tab could only nod mutely.

"There's still a way out," Andy said. "If we had one of the men here from my precinct, living in here, then these people couldn't get in."

The knocking was louder and Tab took a half step backward toward the door. "If there was somebody here now, that would be okay, but Belicher could probably take the thing to the squat court and get occupancy anyway because he has a family. I'll do what I can to help you—but Belicher, he's still my employer."

"Don't open that door," Andy said sharply. "Not until we have this straightened out."

"I have to—what else can I do?" He straightened up and closed his fist with the knucks on it. "Don't try to stop me, Andy. You're a policeman, you know the law about this."

"Tab, must you?" Shirl asked in a low voice.

He turned to her, eyes filled with unhappiness. "We were good friends once, Shirl, and that's the way I'm going to remember it. But you're not going to think much of me after this because I have to do my job. I have to let them in."

"Go ahead—open the damn door," Andy said bitterly, turning his back and walking over to the window.

The Belichers swarmed in. Mr. Belicher was thin, with a strangely shaped head, almost no chin and just enough intelligence to sign his name to the Welfare application. Mrs. Belicher was the support of the family; from the flabby fat of her body came the children, all seven of them, to swell the Relief allotment on which they survived. Number eight was pushing an extra bulge out of the dough of her flesh; it was really number eleven since three of the younger Belichers had perished through indifference or accident. The largest girl, she must have been all of twelve, was carrying the sore-covered infant which stank abominably and cried continuously. The other children shouted at each other now, released from the silence and tension of the dark hall.

"Oh, looka the nice fridge," Mrs. Belicher said, waddling over and opening the door.

"Don't touch that," Andy said, and Belicher pulled him by the arm.

"I like this room—it's not big, you know, but nice. What's in here?" He started toward the open door in the partition.

"That's my room," Andy said, slamming it shut in his face. "Just keep out of there."

"No need to act like that," Belicher said, sidling away quickly like a dog that has been kicked too often. "I got my rights. The law says I can look wherever I want with a squat-order." He moved farther away as Andy took a step toward him. "Not that I'm doubting your word, mister, I believe you. This room here is fine, got a good table, chairs, bed. . . ."

"Those things belong to me. This is an empty room, and a small one at that. It's not big enough for you and all your family."

"It's big enough, all right. We lived in smaller. . . ."

"Andy—stop them! Look—" Shirl's unhappy cry spun Andy around and he saw that two of the boys had found the packets of herbs that Sol had grown so carefully in his window box, and were tearing them open, thinking that it was food of some kind.

"Put these things down," he shouted, but before he could reach them they had tasted the herbs, then spat them out.

"Burn my mouth!" the bigger boy screamed and sprayed the contents of the packet on the floor. The other boy bounced up and down with excitement and began to do the same thing with the rest of the herbs. They twisted away from Andy and before he could stop them the packets were empty.

As soon as Andy turned away, the younger boy, still excited, climbed on the table—his mud-stained foot wrappings leaving filthy smears—and turned up the TV. Blaring music crashed over the screams of the children and the ineffectual calls of their mother. Tab pulled Belicher away as he opened the wardrobe to see what was inside.

"Get these kids out of here," Andy said, white-faced with rage.

"I got a squat-order, I got rights," Belicher shouted, backing away and waving an imprinted square of plastic.

"I don't care what rights you have," Andy told him, opening the hall door. "We'll talk about that when these brats are outside."

Tab settled it by grabbing the nearest child by the scruff of the neck and pushing it out through the door. "Mr. Rusch is right," he said. "The kids can wait outside while we settle this."

Mrs. Belicher sat down heavily on the bed and closed her eyes, as though all this had nothing to do with her. Mr. Belicher retreated against the wall saying something that no one heard or bothered to listen to. There were some shrill cries and angry sobbing from the hall as the last child was expelled.

Andy looked around and realized that Shirl had gone into their room; he heard the key turn in the lock. "I suppose this is it?" he said, looking steadily at Tab.

The bodyguard shrugged helplessly. "I'm sorry, Andy, honest to God I am. What else can I do? It's the law, and if they want to stay here you can't get them out."

"It's the law, it's the law," Belicher echoed tonelessly.

There was nothing Andy could do with his clenched fists and he had to force himself to open them. "Help me carry these things into the other room, will you, Tab?"

"Sure," Tab said, and took the other end of the table. "Try and explain to Shirl about my part in this, will you? I don't think she understands that it's just a job I have to do."

Their footsteps crackled on the dried herbs and seeds that littered the floor and Andy did not answer him.

I am alone in the African street, lost, afraid, and without allies. I understand nothing. Yet this is the street where I was born. I too once delighted in massacre, slavery, castration, and cannibalism, and my conscience told me these things were right. I too once consulted the witch doctor, and accepted his magic, and it was not very long ago. What prevents me today? Nothing prevents me, excepting only the wisdom of my civilization and the conditioning it has brought to my instincts in my lifetime.

—Robert Ardrey, in *African Genesis*

GROANING HINGES OF THE WORLD
by R. A. Lafferty

Eginhard wrote that the Hinges of the World are, the one of them in the Carnic Alps north of the Isarco and quite near high Glockner, and the other one in the Wangerooge in the Frisian Islands off the Weser mouth and under the water of this shelf; and that these hinges are made of iron. It is the Germanies, the whole great country between these hinges, that turns over, he wrote, after either a long generation or a short generation.

The only indication of the turning over is a groaning of the World Hinges too brief to terrify. That which rises out of the Earth has the same appearance in mountains and rivers and towns and people as the land that it replaces. The land and the people do not know that they have turned over, but their neighbors may come to know it. A man looking at the new, after the land had turned over, would not see it different from the old: and yet it would be different. But the places and the persons would have the same names and appearances as those they replaced.

Strabo, however, eight hundred years earlier, wrote that the Hinges of the World are in high Armenia, the one of them on the Albanian extension into the Caspian Sea, the other at Mount Ararat itself (known from the earliest time as the hinge of the world). Strabo wrote that it is the whole Caucasus Mountains that turn over, with all the people and goats: and the hinges on which the region turns are bronze.

But Elpidius claimed that the Hinges of the World are, the one of them at Aneto in Andorra (*anciano Gozne del Mundo*), and the other at Hendaye on the Biscay coast. He stated that it is the Pyrenees that turn over, that their turning is always for a very long generation, and that the Basques who obtain in that region are people from under the earth and are much more Basque-like than those they replace. He wrote that the Hinges of the World are here of rock crystal.

All three of the writers give the name Revolution to this turning over of a region, but lesser authorities have later given that name to less literal turnings. There is something very consistent about the reports of these three men, and there are aspects of their accounts almost too strange not to be true.

But they all lie. How would any of these regions turn over on hinges? And if they have the same appearance in land and people after they have turned over, who would know that they had turned? It would seem that if a man have the same name and appearance after he has turned over, then he is still the same man. As to the deep groaning of the World Hinges which all three authorities state is heard at the time of turnover, why, one hears groanings all the time.

The only region of the world that does in fact turn over is far around the world from all of these. It is in the western Moluccas. One hinge is just north of Berebere on Morotai Island and the other is at Ganedidalem on Jilolo or Halmahera Island. These are the true Hinges of the World and they are made of hard kapok wood well oiled.

All the peoples of this region were peaceful with themselves and their neighbors almost all the time. The people under the world were no more than people in stories to them. There was fire under the islands, of course, and volcanoes on them; and the people under the earth were said to be themselves brands of fire. Well, let them stay under the world then. Let the hinges not turn again!

But one day a fisherman from Obi Island was out in his boat right on the edge of the region that was said to have turned over in the old times. He had pulled in only a few fish in his nets and he had about decided to sail to Jilolo and steal enough fish from the timid people there to fill his boat.

Then he heard a short deep groaning. He felt a shock, and a shock wave. But who pays attention to things like that around the volcano islands? He was uneasy, of course, but a man is supposed to be uneasy several times a day.

He pulled in his net. Then he felt a further shock. This net had been torn in one place and he had tied it together. He had tied it, as he always did, with a *pendek* knot. But now he saw that it was tied with a *panjang* knot which he had never tied in his life. He noticed also that the fish in his net were of a little bit darker color than usual. He wouldn't have noticed this if he hadn't noticed the knot first. In great fear he set his short sail, and he drove his oar as hard as he could to take the boat toward his own Obi Island.

The only region where the *panjang* knot is commonly tied is the region under the world. This region had turned up in the age of the fisherman's ancestors, to the death and destruction of many of them, and now it may have turned up once more. A part of the fisherman's net must have been in the region that turned over, he was that close to the fringe of it. The fisherman knew that the upheaval people would have the same names and appearances as people he knew; he knew also that the whole business might be a high story.

Fast canoes out of Jilolo overtook the fisherman before he was home. He was frightened at first, but when they came closer to overhaul him, he saw that the men in them were friends of his, Jilolo people, the most gentle people in the world. You could push the Jilolos, you could steal their fish, you could steal their fruits, you could even steal their boats, and they would only smile sadly. The fisherman forgot all about the turnover when the gentle Jilolos overtook him.

"Hello, Jilolo men, give me fish, give me fruits," the fisherman said, "or I will run down your canoes and push you into the water. Give me fish. My boat is not near full of fish."

"Hello, our friend," the Jilolo men said to the fisherman. Then they came on board his boat and cut off his head. They were men of the same names and appearances as those he had known, and yet they were different.

The Jilolos tied the fisherman's head onto the prow of the foremost and biggest canoe. "Guide us into the best landing of Obi Island," they told the head. So the head guided them in, telling them whether to veer a little to the east or the west, telling them about the cross-wave and the shoal, telling them how to go right to the landing. (The shy Jilolos had formerly used a poorer landing when they came to Obi Island.)

"Shout a greeting," the men told the head when they were very near the land. "They will know your voice on shore. Tell them to bring out all their spears and fish spears, and the Dutch gun, and stack them all by the landing. Tell them we are their good friends come to play a game with them." So the head shouted it all out.

The Obi men came out and stacked all their spears and the fish spears and the Dutch gun by the landing, chuckling over whatever new game it should be. Weapons had not been used for anything but games for many years.

The Jilolo men came onto shore. They took the spears and the Dutch gun. One of them understood the gun. He shot it three times and killed three of the Obi men with it. Other Jilolo men killed other Obi men with spears and with clubs they brought with them.

"This is the game we play with you," the Jilolos said. They caught twenty of the Obi girls and young women and took them with them. They gave instructions as to what tribute must be brought to them weekly by the Obis. They killed two more Obi men to make sure that their message was understood. Then they went away in their canoes.

And it was all confusion that they left behind them.

One of the Obi men, however, in spite of the killing and confusion, had untied the fisherman's head from the prow of the biggest canoe. Now some of the frightened Obi men took the head with them into the long hut and questioned it as to what this should mean.

"The region has turned over on its hinges," the fisherman's head said, "just as it sometimes turned over and over again in the days of our distant grandfathers. I was out in my boat fishing. I heard the short deep groaning; I felt the shock, and the shock wave. But who pays attention to things like these around the volcano islands. Then I pulled in my net with the few fish in it.

"This net had been torn in one place, and I had tied it together with a *pendek* knot. Now I saw that it was tied with a *panjang* knot, which I never tied in my life, but which the people under the earth tie. I noticed also that the fish in my net were a little darker color than is common. This means that I was on the edge of the region and the region has turned over.

"Oh, my family and my people, it is all misery and death for us

now! The Jilolo men will have the same names and appearances as
those they have displaced, but you see already that they are not the
same. No more will we be able to push the Jilolos down and take their
fish and fruits and boats. We will not be able to push them into the
water or have fun with them. They have taken the bodies of some
of our men with them; they have taken some of our girls and young
women with them; and they will be having fun with both tonight. We
used to make jokes with each other about the stories that we used to
eat each other. It has come back to us now. That whole part of the
world has turned over on its hinges. We die in our woe."

The fisherman's head was in great pain. One of the men gave it a
stick to bite on. And in a little while it died.

And there followed one of the most horrifying ages ever in those
lilac waters. The turned-up Jilolos were the demons, the old slavers
come back. They were like the tearing, meat-eating birds swooping in. They were like bloody dragons. They came one day and took
an Obi man away from his brother. The next day they came again and
said, "Your brother wants to talk to you."

They had a drumhead covered with the brother's skin. They beat
on it till it sounded like the brother's voice booming. That is what
they meant that his brother wanted to talk to him.

These Jilolos gnawed roast meat from men's ribs as they strode
about for mockery. They burned down the huts and the long huts of
the Obi. They did the same thing to the people of Batjan and Misool
and Mangole and Sanana. All the leading men of those places were
hiding in the hills.

The Jilolos said that they would kill nine men for every leading
man who was hiding. Many of the leading men, hearing of this,
came out of their hiding and let themselves be killed to save the lives
of many more. Soon there were only a few leading men left.

The Jilolos cut out the eyes and tongues and gonads of people
and left them blind and mutilated and dying. They roasted some of
the people alive. They are best that way, they said. "How is it that in
the old days we ate only fish and pig and fruit?" the Jilolos asked.
"How have we missed this fine thing so long?"

The Jilolos set fires in the coconut groves and spice bushes and
kapok forests of the five islands. Fires rose over these islands day and
night, brighter even than the volcano fires of Jilolo itself. Anyone who
tried to put out the fire would be burned up in the fire, they said.

They tied sacks over the heads of men before they killed them.
This was to trap their souls and kill them too. They were merciless.

They violated and killed little children. They skinned some people before they killed them. They killed so many people that they took only their eyes and hearts to eat. Carrion birds gobbled down from the high air, and sharks jostled into the waters drawn by more blood than had been known for many ages.

So it went for a year and a day. Whole islands moaned and bled with the abomination of it, and the oceans were black with reeking blood.

There was one old Dutchman who still lived on Obi Island. After the Dutch days, he had gone home to Dutchland. He had missed the really busy seas and ports with the tang of trade to them, and the ordered rich land in all its bright neatness. He had been homesick for many years, so he went home.

But he found that the home seas were cluttered with belching ships that fouled the air (he had forgotten that part); he found the land was overcrowded with Dutchmen all busy and benign (he had forgotten that part too), and the roads and lanes were full of bicycles and motor cars. He found that it was cold and gusty and demanding, and the bright neat colors were not nearly so bright as those of the islands. He discovered that neatness and the appearance of respectability were required of him, and he had long since turned into a loose old rounder. He became homesick for the second time, and he returned to the islands and Obi Island. He had found that he could not Dutch it over the Dutch themselves, but he could still Dutch it over the Obis.

Now the Jilolos demanded that the Obis give up their Dutchman to them, or they would kill one hundred Obis. They wanted to have fun with the Dutchman and then kill him in an unusual way. They wanted to see if Dutch flesh was really prime stuff. So the Obis came sadly to their duty.

"We will have to give you up," they told the Dutchman when they had come to his house in the hills. "We like you, but we don't like you as well as one hundred of ourselves. Come along now. There is no way out of it."

"This Dutchman, about to be given up, will think of a way out of it," the Dutchman said. "A thing that is done can be undone. Can there be found twelve leading men left alive here, and twelve in the peninsula north of Berebere?"

"There are barely that many of us. We are they," the men said. "We believe that there are barely that many leading men left north of Berebere."

"Inform yourselves, and inform them," the Dutchman said. "Each party will go out in twelve fishing boats that have windlass winches for the nets. It will take the power of all the windlasses together to turn the things, and even then it may not work. And both parties will have to do it at exactly the same time."

"How will we know it is the same time, with the distance between the two groups?" the men asked.

"I don't know," the Dutchman said.

But one of the men there had affinity with two large birds of the kind called *radjawall,* who were larger than others of their species and special in several ways. They preyed over the ocean as well as over the land (they were, in fact, sea eagles), they talked more canny than parrots, and they were more intelligent than the *derek-derek,* the crane. The man went out of the Dutchman's house and whistled loudly. The two big birds appeared as two dots in the sky, they came on very rapidly, and then they were there with the men.

"Oh, yes, I've heard of you two fellows," the Dutchman said to the birds. "If one of you were flying high over Ganedidalem and the other over Berebere, could you still see each other at that distance?"

"Yes, if we were high enough, we could still see each other," one of the birds said.

"And would you be too high to see our ready-signal from the shores then?"

"No, we could see that too," the other bird said. "Tell us what you want us to do."

The Dutchman carefully told them about the affair. Then he said, "The one of you fly now to Berebere and find the men there. Tell them how it is. Tell them that we start now and will be at our place in the early morning. Let them be at their place then too. And caution them to be clear of the Hinges when they do it, on the outside of them, or they may find themselves turned over when it happens. In the morning you two birds will give the signal to each other and to us so we can do it together."

The one bird flew off to Berebere. The twelve leading men, each one taking three lesser men with him, cast off in twelve fishing boats. They set sail on the evening wind; and with the wind and the oars going all night, they were off Ganedidalem in the early morning.

They found the great Hinge in an inlet, just where legend had always said it should be. They took the twelve windlass winches off the twelve fishing boats, and the Dutchman rigged them to the kapok-wood axle of the World Hinge. There would be no trouble about the same thing up at Berebere. The men at Berebere are handier and more mechanical than the men of Obi.

Then four men stood at each windlass to throw his weight to the thing. The Dutchman gave the ready signal to the bird in the sky. Then they waited.

One minute later, the bird flared his great wings and began to dive straight down for signal. Long leagues to the north, off Berebere, the other bird did the same thing.

"Heave!" cried the Dutchman. "All heave! For our lives, it is now or it is nevermore with us!" And all heaved at the windlass winches, turning the cranks while the ropes sounded and moaned.

Then began the groaning of the World Hinges, more horrible than could be believed! The Earth shook, and the Island smoked and bawled. This was unnatural, it was a violation. Always before, the hinges had turned from natural forces in the earth that had come to their term and time.

Groaning yet more horrible! The ropes cried like infants from the strain on them, the cranks whined with the sound of hard wood about to shatter. The Hinge groaned a final terrible time. There was the shock! And the shock wave.

Then they were done with it, or they were undone forever.

"Let us go back to Obi Island and wait," the Dutchman said. "I believe that it turned over when the Hinge groaned last and loudest. If the raiding stops, then we have done it. If it has not stopped, then we are dead forever."

"Let us go to Jilolo Island and *not* wait," the Obi men said. "We will have bloody death there, or we will have us a lot of fun."

The Obis with the Dutchman rowed and sailed for Jilolo all day, and came there in the evening. They found Jilolo men. They pushed them down, they stole their fish and fruits and boats, they pushed them in the water and laughed at them. This was the fun they hadn't had for a long time.

These were Jilolos of the same names and appearances as the horrible killers of the last time, but they were different. You could push them down and take advantage of them; you didn't have to be afraid of them. For they were also the men of the same names and appearances of the time before last, and they only smiled sadly when they were robbed and pushed down.

The Obi men called the girls and young women who had been

stolen from them, and took them in the boats with them and went home. So peace returned, and it was all as it had been before with them.

Only not quite.

These girls and young women, robbed from the Obi and now taken back by them, had been on Jilolo when it turned back. It was in reverse with them. With the turning back, they became their own counterparts from under the world, the meanest, most troublesome women ever found anywhere, yet of the same names and appearances as the girls and young women before. They raised hell from one end of Obi to the other when they got home, and they kept it up all their lives.

So it was a troubled peace that came to Obi. Even so, many said it was better than to be killed by the Jilolo. Others said it was about the same thing.

That is the only place, there in the western Moluccas, where the World Hinges do really turn and a whole region may experience this revolution. The other places are almost surely fable.

A man just back from high Armenia says he examined the hinges there and they are bronze turned green with great age. They apparently have not turned since the drying of the flood. And if Armenia would turn over, who would know it? You can turn an Armenian upside down and hardly tell it. Those fellows look about the same on both ends.

As to the Germanies, those hinges in the Carnic Alps and in the Wangerooge are of badly rusted iron. Nobody can tell when they turned last, but should they turn now (the shape they are in) it would make a groaning heard around the world. Besides, if this country had turned in modern centuries, there would have to be some indication of it; some stark frightful thing would have happened there comparable to the revolution of the Jilolos. The people and places, keeping the same names and appearances, would have become immeasurably different in not too subtle ways, would have become violent and appalling. Is there any report of such a thing happening in our own days or those of our fathers?

And in the Pyrenees, is there any indication that they have turned, lately or ever? Rock crystal does not rust, but it does acquire a patina of unuse. Yet one has said of the Canigou, which I take to apply to all the Pyrenees and all the people in them, that it is unchanging forever, but that it is created anew every morning. The Hinges at Aneto and Hendaye either do not turn at all, or they turn every night.

Automobiles are multiplying three times faster than people and five times faster than roads necessary to accommodate them. Freeways are obsolete before completion. If all our registered vehicles were laid end to end, the line would begin to approach in length the total mileage of city streets in the United States. Which suggests why Boston had a traffic jam a few years ago—no special cause—that froze the entire downtown area for five hours. Or why a single New Jersey jam lasted seven hours and tied up a million and a half vehicles.

—David Lyle, in *Esquire*

GAS MASK

by James D. Houston

Charlie Bates didn't mind the freeways much. As he often told his wife when he arrived home from work, he could take them or leave them alone. He listed freeways among those curious obstacle-conveniences with which the world seemed so unavoidably cluttered. Charlie was neither surprised nor dismayed, then, when one summer afternoon about five thirty the eight lanes of traffic around him slowed to a creep and finally to a standstill.

He grew uneasy only when movement resumed half an hour later. His engine was off; the car was in gear; yet it moved forward slowly, as if another car were pushing. Charlie turned around, but the driver behind was turned, too, and the driver beyond him. All the drivers in all the lanes were turned to see who was pushing. Charlie heard his license plate crinkle. He opened his door and stood on the sill.

He was on a high, curving overpass that looked down on a lower overpass and farther down onto a 12-lane straightaway leading to the city's center. As far as Charlie could see in any direction cars were jammed end to end, lane to lane, and nothing moved. The pushing had stopped. Evidently there was nowhere else to push.

He looked into the cars near him. The drivers leaned a little with the curve's sloping bank. Nobody seemed disturbed. They waited quietly. All the engines were off now. Below him the lower levels waited, too—thousands of cars and not a sound, no horns, no one yelling. At first the silence bothered Charlie, frightened him. He decided, however, that it really was the only civilized way to behave. "No use getting worked up," he thought. He climbed back in and closed the door as softly as he could.

As Charlie got used to the silence, he found it actually restful. Another hour passed. Then a helicopter flew over, and a loudspeaker announced, "May I have your attention, please. You are part of a citywide traffic deadlock. It will take at least 24 hours to clear. You have the choice of remaining overnight or leaving your car on the freeway. The city will provide police protection through the crisis."

The copter boomed its message about every 50 yards. A heavy murmur followed it down the freeway. The driver next to Charlie leaned out his window.

"Are they nuts?"

Charlie looked at him.

"They must be nuts. Twenty-four hours to clear a goddamn traffic jam."

Charlie shook his head, sharing the man's bafflement.

"Probably a pileup further down," the man said. "I've seen 'em before. Never takes over an hour or two. I don't know about you, but I'm stickin' it out. If they think I'm gonna leave my goddamn Valiant out here on the freeway, they're all wet."

His name was Arvin Bainbridge. While two more hours passed, he and Charlie chatted about traffic and the world. It was getting dark when Charlie decided he at least ought to phone his wife. Arvin thought the jam would break any minute, so Charlie waited a while longer. Nothing happened.

Finally Charlie climbed out, intending to find a phone booth. He realized, however, that in order to reach the ground he'd have to hike a couple of miles to an exit. Luckily Arvin had a tow rope in a trunk. Charlie tied it to the railing, waved his thanks, swung over the side and hand-over-handed to the second level. From there he slid out onto a high tree limb and shinnied to the ground.

Gazing up at the freeway's massive concrete underside and at Arvin's rope dangling far above him, Charlie knew he'd never climb back. "What the hell," he said to himself, "I might as well go home. The cops'll be around to watch things. Besides, the car's all paid for." He began searching for a bus or a cab. But everything, it seemed, was tied up in the jam.

In a bar where he stopped for a beer to cool off, he learned that every exit, every approach, every lane in the city's complex freeway system was jammed. "And ya know, it's funny," the bartender told him, "there wasn't a single accident. It all happened so gradual, they say. Things slowed down little by little, and the whole town stopped just about at once. Some guys didn't even use their brakes. Just went from one mile an hour to a dead stop."

It took Charlie two hours to walk home. When he arrived his wife, Fay, was frantic.

"Why didn't you call?"

"I started to, honey . . ."

"And what happened to your pants?"

He glanced sheepishly at his torn sharkskin slacks. "I was shinnying down this tree. I guess somebody left a nail in it."

"For God's sake, Charlie, this is no time to kid. If you knew how worried . . ."

"I'm not kidding. You're lucky I got down at all. Some of the guys are still up there—the older guys—the fat ones—couldn't get over the rails. And a lotta guys wouldn't leave. Probably be out all night."

She looked ready to cry, and she stared as if he were insane. "Charlie, please . . ." He put an arm around her and drew her close. "What happened, Charlie? Where have you been?"

He guided her to the sofa and they sat down. His hairy knee stuck up through the torn cloth. "I thought you'd see it on TV or something."

"See *what* on TV?"

While Fay sobbed and sniffled, he told her the whole story. By the time he finished she was sitting up straight and glaring at him.

"Charlie Bates, do you mean you just left our car out on the freeway?"

"What else could I do, honey? I couldn't stay up there all night—not in a Volkswagen. I'd catch cold. I'd be all cramped up."

"You could've got into somebody else's car. This Arvin fellow would have let you. Somebody with a heater or a big back seat or something."

"You can't just barge into somebody else's car and stay overnight, honey. Anyway, I wanted to phone. That's why I came down in the first place."

She rubbed his bare knee. "Oh, Charlie." Leaning against him again she said, "At least nothing happened to *you*. That's the most important thing."

She snuggled next to him, and they were quiet, until she said, "But Charlie, what'll we do?"

"About what?"

"About the car."

"Wait it out, I guess. Wait till tomorrow at least, until they break the jam. Then get back out there. Of course, that won't be as easy as it sounds. Probably have to get over to the nearest approach and hike in—maybe two, three miles of freeway, up the center strip, I suppose —plus getting to the approach itself, which is right in the middle of town. Maybe I can borrow a bike. I don't know quite how we'll . . ."

"Say. Don and Louise have a two-seater. Maybe we can borrow that and both go."

"Maybe," Charlie said wearily. "Let's worry about that tomorrow. I'm bushed."

The next morning Charlie borrowed the big two-seater from Don and Louise, Fay packed a lunch, and they pedaled across the city, figuring to get there fairly early, to be on hand when their car was free, although an early solution was no longer likely. The morning news predicted another 36 hours before traffic would be moving. The jam now included not only the freeways, but all main streets and key intersections, where buses, streetcars and trucks were still entangled. It even extended beyond the city. Police had tried to block incoming traffic, but it was impossible. All highways transversed the city or its net of suburbs. Impatient motorists, discrediting police reports, finally broke the roadblocks, and the confusion was extending in all directions by hundreds of cars an hour.

Charlie and Fay smugly bypassed all that, following a devious route of unblocked streets that he mapped out after watching the news on TV. They pedaled most of the morning. At last they mounted a high bluff and decided to ride an elevator to the roof of an apartment building that rose above the freeway where their car was parked. Charlie brought along a pair of Navy binoculars. From that vantage point they ate lunch and surveyed the curving rows of silent cars.

"Can you see ours, Charlie?"

"Yeah. She looks okay. A little squeezed up, but okay."

"Lemme see."

"Here."

"Gee," Fay said. "Some of those poor men are still sitting out there. Don't they know their wives are worried?"

"Their wives probably heard the news. Everybody must know by now."

"Still worried though, I'll bet." She hugged Charlie and pecked his cheek. "I'm glad you came home." Then, peering again, "I'll bet those men are hungry. Maybe we should take them some sandwiches."

"Take a lot of sandwiches to feed everybody stuck on the freeway, honey."

"I mean for the men right around our car. That Arvin, for instance. You know . . . your friends, sort of."

"I don't really know them that well, Fay."

"Well, we ought to do something."

"Red Cross is probably out," Charlie said. "Isn't that a cross on that helicopter way down there by the city hall? Here, gimme the glasses."

"I'll be darned," Fay said. "It is. They're dropping little packages."

"Here. Lemme see. Yeah. Yeah, that's just what they're doing. Guys are standing on the roofs of their cars, waving. I guess it's been a pretty tough night."

"The poor dears."

Charlie munched a tuna sandwich and scanned the city like a skipper. After a few moments Fay pointed. "Hey look, Charlie. Over that way. A couple more helicopters."

"Where? Down there? Oh, yeah. Couple of military birds, looks like. I guess the Army's out too."

"What're they doing—lifting out one of the cars?"

"No, not a car. It looks like a long, narrow crate. And they're not lifting it, they're lowering it endways. A couple of guys in overalls are down below waiting for it. There. It's down. They're anchoring it to the center strip. Wait a minute. It's not a crate. One of the guys in overalls just opened a door on the front of it, and he's stepping inside. Hey. People are jumping out of their cars and running down the center strip. They're running from everywhere, climbing over hoods. Somebody just knocked over the other guy in overalls. I think there's gonna be a fight. They're really crowding around that door and pushing . . . No . . . I think it's gonna be okay. The guy inside just came out, and he's tacking up a sign over the door. All the men are starting to walk away. The women are lining up along the center strip now."

"The dears."

"A woman just opened the door and stepped inside."

"Oh, Charlie, I'm so glad you came home."

"Me too."

From the rooftop they could hear the police helicopter's periodic messages. By the end of the first day, predictions for clearing the jam were at least two, perhaps three more days. Knowing they should be on hand whenever it broke, yet weary at the very thought of pedaling across the city twice each day to their vantage point and home again, they decided to rent an apartment in the building below them. Fortunately one was available on the top floor, facing the freeway. They moved in that evening, although they had little to move but the binoculars and a thermos. They agreed that Charlie would pedal home the next day to pick up a few necessities, while Fay kept an eye on the car.

The plan worked marvelously. Once situated, they set up a rotation watch—four hours on, four hours off. Charlie figured he could reach the car from the apartment in half an hour if things looked ready to break. He figured he'd have that much warning, by listening to helicopter messages, and watching TV and frequently checking the progress downtown where the cranes worked. Through the binoculars he watched the great jaws lift out cars, vans and buses and drop them over the sides of the freeway. Things would loosen up down there first, he figured, giving him time to bicycle six blocks to the pine tree a mile below his car. Scaling the tree he could reach the top of a 15-foot-high concrete retaining wall and drop to the freeway. From there it was an easy jog up the center strip and around the sloping cloverleaf curve to the overpass.

To be safe Charlie made dry runs over the course a few times each day—down the elevator, onto his bike, up the tree, over the wall, along the freeway, to his car. He'd switch on the engine and warm it for a few minutes, then stroll back, waving to waiting motorists who watched his passage with mixed admiration, envy and disbelief. By the third day the men were stubble-faced, sullen, dark-eyed from fitful sleeping. The women were disheveled, pasty-faced, most of them staring blankly through windshields at nothing. Charlie felt he ought to do something. Sometimes he squatted on the center strip to talk to the man who'd lent him the tow rope.

"How's it going, Arv?"

" 'Bout the same, Charlie."

"Pretty hot out here today, huh?"

" 'Bout like it's been, Charlie. Gettin' used to it, I guess. You probably feel it more than I do. That's a long pull."

"Not so bad anymore. The old legs are shaping up."

"How's your time?"

"Twenty-eight, ten, today."

"Cuttin' it down, hey boy."

"Poco a poco," Charlie said. *"Poco a poco.* It's the elevator that really holds me back though. Slowest elevator I've ever seen."

"You ever thought of waiting down on the sidewalk someplace? The wife could maybe signal out the window when the time comes."

"Say . . ."

"It came to me yesterday," Arvin said, "but I figured you'd thought of it."

"Never entered my head. That's a great idea, Arv." Charlie paused. "I've been meaning to ask you," he went on. "Why don't you come up to the apartment to meet Fay? I've told her about you. You'd like her, I know. We could have a couple of drinks and just relax for a while."

"Well . . . that's real nice of you, Charlie. But . . . I'm not sure. The trouble is, you never know when the thing's gonna break loose."

"I've got that two-seater, Arv. If anything happens, we can pedal back over here in no time. Cuttin' it down every trip, ya know. C'mon. It'd be good for you to get away."

"I'd like to, Charlie, I really would. But . . . to be honest, I haven't had this car very long. I'm still making payments, and . . . well, I just feel like I ought to stick pretty close to it."

"I know how you feel, Arv. In a way I don't blame you. I get a little jumpy myself—especially at night when I can't see much. But look, if you change your mind, I'll be back this afternoon."

"Thanks, Charlie."

"See ya later, Arv. And thanks for that idea."

"My pleasure, Charlie. Hate to have you miss your car when the action starts."

Taking Arvin's advice, Charlie spent most of each day sitting on a bus-stop bench across the street from the apartment house.

At last, on the afternoon of the sixth day after traffic stopped, Fay's white handkerchief appeared in the 12th-floor window. Charlie's bike stood before him in the gutter. He mounted it over the back wheel, like a pony-express rider. In a moment he was off and pedaling hard for the pine tree.

From blocks away he could hear the now unfamiliar roar of a thousand engines. As he gained the top of the concrete wall and poised ready to drop, a cloud of exhaust smoke swirled up and blinded him. It stung his eyes. He began to cough. He dropped anyway, sure of the route he must follow, even if he couldn't see. Gasping and wiping his eyes he clambered over hoods toward the center strip. The smoke didn't abate. It puffed and spurted, choking Charlie. Every driver was gunning his engine, warming up for takeoff. In a panic that he'd miss his car, that it would be carried away in the advancing stream, Charlie stumbled blindly upward, deafened by the sputtering thunder of long-cold cylinders, nauseated by fumes, confused by the semidarkness of gray, encompassing billows.

The cars disappeared. It seemed he staggered through the smoke for hours. He nearly forgot why he was there, until he heard a yell behind him: "Hey, Charlie! Where ya goin'?"

"That you, Arv?"

"Yeah. You nearly passed your car."

"This damn smoke."

"Helluva thing, isn't it?"

Arv was elated. Through the veil of fumes that curled up from under Arvin's car, Charlie could see a wild expectancy lighting the haggard eyes. His yellowed teeth grinned behind the beard.

"What's happening?" Charlie said, still gasping, hanging onto Arvin's aerial while his lungs convulsed.

"Looks like we're moving out. Better warm up."

"When did you get the signal?"

"No real signal," Arvin shouted, "but everybody down the line started up, so I started up. Things ought to get going anytime."

"Have you moved at all?"

"Not yet, but you better get the old engine warmed up, Charlie. We're on our way, boy! We're on our way!"

Coughing and crying Charlie staggered to his car, climbed in and started it. He accelerated a few times, then leaned forward to rest his head on the steering wheel, as nausea overcame him. The noise around him would split his eardrums, he thought. He passed out.

When he came to he was staring through the wheel at his gas gauge: nearly empty. He looked around. It seemed less noisy. The smoke had cleared a little. He could see vague outlines of cars in the next lane. None had moved. He switched off his engine. Evidently others were doing the same. The rumble of engines diminished perceptibly from moment to moment. Within minutes after he came to, it was quiet again. There was little wind. The smoke thinned slowly. Only gradually did he discern shapes around him. Behind him he saw a driver sprawled across the hood, chest heaving. In front of him a man and woman were leaning glassy-eyed against their car. And in the next lane he heard the wheezing rattle of a man retching. He turned and saw Arvin leaning out his open car door into the gutter.

The police helicopter droned toward them, hovered, sucking up smoke, and announced, "Please turn off your engines. Please turn off your engines. The deadlock will not be cleared for at least another 36 hours. You will be alerted well in advance of starting time. Please turn off your engines."

No one seemed to listen. The helicopter passed on. Charlie climbed out, still queasy but able to stand. Arvin was sitting on the edge of his seat now, bent forward with his head in his hands.

"Hey, Arv. You okay?" Charlie looked down at him for several moments before the answer came.

"Yeah, I guess so."

"False alarm, huh?"

Arv grunted.

"Looks like tomorrow might be the day, though," Charlie said.

Arv nodded, then raised his head slowly. His eyes were dark, weary, defeated. All hope had left him. Deep creases of fatigue lined his cheeks and forehead. His beard was scraggly and unkempt. He looked terribly old. His voice was hoarse and feeble as he said, "But, Charlie . . . what if it's not tomorrow? What're we gonna do, for God's sake? It's been six days."

Compassion welled up in Charlie. He said, "Look, Arv. You heard

the last announcement. It'll be at least another 36 hours. Why don't
you come up to the place and lay down for a while?"

A little light brightened Arvin's eyes. His mouth turned faintly
toward a smile, as if remembering some long-gone pleasure. But
he said, "I can't, Charlie." He raised his shoulders helplessly.

Charlie nodded slowly. "I know, Arv. I know." After a pause he
said, "I guess I'll see you this afternoon then." He waited for Arvin's
reply, but his head had fallen again into the palms of his hands, and
he sat there swaying. Charlie walked away.

Most of the smoke had cleared. The heavy silence was broken
occasionally by distant groans, staccato coughs. All around him, down
the curve he would walk, on the other freeways that snaked so gracefully below him, in among the rows of dusty cars, he saw people
sprawled, hunched, prone on the center strip, folded over fenders,
hanging out windows, wheezing, staring, stunned.

He picked his way to the concrete wall, scaled it and left the dev-
astation behind. He knew, though, he'd have to return, perhaps several times. No one could tell when it would be over. The police
reports were meaningless. He returned to the apartment to console
Fay, who felt guilty about sending him on a wild-goose chase. Then
he pedaled downtown to a war-surplus store. His lungs still burned
from the smoke. He decided to buy Arvin a gas mask and one for
himself.

How It Could Get Worse
#2

Most of the people who are going to die in the greatest cataclysm in the history of man have already been born. More than three and a half billion people already populate our moribund globe, and about half of them are hungry. . . . It took several million years for the population to reach a total of two billion people in 1930 while *a second two billion will have been added by 1975!* By that time some experts feel that food shortages will have escalated the present level of world hunger and starvation into famines of unbelievable proportions. Other experts, more optimistic, think the ultimate food-population collision will not occur until the decade of the 1980's. Of course more massive famine may be avoided if other events cause a prior rise in the human death rate.

—Paul R. Ehrlich, in *Ramparts*

WEDNESDAY, NOVEMBER 15, 1967
by Geo. Alec Effinger

Summer to winter
  bridge of red and yellow leaves.
  Love changes to love.

—*Geo. Alec Effinger*
11/15/67

It is Wednesday, November 15th, 1967.

What am I going to do with this notebook? I mean, you out there already know what I did with it, you my chittering insect audience, but the problem is still and unfortunately mine. I will place this under a crusting wet rock, I will throw it into the rotting sea in a bottle. I will carry it with me as I madden, chewing with my bloody teeth on the heavy cardboard cover, and when I fall at last it will fall, too. You will find it near the green bones of my hand when my peat bog cairn is exhumed.

It is 15 November, '67, and I can warn you that it's going to stay that way indefinitely. That's what it says up at the top of the page. It's the only page I've got with a date on it, so I hope you like it. Do you know of 1967? Is there some racially collective-unconscious jog when you see that date? Maybe I'm being optimistic; maybe you'll find this fifteen minutes after I take my mask off. In that case, where were *you* on Wednesday, November 15th, 1967? We're having an ecological disaster. In 1967 nearly everyone could recognize the word "ecology" as one of those *Reader's Digest* Power Words. The more erudite thought it had something to do with the study of the derivation of words.

Thus, the disaster.

And there's no need for me to go on about the disaster itself; I'm sure that you there in the far future click your mandibles in appreciation of the efficiency and finesse with which we carried out our disaster. Certainly there have been others, but even I can marvel at our own dexterity.

So, for your edification and viewing pleasure I have to decide what I'm going to do with this notebook.

* * *

Our first child was born on November 15th, 1967. I watched my wife's eyebrows moving above her mask, and her forehead as it wrinkled in her labor. I was, of course, helpless. I always am, I am now. But we had a doctor there, for which I am grateful. He held my son up to me and I suppose that I smiled beneath my respirator. Georgie cried, I guess; they all do. They're supposed to. I've never really liked babies, they make me feel uncomfortable when they cry. Dia always told me that that's what babies are *for*. I used to love her. Anyway, I recall thinking that his tears were probably hurting him, running down his cheeks in the thick air, hydrogen chloride or sulfur dioxide or something dissolving in the water and etching those furrows permanently into his face. By this time there weren't any more masks being manufactured, of course, and we couldn't find one for Georgie. He died in about an hour. I squeezed Dia's hand.

* * *

I wander about this poor, ravaged world of ours, and I whistle as I travel. What unholy beauty, in the rusty earth, the grayed yellow, painful sky, the wombwall of the nighttime "heavens." Very charming, and gruesomely quieting, as the ambulance sirens used to be quieting. I remember that I wanted to be a poet. I was going to school to learn how when the disaster occurred, catching me not completely prepared:

> Nothing in the crannied wall
> I see you in the crannies;
> I see you atop the bricks above,
>   and under stones,
> And I wonder, lately,
> At how much more
>   cranny
> There is
> Than wall.

—Geo. Alec Effinger
11/15/67

Last night I dreamed the strangest dream. I dreamed that as I traveled the splintered skeleton of our once-proud nation I came upon that mythic and dearly loved statistic, the pile of shattered automobiles that stretches into the clouds, from Detroit beyond the moon. And it seemed to me that I began to climb that tower, seeking to leave the lifeless world of my birth, to reach a newer and unspoiled planet to take up my life. And as I labored upward in my dream, I became weary, so that I had to stop and rest; I entered the stranded hulk of a metal-flake burgundy Pontiac Catalina, thrown up into the sky by the exigencies of advertising. I laid myself down on the plastic seat cover for to take my rest, and in my dream I dreamed again.

It seemed, in my dream's dream, that I looked out the car's windshield, through the spider web-work of cracks, and down to the ground. The painted steel relics misted and disappeared as I watched, and I stood suddenly on the verge of a great plateau, looking down into a gently sloping valley tacked over with a forest of lightest spring green. Through the middle of the valley ran a small river, rushing over rocks with foam of pure white, running to royal blue in the current's deeper middle, flashing clean and clear spray, sparkling under the sun. The entire scene made me glad, so that I forgot my true situation, and embraced this illusion with all my heart. I sat down in the dewy grass at the edge of my plateau, and considered the valley in all its aspects, thanking God that the world was not yet *totally* ruined.

I watched the river coursing its way for some time, delighted in my dream-fogged mind, until I began to see hints of strange things flickering just below the surface of the flood. From my elevated position I thought that I could see the veriest animal borne by the current. It seemed that no protozoan, no tiny dot of living plasm was too small for my imagined powers of observation. I saw each semi-living virus, each bacterial mote, every single-celled, thrashing organism as it sped through its life cycle in the river's amniotic broth, and I marveled. Slowly I became aware that I was watching not only the crazy microscopic lives in all their rich variety, but also their intangible community. Their interrelations, as insubstantial as that concept sounds, seemed to me in my vision to take on its own formal gestalt, and loomed above them (and me) as some benign and yet-incomplete Idea. I knew that I saw the birth of God.

And in their random motions I saw the animalcula grow, slowly and deliberately. I watched passively and intrigued as the phyla developed; each step followed in preordained fashion, and the river hosted an ever more complex assortment of creatures. Individuals of the new orders were larger and, therefore, ever more voracious than their evolutionary precursors. It occurred to me that as each newly distinct grouping of animals took over the precarious position of eminence it seemed, through its peculiar sort of adaptive traits, to be able to hold that position forever. But no; no sooner did one level of organism gain mastery than another came along better equipped to fill the environment with its offspring. And, always, the conqueror grew larger.

I was entranced by the parade of living things, drunk on the majesty and logic to such an extent that I gave no notice to the especially momentous advancements, such as the appearance of the chordates, or (I must admit) their epochal abandonment of the water entirely for the unproved benefits of dry land. So totally fascinated was I that I only came to my senses when I became aware of the massive reptiles that browsed the water's edge.

The monstrous, swaying beasts that I watched were dinosaurs, whose existence I had previously accepted only intellectually. I was shocked by their size, their aura of latent power, and the brutal and vicious competition among the carnivores. Knowing their fate I was somewhat saddened by the apparent confidence (though this may be my own anthropomorphic projection) with which they clutched the earth to themselves as solely their own. Nevertheless, the vast span of their ascendency, those fearful millions of years, passed for me in an hour.

Already, I dreamed, the impulse to grow had died; the dinosaurs had vanished. Where? In my fancy I answered myself: gone to wherever these mammals have come from. The warm-blooded creatures had received the reptiles' abandoned mantle of superiority, and begun the downward trend in size. They bred quickly, filling the valley with their numbers, overrunning the forest in their perplexing variations. And, of course, after a time I saw that the hominids were developing. I could not suppress my feeling of joy, that I should at last have human company in this most beautiful of earth's precincts; I awaited impatiently the emergence of the true, intelligent, modern man.

It did not take long. Before I could call out to them, so quickly did the scale of time accelerate, I saw that they were building cities in the garden, and even as I sought to find a way down from the plateau into the valley I saw that the sky above was darkening with the industrial smokes that I knew so well, and the greenery of the valley had turned to a dull and unmoving gray or red-brown. With utter sadness I turned my back on the ruined valley, walking along the plateau in search of another unspoiled district. . . .

From my dream's dream I awoke, and discovered that I was not, in truth, on that magic table of rock, but returned to the interior of the wasted automobile. I sighed heavily, knowing in my fantasy that such a valley was beyond the hope of my diseased world. Not fully rested, but anxious that I be on my way, I climbed outside once again and took up my arduous journey up the monument of man's labor. The automobiles stood like the solitary headstone in the planetwide cemetery of our race, and of all the living things that we had doomed along with ourselves. But of course it was far too late for vain regrets or even poetic reevaluations, and I worked only at escaping the dead past and the dead present.

The winds grew cold, for I had climbed high up above the earth, clinging to crushed fenders or corroding door handles. I never looked downward, but in my dream I saw myself inching up the spire of steel, while below the restless, gritty clouds filled the air and hid the ground. I was suffering with the cold, and the thinness of the atmosphere made it even more difficult to breathe. In a little while I had to stop again for lack of air, and I found that I was exhausted, unable either to continue upward to my goal or turn back. I could not breathe at all; even the poison winds had forsaken me, rarified and too noxious to support my life. The dream turned to nightmare as I struggled to fill my lungs without success.

I awoke into my reality with a cry, finding that in my sleeping troubles I had managed to remove my mask. I do not know how long I had been breathing the "air," but certainly long enough to make this narrative appreciably shorter.

>   On trees, on houses
>   first snowfall sings to my eyes.
>   And it dances, too!
>   —*Geo. Alec Effinger*
>   11/15/67

* * *

"Why, Uncle Caleb! What you doing up so early?"

"Thought I'd come down and watch them damn bugs. Can't sleep knowin' they're out there. Looks like it's goin' to be a hard winter."

"Guess so. Dad sent away for some more bug killer, but I think he's goin' to need an awful lot."

"Probably ordered an awful lot."

"Guess so. Which plague is this now, four or five?"

"Don't rightly know. I lost track a while ago. I just sit and watch them these days. Fella down to the store says them bugs is the fault of people like your dad."

"You mean Hawkins, the loony scientist? He's always sayin' stuff like that. Don't make much sense most of the time."

"I don't know. I heard that Hawkins fella talkin' about it to Old Man Durfee last week. Sounds like that bug killer your dad ordered kills off more'n just bugs. Seems like it kills off all the stuff that ought to be eatin' the bugs natural, like birds. And then the bugs start breedin' so fast, why, if any of 'em don't mind the poison then in a little while you got millions of 'em that don't mind it. But that don't bring the birds back. Your dad's just makin' things worse."

"But . . . if that loony Hawkins is right, then . . . then we're in a pile of trouble!"

"Yep."

"Well, it's scientists like him that's got us here in the first place. He ought to be figurin' somethin' out that'll kill the bugs, instead of just sittin' around tellin' us 'I told you so.' "

"No, Billy, it isn't the fault of the scientist. No, it's our fault entirely for taking the marvelous fruits of their labor and ignoring the warnings that went with them. The scientists have always been the friend of mankind, but in our own ignorance and greed we have corrupted all their best intentions. *And it's gotten us so far into hot water even they won't be able to help this time.*"

"But what can we do, Uncle Caleb?"

"We'll do what we've always done, boy. We'll pray."

* * *

So if anything gets through, it'll be the bugs. Maybe I should write out a note and slip it under the carapace of a katydid (if I can find one); "Take this to your master," like good old Rin Tin Tin.

My hysterical imagination says no, it doesn't have to be that way at all. Insects are a good bet, continuing the downward trend in size until the earth is covered with semi-aware replicating soup. But maybe the world is to be inherited by a subtle and strange new sort of life, where DNA is effectively replaced by some other substance that works as well. An ironic, asymmetric molecule, formed by the perverted mating of DDT and 2, 4, 5-T, for instance. I like that: giant shimmering crystals slinking the horizon are infinitely preferable to the clacking insectivora that I picture you as being. Did you have to wait eons to grow thumbs before you could dig this up?

And were you expecting a last, melancholic warning? Well, never mind. I will not speak to you across the gulf of ages with the voice of experience, counseling you to Be Good. You're not dead, but I am. What the hell, why don't you die, too? All you're going to get out of this are a few fables as my mood shifts toward screaming crazyhood.

* * *

As the last living representative of mankind (not, you understand, by actual count of noses, but by legislation) I have decided to strike certain words from the living language, never to be used again. This decision was reached early this evening and made public at a specially convened news conference here on the Upper West Side. A high-level cabinet spokesman, after rereading the previous entries in this notebook, listed the proscribed vocabulary as follows:

> ecology
> sulfur dioxide
> statistic
> advertising
> plastic
> God
> superiority
> modern
> industrial
> scientist
> hot water
> (DDT) + (2, 4, 5-T)
> mankind

Already as I look over the list I am unsure what the words mean. They will not be used again by me, and, thus, by anyone. Failure to comply with this directive incurs no special penalty. We'll take your word. It doesn't make any difference, anyway.

In case of a tie, duplicate prizes will be awarded.

* * *

Dia dying. It looks very nice here on the page. A euphonious phrase; it's the sort of thing that turns into a poem if you're not careful. Somehow I don't feel up to writing a poem on the asphyxiation of my wife.

I recall it very well. It was very close to the end. We were on the subway (the city wasn't running them, then. I don't know who was. Not many people were taking them. It was pretty foul down there. Just us people that had to get somewhere, and the flipped who were doing themselves in, without masks at all), sitting across from a

Puerto Rican family. All six of them were crying. Suddenly Dia grabbed my hand; I turned to her, starting to whisper something. She shook her head. Her blue eyes were wet, her eyebrows pressed together so tightly that they turned up over the bridge of her nose. I remember noticing her hair, which was hanging in wet, dirty strands. It used to look like blond mist when she brushed it.

"I think . . . Piglet, I . . . hey, I can't *breathe* anymore!" she cried.

I can remember, damn it, when I wrote that I could *feel* the same cold shock down at the base of my spine, running up the inside of me, and I don't like it any better now.

"Look, I don't know . . . be quiet, maybe keep your breathing down. We can get off at the next. . . ."

She stretched, half standing, shaking her head and crying. I could hear her alternately sobbing and choking. She grabbed at the air with stiff fingers, trying to claw hold of something that would help her *live,* and all the time I was helpless, feeling entirely unnatural, like I was watching a movie. It couldn't be happening to Dia. Somebody in a book, maybe, but not *Dia.* She bent over finally and retched into her mask. I didn't know what to do then. I was holding her hand, rubbing the back of her neck, maybe I was crying, too. She certainly couldn't breathe with her mask filled, and she threw it off. I tried to give her mine, but she held my arms down.

She looked at me wildly, her lips moved below her mottled red and blue face. I shook my head and it kept on buzzing. Dia leaned toward me, her eyelids drooped, and her head fell onto my shoulder.

The people across from me on the train looked away. For eight stops they wouldn't meet my eyes. Like it was five years ago and I was some kind of wino, embarrassing them.

I held her through three boroughs, until we got back to Manhattan. I carried her body out into the Fourth Street station. I'm not very strong, but I carried her up the stairs and along the Avenue of the Americas to Eighth Street. There was no one around, and the sky was slightly green. I had to stop often to rest.

I finally got Dia's body to the Marboro Book Store on Eighth Street. I mean, this is where we first met. Wednesday, November 15th, 1967. I worked in the store then. It wasn't so long ago.

I scooped all the trash and books from the counter in the front of the store, and laid her body on it. I rested her head on a couple of thick copies of *Paperback Books in Print*. I wish that I could have left her and Georgie together, but I don't know what happened to our baby's corpse. As an afterthought I put a paperback copy of my first novel in her hand. I kissed her.

That was Dia, my wife. Sept. 3, 1945–Nov. 15, 1967.

I had to get that all out. I don't know what kind of reaction this will spring from you. Surely nothing emotional (damn it, it wouldn't get the least bit of emotion out of another human being right *now,* if there were any); and I really can't use anything else that serves you instead. Now my baby's dead, and my wife, and, well . . . me. Let me tell you that I'm starting to get pretty worked up over *that.*

But I wouldn't want you to think that I'm starting to feel sorry for myself. It's not pity that I'm looking for. I can't breathe pity.

> Empty police car
> and on its red dome, resting,
> a white butterfly!
>
> —*Geo. Alec Effinger*
> *11/15/67*

A spring haiku, that. And a bit of a cheat. Haiku are best when written at the moment of inspiration, as a short sketch of some emotionally involving event. Well, there's plenty of empty cars around, but I haven't seen a butterfly in quite a while. I don't expect to.

The poem is strange to me. Its irony is entirely bioeconomic, now, and five years ago the emphasis was purely political.

There's never a cop around when you need one.

* * *

It's a brand-new day.

The sun doesn't rise in the east anymore. Instead, the sky right overhead turns from brown-black to a sick eggyolk and ash color, as if someone were slowly turning up the houselights. It's less dramatic this way, and if you're not careful (which I'm not) you have no idea what time of day it is. Then the days go, and the weeks. I don't suppose that I'll have to worry about months.

I've been wandering around quite a bit, living uptown for old times' sake. Up in our old apartment on 87th Street. But now I guess I'll head back downtown, the old bull elephant trekking to his final *reward*, searching for that fabulous boneyard. Old elephant, *circumspice!* It's all yours, man!

Heading back downtown. Gonna lay these tired ol' bones up on that counter. It's getting to be about that time, I suppose. Gonna see my gal. She so fine.

Various Horsemen are abroad, doing their various Apocalyptic things. I'm staying strictly to the West Side. If I caught so much as a glimpse of the 59th Street Bridge, why, I'd start to feeling groovy. That's all I need.

Oh, please, stay by me, Diana. (Oh, my darling, you're the most.)

Wow. I do believe maybe I'll go lie down for a while.

* * *

I think I'm going weird.

I just read that nonsense up there. It's a bad sign. Hey, you out there. You there, in the impervious protein chitinous exoskeleton. Yeah, you; the homoptera who inherit the earth. Hey, like what's happening? I got this sore throat, and I'm all swollen up on my neck, and under my arms, and in my, uh, groin.

You know what a groin is? Well, I'm not going to be the one to tell you, either. Let it be an unsolvable historical mystery. Like the enigma of the lost Roanoke calumny.

Maybe I have caught some loathsome disease from these little buglies crawling around on my skin who will some day be you. Thanks a lot. Well, anyway, *that* one won't be you. He dead.

Me too.

* * *

Clip this out, sign it, and send it to your Congressman:

Dear Congressman:
I *support* the despoiling and rape of our irreplaceable natural resources.

Very truly yours,
(signed)——

DON'T DELAY! DO IT TODAY!

(Void where prohibited, licensed, or taxed. Offer expires
November 15, 1967)

* * *

But, you know, now that I feel a little better, I realize that things
really aren't that bad. Perhaps I was maximizing my discomforts.
Being the only person left has its advantages. The traffic problem
is, at last, solved; the population boom has leveled off; I have an interesting position that allows me to keep my own hours, with periodic
vacations and many other fringes; brother no longer lifts sword
against brother; and I can get good seats to any show in town:

> The current disaster suffered quite a bit, in my opinion, from
> all the excited press it received before the actual opening. But
> be that as it may, I'm quite certain that there is still enough en-
> thusiasm in the production to impress even the most sophisti-
> cated and jaded observer. It is *definitely* worth the time to
> investigate.
> The tendency is toward REALISM, a trend quite at odds with
> the current crop of modish theater to which we have been
> "treated" in recent seasons, and the realistic turn is one which
> I, personally, endorse. It is a refreshing respite from the self-
> consciously *kicky* or (at the opposite extreme) the altogether
> precious. At times certain elements of the staging become ob-
> trusive, to the detriment of the overall effect; but generally speak-
> ing the disaster is a remarkably well conceived and, above all
> else, *professionally* executed affair. Although it attempts to deal
> with absolutely *every* aspect of our environmental disintegration
> —and succeeds—the direction never becomes heavy-handed. One
> is always made subtly aware of the interrelations of all those en-
> vironmental factors, to a degree that was undreamed of before,
> and without sacrificing the total devotion to the basic, the simple,
> and, always, the natural.
> There is an awesome ambience, an atmosphere of anger but
> not sorrow, that strikes the viewer almost before the curtain rises.
> One is continuously asking, "What is the point?" during the early

moments. But then it becomes clear: there is no moral; the disaster is an exhibit and not at all an entertainment. The audience is invited to observe and to form its own aesthetic correlations. But never is there the editorializing, intrusive author that so often spoils this sort of thing for me.

The pace is sluggish at first, but one is given such a fascinating wealth of visual detail that one hardly notices. And then the direction accelerates breathtakingly until the end (there is no intermission), leaving the viewer literally gasping. As the first legitimately mounted example of this sort, it comes off splendidly, and so all-encompassing in scope is it that I do not at all fear a rash of lesser, cheaper imitations. This disaster does it all.

The cast is as a whole fresh, vigorous, and exciting; the members produce a startling sense of credibility unusual for any such large-scale effort as this. The unhuman portion of the cast is by no means less spectacular. The dead fish, birds, rodents, and people strewn across the stage provide their own commentary, by turns ironic, poignant, horrible, and threatening, but not without humor as well.

The lighting and choreography (both uncredited, for some obscure reason) were, for me, unsuccessful, evidently striving for some ultra-arty effect that seemed to be contraproductive to the total concept. Similarly the sets, by Ming Cho Lee, while impressive and sensitively subdued, seemed to stress too heavily the *O tempora! O mores!* aspect of the show.

And, finally, what can one say about the deft touch of Mike Nichols? His direction is superb, as always, building the occasionally scant or implausible material to continuous, climactic, show-stopping moments. This may well be the culmination of his remarkable career; surely it will be hard to go beyond it.

This is one you can't miss.

–Reviewed by Geo. Alec Effinger
(Closed, 11/15/67)

I see by my swollen brown tongue that the sun is beginning its downward plunge. Wednesday, November 15th, 1967, is drawing to its close. I, for one (and all), am sorry to see it go. It was a good day, and I won't see its like around again. Therefore, no Romantic thoughts of new days dawning, etc., mainly because they won't be

mine, so who gives a damn? I am fevered, and although my arms and
legs ache like crazy, I am seized with a strange desire to *dance*.
    Are you havin' a *good* time?
    I sure am.

> Summer of my life:
>   how will I feel when I see
>   leaves wither and fall?
>   —*Geo. Alec Effinger*
>   11/15/67

Yes. Well. I know, I guess.

DON'T DIE FLORIDA
We Need You.

You can be sure we'll all feel it if Florida plunges into ecological collapse. And that's what's about to happen to the Sunshine State. It's beginning to feel Nature's own backlash. A backlash strong enough to turn this citadel of tourism, beefsteaks, winter vegetables, and wealth into an environmental corpse.

The Sierra Club believes this crisis warrants a book. Now we have that book. It's called *Everglades*.

—from an advertisement in
Scientific American

THE CAGE OF SAND
by J. G. Ballard

At sunset, when the vermilion glow reflected from the dunes along the horizon fitfully illuminated the white faces of the abandoned hotels, Bridgman stepped on to his balcony and looked out over the long stretches of cooling sand as the tides of purple shadow seeped across them. Slowly, extending their slender fingers through the shallow saddles and depressions, the shadows massed together like gigantic combs, a few phosphorescing spurs of obsidian isolated for a moment between the tines, and then finally coalesced and flooded in a solid wave across the half-submerged hotels. Behind the silent façades, in the tilting sand-filled streets which had once glittered with cocktail bars and restaurants, it was already night. Haloes of moon-

light beaded the lamp-standards with silver dew, and draped the
shuttered windows and slipping cornices like a frost of frozen gas.

As Bridgman watched, his lean bronzed arms propped against the
rusting rail, the last whorls of light sank away into the cerise funnel
withdrawing below the horizon, and the first wind stirred across the
dead Martian sand. Here and there miniature cyclones whirled about
a sandspur, drawing off swirling feathers of moon-washed spray, and
a nimbus of white dust swept across the dunes and settled in the dips
and hollows. Gradually the drifts accumulated, edging towards the
former shoreline below the hotels. Already the first four floors had
been inundated, and the sand now reached up to within two feet of
Bridgman's balcony. After the next sandstorm he would be forced
yet again to move to the floor above.

"Bridgman!"

The voice cleft the darkness like a spear. Fifty yards to his right,
at the edge of the derelict sand-break he had once attempted to build
below the hotel, a square stocky figure wearing a pair of frayed cotton
shorts waved up at him. The moonlight etched the broad sinewy
muscles of his chest, the powerful bowed legs sinking almost to their
calves in the soft Martian sand. He was about forty-five years old, his
thinning hair close-cropped so that he seemed almost bald. In his
right hand he carried a large canvas hold-all.

Bridgman smiled to himself. Standing there patiently in the moonlight below the derelict hotel, Travis reminded him of some long-
delayed tourist arriving at a ghost resort years after its extinction.

"Bridgman, are you coming?" When the latter still leaned on his
balcony rail, Travis added: "The next conjunction is tomorrow."

Bridgman shook his head, a rictus of annoyance twisting his mouth.
He hated the bi-monthly conjunctions, when all seven of the derelict
satellite capsules still orbiting the Earth crossed the sky together.
Invariably on these nights he remained in his room, playing over the
old memo-tapes he had salvaged from the submerged chalets and
motels further along the beach (the hysterical "This is Mamie Gold-
berg, 62955 Cocoa Boulevard, I really wanna protest against this
crazy evacuation . . ." or resigned "Sam Snade here, the Pontiac
convertible in the back garage belongs to anyone who can dig it out").
Travis and Louise Woodward always came to the hotel on the conjunction nights—it was the highest building in the resort, with an unrestricted view from horizon to horizon—and would follow the seven

converging stars as they pursued their endless courses around the globe. Both would be oblivious of everything else, which the wardens knew only too well, and they reserved their most careful searches of the sand sea for these bi-monthly occasions. Invariably Bridgman found himself forced to act as lookout for the other two.

"I was out last night," he called down to Travis. "Keep away from the northeast perimeter fence by the Cape. They'll be busy repairing the track."

Most nights Bridgman divided his time between excavating the buried motels for caches of supplies (the former inhabitants of the resort area had assumed the government would soon rescind its evacuation order) and disconnecting the sections of metal roadway laid across the desert for the wardens' jeeps. Each of the squares of wire mesh was about five yards wide and weighed over three hundred pounds. After he had snapped the lines of rivets, dragged the sections away and buried them among the dunes he would be exhausted, and spend most of the next day nursing his strained hands and shoulders. Some sections of the track were now permanently anchored with heavy steel stakes, and he knew that sooner or later they would be unable to delay the wardens by sabotaging the roadway.

Travis hesitated, and with a noncommittal shrug disappeared among the dunes, the heavy tool-bag swinging easily from one powerful arm. Despite the meager diet which sustained him, his energy and determination seemed undiminished—in a single night Bridgman had watched him dismantle twenty sections of track and then loop together the adjacent limbs of a crossroad, sending an entire convoy of six vehicles off into the wastelands to the south.

Bridgman turned from the balcony, then stopped when a faint tang of brine touched the cool air. Ten miles away, hidden by the lines of dunes, was the sea, the long green rollers of the middle Atlantic breaking against the red Martian strand. When he had first come to the beach five years earlier there had never been the faintest scent of brine across the intervening miles of sand. Slowly, however, the Atlantic was driving the shore back to its former margins. The tireless shoulder of the Gulf Stream drummed against the soft Martian dust and piled the dunes into grotesque rococo reefs which the wind carried away into the sand-sea. Gradually the ocean was returning, reclaiming its great smooth basin, sifting out the black quartz and

Martian obsidian which would never be wind-borne and drawing these down into its deeps. More and more often the stain of brine would hang on the evening air, reminding Bridgman why he had first come to the beach and removing any inclination to leave.

Three years earlier he had attempted to measure the rate of approach, by driving a series of stakes into the sand at the water's edge, but the shifting contours of the dunes carried away the colored poles. Later, using the promontory at Cape Canaveral, where the old launching gantries and landing ramps reared up into the sky like derelict pieces of giant sculpture, he had calculated by triangulation that the advance was little more than thirty yards per year. At this rate—without wanting to, he had automatically made the calculation—it would be well over five hundred years before the Atlantic reached its former littoral at Cocoa Beach. Though discouragingly slow, the movement was nonetheless in a forward direction, and Bridgman was happy to remain in his hotel ten miles away across the dunes, conceding towards its time of arrival the few years he had at his disposal.

Later, shortly after Louise Woodward's arrival, he had thought of dismantling one of the motel cabins and building himself a small chalet by the water's edge. But the shoreline had been too dismal and forbidding. The great red dunes rolled on for miles, cutting off half the sky, dissolving slowly under the impact of the slate-green water. There was no formal tide line, but only a steep shelf littered with nodes of quartz and rusting fragments of Mars rockets brought back with the ballast. He spent a few days in a cave below a towering sand reef, watching the long galleries of compacted red dust crumble and dissolve as the cold Atlantic stream sluiced through them, collapsing like the decorated colonnades of a baroque cathedral. In the summer the heat reverberated from the hot sand as from the slag of some molten sun, burning the rubber soles from his boots, and the light from the scattered flints of washed quartz flickered with diamond hardness. Bridgman had returned to the hotel grateful for his room overlooking the silent dunes.

Leaving the balcony, the sweet smell of brine still in his nostrils, he went over to the desk. A small cone of shielded light shone down over the tape recorder and rack of spools. The rumble of the wardens' unsilenced engines always gave him at least five minutes' warning of their arrival, and it would have been safe to install another lamp in the room—there were no roadways between the hotel and the sea, and from a distance any light reflected onto the balcony was indistinguishable from the corona of glimmering phosphors which hung over the sand like myriads of fireflies. However, Bridgman preferred to sit in the darkened suite, enclosed by the circle of books on the makeshift shelves, the shadow-filled air playing over his shoulders through the long night as he toyed with the memo-tapes, fragments of a vanished and unregretted past. By day he always drew the blinds, immolating himself in a world of perpetual twilight.

Bridgman had easily adapted himself to his self-isolation, soon evolved a system of daily routines that gave him the maximum of time to spend on his private reveries. Pinned to the walls around him were a series of huge white-prints and architectural drawings, depicting various elevations of a fantastic Martian city he had once designed, its glass spires and curtain walls rising like heliotropic jewels from the vermilion desert. In fact, the whole city was a vast piece of jewelry, each elevation brilliantly visualized but as symmetrical, and ultimately as lifeless, as a crown. Bridgman continuously retouched the drawings, inserting more and more details, so that they almost seemed to be photographs of an original.

Most of the hotels in the town—one of a dozen similar resorts buried by the sand which had once formed an unbroken strip of motels, chalets and five-star hotels thirty miles to the south of Cape Canaveral—were well stocked with supplies of canned food abandoned when the area was evacuated and wired off. There were ample reservoirs and cisterns filled with water, apart from a thousand intact cocktail bars six feet below the surface of the sand. Travis had excavated a dozen of these in search of his favorite vintage bourbon. Walking out across the desert behind the town one would suddenly find a short flight of steps cut into the annealed sand and crawl below an occluded sign announcing "The Satellite Bar" or "The Orbit Room" into the inner sanctum, where the jetting deck of a chromium bar had been cleared as far as the diamond-paned mirror freighted with its rows of bottles and figurines. Bridgman would have been glad to see them left undisturbed.

The whole trash of amusement arcades and cheap bars on the outskirts of the beach resorts were a depressing commentary on the original space flights, reducing them to the level of monster sideshows at a carnival.

Outside his room, steps sounded along the corridor, then slowly climbed the stairway, pausing for a few seconds at every landing. Bridgman lowered the memo-tape in his hand, listening to the familiar tired footsteps. This was Louise Woodward, making her invariable evening ascent to the roof ten stories above. Bridgman glanced to the timetable pinned to the wall. Only two of the satellites would be visible, between 12:25 and 12:35 a.m., at an elevation of 62 degrees in the southwest, passing through Cetus and Eridanus, neither of them containing her husband. Although the siting was two hours away, she was already taking up her position, and would remain there until dawn.

Bridgman listened wanly to the feet recede slowly up the stairwell. All through the night the slim pale-faced woman would sit out under the moonlit sky, as the soft Martian sand her husband had given his life to reach sifted around her in the dark wind, stroking her faded hair like some mourning mariner's wife waiting for the sea to surrender her husband's body. Travis usually joined her later, and the two of them sat side by side against the elevator house, the frosted letters of the hotel's neon sign strewn around their feet like the fragments of a dismembered zodiac, then at dawn made their way down into the shadow-filled streets to their eyries in the nearby hotels.

Initially Bridgman often joined their nocturnal vigil, but after a few nights he began to feel something repellent, if not actually ghoulish, about their mindless contemplation of the stars. This was not so much because of the macabre spectacle of the dead astronauts orbiting the planet in their capsules, but because of the curious sense of unspoken communion between Travis and Louise Woodward, almost as if they were celebrating a private rite to which Bridgman could never be initiated. Whatever their original motives, Bridgman sometimes suspected that these had been overlaid by other, more personal ones.

Ostensibly, Louise Woodward was watching her husband's satellite in order to keep alive his memory, but Bridgman guessed that the memories she unconsciously wished to perpetuate were those of herself twenty years earlier, when her husband had been a celebrity and she herself courted by magazine columnists and TV reporters. For fifteen years after his death—Woodward had been killed testing a new lightweight launching platform—she had lived a nomadic existence, driving restlessly in her cheap car from motel to motel across the continent, following her husband's star as it disappeared into the eastern night, and had at last made her home at Cocoa Beach in sight of the rusting gantries across the bay.

Travis's real motives were probably more complex. To Bridgman, after they had known each other for a couple of years, he had confided that he felt himself bound by a debt of honor to maintain a watch over the dead astronauts for the example of courage and sacrifice they had set him as a child (although most of them had been piloting their wrecked capsules for fifty years before Travis's birth), and that now they were virtually forgotten he must singlehandedly keep alive the fading flame of their memory. Bridgman was convinced of his sincerity.

Yet later, going through a pile of old news magazines in the trunk of a car he excavated from a motel port, he came across a picture of Travis wearing an aluminum pressure suit and learned something more of his story. Apparently Travis had at one time been himself an astronaut—or rather, a would-be astronaut. A test pilot for one of the civilian agencies setting up orbital relay stations, his nerve had failed him a few seconds before the last "hold" of his countdown, a moment of pure unexpected funk that cost the company some five million dollars.

Obviously it was his inability to come to terms with this failure of character, unfortunately discovered lying flat on his back on a contour couch two hundred feet above the launching pad, which had brought Travis to Canaveral, the abandoned Mecca of the first heroes of astronautics.

Tactfully Bridgman had tried to explain that no one would blame him for this failure of nerve—less his responsibility than that of the selectors who had picked him for the flight, or at least the result of an unhappy concatenation of ambiguously worded multiple-choice questions (crosses in the wrong boxes, some heavier to bear and harder to open than others! Bridgman had joked sardonically to himself). But Travis seemed to have reached his own decision about himself. Night after night, he watched the brilliant funerary convoy weave its gilded pathway towards the dawn sun, salving his own failure by identifying it with the greater, but blameless, failure of the seven astronauts. Travis still wore his hair in the regulation "Mohican" cut of the spaceman, still kept himself in perfect physical trim by the vigorous routines he had practiced before his abortive flight.

Sustained by the personal myth he had created, he was now more or less unreachable.

"Dear Harry, I've taken the car and deposit box. Sorry it should end like—"

Irritably, Bridgman switched off the memo-tape and its recapitulation of some thirty-year-old private triviality. For some reason he seemed unable to accept Travis and Louise Woodward for what they were. He disliked this failure of compassion, a nagging compulsion to expose other people's motives and strip away the insulating sheaths around their naked nerve strings, particularly as his own motives for being at Cape Canaveral were so suspect. Why was *he* there, what failure was *he* trying to expiate? And why choose Cocoa Beach as his penitential shore? For three years he had asked himself these questions so often that they had ceased to have any meaning, like a fossilized catechism or the blunted self-recrimination of a paranoic.

He had resigned his job as the chief architect of a big space development company after the large government contract on which the firm depended, for the design of the first Martian city-settlement, was awarded to a rival consortium. Secretly, however, he realized that his resignation had marked his unconscious acceptance that despite his great imaginative gifts he was unequal to the specialized and more prosaic tasks of designing the settlement. On the drawing board, as elsewhere, he would always remain earthbound.

His dreams of building a new gothic architecture of launching ports and controls gantries, of being the Frank Lloyd Wright and Le Corbusier of the first city to be raised outside Earth, faded forever, but leaving him unable to accept the alternative of turning out endless plans for low-cost hospitals in Ecuador and housing estates in Tokyo. For a year he had drifted aimlessly, but a few color photographs of the vermilion sunsets at Cocoa Beach and a news story about the recluses living on in the submerged motels had provided a powerful compass.

He dropped the memo-tape into a drawer, making an effort to accept Louise Woodward and Travis on their own terms, a wife keeping watch over her dead husband and an old astronaut maintaining a solitary vigil over the memories of his lost comrades-in-arms.

The wind gusted against the balcony window, and a light spray of sand rained across the floor. At night dust storms churned along the beach. Thermal pools isolated by the cooling desert would suddenly accrete like beads of quicksilver and erupt across the fluffy sand in miniature tornadoes.

Only fifty yards away, the dying cough of a heavy diesel cut through the shadows. Quickly Bridgman turned off the small desk light, grateful for his meanness over the battery packs plugged into the circuit, then stepped to the window.

At the leftward edge of the sand break, half-hidden in the long shadows cast by the hotel, was a large tracked vehicle with a low camouflaged hull. A narrow observation bridge had been built over the bumpers directly in front of the squat snout of the engine housing, and two of the beach wardens were craning up through the plexiglass windows at the balconies of the hotel, shifting their binoculars from room to room. Behind them, under the glass dome of the extended driving cabin, were three more wardens, controlling an outboard spotlight. In the center of the bowl a thin mote of light pulsed with the rhythm of the engine, ready to throw its powerful beam into any of the open rooms.

Bridgman hid back behind the shutters as the binoculars focused upon the adjacent balcony, moved to his own, hesitated, and passed to the next. Exasperated by the sabotaging of the roadways, the wardens had evidently decided on a new type of vehicle. With their four broad tracks, the huge squat sand-cars would be free of the mesh roadways and able to rove at will through the dunes and sand hills.

Bridgman watched the vehicle reverse slowly, its engine barely varying its deep base growl, then move off along the line of hotels, almost indistinguishable in profile among the shifting dunes and hillocks. A hundred yards away, at the first intersection, it turned towards the main boulevard, wisps of dust streaming from the metal cleats like thin spumes of steam. The men in the observation bridge were still watching the hotel. Bridgman was certain that they had seen a reflected glimmer of light, or perhaps some movement of Louise Woodward's on the roof. However reluctant to leave the car and be contaminated by the poisonous dust, the wardens would not hesitate if the capture of one of the beachcombers warranted it.

Racing up the staircase, Bridgman made his way to the roof, crouching below the windows that overlooked the boulevard. Like a huge crab, the sand-car had parked under the jutting overhang of the big department store opposite. Once fifty feet from the ground, the concrete lip was now separated from it by little more than six or seven feet, and the sand-car was hidden in the shadows below it, engine silent. A single movement in a window, or the unexpected return of Travis, and the wardens would spring from the hatchways, their long-handled nets and lassos pinioning them around the necks and ankles. Bridgman remembered one beachcomber he had seen flushed from his motel hideout and carried off like a huge twitching spider at the center of a black rubber web, the wardens with their averted faces and masked mouths like devils in an abstract ballet.

Reaching the roof, Bridgman stepped out into the opaque white moonlight. Louise Woodward was leaning on the balcony, looking out towards the distant, unseen sea. At the faint sound of the door creaking she turned and began to walk listlessly around the roof, her pale face floating like a nimbus. She wore a freshly ironed print dress she had found in a rusty spin drier in one of the launderettes, and her streaked blond hair floated out lightly behind her on the wind.

"Louise!"

Involuntarily she started, tripping over a fragment of the neon sign, then moved backwards towards the balcony overlooking the boulevard.

"Mrs. Woodward!" Bridgman held her by the elbow, raised a hand to her mouth before she could cry out. "The wardens are down below. They're watching the hotel. We must find Travis before he returns."

Louise hesitated, apparently recognizing Bridgman only by an effort, and her eyes turned up to the black marble sky. Bridgman looked at his watch; it was almost 12:35. He searched the stars in the southwest.

Louise murmured: "They're nearly here now, I must see them. Where is Travis, he should be here?"

Bridgman pulled at her arm. "Perhaps he saw the sand-car. Mrs. Woodward, we should leave."

Suddenly she pointed up at the sky, then wrenched away from him and ran to the rail. "There they are!"

Fretting, Bridgman waited until she had filled her eyes with the two companion points of light speeding from the western horizon. These were Merril and Pokrovski—like every schoolboy he knew the sequences perfectly, a second system of constellations with a more complex but far more tangible periodicity and precession—the Castor and Pollux of the orbiting zodiac, whose appearance always heralded a full conjunction the following night.

Louise Woodward gazed up at them from the rail, the rising wind lifting her hair off her shoulders and entraining it horizontally behind her head. Around her feet the red Martian dust swirled and rustled, silting over the fragments of the old neon sign, a brilliant pink spume streaming from her long fingers as they moved along the balcony ledge. When the satellites finally disappeared among the stars along the horizon, she leaned forwards, her face raised to the milk-blue moon as if to delay their departure, then turned back to Bridgman, a bright smile on her face.

His earlier suspicions vanishing, Bridgman smiled back at her encouragingly. "Roger will be here tomorrow night, Louise. We must be careful the wardens don't catch us before we see him."

He felt a sudden admiration for her, at the stoical way she had sustained herself during her long vigil. Perhaps she thought of Woodward as still alive, and in some way was patiently waiting for him to return? He remembered her saying once: "Roger was only a boy when he took off, you know, I feel more like his mother now," as if frightened how Woodward would react to her dry skin and fading hair, fearing that he might even have forgotten her. No doubt the death she visualized for him was of a different order than the mortal kind.

Hand in hand, they tiptoed carefully down the flaking steps, jumped down from a terrace window into the soft sand below the windbreak. Bridgman sank to his knees in the fine silver moon-dust, then waded up to the firmer ground, pulling Louise after him. They climbed through a breach in the tilting palisades, then ran away from the line of dead hotels looming like skulls in the empty light.

"Paul, wait!" Her head still raised to the sky, Louise Woodward fell to her knees in a hollow between two dunes, with a laugh stumbled after Bridgman as he raced through the dips and saddles. The wind was now whipping the sand off the higher crests, flurries of dust spurting like excited wavelets. A hundred yards away, the town was a fading film set, projected by the camera obscura of the sinking moon. They were standing where the long Atlantic seas had once been ten fathoms deep, and Bridgman could scent again the tang of brine among the flickering whitecaps of dust, phosphorescing like shoals of animalcula. He waited for any sign of Travis.

"Louise, we'll have to go back to the town. The sandstorms are blowing up, we'll never see Travis here."

They moved back through the dunes, then worked their way among the narrow alleyways between the hotels to the northern gateway to the town. Bridgman found a vantage point in a small apartment block, and they lay down looking out below a window lintel into the sloping street, the warm sand forming a pleasant cushion. At the intersections the dust blew across the roadway in white clouds, obscuring the wardens' beach-car parked a hundred yards down the boulevard.

Half an hour later an engine surged, and Bridgman began to pile sand into the interval in front of them. "They're going. Thank God!"

Louise Woodward held his arm. "Look!"

Fifty feet away, his white vinyl suit half-hidden in the dust clouds, one of the wardens was advancing slowly towards them, his lasso twirling lightly in his hand. A few feet behind was a second warden, craning up at the windows of the apartment block with his binoculars.

Bridgman and Louise crawled back below the ceiling, then dug their way under a transom into the kitchen at the rear. A window opened onto a sand-filled yard, and they darted away through the lifting dust that whirled between the buildings.

Suddenly, around a corner, they saw the line of wardens moving down a side street, the sand-car edging along behind them. Before Bridgman could steady himself a spasm of pain seized his right calf, contorting the gastrocnemius muscle, and he fell to one knee. Louise Woodward pulled him back against the wall, then pointed at a squat, bow-legged figure trudging towards them along the curving road into town.

"Travis—"

The tool-bag swung from his right hand, and his feet rang faintly on the wire-mesh roadway. Head down, he seemed unaware of the wardens hidden by a bend in the road.

"Come on!" Disregarding the negligible margin of safety, Bridgman clambered to his feet and impetuously ran out into the center of the street. Louise tried to stop him, and they had covered only ten yards before the wardens saw them. There was a warning shout, and the spotlight flung its giant cone down the street. The sand-car surged forward, like a massive dust-covered bull, its tracks clawing at the sand.

"Travis!" As Bridgman reached the bend, Louise Woodward ten yards behind, Travis looked up from his reverie, then flung the tool-bag over one shoulder and raced ahead of them towards the clutter of motel roofs protruding from the other side of the street. Lagging behind the others, Bridgman again felt the cramp attack his leg, broke off into a painful shuffle. When Travis came back for him Bridgman tried to wave him away, but Travis pinioned his elbow and propelled him forward like an attendant straight-arming a patient.

The dust swirling around them, they disappeared through the fading streets and out into the desert, the shouts of the beach-wardens lost in the roar and clamor of the baying engine. Around them, like the strange metallic flora of some extra-terrestrial garden, the old neon signs jutted from the red Martian sand—"Satellite Motel," "Planet Bar," "Mercury Motel." Hiding behind them, they reached the scrub-covered dunes on the edge of the town, then picked up one of the trails that led away among the sand-reefs. There, in the deep grottos of compacted sand which hung like inverted palaces, they waited until the storm subsided. Shortly before dawn the wardens abandoned their search, unable to bring the heavy sand-car onto the disintegrating reef.

Contemptuous of the wardens, Travis lit a small fire with his ciga-rette lighter, burning splinters of driftwood that had gathered in the gullies. Bridgman crouched beside it, warming his hands.

"This is the first time they've been prepared to leave the sand-car," he remarked to Travis. "It means they're under orders to catch us."

Travis shrugged. "Maybe. They're extending the fence along the beach. They probably intend to seal us in forever."

"What?" Bridgman stood up with a sudden feeling of uneasiness. "Why should they? Are you sure? I mean, what would be the point?"

Travis looked up at him, a flicker of dry amusement on his bleached face. Wisps of smoke wreathed his head, curled up past the serpen-tine columns of the grotto to the winding interval of sky a hundred feet above. "Bridgman, forgive me saying so, but if you want to leave here, you should leave now. In a month's time you won't be able to."

Bridgman ignored this, and searched the cleft of dark sky over-head, which framed the constellation Scorpio, as if hoping to see a reflection of the distant sea. "They must be crazy. How much of this fence did you see?"

"About eight hundred yards. It won't take them long to complete. The sections are prefabricated, about forty feet high." He smiled ironically at Bridgman's discomfort. "Relax, Bridgman. If you do want to get out, you'll always be able to tunnel underneath it."

"I don't want to get out," Bridgman said coldly. "Damn them, Travis, they're turning the place into a zoo. You know it won't be the same with a fence all the way around it."

"A corner of Earth that is forever Mars." Under the high forehead, Travis's eyes were sharp and watchful. "I see their point. There hasn't been a fatal casualty now"—he glanced at Louise Woodward, who was strolling about in the colonnades "—for nearly twenty years, and passenger rockets are supposed to be as safe as commuters' trains. They're quietly sealing off the past, Louise and I and you with it. I suppose it's pretty considerate of them not to burn the place down with flame throwers. The virus would be a sufficient excuse. After all, we three are probably the only reservoirs left on the planet." He picked up a handful of red dust and examined the fine crystals with a somber eye. "Well, Bridgman, what are you going to do?"

His thoughts discharging themselves through his mind like frantic signal flares, Bridgman walked away without answering.

Behind them, Louise Woodward wandered among the deep galleries of the grotto, crooning to herself in a low voice to the sighing rhythms of the whirling sand.

The next morning they returned to the town, wading through the deep drifts of sand that lay like a fresh fall of red snow between the hotels and stores, coruscating in the brilliant sunlight. Travis and Louise Woodward made their way towards their quarters in the motels further down the beach. Bridgman searched the still, crystal air for any signs of the wardens, but the sand-car had gone, its tracks obliterated by the storm.

In his room he found their calling card.

A huge tide of dust had flowed through the french windows and submerged the desk and bed, three feet deep against the rear wall. Outside the sand break had been inundated, and the contours of the desert had completely altered, a few spires of obsidian marking its former perspectives like bouys on a shifting sea. Bridgman spent the morning digging out his books and equipment, dismantled the electrical system and its batteries and carried everything to the room above. He would have moved to the penthouse on the top floor, but his lights would have been visible for miles.

Settling into his new quarters, he switched on the tape recorder, heard a short clipped message in the brisk voice which had shouted orders at the wardens the previous evening. "Bridgman, this is Major Webster, deputy commandant of Cocoa Beach Reservation. On the instructions of the Anti-Viral Subcommittee of the UN General Assembly we are now building a continuous fence around the beach area. On completion no further egress will be allowed, and anyone escaping will be immediately returned to the reservation. Give yourself up now, Bridgman, before—"

Bridgman stopped the tape, then reversed the spool and erased the message, staring angrily at the instrument. Unable to settle down to the task of rewiring the room's circuits, he paced about, fiddling with the architectural drawings propped against the wall. He felt restless and hyper-excited, perhaps because he had been trying to repress, not very successfully, precisely those doubts of which Webster had now reminded him.

He stepped onto the balcony and looked out over the desert, at the red dunes rolling to the windows directly below. For the fourth time he had moved up a floor, and the sequence of identical rooms he had occupied were like displaced images of himself seen through a prism. Their common focus, that elusive final definition of himself which he had sought for so long, still remained to be found. Timelessly the sand swept towards him, its shifting contours, approximating more closely than any other landscape he had found to complete psychic zero, enveloping his past failures and uncertainties, masking them in its enigmatic canopy.

Bridgman watched the red sand flicker and fluoresce in the steepening sunlight. He would never see Mars now, and redress the implicit failure of talent, but a workable replica of the planet was contained within the beach area.

Several million tons of the Martian topsoil had been ferried in as ballast some fifty years earlier, when it was feared that the continuous firing of planetary probes and space vehicles, and the transportation of bulk stores and equipment to Mars would fractionally lower the gravitational mass of the Earth and bring it into a tighter orbit around the Sun. Although the distance involved would be little more than a few millimeters, and barely raise the temperature of the atmosphere, its cumulative effects over an extended period might have resulted in a loss into space of the tenuous layers of the outer atmosphere, and of the radiological veil which alone made the biosphere habitable.

Over a twenty-year period a fleet of large freighters had shuttled to and from Mars, dumping the ballast into the sea near the landing grounds of Cape Canaveral. Simultaneously the Russians were filling in a small section of the Caspian Sea. The intention had been that the ballast should be swallowed by the Atlantic and Caspian waters, but all too soon it was found that the microbiological analysis of the sand had been inadequate.

At the Martian polar caps, where the original water vapor in the atmosphere had condensed, a residue of ancient organic matter formed the topsoil, a fine sandy loess containing the fossilized spores of the giant lichens and mosses which had been the last living organisms on the planet millions of years earlier. Embedded in these spores were the crystal lattices of the viruses which had once preyed on the plants, and traces of these were carried back to Earth with the Canaveral and Caspian ballast.

A few years afterwards a drastic increase in a wide range of plant diseases was noticed in the southern states of America and in the Kazakhstan and Turkmenistan republics of the Soviet Union. All over Florida there were outbreaks of blight and mosaic disease, orange plantations withered and died, stunted palms split by the roadside like dried banana skins, manila grass stiffened into paper spears in the summer heat. Within a few years the entire peninsula was transformed into a desert. The swampy jungles of the Everglades became bleached and dry, the rivers cracked husks strewn with the gleaming skeletons of crocodiles and birds, the forests petrified.

The former launching ground at Canaveral was closed, and shortly afterwards the Cocoa Beach resorts were sealed off and evacuated, billions of dollars of real estate were abandoned to the virus. Fortunately never virulent to animal hosts, its influence was confined to within a small radius of the original loess which had borne it, unless ingested by the human organism, when it symbioted with the bacteria in the gut flora, benign and unknown to the host, but devastating to vegetation thousands of miles from Canaveral if returned to the soil.

Unable to rest despite his sleepless night, Bridgman played irritably with the tape recorder. During their close escape from the wardens he had more than half-hoped they would catch him. The mysterious leg cramp was obviously psychogenic. Although unable to accept consciously the logic of Webster's argument, he would willingly have conceded to the fait accompli of physical capture, gratefully submitted to a year's quarantine at the Parasitological Cleansing Unit at Tampa, and then returned to his career as an architect, chastened but accepting his failure.

As yet, however, the opportunity for surrender had failed to offer itself. Travis appeared to be aware of his ambivalent motives; Bridgman noticed that he and Louise Woodward had made no arrangements to meet him that evening for the conjunction.

In the early afternoon he went down into the streets, plowed through the drifts of red sand, following the footprints of Travis and Louise as they wound in and out of the side streets, finally saw them disappear into the coarser, flintlike dunes among the submerged motels to the south of the town. Giving up, he returned through the empty, shadowless streets, now and then shouted up into the hot air, listening to the echoes boom away among the dunes.

Later that afternoon he walked out towards the northeast, picking his way carefully through the dips and hollows, crouching in the pools of shadow whenever the distant sounds of the construction gangs along the perimeter were carried across to him by the wind. Around him, in the great dust basins, the grains of red sand glittered like diamonds. Barbs of rusting metal protruded from the slopes, remnants of Mars satellites and launching stages which had fallen onto the Martian deserts and then been carried back again to Earth. One fragment which he passed, a complete section of hull plate like a concave shield, still carried part of an identification numeral, and stood upright in the dissolving sand like a door into nowhere.

Just before dusk he reached a tall spur of obsidian that reared up into the tinted cerise sky like the spire of a ruined church, climbed up among its jutting cornices and looked out across the intervening two or three miles of dunes to the perimeter. Illuminated by the last light, the metal grilles shone with a roseate glow like fairy portcullises on the edge of an enchanted sea. At least half a mile of the fence had been completed, and as he watched another of the giant prefabricated sections was cantilevered into the air and staked to the ground. Already the eastern horizon was cut off by the encroaching fence, the enclosed Martian sand like the gravel scattered at the bottom of a cage.

Perched on the spur, Bridgman felt a warning tremor of pain in his calf. He leapt down in a flurry of dust, without looking back made off among the dunes and reefs.

Later, as the last baroque whorls of the sunset faded below the horizon, he waited on the roof for Travis and Louise Woodward, peering impatiently into the empty moon-filled streets.

Shortly after midnight, at an elevation of 35 degrees in the southwest, between Aquila and Ophiuchus, the conjunction began. Bridgman continued to search the streets, and ignored the seven points of speeding light as they raced towards him from the horizon like an invasion from deep space. There was no indication of their convergent orbital pathways, which would soon scatter them thousands of miles apart, and the satellites moved as if they were always together, in the tight configuration Bridgman had known since childhood, like a lost zodiacal emblem, a constellation detached from the celestial sphere and forever frantically searching to return to its place.

"Travis! Confound you!" With a snarl, Bridgman swung away from the balcony and moved along to the exposed section of rail behind the elevator head. To be avoided like a pariah by Travis and Louise Woodward forced him to accept that he was no longer a true resident of the beach and now existed in a no-man's-land between them and the wardens.

The seven satellites drew nearer, and Bridgman glanced up at them cursorily. They were disposed in a distinctive but unusual pattern resembling the Greek letter *chi,* a limp cross, a straight lateral member containing four capsules more or less in line ahead—Connolly, Tkachev, Merril and Maiakovski—bisected by three others forming with Tkachev an elongated Z—Pokrovski, Woodward and Brodisnek. The pattern had been variously identified as a hammer and sickle, an eagle, a swastika, and a dove, as well as a variety of religious and runic emblems, but all these were being defeated by the advancing tendency of the older capsules to vaporize.

It was this slow disintegration of the aluminum shells that made them visible—it had often been pointed out that the observer on the ground was looking, not at the actual capsule, but at a local field of vaporized aluminum and ionized hydrogen peroxide gas from the ruptured altitude jets now distributed within half a mile of each of the capsules. Woodward's, the most recently in orbit, was a barely perceptible point of light. The hulks of the capsules, with their perfectly preserved human cargoes, were continually dissolving, and a wide fan of silver spray opened out in a phantom wake behind Merril and Pokrovski (1998 and 1999), like a double star transforming itself into a nova in the center of a constellation. As the mass of the capsules diminished they sank into a closer orbit around the earth, would soon touch the denser layers of the atmosphere and plummet to the ground.

Bridgman watched the satellites as they moved towards him, his irritation with Travis forgotten. As always, he felt himself moved by the eerie but strangely serene spectacle of the ghostly convoy endlessly circling the dark sea of the midnight sky, the long-dead astronauts converging for the ten-thousandth time upon their brief rendezvous and then setting off upon their lonely flight paths around the perimeter of the ionosphere, the tidal edge of the beachway into space which had reclaimed them.

How Louise Woodward could bear to look up at her husband he had never been able to understand. After her arrival he once invited her to the hotel, remarking that there was an excellent view of the beautiful sunsets, and she had snapped back bitterly: "Beautiful? Can you imagine what it's like looking up at a sunset when your husband's spinning round through it in his coffin?"

This reaction had been a common one when the first astronauts had died after failing to make contact with the launching platforms in fixed orbit. When these new stars rose in the west an attempt had been made to shoot them down—there was the unsettling prospect of the skies a thousand years hence, littered with orbiting refuse—but later they were left in this natural graveyard, forming their own monument.

Obscured by the clouds of dust carried up into the air by the sandstorm, the satellites shone with little more than the intensity of second-magnitude stars, winking as the reflected light was interrupted by the lanes of stratocirrus. The wake of diffusing light behind Merril and Pokrovski which usually screened the other capsules seemed to have diminished in size, and he could see both Maiakovski and Brodisnek clearly for the first time in several months. Wondering whether Merril or Pokrovski would be the first to fall from orbit, he looked towards the center of the cross as it passed overhead.

With a sharp intake of breath, he tilted his head back. In surprise he noticed that one of the familiar points of light was missing from the center of the group. What he had assumed to be an occlusion of the conjoint vapor trails by dust clouds was simply due to the fact that one of the capsules—Merril's, he decided, the third of the line ahead—had fallen from its orbit.

Head raised, he sidestepped slowly across the roof, avoiding the pieces of rusting neon sign, following the convoy as it passed overhead and moved towards the eastern horizon. No longer overlayed by the wake of Merril's capsule, Woodward's shone with far greater clarity, and almost appeared to have taken the former's place, although he was not due to fall from orbit for at least a century.

In the distance somewhere an engine growled. A moment later, from a different quarter, a woman's voice cried out faintly. Bridgman moved to the rail, over the intervening rooftops saw two figures silhouetted against the sky on the elevator head of an apartment block, then heard Louise Woodward call out again. She was pointing up at the sky with both hands, her long hair blown about her face, Travis trying to restrain her. Bridgman realized that she had misconstrued Merril's descent, assuming that the fallen astronaut was her husband. He climbed onto the edge of the balcony, watching the pathetic tableau on the distant roof.

Again, somewhere among the dunes, an engine moaned. Before Bridgman could turn around, a brilliant blade of light cleaved the sky in the southwest. Like a speeding comet, an immense train of vaporizing particles stretching behind it to the horizon, it soared towards them, the downward curve of its pathway clearly visible. Detached from the rest of the capsules, which were now disappearing among the stars along the eastern horizon, it was little more than a few miles off the ground.

Bridgman watched it approach, apparently on a collision course with the hotel. The expanding corona of white light, like a gigantic signal flare, illuminated the rooftops, etching the letters of the neon signs over the submerged motels on the outskirts of the town. He ran for the doorway, as he raced down the stairs saw the glow of the descending capsule fill the somber streets like a hundred moons. When he reached his room, sheltered by the massive weight of the hotel, he watched the dunes in front of the hotel light up like a stage set. Three hundred yards away the low camouflaged hull of the wardens' beach-car was revealed poised on a crest, its feeble spotlight drowned by the glare.

With a deep metallic sigh, the burning catafalque of the dead astronaut soared overhead, a cascade of vaporizing metal pouring from its hull, filling the sky with incandescent light. Reflected below it, like an expressway illuminated by an aircraft's spotlights, a long lane of light several hundred yards in width raced out into the desert towards the sea. As Bridgman shielded his eyes, it suddenly erupted in a tremendous explosion of detonating sand. A huge curtain of white dust lifted into the air and fell slowly to the ground. The sounds of the impact rolled against the hotel, mounting in a sustained crescendo that drummed against the windows. A series of smaller explosions flared up like opalescent fountains. All over the desert fires flickered briefly where fragments of the capsule had been scattered. Then the noise subsided, and an immense glistening pall of phosphorescing gas hung in the air like a silver veil, particles within it beading and winking.

Two hundred yards away across the sand was the running figure of Louise Woodward, Travis twenty paces behind her. Bridgman watched them dart in and out of the dunes, then abruptly felt the cold spotlight of the beach-car hit his face and flood the room behind him. The vehicle was moving straight towards him, two of the wardens, nets and lassos in hand, riding the outboard.

Quickly Bridgman straddled the balcony, jumped down into the sand and raced towards the crest of the first dune. He crouched and ran on through the darkness as the beam probed the air. Above, the glistening pall was slowly fading, the particles of vaporized metal sifting towards the dark Martian sand. In the distance the last echoes of the impact were still reverberating among the hotels of the beach colonies further down the coast.

Five minutes later he caught up with Louise Woodward and Travis. The capsule's impact had flattened a number of the dunes, forming a shallow basin some quarter of a mile in diameter, and the surrounding slopes were scattered with the still glowing particles, sparkling like fading eyes. The beach-car growled somewhere four or five hundred yards behind him, and Bridgman broke off into an exhausted walk. He stopped beside Travis, who was kneeling on the ground, breath pumping into his lungs. Fifty yards away Louise Woodward was running up and down, distraughtly gazing at the fragments of smouldering metal. For a moment the spotlight of the approaching beach-car illuminated her, and she ran away among the dunes. Bridgman caught a glimpse of the inconsolable anguish in her face.

Travis was still on his knees. He had picked up a piece of the oxidized metal and was pressing it together in his hands.

"Travis, for God's sake tell her! This was Merril's capsule, there's no doubt about it! Woodward's still up there."

Travis looked up at him silently, his eyes searching Bridgman's face. A spasm of pain tore his mouth, and Bridgman realized that the barb of steel he clasped reverently in his hands was still glowing with heat.

"Travis!" He tried to pull the man's hands apart, the pungent stench of burning flesh gusting into his face, but Travis wrenched away from him. "Leave her alone, Bridgman! Go back with the wardens!"

Bridgman retreated from the approaching beach-car. Only thirty yards away, its spotlight filled the basin. Louise Woodward was still searching the dunes. Travis held his ground as the wardens jumped down from the car and advanced towards him with their nets, his bloodied hands raised at his sides, the steel barb flashing like a dagger. At the head of the wardens, the only one unmasked, was a trim, neat-featured man with an intent, serious face. Bridgman guessed that this was Major Webster, and that the wardens had known of the impending impact and hoped to capture them, and Louise in particular, before it occurred.

Bridgman stumbled back towards the dunes at the edge of the basin. As he neared the crest he trapped his foot in a semicircular plate of metal, sat down and freed his heel. Unmistakably it was part of a control panel, the circular instrument housings still intact.

Overhead the pall of glistening vapor had moved off to the northeast, and the reflected light was directly over the rusting gantries of the former launching site at Cape Canaveral. For a few fleeting seconds the gantries seemed to be enveloped in a sheen of silver, transfigured by the vaporized body of the dead astronaut, diffusing over them in a farewell gesture, his final return to the site from which he had set off to his death a century earlier. Then the gantries sank again into their craggy shadows, and the pall moved off like an immense wraith towards the sea, barely distinguishable from the star glow.

Down below Travis was sitting on the ground surrounded by the wardens. He scuttled about on his hands like a frantic crab, scooping handfuls of the virus-laden sand at them. Holding tight to their masks, the wardens maneuvered around him, their nets and lassos at the ready. Another group moved slowly towards Bridgman.

Bridgman picked up a handful of the dark Martian sand beside the instrument panel, felt the soft glowing crystals warm his palm. In his mind he could still see the silver-sheathed gantries of the launching site across the bay, by a curious illusion almost identical with the Martian city he had designed years earlier. He watched the pall disappear over the sea, then looked around at the other remnants of Merril's capsule scattered over the slopes. High in the western night, between Pegasus and Cygnus, shone the distant disc of the planet Mars, which for both himself and the dead astronaut had served for so long as a symbol of unattained ambition. The wind stirred softly through the sand, cooling this replica of the planet which lay passively around him, and at last he understood why he had come to the beach and been unable to leave it.

Twenty yards away Travis was being dragged off like a wild dog, his thrashing body pinioned in the center of a web of lassos. Louise Woodward had run away among the dunes towards the sea, following the vanished gas cloud.

In a sudden excess of refound confidence, Bridgman drove his fist into the dark sand, buried his forearm like a foundation pillar. A flange of hot metal from Merril's capsule burned his wrist bonding him to the spirit of the dead astronaut. Scattered around him on the Martian sand, in a sense Merril had reached Mars after all.

"Damn it!" he cried exultantly to himself as the wardens' lassos stung his neck and shoulders. "We made it!"

"Then there shall be signs in Heaven"—
This much in the text is given,
Worthy of the sinner's heeding:
But the other signs preceding
Earth's Last Judgment and destruction,
And its fiery reconstruction,
May be drawn from other channels;
For we read in Hebrew annals
That there shall be altogether
Fifteen Judgment days; but whether
Following or interpolated,
Jerome saith, is nowhere stated.

—Sebastian Evans, in "The Fifteen Days of Judgment"

ACCIDENT VERTIGO

by Kenward Elmslie

Another continent!

Nothing but solitaries around one. One finishes one's coffee, one's lip is bleeding from a metal sliver imbedded in the sugar cube which refuses to dissolve however hard one hacks it with one's spoon, and the spoon handle bends if much pressure is exerted, until it is curved, like an old-fashioned baby spoon. So what is there to do but proceed to the nearest newsstand. All the newspapers have identical headlines: "Accident Vertigo." It's the main topic at parties, or in stalled vehicles, or in cabaret shows in the red-light district—("I dunno where to go. Got Big A Vertigo . . .")—time for a relaxing cigarette. The match tip splits, and part of it arcs into a pile of cheap green magazines, the printing machine of which must be on the blink too, as one can dimly see its feature article entitled—is that an "I"—and another "I"—is that "GO"—how simple: "VERTIGO"—and that smudged part must be—it isn't smudged at all! It's a paperweight that the vendor's just moved, a joke piece of dog excrement disguised as a cucumber, a popular gift item in the area, made of plastic, hein, hein? So plastic it catches fire, WHOOSH! Flames abetted by the bottle of bootleg wheat-mash-and-ether-and-rubbing alcohol the old man is holding out teasingly to the woman selling pencils on the platform with kiddie-car wheels. Where are all the solitaries? Racing down the street, yes, the newsstand's on fire, and the refuse trough next to it— the pencil woman's propelling her platform, the vendor and the bootlegger are struggling to get out of their overcoats—the fur collars are on fire—but their speed only fans the flames—a tractor's gone berserk —it's hit them—one flattens oneself against a government building— the wall buckles, a family leap in front of one (how lucky they were watching the passing scene from the ornate iron balcony that narrowly misses one as it crashes to the sidewalk) and run off into the night, hobbling, quickly inventing a rabbity way of avoiding the tractor— more coffee? The loudspeakers of the avenue have interrupted a medley of riverboat hosannah songs (needless to say at the wrong tempo, due to a mechanical failure, so they sound like dirges) and are promising free coffee to anyone in the vicinity whose first name contains the syllable "vert." Most likely, this is part of a campaign to change people's responses to such words as "vertigo" and "accident." A blind woman throws her white cane in the air: Vera, my name is Vera, goodness how lucky. She steps into the street—and vanishes! A manhole: the lids split in two if stepped on if one weighs more than eighty pounds—the sign says so, stencilled on the gutter. Ah, she's clambering out now, cursing everyone and his Dutch uncle.

Another continent!
Solitaries fretting interminably about damaged candybars with dead leaves and wasps in them—the manufacturer insists these are one-in-a-million lucky prizes, if one plants the leaves, mulching them with ten more crumbled candybars, and then injects the wasps with a side-product (hypodermic already filled) called "Vertigo"—

Another continent!
Rife with rumors, rumors of new regulations! Is this Harappa? Yuss, it is Harappa as your teecket steepulates. But this is Mohenjo-Daro, with its famed red domes, not to mention the Mohenjo-Daro-

esque sutras being angrily shouted by the crowd outside this rickshaw! Yes, it is that too: Harrappa, Mohenjo-Daro, Mohenjo-Daro-Harrapa. It is a peeriod of transeetion. Yuss?

Nothing to do but sell one's belongings and move to a new commune in the ice-lands. The solitaries whom one joins, who have the same idea, are already laughing at their having fretted about their candybars named ACCIDENT (printed in yellow streak-of-lightning lettering), piled high in their closets, half-gnawed, with tooth marks that will actually be a useful record in case they need dental care (icy winds are bad for porous enamel, which is a *fait accompli* (free) according to the new regulations, along with hoes, rakes, shovels, palmetto slats, and valuable varicolored corn seeds from the vaults of The Memories, which the commune has been promised access to seven days a week (free), not directly, but via a feeder station that is being hurried to completion, barring certain technical difficulties that have arisen, namely—gourd notions. Gourd notions? Who knows what that was, before it got garbled by a series of transmission experts —god notions? Hoarded rations? Border of oceans? Yuss, border condeetions. The excited voices of the solitaries, burbling around one! Soon these tubular environments (M they're called, just M)— ("Twelve new M this week, Hashville, Roston, Yrie, Vontpelier, Mt. Paul")—("Why hasn't the west more M?")—("Wait for next week, bub!")—one watches the cube sliver in one's coffee suspiciously —from the lip-pomade that was to have healed the cut, one has caught a skin fungus condition (brown specks that produce "spores" each summer, giving one's skin a rough sandpaper texture)—ah, safe! no sliver, one swallows the last of the tepid cube with oily Paisley patterns on its surface (good! detergent residue most likely)—

"My throat's on fire, my throat's on fire!"—the waitress and counterman dive for the floor, lay there, face down as the coffee machine explodes, jetting steam—the specialist says the lip "spores" are not at fault here, the throat was aggravated by "spores" from the improperly washed cup, as certain ingredients of the detergent combined with certain ingredients in the cube (ought not to have been in it)— the sugar manufacturer obligingly traces them to "unclean" trucks: particles of dust adhered to shipments of alfalfa—it's all immaterial! Time for—another continent! Time for the commune with its guaranteed implements, its solitaries, and access to The Memories. Yes, soon those tubular environments will dot the land. Tpringfield! Zampa! Gew Orleans! Itlanta! Theyenne! Mms they're now called, jocularly, Mms—by the other solitaries. New regulations! Mmms they're now called, Mmms. Not in personal conversation anymore—speeches mainly. And that's not the only change. New regulations! No implements. No access to the feeder station except for ten minutes every Sunday a.m. at 11—which is just when the inhabitants of the island the feeder station is located on prohibit all communiqués to or from the outside world. From 11 a.m. to 12 noon, they sit on the rocks, facing the very continent we are on, and repeat the Stone Mantras silently to themselves.

Stone, oh, stone of stone, stone of stone stone,
Stone, oh, stone of stone, stone of stone stone stone,
Stone, oh, stone of stone, stone, oh, stone stone stone of stone

All, all immaterial. The regulations have changed again—the commune's area has been assigned to a financieress (the solitaries hiss "financieress, financieress" so it sounds like "things are getting serious") who has been given the commune's harvests going back seven years. Harvests! *What* harvests! Now those tubular environments are muttered about reverently—Mmmms. Generally in spring, one hears it murmured, someone on the other side of the glacier, one of the original solitaries, getting some sun, resting up for summer: Santa Claus and sleighs and bobbing for pale-green health lozenges jocularly referred to as "Accidents." The commune is referred to as "Vertigo." Perhaps some deep-seated need on the part of the solitaries to mention the inevitable, and therefore possibly prevent it from ever happening. Debts! Piled on debts! Debts! They're as bad as the blizzards that add new and higher levels of snow each year, so that one must continually build additions on top of old roofs to provide substandard living quarters, cubbyholes whole units of solitaries are forced to share in shifts, one cuts a door through to the surface—by the time it's finished, it's impossible to open it—the drifts outside press against it. The widow's walk (first year) that came to be regarded as such an oddity (wasted labor), is now a sub-sub-sub basement, with clumsy drawings pasted on the inside of the windows, scenes of green plateaus, with elks grazing, and throngs gathering for a picnic, with athletic competitions and contests of all sorts—a fine den to relax in under the gales. The expenses though! The outlay! The financieress proves to be understanding—she knows reinforcements and buttresses come dear these days. Wouldn't it be simpler to start afresh? She cancels the debts. On the spot, she is dubbed Mmmmmm. MMMMMM. That's the design decided on for New Vertigo; units of six row houses of double arches, with a snow trough between the arches, snow which will be instantly melted by gas burners at intervals in the trough. New seed arrives—butterbeans, from the vaults of The Memories (no one mentions *them* anymore) to which she has constant access by means of a private system of relayed impulses, the nature of which she is not at liberty to divulge. At last, another continent. New lodgments, new eatments, vistas, and a future of green fields that will chomp up the glaciers, tendrils that will "ossify the snow particles."

All, all immaterial. The regulations have changed again. She is not the financieress! She is a political-socio-economic opportunist of the rankest order! The genuine financieress arrives, after a saga of mishaps (waylaid, a period in an asylum in a forest, cafeteria work, saves enough to approach a first-rate legal adviser, fights her way through the courts, success!)—and is not pleased by the layout, not pleased at all. New debts! Back to the old, buried dwellings that now need new extensions upward with egresses to the surface. Trapdoor egresses at the end of a series of ladders, one on top of the other. Egresses that are never used, for the financieress refuses to underwrite the expense of top-grade preservatives for the butterbeans. And how else can they reach the cities to the north? From her lean-to, she smells the rancid night air, and announces to us solitaries:

"White fungi are spreading along the new gullies.
Nothing wriggles in the labs with ticketed jellies.
Trinkets—human hair plaited into flower offerings—
thank you for them. I have been in touch with the Mings,

and they will set up here a vast pleasure park,
of rocks and snow and silence and winds and the dark,
one solitary will be chosen per year—by lot.
Good-bye. Amnesty! No one will be shot."

It is well to be in the flatlands of Texas, my hands resting spread out on my thighs as I sit, trapdoor overhead, immobile as a quiet and composed Egyptian posing for a bas-relief of his ruler, phone propped on my upraised shoulder, head bent down, eyes following the bobbing.

Another continent.

Feb 8, 1772

Dear Sir,

When I ride about in the winter, and see such prodigious flocks of various kinds of birds, I cannot help admiring at these congregation, and wishing that it was in my power to account for those appearances almost peculiar to the season. The two great motives which regulate the proceedings of the brute creation are love and hunger. . . . As to love, that is out of the question at a time of the year when that soft passion is not indulged. . . .

Now as to the business of food: as these animals are actuated by instinct to hunt for necessary food, they should not, one would suppose, crowd together in pursuit of sustenance at a time when it is most likely to fail: yet such associations do take place in hard weather chiefly, and thicken as the severity increases. As some kind of self-interest and self-defense is no doubt the motive for the proceeding, may it not arise from the helplessness of their state in such rigorous seasons; as men crowd together, when under great calamities, though they know not why?

—Gilbert White in *The Natural History of Selborne*

THE BIRDS

by Daphne du Maurier

On December the third the wind changed overnight and it was winter. Until then the autumn had been mellow, soft. The leaves had lingered on the trees, golden-red, and the hedgerows were still green. The earth was rich where the plow had turned it.

Nat Hocken, because of a wartime disability, had a pension and did not work full time at the farm. He worked three days a week, and they gave him the lighter jobs: hedging, thatching, repairs to the farm buildings.

Although he was married, with children, his was a solitary disposition; he liked best to work alone. It pleased him when he was given a bank to build up, or a gate to mend at the far end of the peninsula, where the sea surrounded the farmland on either side. Then, at midday, he would pause and eat the pasty that his wife had baked for him, and, sitting on the cliff's edge, would watch the birds. Autumn was best for this, better than spring. In spring the birds flew inland, purposeful, intent; they knew where they were bound, the rhythm and ritual of their life brooked no delay. In autumn those that had not migrated overseas but remained to pass the winter were caught up in the same driving urge, but because migration was denied them followed a pattern of their own. Great flocks of them came to the peninsula, restless, uneasy, spending themselves in ·motion; now wheeling, circling in the sky, now settling to feed on the rich newturned soil, but even when they fed it was as though they did so without hunger, without desire. Restlessness drove them to the skies again.

Black and white, jackdaw and gull, mingled in strange partnership, seeking some sort of liberation, never satisfied, never still. Flocks of starlings, rustling like silk, flew to fresh pasture, driven by the same necessity of movement, and the smaller birds, the finches and the larks, scattered from tree to hedge as if compelled.

Nat watched them, and he watched the sea birds too. Down in the bay they waited for the tide. They had more patience. Oyster catchers, redshank, sanderling, and curlew watched by the water's edge; as the slow sea sucked at the shore and then withdrew, leaving the strip of seaweed bare and the shingle churned, the sea birds raced and ran upon the beaches. Then that same impulse to flight seized upon them too. Crying, whistling, calling, they skimmed the placid sea and left the shore. Make haste, make speed, hurry and begone; yet where, and to what purpose? The restless urge of autumn, unsatisfying, sad, had put a spell upon them and they must flock, and wheel, and cry; they must spill themselves of motion before winter came.

"Perhaps," thought Nat, munching his pasty by the cliff's edge, "a message comes to the birds in autumn, like a warning. Winter is coming. Many of them perish. And like people who, apprehensive of death before their time, drive themselves to work or folly, the birds do likewise."

The birds had been more restless than ever this fall of the year, the agitation more marked because the days were still. As the tractor traced its path up and down the western hills, the figure of the farmer silhouetted on the driving seat, the whole machine and the man upon it would be lost momentarily in the great cloud of wheeling, crying birds. There were many more than usual, Nat was sure of this. Always, in autumn, they followed the plow, but not in great flocks like these, nor with such clamor.

Nat remarked upon it when hedging was finished for the day. "Yes," said the farmer, "there are more birds about than usual; I've noticed it too. And daring, some of them, taking no notice of the tractor. One or two gulls came so close to my head this afternoon I thought they'd knock my cap off! As it was, I could scarcely see what I was doing, when they were overhead and I had the sun in my eyes. I have a notion the weather will change. It will be a hard winter. That's why the birds are restless."

Nat, tramping home across the fields and down the lane to his cottage, saw the birds still flocking over the western hills, in the last glow of the sun. No wind, and the gray sea calm and full. Campion in bloom yet in the hedges, and the air mild. The farmer was right, though, and it was that night the weather turned. Nat's bedroom faced east. He woke just after two and heard the wind in the chimney. Not the storm and bluster of a sou' westerly gale, bringing the rain, but east wind, cold and dry. It sounded hollow in the chimney, and a loose slate rattled on the roof. Nat listened, and he could hear the sea roaring in the bay. Even the air in the small bedroom had turned chill; a draught came under the skirting of the door, blowing upon the bed. Nat drew the blanket round him, leant closer to the back of his sleeping wife, and stayed wakeful, watchful, aware of misgiving without cause.

Then he heard the tapping on the window. There was no creeper on the cottage walls to break loose and scratch upon the pane. He listened, and the tapping continued until, irritated by the sound, Nat got out of bed and went to the window. He opened it, and as he did so something brushed his hand, jabbing at his knuckles, grazing the skin. Then he saw the flutter of the wings and it was gone, over the roof, behind the cottage.

It was a bird; what kind of bird he could not tell. The wind must have driven it to shelter on the sill.

He shut the window and went back to bed, but, feeling his knuckles wet, put his mouth to the scratch. The bird had drawn blood. Frightened, he supposed, and bewildered, the bird, seeking shelter, had stabbed at him in the darkness. Once more he settled himself to sleep.

Presently the tapping came again, this time more forceful, more insistent, and now his wife woke at the sound and, turning in the bed, said to him, "See to the window, Nat, it's rattling."

"I've already seen to it," he told her; "there's some bird there trying to get in. Can't you hear the wind? It's blowing from the east, driving the birds to shelter."

"Send them away," she said, "I can't sleep with that noise."

He went to the window for the second time, and now when he opened it there was not one bird upon the sill but half a dozen; they flew straight into his face, attacking him.

He shouted, striking out at them with his arms, scattering them; like the first one, they flew over the roof and disappeared. Quickly he let the window fall and latched it.

"Did you hear that?" he said. "They went for me. Tried to peck my eyes." He stood by the window, peering into the darkness, and could see nothing. His wife, heavy with sleep, murmured from the bed.

"I'm not making it up," he said, angry at her suggestion. "I tell you the birds were on the sill, trying to get into the room."

Suddenly a frightened cry came from the room across the passage where the children slept.

"It's Jill," said his wife, roused at the sound, sitting up in bed. "Go to her, see what's the matter."

Nat lit the candle, but when he opened the bedroom door to cross the passage the draught blew out the flame.

There came a second cry of terror, this time from both children, and stumbling into their room, he felt the beating of wings about him in the darkness. The window was wide open. Through it came the birds, hitting first the ceiling and the walls, then swerving in midflight, turning to the children in their beds.

"It's all right, I'm here," shouted Nat, and the children flung themselves, screaming, upon him, while in the darkness the birds rose and dived and came for him again.

"What is it, Nat, what's happened?" his wife called from the further bedroom, and swiftly he pushed the children through the door to the passage and shut it upon them, so that he was alone now in their bed-room with the birds.

He seized a blanket from the nearest bed and, using it as a weapon, flung it to right and left about him in the air. He felt the thud of bodies, heard the fluttering of wings, but they were not yet defeated, for again and again they returned to the assault, jabbing his hands, his head, the little stabbing beaks sharp as pointed forks. The blanket became a weapon of defense; he wound it about his head, and then in greater darkness beat at the birds with his bare hands. He dared not stumble to the door and open it, lest in doing so the birds should follow him.

How long he fought with them in the darkness he could not tell, but at last the beating of the wings about him lessened and then with-drew, and through the density of the blanket he was aware of light. He waited, listened; there was no sound except the fretful crying of one of the children from the bedroom beyond. The fluttering, the whirring of the wings had ceased.

He took the blanket from his head and stared about him. The cold gray morning light exposed the room. Dawn and the open window had called the living birds; the dead lay on the floor. Nat gazed at the little corpses, shocked and horrified. They were all small birds, none of any size; there must have been fifty of them lying there upon the floor. There were robins, finches, sparrows, blue tits, larks, and bram-blings, birds that by nature's law kept to their own flock and their own territory, and now, joining one with another in their urge for battle, had destroyed themselves against the bedroom walls, or in the strife had been destroyed by him. Some had lost feathers in the fight; others had blood, his blood, upon their beaks.

Sickened, Nat went to the window and stared out across his patch of garden to the fields.

It was bitter cold, and the ground had all the hard black look of frost. Not white frost, to shine in the morning sun, but the black frost that the east wind brings. The sea, fiercer now with the turning tide, white-capped and steep, broke harshly in the bay. Of the birds there was no sign. Not a sparrow chattered in the hedge beyond the garden gate, no early missel thrush or blackbird pecked on the grass for worms. There was no sound at all but the east wind and the sea.

Nat shut the window and the door of the small bedroom, and went back across the passage to his own. His wife sat up in one bed, one child asleep beside her, the smaller in her arms, his face bandaged.

The curtains were tightly drawn across the window, the candles lit. Her face looked garish in the yellow light. She shook her head for silence.

"He's sleeping now," she whispered, "but only just. Something must have cut him, there was blood at the corner of his eyes. Jill said it was the birds. She said she woke up, and the birds were in the room."

His wife looked up at Nat, searching his face for confirmation. She looked terrified, bewildered, and he did not want her to know that he was also shaken, dazed almost, by the events of the past few hours.

"There are birds in there," he said, "dead birds, nearly fifty of them. Robins, wrens, all the little birds from hereabouts. It's as though a madness seized them, with the east wind." He sat down on the bed beside his wife, and held her hand. "It's the weather," he said, "it must be that, it's the hard weather. They aren't the birds, maybe, from here around. They've been driven down from up-country."

"But, Nat," whispered his wife, "it's only this night that the weather turned. There's been no snow to drive them. And they can't be hungry yet. There's food for them out there in the fields."

"It's the weather," repeated Nat. "I tell you, it's the weather."

His face, too, was drawn and tired, like hers. They stared at one another for a while without speaking.

"I'll go downstairs and make a cup of tea," he said.

The sight of the kitchen reassured him. The cups and saucers, neatly stacked upon the dresser, the table and chairs, his wife's roll of knitting on her basket chair, the children's toys in a corner cupboard.

He knelt down, raked out the old embers, and relit the fire. The glowing sticks brought normality, the steaming kettle and the brown teapot comfort and security. He drank his tea, carried a cup up to his wife. Then he washed in the scullery, and, putting on his boots, opened the back door.

The sky was hard and leaden, and the brown hills that had gleamed in the sun the day before looked dark and bare. The east wind, like a razor, stripped the trees, and the leaves, crackling and dry, shivered and scattered with the wind's blast. Nat stubbed the earth with his boot. It was frozen hard. He had never known a change so swift and sudden. Black winter had descended in a single night.

The children were awake now. Jill was chattering upstairs and young Johnny crying once again. Nat heard his wife's voice, soothing, comforting. Presently they came down. He had breakfast ready for them, and the routine of the day began.

"Did you drive away the birds?" asked Jill, restored to calm because of the kitchen fire, because of day, because of breakfast.

"Yes, they've all gone now," said Nat. "It was the east wind brought them in. They were frightened and lost, they wanted shelter."

"They tried to peck us," said Jill. "They went for Johnny's eyes."

"Fright made them do that," said Nat. "They didn't know where they were in the dark bedroom."

"I hope they won't come again," said Jill. "Perhaps if we put bread for them outside the window they will eat that and fly away."

She finished her breakfast and then went for her coat and hood, her schoolbooks and her satchel. Nat said nothing, but his wife looked at him across the table. A silent message passed between them.

"I'll walk with her to the bus," he said. "I don't go to the farm today."

And while the child was washing in the scullery he said to his wife, "Keep all the windows closed, and the doors too. Just to be on the safe side. I'll go to the farm. Find out if they heard anything in the night." Then he walked with his small daughter up the lane. She seemed to have forgotten her experience of the night before. She danced ahead of him, chasing the leaves, her face whipped with the cold and rosy under the pixie hood.

"Is it going to snow, Dad?" she said. "It's cold enough."

He glanced up at the bleak sky, felt the wind tear at his shoulders. "No," he said, "it's not going to snow. This is a black winter, not a white one."

All the while he searched the hedgerows for the birds, glanced over the top of them to the fields beyond, looked to the small wood above the farm where the rooks and jackdaws gathered. He saw none.

The other children waited by the bus stop, muffled, hooded like Jill, the faces white and pinched with cold.

Jill ran to them, waving. "My Dad says it won't snow," she called, "it's going to be a black winter."

She said nothing of the birds. She began to push and struggle with another little girl. The bus came ambling up the hill. Nat saw her on to it, then turned and walked back towards the farm. It was not his day for work, but he wanted to satisfy himself that all was well. Jim, the cowman, was clattering in the yard.

"Boss around?" asked Nat.

"Gone to market," said Jim. "It's Tuesday, isn't it?"

He clumped off round the corner of a shed. He had no time for Nat. Nat was said to be superior. Read books, and the like. Nat had forgotten it was Tuesday. This showed how the events of the preceding night had shaken him. He went to the back door of the farmhouse and heard Mrs. Trigg singing in the kitchen, the wireless making a background to her song.

"Are you there, missus?" called out Nat.

She came to the door, beaming, broad, a good-tempered woman. "Hullo, Mr. Hocken," she said. "Can you tell me where this cold is coming from? Is it Russia? I've never seen such a change. And it's going on, the wireless says. Something to do with the Arctic Circle."

"We didn't turn on the wireless this morning," said Nat. "Fact is, we had trouble in the night."

"Kiddies poorly?"

"No . . ." He hardly knew how to explain it. Now, in daylight, the battle of the birds would sound absurd.

He tried to tell Mrs. Trigg what had happened, but he could see from her eyes that she thought his story was the result of a nightmare.

"Sure they were real birds," she said, smiling, "with proper feathers and all? Not the funny-shaped kind that the men see after closing hours on a Saturday night?"

"Mrs. Trigg," he said, "there are fifty dead birds, robins, wrens, and such, lying low on the floor of the children's bedroom. They went for me; they tried to go for young Johnny's eyes."

Mrs. Trigg stared at him doubtfully.

"Well there, now," she answered. "I suppose the weather brought them. Once in the bedroom, they wouldn't know where they were to. Foreign birds maybe, from that Arctic Circle."

"No," said Nat, "they were the birds you see about here every day."

"Funny thing," said Mrs. Trigg, "no explaining it, really. You ought to write up and ask the *Guardian*. They'd have some answer for it. Well, I must be getting on."

She nodded, smiled, and went back into the kitchen.

Nat, dissatisfied, turned to the farm gate. Had it not been for those corpses on the bedroom floor, which he must now collect and bury somewhere, he would have considered the tale exaggeration too.

Jim was standing by the gate.

"Had any trouble with the birds?" asked Nat.

"Birds? What birds?"

"We got them up our place last night. Scores of them, came in the children's bedroom. Quite savage they were."

"Oh?" It took time for anything to penetrate Jim's head. "Never heard of birds acting savage," he said at length. "They get tame-like, sometimes. I've seen them come to the windows for crumbs."

"These birds last night weren't tame."

"No? Cold, maybe. Hungry. You put out some crumbs."

Jim was no more interested than Mrs. Trigg had been. It was, Nat thought, like air raids in the war. No one down this end of the country knew what the Plymouth folk had seen and suffered. You had to endure something yourself before it touched you. He walked back along the lane and crossed the stile to his cottage. He found his wife in the kitchen with young Johnny.

"See anyone?" she asked.

"Mrs. Trigg and Jim," he answered. "I don't think they believed me. Anyway, nothing wrong up there."

"You might take the birds away," she said. "I daren't go into the room to make the beds until you do. I'm scared."

"Nothing to scare you now," said Nat. "They're dead, aren't they?"

He went up with a sack and dropped the stiff bodies into it, one by one. Yes, there were fifty of them, all told. Just the ordinary common birds of the hedgerow, nothing as large even as a thrush. It must have been fright that made them act the way they did. Blue tits, wrens —it was incredible to think of the power of their small beaks jabbing at his face and hands the night before. He took the sack out into the garden and was faced now with a fresh problem. The ground was too hard to dig. It was frozen solid, yet no snow had fallen, nothing had happened in the past hours but the coming of the east wind. It was unnatural, queer. The weather prophets must be right. The change was something connected with the Arctic Circle.

The wind seemed to cut him to the bone as he stood there uncertainly, holding the sack. He could see the white-capped seas breaking down under in the bay. He decided to take the birds to the shore and bury them.

When he reached the beach below the headland he could scarcely stand, the force of the east wind was so strong. It hurt to draw breath, and his bare hands were blue. Never had he known such cold, not in all the bad winters he could remember. It was low tide. He crunched his way over the shingle to the softer sand and then, his back to the wind, ground a pit in the sand with his heel. He meant to drop the birds into it, but as he opened up the sack the force of the wind carried them, lifted them, as though in flight again, and they were blown away from him along the beach, tossed like feathers, spread and scattered, the bodies of the fifty frozen birds. There was something ugly in the sight. He did not like it. The dead birds were swept away from him by the wind.

"The tide will take them when it turns," he said to himself.

He looked out to sea and watched the crested breakers, combing green. They rose stiffly, curled, and broke again, and because it was ebb tide the roar was distant, more remote, lacking the sound and thunder of the flood.

Then he saw them. The gulls. Out there, riding the seas.

What he had thought at first to be the whitecaps of the waves were gulls. Hundreds, thousands, tens of thousands . . . They rose and fell in the trough of the seas, heads to the wind, like a mighty fleet at anchor, waiting on the tide. To eastward, and to the west, the gulls were there. They stretched as far as his eye could reach, in close formation, line upon line. Had the sea been still they would have covered the bay like a white cloud, head to head, body packed to body. Only the east wind, whipping the sea to breakers, hid them from the shore.

Nat turned and, leaving the beach, climbed the steep path home. Someone should know of this. Someone should be told. Something was happening, because of the east wind and the weather, that he did not understand. He wondered if he should go to the call box by the bus stop and ring up the police. Yet what could they do? What could anyone do? Tens of thousands of gulls riding the sea there in the bay because of storm, because of hunger. The police would think him mad, or drunk, or take the statement from him with great calm. "Thank you. Yes, the matter has already been reported. The hard weather is driving the birds inland in great numbers." Nat looked about him. Still no sign of any other bird. Perhaps the cold had sent them all from upcountry? As he drew near to the cottage his wife came to meet him at the door. She called to him, excited. "Nat," she said, "it's on the wireless. They've just read out a special news bulletin. I've written it down."

"What's on the wireless?" he said.

"About the birds," she said. "It's not only here, it's everywhere. In London, all over the country. Something has happened to the birds."

Together they went into the kitchen. He read the piece of paper lying on the table.

"Statement from the Home Office at 11 a.m. today. Reports from all over the country are coming in hourly about the vast quantity of birds flocking above towns, villages, and outlying districts, causing obstruction and damage and even attacking individuals. It is thought that the Arctic airstream, at present covering the British Isles, is causing birds to migrate south in immense numbers, and that intense hunger may drive these birds to attack human beings. Householders are warned to see to their windows, doors, and chimneys, and to take reasonable precautions for the safety of their children. A further statement will be issued later."

A kind of excitement seized Nat; he looked at his wife in triumph.

"There you are," he said. "Let's hope they'll hear that at the farm. Mrs. Trigg will know it wasn't any story. It's true. All over the country. I've been telling myself all morning there's something wrong. And just now, down on the beach, I looked out to sea and there are gulls, thousands of them, tens of thousands—you couldn't put a pin between their heads—and they're all out there, riding on the sea, waiting."

"What are they waiting for, Nat?" she asked.

He stared at her, then looked down again at the piece of paper. "I don't know," he said slowly. "It says here the birds are hungry."

He went over to the drawer where he kept his hammer and tools.

"What are you going to do, Nat?"

"See to the windows and the chimneys too, like they tell you."

"You think they would break in, with the windows shut? Those sparrows and robins and such? Why, how could they?"

He did not answer. He was not thinking of the robins and the sparrows. He was thinking of the gulls. . . .

He went upstairs and worked there the rest of the morning, boarding the windows of the bedrooms, filling up the chimney bases. Good job it was his free day and he was not working at the farm. It reminded him of the old days, at the beginning of the war. He was not married then, and he had made all the blackout boards for his mother's house in Plymouth. Made the shelter too. Not that it had been of any use when the moment came. He wondered if they would take these precautions up at the farm. He doubted it. Too easygoing, Harry Trigg and his missus. Maybe they'd laugh at the whole thing. Go off to a dance or a whist drive.

"Dinner's ready." She called him, from the kitchen.

"All right. Coming down."

He was pleased with his handiwork. The frames fitted nicely over the little panes and at the bases of the chimneys.

When dinner was over and his wife was washing up, Nat switched on the one o'clock news. The same announcement was repeated, the one which she had taken down during the morning, but the news bulletin enlarged upon it. "The flocks of birds have caused dislocation in all areas," read the announcer, "and in London the sky was so dense at ten o'clock this morning that it seemed as if the city was covered by a vast black cloud.

"The birds settled on rooftops, on window ledges, and on chimneys. The species included blackbird, thrush, the common house sparrow, and, as might be expected in the metropolis, a vast quantity of pigeons and starlings, and that frequenter of the London river, the blackheaded gull. The sight has been so unusual that traffic came to a standstill in many thoroughfares, work was abandoned in shops and offices, and the streets and pavements were crowded with people standing about to watch the birds."

Various incidents were recounted, the suspected reason of cold and hunger stated again, and warnings to householders repeated. The announcer's voice was smooth and suave. Nat had the impression that this man, in particular, treated the whole business as he would an elaborate joke. There would be others like him, hundreds of them, who did not know what it was to struggle in darkness with a flock of birds. There would be parties tonight in London, like the ones they gave on election nights. People standing about, shouting and laughing, getting drunk. "Come and watch the birds!"

Nat switched off the wireless. He got up and started work on the kitchen windows. His wife watched him, young Johnny at her heels.

"What, boards for down here too?" she said. "Why, I'll have to light up before three o'clock. I see no call for boards down here."

"Better be sure than sorry," answered Nat. "I'm not going to take any chances."

"What they ought to do," she said, "is to call the Army out and shoot the birds. That would soon scare them off."

"Let them try," said Nat. "How'd they set about it?"

"They have the Army to the docks," she answered, "when the dockers strike. The soldiers go down and unload the ships."

"Yes," said Nat, "and the population of London is eight million or more. Think of all the buildings, all the flats and houses. Do you think they've enough soldiers to go round shooting birds from every roof?"

"I don't know. But something should be done. They ought to do something."

Nat thought to himself that "they" were no doubt considering the problem at that very moment, but whatever "they" decided to do in London and the big cities would not help the people here, three hundred miles away. Each householder must look after his own.

"How are we off for food?" he said.

"Now, Nat, whatever next?"

"Never mind. What have you got in the larder?"

"It's shopping day tomorrow, you know that. I don't keep uncooked food hanging about, it goes off. Butcher doesn't call till the day after. But I can bring back something when I go in tomorrow."

Nat did not want to scare her. He thought it possible that she might not go to town tomorrow. He looked in the larder for himself, and in the cupboard where she kept her tins. They would do for a couple of days. Bread was low.

"What about the baker?"

"He comes tomorrow too."

He saw she had flour. If the baker did not call she had enough to bake one loaf.

"We'd be better off in old days," he said, "when the women baked twice a week, and had pilchards salted, and there was food for a family to last a siege, if need be."

"I've tried the children with tinned fish, they don't like it," she said.

Nat went on hammering the boards across the kitchen windows. Candles. They were low in candles too. That must be another thing she meant to buy tomorrow. Well, it could not be helped. They must go early to bed tonight. That was, if . . .

He got up and went out of the back door and stood in the garden, looking down towards the sea. There had been no sun all day, and now, at barely three o'clock, a kind of darkness had already come, the sky sullen, heavy, colorless like salt. He could hear the vicious sea drumming on the rocks. He walked down the path, halfway to the beach. And then he stopped. He could see the tide had turned. The rock that had shown in midmorning was now covered, but it was not the sea that held his eyes. The gulls had risen. They were circling, hundreds of them, thousands of them, lifting their wings against the wind. It was the gulls that made the darkening of the sky. And they were silent. They made not a sound. They just went on soaring and circling, rising, falling, trying their strength against the wind.

Nat turned. He ran up the path, back to the cottage.

"I'm going for Jill," he said. "I'll wait for her at the bus stop."

"What's the matter?" asked his wife. "You've gone quite white."

"Keep Johnny inside," he said. "Keep the door shut. Light up now, and draw the curtains."

"It's only just gone three," she said.

"Never mind. Do what I tell you."

He looked inside the tool shed outside the back door. Nothing there of much use. A spade was too heavy, and a fork no good. He took the hoe. It was the only possible tool, and light enough to carry.

He started walking up the lane to the bus stop, and now and again glanced back over his shoulder.

The gulls had risen higher now, their circles were broader, wider, they were spreading out in large formation across the sky.

He hurried on; although he knew the bus would not come to the top of the hill before four o'clock he had to hurry. He passed no one on the way. He was glad of this. No time to stop and chatter.

At the top of the hill he waited. He was much too soon. There was half an hour still to go. The east wind came whipping across the fields from the higher ground. He stamped his feet and blew upon his hands. In the distance he could see the clay hills, white and clean, against the heavy pallor of the sky. Something black rose from behind them, like a smudge at first, then widening, becoming deeper, and the smudge became a cloud, and the cloud divided again into five other clouds, spreading north, east, south, and west, and they were not clouds at all; they were birds. He watched them travel across the sky, and as one section passed overhead, within two or three hundred feet of him, he knew, from their speed, they were bound inland, up-country; they had no business with the people here on the peninsula. They were rooks, crows, jackdaws, magpies, jays, all birds that usually preyed upon the smaller species; but this afternoon they were bound on some other mission.

"They've been given the towns," thought Nat; "they know what they have to do. We don't matter so much here. The gulls will serve for us. The others go to the towns."

He went to the call box, stepped inside, and lifted the receiver. The exchange would do. They would pass the message on.

"I'm speaking from Highway," he said, "by the bus stop. I want to report large formations of birds travelling upcountry. The gulls are also forming in the bay."

"All right," answered the voice, laconic, weary.

"You'll be sure and pass this message on to the proper quarter?"

"Yes . . . yes . . ." Impatient now, fed up. The buzzing note resumed.

"She's another," thought Nat, "she doesn't care. Maybe she's had to answer calls all day. She hopes to go to the pictures tonight. She'll squeeze some fellow's hand, and point up at the sky, and say, 'Look at all them birds!' She doesn't care."

The bus came lumbering up the hill. Jill climbed out, and three or four other children. The bus went on towards the town.

"What's the hoe for, Dad?"

They crowded around him, laughing, pointing.

"I just brought it along," he said. "Come on now, let's get home. It's cold, no hanging about. Here, you. I'll watch you across the fields, see how fast you can run."

He was speaking to Jill's companions, who came from different families, living in the council houses. A short cut would take them to the cottages.

"We want to play a bit in the lane," said one of them.

"No, you don't. You go off home or I'll tell your Mammy."

They whispered to one another, round-eyed, then scuttled off across the fields. Jill stared at her father, her mouth sullen.

"We always play in the lane," she said.

"Not tonight, you don't," he said. "Come on now, no dawdling."

He could see the gulls now, circling the fields, coming in towards the land. Still silent. Still no sound.

"Look, Dad, look over there, look at all the gulls."

"Yes. Hurry, now."

"Where are they flying to? Where are they going?"

"Upcountry, I dare say. Where it's warmer."

He seized her hand and dragged her after him along the lane.

"Dad, what is it? What are the gulls doing?"

The gulls were copying the rooks and crows. They were spreading out in formation across the sky. They headed, in bands of thousands, to the four compass points.

"Dad, what is it? What are the gulls doing?"

They were not intent upon their flight, as the crows, as the jackdaws had been. They still circled overhead. Nor did they fly so high. It was as though they waited upon some signal. As though some decision had yet to be given. The order was not clear.

"Do you want me to carry you, Jill? Here, come pick-a-back."

This way he might put on speed; but he was wrong. Jill was heavy.

She kept slipping. And she was crying too. His sense of urgency, of fear, had communicated itself to the child.

"I wish the gulls would go away. I don't like them. They're coming closer to the lane."

He put her down again. He started running, swinging Jill after him. As they went past the farm turning he saw the farmer backing his car out of the garage. Nat called to him.

"Can you give us a lift?" he said.

"What's that?"

Mr. Trigg turned in the driving seat and stared at them. Then a smile came to his cheerful, rubicund face.

"It looks as though we're in for some fun," he said. "Have you seen the gulls? Jim and I are going to take a crack at them. Everyone's gone bird-crazy, talking of nothing else. I hear you were troubled in the night. Want a gun?"

Nat shook his head.

The small car was packed. There was just room for Jill, if she crouched on top of petrol tins on the back seat.

"I don't want a gun," said Nat, "but I'd be obliged if you'd run Jill home. She's scared of the birds."

He spoke briefly. He did not want to talk in front of Jill.

"OK," said the farmer, "I'll take her home. Why don't you stop behind and join the shooting match? We'll make the feathers fly."

Jill climbed in, and, turning the car, the driver sped up the lane. Nat followed after. Trigg must be crazy. What use was a gun against a sky of birds?

Now Nat was not responsible for Jill, he had time to look about him. The birds were circling still above the fields. Mostly herring gull, but the black-backed gull amongst them. Usually they kept apart. Now they were united. Some bond had brought them together. It was the black-backed gull that attacked the smaller birds, and even newborn lambs, so he'd heard. He'd never seen it done. He remembered this now, though, looking above him in the sky. They were coming in towards the farm. They were circling lower in the sky, and the black-backed gulls were to the front. The black-backed gulls were leading. The farm, then, was their target. They were making for the farm.

Nat increased his pace towards his own cottage. He saw the farmer's car turn and come back along the lane. It drew up beside him with a jerk.

"The kid has run inside," said the farmer. "Your wife was watching for her. Well, what do you make of it? They're saying in town the Russians have done it. The Russians have poisoned the birds."

"How could they do that?" asked Nat.

"Don't ask me. You know how stories get around. Will you join my shooting match?"

"No, I'll get along home. The wife will be worried else."

"My missus says if you could eat gull there'd be some sense in it," said Trigg, "we'd have roast gull, baked gull, and pickle 'em into the bargain. You wait until I let off a few barrels into the brutes. That'll scare 'em."

"Have you boarded your windows?" asked Nat.

"No. Lot of nonsense. They like to scare you on the wireless. I've had more to do today than to go round boarding up my windows."

"I'd board them now, if I were you."

"Garn. You're windy. Like to come to our place to sleep?"

"No, thanks all the same."

"All right. See you in the morning. Give you a gull breakfast."

The farmer grinned and turned his car to the farm entrance.

Nat hurried on. Past the little wood, past the old barn, and then across the stile to the remaining field.

As he jumped the stile he heard the whir of wings. A black-backed gull dived down at him from the sky, missed, swerved in flight, and rose to dive again. In a moment it was joined by others, six, seven, a dozen, black-backed and herring mixed. Nat dropped his hoe. The hoe was useless. Covering his head with his arms, he ran towards the cottage. They kept coming at him from the air, silent save for the beating wings. The terrible, fluttering wings. He would feel the blood on his hands, his wrists, his neck. Each stab of a swooping beak tore his flesh. If only he could keep them from his eyes. Nothing else mattered. He must keep them from his eyes. They had not learnt yet how to cling to a shoulder, how to rip clothing, how to dive in mass upon the head, upon the body. But with each dive, with each attack, they became bolder. And they had no thought for themselves. When they dived low and missed, they crashed, bruised and broken, on the ground. As Nat ran he stumbled, kicking their spent bodies in front of him.

He found the door; he hammered upon it with his bleeding hands. Because of the boarded windows no light shone. Everything was dark.

"Let me in," he shouted, "it's Nat. Let me in."

He shouted loud to made himself heard above the whir of the gulls' wings.

Then he saw the gannet, poised for the dive, above him in the sky. The gulls circled, retired, soared, one after another, against the wind. Only the gannet remained. One single gannet above him in the sky. The wings folded suddenly to its body. It dropped like a stone. Nat screamed, and the door opened. He stumbled across the threshold, and his wife threw her weight against the door.

They heard the thud of the gannet as it fell.

His wife dressed his wounds. They were not deep. The backs of his hands had suffered most, and his wrists. Had he not worn a cap they would have reached his head. As to the gannet . . . the gannet could have split his skull.

The children were crying, of course. They had seen the blood on their father's hands.

"It's all right now," he told them. "I'm not hurt. Just a few scratches. You play with Johnny, Jill. Mammy will wash these cuts."

He half shut the door to the scullery so that they could not see. His wife was ashen. She began running water from the sink.

"I saw them overhead," she whispered. "They began collecting just as Jill ran in with Mr. Trigg. I shut the door fast, and it jammed. That's why I couldn't open it at once when you came."

"Thank God they waited for me," he said. "Jill would have fallen at once. One bird alone would have done it."

Furtively, so as not to alarm the children, they whispered together as she bandaged his hands and the back of his neck.

"They're flying inland," he said, "thousands of them. Rooks, crows, all the bigger birds. I saw them from the bus stop. They're making for the towns."

"But what can they do, Nat?"

"They'll attack. Go for everyone out in the streets. Then they'll try the windows, the chimneys."

"Why don't the authorities do something? Why don't they get the Army, get machine guns, anything?"

"There's been no time. Nobody's prepared. We'll hear what they have to say on the six o'clock news."

Nat went back into the kitchen, followed by his wife. Johnny was playing quietly on the floor. Only Jill looked anxious.

"I can hear the birds," she said. "Listen, Dad."

Nat listened. Muffled sounds came from the windows, from the door. Wings brushing the surface, sliding, scraping, seeking a way of entry. The sound of many bodies, pressed together, shuffling on the sills. Now and again came a thud, a crash, as some bird dived and fell. "Some of them will kill themselves that way," he thought, "but not enough. Never enough."

"All right," he said aloud, "I've got boards over the windows, Jill. The birds can't get in."

He went and examined all the windows. His work had been thorough. Every gap was closed. He would make extra certain, however. He found wedges, pieces of old tin, strips of wood and metal, and fastened them at the sides to reinforce the boards. His hammering helped to deafen the sound of the birds, the shuffling, the tapping, and more ominous—he did not want his wife or the children to hear it —the splinter of cracked glass.

"Turn on the wireless," he said. "Let's have the wireless."

This would drown the sound also. He went upstairs to the bedrooms and reinforced the windows there. Now he could hear the birds on the roof, the scraping of claws, a sliding, jostling sound.

He decided they must sleep in the kitchen, keep up the fire, bring down the mattresses, and lay them out on the floor. He was afraid of the bedroom chimneys. The boards he had placed at the chimney bases might give way. In the kitchen they would be safe because of the fire. He would have to make a joke of it. Pretend to the children they were playing at camp. If the worst happened, and the birds forced an entry down the bedroom chimneys, it would be hours, days perhaps, before they could break down the doors. The birds would be imprisoned in the bedrooms. They could do no harm there. Crowded together, they would stifle and die.

He began to bring the mattresses downstairs. At the sight of them his wife's eyes widened in apprehension. She thought the birds had already broken in upstairs.

"All right," he said cheerfully, "we'll all sleep together in the kitchen tonight. More cozy here by the fire. Then we shan't be worried by those silly old birds tapping at the windows."

He made the children help him rearrange the furniture, and he took the precaution of moving the dresser, with his wife's help, across the window. It fitted well. It was an added safeguard. The mattresses could now be lain, one beside the other, against the wall where the dresser had stood.

"We're safe enough now," he thought. "We're snug and tight, like an air-raid shelter. We can hold out. It's just the food that worries me.

Food, and coal for the fire. We've enough for two or three days, not more. By that time . . ."

No use thinking ahead as far as that. And they'd be giving directions on the wireless. People would be told what to do. And now, in the midst of many problems, he realized that it was dance music only coming over the air. Not Children's Hour, as it should have been. He glanced at the dial. Yes, they were on the Home Service all right. Dance records. He switched to the Light program. He knew the reason. The usual programs had been abandoned. This only happened at exceptional times. Elections and such. He tried to remember if it had happened in the war, during the heavy raids on London. But of course. The B.B.C. was not stationed in London during the war. The programs were broadcast from other, temporary quarters. "We're better off here," he thought; "we're better off here in the kitchen, with the windows and the doors boarded, than they are up in the towns. Thank God we're not in the towns."

At six o'clock the records ceased. The time signal was given. No matter if it scared the children, he must hear the news. There was a pause after the pips. Then the announcer spoke. His voice was solemn, grave. Quite different from midday.

"This is London," he said. "A National Emergency was proclaimed at four o'clock this afternoon. Measures are being taken to safeguard the lives and property of the population, but it must be understood that these are not easy to effect immediately, owing to the unforeseen and unparalleled nature of the present crisis. Every householder must take precautions to his own building, and where several people live together, as in flats and apartments, they must unite to do the utmost they can to prevent entry. It is absolutely imperative that every individual stay indoors tonight and that no one at all remain on the streets, or roads, or anywhere without doors. The birds, in vast numbers, are attacking anyone on sight, and have already begun an assault upon buildings; but these, with due care, should be impenetrable. The population is asked to remain calm and not to panic. Owing to the exceptional nature of the emergency, there will be no further transmission from any broadcasting station until 7 a.m. tomorrow."

They played the National Anthem. Nothing more happened. Nat switched off the set. He looked at his wife. She stared back at him.

"What's it mean?" said Jill. "What did the news say?"

"There won't be any more programs tonight," said Nat. "There's been a breakdown at the B.B.C."

"Is it the birds?" asked Jill. "Have the birds done it?"

"No," said Nat, "it's just that everyone's very busy, and then of course they have to get rid of the birds, messing everything up, in the towns. Well, we can manage without the wireless for one evening."

"I wish we had a gramophone," said Jill, "that would be better than nothing."

She had her face turned to the dresser backed against the windows. Try as they did to ignore it, they were all aware of the shuffling, the stabbing, the persistent beating and sweeping of wings.

"We'll have supper early," suggested Nat, "something for a treat. Ask Mammy. Toasted cheese, eh? Something we all like?"

He winked and nodded at his wife. He wanted the look of dread, of apprehension, to go from Jill's face.

He helped with the supper, whistling, singing, making as much clatter as he could, and it seemed to him that the shuffling and the tapping were not so intense as they had been at first. Presently he went to the bedrooms and listened, and he no longer heard the jostling for place upon the roof.

"They've got reasoning powers," he thought; "they know it's hard to break in here. They'll try elsewhere. They won't waste their time with us."

Supper passed without incident, and then, when they were clearing away, they heard a new sound, droning, familiar, a sound they all knew and understood.

His wife looked up at him, her face alight. "It's planes," she said; "they're sending out planes after the birds. That's what I said they ought to do all along. That will get them. Isn't that gunfire? Can't you hear guns?"

It might be gunfire out at sea. Nat could not tell. Big naval guns might have an effect upon the gulls out at sea, but the gulls were inland now. The guns couldn't shell the shore because of the population.

"It's good, isn't it," said his wife, "to hear the planes?" And Jill, catching her enthusiasm, jumped up and down with Johnny. "The planes will get the birds. The planes will shoot them."

Just then they heard a crash about two miles distant, followed by a second, then a third. The droning became more distant, passed away out to sea.

"What was that?" asked his wife. "Were they dropping bombs on the birds?"

"I don't know," answered Nat. "I don't think so."

He did not want to tell her that the sound they had heard was the crashing of aircraft. It was, he had no doubt, a venture on the part of the authorities to send out reconnaissance forces, but they might have known the venture was suicidal. What could aircraft do against birds that flung themselves to death against propeller and fuselage, but hurtle to the ground themselves? This was being tried now, he supposed, over the whole country. And at a cost. Someone high up had lost his head.

"Where have the planes gone, Dad?" asked Jill.

"Back to base," he said. "Come on, now, time to tuck down for bed."

It kept his wife occupied, undressing the children before the fire, seeing to the bedding, one thing and another, while he went round the cottage again, making sure that nothing had worked loose. There was no further drone of aircraft, and the naval guns had ceased. "Waste of life and effort," Nat said to himself. "We can't destroy enough of them that way. Cost too heavy. There's always gas. Maybe they'll try spraying with gas, mustard gas. We'll be warned first, of course, if they do. There's one thing, the best brains of the country will be onto it tonight."

Somehow the thought reassured him. He had a picture of scientists, naturalists, technicians, and all those chaps they called the backroom boys, summoned to a council; they'd be working on the problem now. This was not a job for the government, for the chiefs of staff—they would merely carry out the orders of the scientists.

"They'll have to be ruthless," he thought. "Where the trouble's worst they'll have to risk more lives, if they use gas. All the livestock, too, and the soil—all contaminated. As long as everyone doesn't panic. That's the trouble. People panicking, losing their heads. The B.B.C. was right to warn us of that."

Upstairs in the bedrooms all was quiet. No further scraping and stabbing at the windows. A lull in battle. Forces regrouping. Wasn't that what they called it in the old wartime bulletins? The wind hadn't dropped, though. He could still hear it roaring in the chimneys. And the sea breaking down on the shore. Then he remembered the tide. The tide would be on the turn. Maybe the lull in battle was because of the tide. There was some law the birds obeyed, and it was all to do with the east wind and the tide.

He glanced at his watch. Nearly eight o'clock. It must have gone high water an hour ago. That explained the lull: the birds attacked with the flood tide. It might not work that way inland, upcountry, but it seemed as if it was so this way on the coast. He reckoned the time limit in his head. They had six hours to go without attack. When the tide turned again, around one-twenty in the morning, the birds would come back. . . .

There were two things he could do. The first to rest, with his wife and the children, and all of them snatch what sleep they could, until the small hours. The second to go out, see how they were faring at the farm, see if the telephone was still working there, so that they might get news from the exchange.

He called softly to his wife, who had just settled the children. She came halfway up the stairs and he whispered to her.

"You're not to go," she said at once, "you're not to go and leave me alone with the children. I can't stand it."

Her voice rose hysterically. He hushed her, calmed her.

"All right," he said, "all right. I'll wait till morning. And we'll get the wireless bulletin then too, at seven. But in the morning, when the tide ebbs again, I'll try for the farm, and they may let us have bread and potatoes, and milk too."

His mind was busy again, planning against emergency. They would not have milked, of course, this evening. The cows would be standing by the gate, waiting in the yard, with the household inside, battened behind boards, as they were here at the cottage. That is, if they had time to take precautions. He thought of the farmer, Trigg, smiling at him from the car. There would have been no shooting party, not tonight.

The children were asleep. His wife, still clothed, was sitting on her mattress. She watched him, her eyes nervous.

"What are you going to do?" she whispered.

He shook his head for silence. Softly, stealthily, he opened the back door and looked outside.

It was pitch dark. The wind was blowing harder than ever, coming in steady gusts, icy, from the sea. He kicked at the step outside the door. It was heaped with birds. There were dead birds everywhere. Under the windows, against the walls. These were the suicides, the divers, the ones with broken necks. Wherever he looked he saw dead birds. No trace of the living. The living had flown seaward with the turn of the tide. The gulls would be riding the seas now, as they had done in the forenoon.

In the far distance, on the hill where the tractor had been two days before, something was burning. One of the aircraft that had crashed; the fire, fanned by the wind, had set light to a stack.

He looked at the bodies of the birds, and he had a notion that if he heaped them, one upon the other, on the window sills they would make added protection for the next attack. Not much, perhaps, but something. The bodies would have to be clawed at, pecked, and dragged aside before the living birds could gain purchase on the sills and attack the panes. He set to work in the darkness. It was queer; he hated touching them. The bodies were still warm and bloody. The blood matted their feathers. He felt his stomach turn, but he went on with his work. He noticed grimly that every windowpane was shattered. Only the boards had kept the birds from breaking in. He stuffed the cracked panes with the bleeding bodies of the birds.

When he had finished he went back into the cottage. He barricaded the kitchen door, made it doubly secure. He took off his bandages, sticky with the birds' blood, not with his own cuts, and put on fresh plaster.

His wife had made him cocoa and he drank it thirstily. He was very tired.

"All right," he said, smiling, "don't worry. We'll get through."

He lay down on his mattress and closed his eyes. He slept at once. He dreamt uneasily, because through his dreams there ran a thread of something forgotten. Some piece of work, neglected, that he should have done. Some precaution that he had known well but had not taken, and he could not put a name to it in his dreams. It was connected in some way with the burning aircraft and the stack upon the hill. He went on sleeping, though; he did not awake. It was his wife shaking his shoulder that awoke him finally.

"They've begun," she sobbed, "they've started this last hour. I can't listen to it any longer alone. There's something smelling bad too, something burning."

Then he remembered. He had forgotten to make up the fire. It was smouldering, nearly out. He got up swiftly and lit the lamp. The hammering had started at the windows and the doors, but it was not that he minded now. It was the smell of singed feathers. The smell filled the kitchen. He knew at once what it was. The birds were coming down the chimney, squeezing their way down to the kitchen range.

He got sticks and paper and put them on the embers, then reached for the can of paraffin.

"Stand back," he shouted to his wife. "We've got to risk this."

He threw the paraffin on the fire. The flame roared up the pipe, and down upon the fire fell the scorched, blackened bodies of the birds. The children woke, crying. "What is it?" said Jill. "What's happened?"

Nat had no time to answer. He was raking the bodies from the chimney, clawing them out on to the floor. The flames still roared, and the danger of the chimney catching fire was one he had to take. The flames would send away the living birds from the chimney top. The lower joint was the difficulty, though. This was choked with the smouldering, helpless bodies of the birds caught by fire. He scarcely heeded the attack on the windows and the door: let them beat their wings, break their beaks, lose their lives, in the attempt to force an entry into his home. They would not break in. He thanked God he had one of the old cottages, with small windows, stout walls. Not like the new council houses. Heaven help them up the lane in the new council houses.

"Stop crying," he called to the children. "There's nothing to be afraid of, stop crying."

He went on raking at the burning, smouldering bodies as they fell into the fire.

"This'll fetch them," he said to himself, "the draught and the flames together. We're all right, as long as the chimney doesn't catch. I ought to be shot for this. It's all my fault. Last thing, I should have made up the fire. I knew there was something."

Amid the scratching and tearing at the window boards came the sudden homely striking of the kitchen clock. Three a.m. A little more than four hours yet to go. He could not be sure of the exact time of high water. He reckoned it would not turn much before half-past seven, twenty to eight.

"Light up the Primus," he said to his wife. "Make us some tea, and the kids some cocoa. No use sitting around doing nothing."

That was the line. Keep her busy, and the children too. Move about, eat, drink; always best to be on the go.

He waited by the range. The flames were dying. But no more blackened bodies fell from the chimney. He thrust his poker up as far as it could go and found nothing. It was clear. The chimney was clear. He wiped the sweat from his forehead.

"Come on now, Jill," he said, "bring me some more sticks. We'll have a good fire going directly." She wouldn't come near him, though. She was staring at the heaped singed bodies of the birds.

"Never mind them," he said, "we'll put those in the passage when I've got the fire steady."

The danger of the chimney was over. It could not happen again, not if the fire was kept burning day and night.

"I'll have to get more fuel from the farm tomorrow," he thought. "This will never last. I'll manage, though. I can do all that with the ebb tide. It can be worked, fetching what we need, when the tide's turned. We've just got to adapt ourselves, that's all."

They drank tea and cocoa and ate slices of bread and Bovril. Only half a loaf left, Nat noticed. Never mind though, they'd get by.

"Stop it," said young Johnny, pointing to the windows with his spoon, "stop it, you old birds."

"That's right," said Nat, smiling, "we don't want the old beggars, do we? Had enough of 'em."

They began to cheer when they heard the thud of the suicide birds.

"There's another, Dad," cried Jill, "he's done for."

"He's had it," said Nat. "There he goes, the blighter."

This was the way to face up to it. This was the spirit. If they could keep this up, hang on like this until seven, when the first news bulletin came through, they would not have done too badly.

"Give us a fag," he said to his wife. "A bit of smoke will clear away the smell of the scorched feathers."

"There's only two left in the packet," she said. "I was going to buy you some from the Co-op."

"I'll have one," he said, "t'other will keep for a rainy day."

No sense trying to make the children rest. There was no rest to be got while the tapping and the scratching went on at the windows. He sat with one arm round his wife and the other round Jill, with Johnny on his mother's lap and the blankets heaped about them on the mattress.

"You can't help admiring the beggars," he said; "they've got persistence. You'd think they'd tire of the game, but not a bit of it."

Admiration was hard to sustain. The tapping went on and on and a new rasping note struck Nat's ear, as though a sharper beak than any hitherto had come to take over from its fellows. He tried to remember the names of birds; he tried to think which species would go for this particular job. It was not the tap of the woodpecker. That would be light and frequent. This was more serious, because if it continued long the wood would splinter as the glass had done. Then he remembered the hawks. Could the hawks have taken over from the gulls? Were there buzzards now upon the sills, using talons as well as beaks? Hawks, buzzards, kestrels, falcons—he had forgotten the birds of prey. He had forgotten the gripping power of the birds of prey. Three hours to go, and while they waited, the sound of the splintering wood, the talons tearing at the wood.

Nat looked about him, seeing what furniture he could destroy to fortify the door. The windows were safe because of the dresser. He was not certain of the door. He went upstairs, but when he reached the landing he paused and listened. There was a soft patter on the floor of the children's bedroom. The birds had broken through. . . . He put his ear to the door. No mistake. He could hear the rustle of wings and the light patter as they searched the floor. The other bedroom was still clear. He went into it and began bringing out the furniture, to pile at the head of the stairs should the door of the children's bedroom go. It was a preparation. It might never be needed. He could not stack the furniture against the door, because it opened inward. The only possible thing was to have it at the top of the stairs.

"Come down, Nat, what are you doing?" called his wife.

"I won't be long," he shouted. "Just making everything shipshape up here."

He did not want her to come; he did not want her to hear the pattering of the feet in the children's bedroom, the brushing of those wings against the door.

At five-thirty he suggested breakfast, bacon and fried bread, if only to stop the growing look of panic in his wife's eyes and to calm the fretful children. She did not know about the birds upstairs. The bedroom, luckily, was not over the kitchen. Had it been so, she could not have failed to hear the sound of them up there, tapping the boards. And the silly, senseless thud of the suicide birds, the death and glory boys, who flew into the bedroom, smashing their heads against the walls. He knew them of old, the herring gulls. They had no brains. The black-backs were different; they knew what they were doing. So did the buzzards, the hawks . . .

He found himself watching the clock, gazing at the hands that went so slowly round the dial. If his theory was not correct, if the attack did not cease with the turn of the tide, he knew they were beaten. They could not continue through the long day without air, without rest, without more fuel, without . . . His mind raced. He knew there were so many things they needed to withstand siege. They were not fully prepared. They were not ready. It might be that it would be safer in the towns after all. If he could get a message through on the farm telephone to his cousin, only a short journey by train upcountry, they might be able to hire a car. That would be quicker—hire a car between tides . . .

His wife's voice, calling his name, drove away the sudden, desperate desire for sleep.

"What is it? What now?" he said sharply.

"The wireless," said his wife. "I've been watching the clock. It's nearly seven."

"Don't twist the knob," he said, impatient for the first time. "It's on the Home where it is. They'll speak from the Home."

They waited. The kitchen clock struck seven. There was no sound. No chimes, no music. They waited until a quarter past, switching to the Light. The result was the same. No news bulletin came through.

"We've heard wrong," he said. "They won't be broadcasting until eight o'clock."

They left it switched on, and Nat thought of the battery, wondered how much power was left in it. It was generally recharged when his wife went shopping in the town. If the battery failed they would not hear the instructions.

"It's getting light," whispered his wife. "I can't see it, but I can feel it. And the birds aren't hammering so loud."

She was right. The rasping, tearing sound grew fainter every moment. So did the shuffling, the jostling for place upon the step, upon the sills. The tide was on the turn. By eight there was no sound at all. Only the wind. The children, lulled at last by the stillness, fell asleep. At half-past eight Nat switched the wireless off.

"What are you doing? We'll miss the news," said his wife.

"There isn't going to be any news," said Nat. "We've got to depend upon ourselves."

He went to the door and slowly pulled away the barricades. He drew the bolts and, kicking the bodies from the step outside the door, breathed the cold air. He had six working hours before him, and he knew he must reserve his strength for the right things, not waste it in any way. Food, and light, and fuel; these were the necessary things. If he could get them in sufficiency, they could endure another night.

He stepped into the garden, and as he did so he saw the living birds. The gulls had gone to ride the sea, as they had done before; they sought sea food, and the buoyancy of the tide, before they returned to the attack. Not so the land birds. They waited and watched. Nat saw them, on the hedgerows, on the soil, crowded in the trees, outside in the field, line upon line of birds, all still, doing nothing.

He went to the end of his small garden. The birds did not move. They went on watching him.

"I've got to get food," said Nat to himself. "I've got to go to the farm to find food."

He went back to the cottage. He saw to the windows and the doors. He went upstairs and opened the children's bedroom. It was empty, except for the dead birds on the floor. The living were out there, in the garden, in the fields. He went downstairs.

"I'm going to the farm," he said.

His wife clung to him. She had seen the living birds from the open door.

"Take us with you," she begged. "We can't stay here alone. I'd rather die than stay here alone."

He considered the matter. He nodded.

"Come on, then," he said. "Bring baskets, and Johnny's pram. We can load up the pram."

They dressed against the biting wind, wore gloves and scarves. His wife put Johnny in the pram. Nat took Jill's hand.

"The birds," she whimpered, "they're all out there in the fields."

"They won't hurt us," he said, "not in the light."

They started walking across the field towards the stile, and the birds did not move. They waited, their heads turned to the wind.

When they reached the turning to the farm, Nat stopped and told his wife to wait in the shelter of the hedge with the two children.

"But I want to see Mrs. Trigg," she protested. "There are lots of things we can borrow if they went to market yesterday; not only bread, and . . ."

"Wait here," Nat interrupted. "I'll be back in a moment."

The cows were lowing, moving restlessly in the yard, and he could see a gap in the fence where the sheep had knocked their way through, to roam unchecked in the front garden before the farmhouse. No smoke came from the chimneys. He was filled with misgivings. He did not want his wife or the children to go down to the farm.

"Don't gib now," said Nat, harshly, "do what I say."

She withdrew with the pram into the hedge, screening herself and the children from the wind.

He went down alone to the farm. He pushed his way through the herd of bellowing cows, which turned this way and that, distressed, their udders full. He saw the car standing by the gate, not put away in the garage. The windows of the farmhouse were smashed. There were many dead gulls lying in the yard and around the house. The living birds perched on the group of trees behind the farm and on the roof of the house. They were quite still. They watched him.

Jim's body lay in the yard . . . what was left of it. When the birds had finished, the cows had trampled him. His gun was beside him. The door of the house was shut and bolted, but as the windows were smashed it was easy to lift them and climb through. Trigg's body was close to the telephone. He must have been trying to get through to the exchange when the birds came for him. The receiver was hanging loose, the instrument torn from the wall. No sign of Mrs. Trigg. She would be upstairs. Was it any use going up? Sickened, Nat knew what he would find.

"Thank God," he said to himself, "there were no children."

He forced himself to climb the stairs, but halfway he turned and descended again. He could see her legs protruding from the open bedroom door. Beside her were the bodies of the black-backed gulls, and an umbrella, broken.

"It's no use," thought Nat, "doing anything. I've only got five hours, less than that. The Triggs would understand. I must load up with what I can find."

He tramped back to his wife and children.

"I'm going to fill up the car with stuff," he said. "I'll put coal in it, and paraffin for the Primus. We'll take it home and return for a fresh load."

"What about the Triggs?" asked his wife.

"They must have gone to friends," he said.

"Shall I come and help you, then?"

"No; there's a mess down there. Cows and sheep all over the place. Wait, I'll get the car. You can sit in it."

Clumsily he backed the car out of the yard and into the lane. His wife and the children could not see Jim's body from there.

"Stay here," he said, "never mind the pram. The pram can be fetched later. I'm going to load the car."

Her eyes watched his all the time. He believed she understood, otherwise she would have suggested helping him to find the bread and groceries.

They made three journeys altogether, backwards and forwards between their cottage and the farm, before he was satisfied they had everything they needed. It was surprising, once he started thinking, how many things were necessary. Almost the most important of all was planking for the windows. He had to go round searching for timber. He wanted to renew the boards on all the windows at the cottage. Candles, paraffin, nails, tinned stuff; the list was endless. Besides all that, he milked three of the cows. The rest, poor brutes, would have to go on bellowing.

On the final journey he drove the car to the bus stop, got out, and went to the telephone box. He waited a few minutes, jangling the receiver. No good, though. The line was dead. He climbed on to a bank and looked over the countryside, but there was no sign of life at all, nothing in the fields but the waiting, watching birds. Some of them slept—he could see the beaks tucked into the feathers.

"You'd think they'd be feeding," he said to himself, "not just standing in that way."

Then he remembered. They were gorged with food. They had eaten their fill during the night. That was why they did not move this morning. . . .

No smoke came from the chimneys of the council houses. He thought of the children who had run across the fields the night before.

"I should have known," he thought; "I ought to have taken them home with me."

He lifted his face to the sky. It was colorless and gray. The bare trees on the landscape looked bent and blackened by the east wind. The cold did not affect the living birds waiting out there in the fields.

"This is the time they ought to get them," said Nat; "they're a sitting target now. They must be doing this all over the country. Why don't our aircraft take off now and spray them with mustard gas? What are all our chaps doing? They must know, they must see for themselves."

He went back to the car and got into the driver's seat.

"Go quickly past that second gate," whispered his wife. "The postman's lying there. I don't want Jill to see."

He accelerated. The little Morris bumped and rattled along the lane. The children shrieked with laughter.

"Up-a-down, up-a-down," shouted young Johnny.

It was a quarter to one by the time they reached the cottage. Only an hour to go.

"Better have cold dinner," said Nat. "Hot up something for yourself and the children, some of that soup. I've no time to eat now. I've got to unload all this stuff."

He got everything inside the cottage. It could be sorted later. Give them all something to do during the long hours ahead. First he must see to the windows and the doors.

He went round the cottage methodically, testing every window, every door. He climbed on to the roof also, and fixed boards across every chimney, except the kitchen. The cold was so intense he could hardly bear it, but the job had to be done. Now and again he would look up, searching the sky for aircraft. None came. As he worked he cursed the inefficiency of the authorities.

"It's always the same," he muttered, "they always let us down. Muddle, muddle, from the start. No plan, no real organization. And we don't matter down here. That's what it is. The people upcountry have priority. They're using gas up there, no doubt, and all the aircraft. We've got to wait and take what comes."

He paused, his work on the bedroom chimney finished, and looked out to sea. Something was moving out there. Something gray and white amongst the breakers.

"Good old Navy," he said, "they never let us down. They're coming down-channel, they're turning in the bay."

He waited, straining his eyes, watering in the wind, towards the sea. He was wrong, though. It was not ships. The Navy was not there. The gulls were rising from the sea. The massed flocks in the fields, with ruffled feathers, rose in formation from the ground and, wing to wing, soared upwards to the sky.

The tide had turned again.

Nat climbed down the ladder and went inside the kitchen. The family were at dinner. It was a little after two. He bolted the door, put up the barricade, and lit the lamp.

"It's nighttime," said young Johnny.

His wife had switched on the wireless once again, but no sound came from it.

"I've been all round the dial," she said, "foreign stations, and that lot. I can't get anything."

"Maybe they have the same trouble," he said, "maybe it's the same right through Europe."

She poured out a plateful of the Triggs' soup, cut him a large slice of the Triggs' bread, and spread their dripping upon it.

They ate in silence. A piece of the dripping ran down young Johnny's chin and fell on to the table.

"Manners, Johnny," said Jill, "you should learn to wipe your mouth."

The tapping began at the windows, at the door. The rustling, the jostling, the pushing for position on the sills. The first thud of the suicide gulls upon the step.

"Won't America do something?" said his wife. "They've always been our allies, haven't they? Surely America will do something?"

Nat did not answer. The boards were strong against the windows, and on the chimneys too. The cottage was filled with stores, with fuel, with all they needed for the next few days. When he had finished dinner he would put the stuff away, stack it neatly, get everything shipshape, handy-like. His wife could help him, and the children too. They'd tire themselves out, between now and a quarter to nine, when the tide would ebb; then he'd tuck them down on their mattresses, see that they slept good and sound until three in the morning.

He had a new scheme for the windows, which was to fit barbed wire in front of the boards. He had brought a great roll of it from the farm. The nuisance was, he'd have to work at this in the dark, when the lull came between nine and three. Pity he had not thought of it before. Still, as long as the wife slept, and the kids, that was the main thing.

The smaller birds were at the window now. He recognized the light tap-tapping of their beaks and the soft brush of their wings. The hawks ignored the windows. They concentrated their attack upon the door. Nat listened to the tearing sound of splintering wood, and wondered how many million years of memory were stored in those little brains, behind the stabbing beaks, the piercing eyes, now giving them this instinct to destroy mankind with all the deft precision of machines.

"I'll smoke that last fag," he said to his wife. "Stupid of me, it was the one thing I forgot to bring back from the farm."

He reached for it, switched on the silent wireless. He threw the empty packet on the fire, and watched it burn.

The transcending issue beginning to emerge through the smog and confusion is one even more fundamental than the old issue about the governability of American cities. This remains a related and vital question, generally answered in the negative by political scientists. . . .

The new issue involves survival. Is the city livable? New York's recent experiences suggest a negative reply here as well. The city is not altogether livable now. It will become less so in the future. . . .

—from an editorial in the New York *Times*

DO IT FOR MAMA!
CONCERNING DOGS, MEN & MANHATTAN:
24 HOURS OF VIOLENCE & TRAGEDY

by *Jerrold J. Mundis*

At 12:40 p.m. on Tuesday, September 13, Patrolmen Gerald O'Malley and Walter Ensley knocked on the door of an apartment on Mulberry Street. They were admitted by Joseph D'Agostino, an unemployed longshoreman. His wife was sitting on a sofa in the living room at the end of a hall. She held a beagle in her lap, and she was crying. D'Agostino smiled at the policemen and asked, "This is a joke, right? You guys ain't really lookin' to take my dog." Patrolman Ensley answered that it was their duty to confiscate the animal in accordance with Section 161.05 of the Health Code—unless the D'Agostinos could produce a certificate of authorization from the Environmental Protection Administration. D'Agostino said he couldn't, and then offered the policemen a $50 bribe, which they refused. The longshoreman stepped aside and motioned them toward the living room. He said to his wife, "I'm sorry, baby. There's no other way." As the officers passed through the arch at the end of the hall, they were assaulted from both sides by three men who had been in hiding, and by D'Agostino from the rear. They were savagely beaten with pipes and heavy pieces of dowling and kicked with steel-toed work boots. Then, bleeding and insensible, they were dragged from the building and dumped in the gutter.

It was the first major incident of what has come to be known throughout this nation, and in many foreign countries as well, as "Bloody Tuesday."

Six weeks have passed, and now an uneasy peace prevails in the city. The New Yorker in the street has reassumed his traditional mask of detachment, his formal and sometimes cold politeness. But within him still roils the maelstrom of shame and hatred that is September 13's legacy. Scattered incidents of violence have erupted since then, but police have damped them quickly, and in several cases even passersby have sprung forward to pull the combatants apart. Such willingness to become involved is new to the people of New York, where 30 persons once increased the volume of their radios and television sets so they would not have to listen to the screams of a young woman being stabbed to death in front of their building. The reason is simple: They are willing to chance minor personal injury in order to stave off the immensely more frightening consequences of a recurrence of the events of last month.

As Decoration or Memorial Day has a greater reality than the date May 30th, so also has Bloody Tuesday brutally supplanted September 13th.

Section 161.05 of the Health Code was passed by the City Council in March of this year. It reads: "No person shall cause or allow a dog or other member of the canine family to be owned, kept, maintained, possessed or controlled in his own residence or in the residencies of his agents, tenants or lessees except as provided for in the Regulations of the Environmental Protection Administration. Persons violating this section will be guilty of a misdemeanor and subject to a fine of not less than $500 nor more than $1,000 and/or imprisonment of not less than six months, nor more than one year." The regulations of the Environmental Protection Administration, approved and passed on the same day, dictate that authorization will be given only to dogs who are (1) guides for the blind, (2) necessary for the mental or emotional health of the owner (as attested to by an affidavit from a licensed psychiatrist), or (3) essential to the owner's personal safety or that of his business (as confirmed by written statement from the commanding officer of the applicant's police precinct). It was estimated that these conditions would permit not more than 3,500 dogs to remain in the city.

This legislation was the culmination of a struggle between pro- and anti-dog forces that has gripped New York with the power of an *idée fixe* for more than a decade. The issue has been contested in public hearings, judicial chambers, bars, supermarkets, subways and taxies, in hippie pads and sumptuous penthouses, at dinner parties and on street corners. It has received more media air time and column space in New York City than has the controversial Latin American war, including the President's decision last year to resume the bombing of Bolivia, Chile, and Argentina. It has directly influenced a half a dozen major political careers and several more minor ones. The liberal and popular Alastair MacDonnel, for example, who followed John Lindsay into Gracie Mansion in 1974, was defeated after one term in a hard and bitter campaign by Nicholas Spinelli. Spinelli, a grass-roots conservative, beat a single and ever loudening drum throughout the fight — BAN THE DOGS! BAN THE DOGS!

New York remains a fundamentally liberal city, but still it awarded Spinelli the mayoralty; there are simply more dog haters than dog lovers.

Bloody Tuesday was brought to a halt within 24 hours by an emergency session of the City Council. But by then the tally had already risen to:

*43 persons dead.

*387 persons injured.

*8 women raped.

*6 buildings burned.

*56 apartments reduced to shambles.

*700 windows broken.

*16 vehicles demolished.

*300 to 500 dogs slaughtered before the eyes of their horror-stricken owners.

Professional criminals took swift advantage of the city-wide confusion. Armed robbery was reported at 12 times its normal rate, burglary at 8, vehicle theft at 2, and petty larceny at a staggering 21.

DIM is an acronym for Dogs Inimical to Man, Inc., an international anti-dog organization headquartered in New York City. It is commonly understood that the initials were taken from a movie of the late 1960's, *Midnight Cowboy,* in which a woman led her bejeweled poodle to the curb and anxiously urged the creature to "Do it for mama!" DIM's unofficial but traditional rallying cry is that same derisory request. DIM was founded in late 1971 by a handful of private citizens who were inspired by a New York *Post* editorial entitled "Filth City." Pete Hamill, author of the editorial, was one of the first public figures to spotlight the growing problem of dogs in modern cities, and he stated that if no other solution could be found, "we could declare a bounty and start shooting them." This suggestion was in good part capricious, but it was also pathetically prophetic.

Dog lovers at first dismissed DIM as a distasteful but harmless crank organization. Few understood the depth and intensity of the anti-dog sentiment that lay waiting to be tapped in New York, and in many other cities as well. Within 18 months DIM had recruited 15,-000 members (at a $15 initiation fee, and annual dues of $10) and had authorized chapters in Chicago, Los Angeles and Miami. By 1977 it was a strong social and political force actively supported by seven million members; its central offices occupied a new eight-story steel and glass building on Lexington Avenue; it had chapters in 21 American cities and six foreign countries. Its efforts, it is generally agreed, were the deciding factor in the election of Mayor Nicholas Spinelli.

DIM selected New York City as its test case and waged an extended, arduous, sometimes vicious, and hugely expensive campaign. Politicians, ecologists, city planners, psychiatrists, sociologists, pediatricians, social workers and experts from a wide variety of other disciplines testified against dogs alongside large numbers of private citizens at public hearings and in open forums. DOG (a loosely knit and poorly structured organization formed to defend canine "citizens") produced its own expert and sympathetic witnesses.

Statisticians were baffled in attempts to draw social, economic and ethnic profiles of dog haters and dog lovers. Allegiance was unpredictable: $75,000 a year portfolio managers found themselves ranked side by side with Maoist revolutionaries, and both were as likely to view the dog as anathema as they were to see him as an integral part of human existence.

DIM presented an horrific picture. While the city's human population increased by only 13% between 1970 and 1980 (eight million to nine million), the canine population rose by 50%, swelling from 500,000 to a formidable 750,000 animals—one dog for every 12 humans, one dog for every three families. In 1982, 46,000 New Yorkers (as opposed to 33,000 in 1970) were bitten seriously enough to require medical attention. Each day, dogs released 12,000 quarts of urine and dropped 281,000 pounds of excrement onto the streets. "That gives us a million gallons of p—s each year," said Timothy Flanagan, chief of the Uniformed Sanitation Workers. "Most of it dries up or gets washed into the sewers when it rains, but we still get *a hundred and two million pounds of c—p* that's gotta be hauled away! Everyone complains we don't pick up their garbage. Hell, we're too busy cleanin' up their dogs—t!" City Health Commissioner Lawrence Reid said, "One needn't be a medical man, or even be aware of the gruesome specifics, to know that all that waste material is a health hazard. I don't know how we've escaped a plague thus far."

Other experts did not eschew specifics. Toxocara canis, one disease cited, attacks and can do severe damage to the human victim's liver, lungs, and eyes. Leptospirosis is an infection frequently involved with aseptic meningitis. Dogs can infect humans with scabies and ringworm. And an epidemic of rabies, DIM claimed, is also a constant hazard.

Louis G. Foster, director of the Metropolitan Museum of Art, stated: "Dogs commit aesthetic atrocities against the city. Their residue offends the eye whether it is piled atop the summer concrete, or blemishing the winter snow. One must be a talented obstacle runner to avoid befouling one's shoes with the stuff. And bluntly . . . it stinks. Lord, how it stinks!"

Dogs are also sources of noise pollution, DIM pointed out. Throughout the city, from crowded tenement rooms to co-ops with river views, they bark and growl behind closed doors at the slightest sound. They hurl ear-punishing challenges at each other on the streets. They whine and scream with loneliness when their masters are away. The passage of a police or fire siren creates great, spreading waves of howls and wails that linger long in the night.

Many owners allow their pets to walk off leash; these dogs frequently menace or bowl people over, leap up in friendliness and soil clothes, or dash across streets, causing traffic accidents as motorists swerve to avoid them. DIM advises its members: "You, the driver, have the right of way: assert it." Sports players, strollers, nature lovers and mothers with small children have been forced out of the parks by hordes of dogs unleashed for exercise.

Attack-trained dogs are a very serious problem. In 1970 there were 4,000 of these beasts in the city, in 1980 more than 10,000; and DIM claims the number has now risen to 14,000. These animals have been purchased in response to a mushrooming crime rate. Among other frightening statistics, the current odds are 1 in 5 that the average citizen will be robbed at gunpoint or mugged if he does not reach the sanctuary of his home by nightfall. A well-bred and properly trained attack-dog is an effective and *safe* defense against crime. He will attack only when commanded, or if his master is assaulted. Unfortunately, the skyrocketing demand for canine protection has caused a boom of unqualified "trainers," whose simple technique is to abuse a dog so savagely that he becomes a man-hater intent on tearing apart everyone but his master, and even him sometimes; less than a third of New York City's attack-dogs have been competently trained; the rest are serious threats to the general public. Such animals have mutilated and inflicted serious and permanent damage upon many citizens.

Wisely, the DOG forces did not attempt to deny the problem, or even its magnitude. "Of course there are great difficulties," said Marcus Crozier, Manhattan Borough president, and himself the owner of two golden Labrador retrievers. "Solutions must be found, and soon. But proscribing dogs from the city is patently absurd. By the same reasoning, we should solve our poverty problem by banishing the poor." This argument stood in DIM's path like a snarling dog for some time; it suggested to the unsure citizen that a canine purge would be an evasion of responsibility, an admission of failure, a cop-out. DOG also admitted that the brutalized, and therefore brutal, animals being sold as attack-dogs were a definite menace. But the answer, they claimed, lay in the establishment of an agency to control standards, license qualified trainers and certify the stability of finished dogs. So far as the bites of run-of-the-mill animals were concerned, these were usually of negligible severity, requiring little more treatment than a good cleaning and a Band-Aid. Dozens of professional trainers, behavioral psychologists, cynologists, and naturalists insisted there are very few renegade or truly vicious dogs. "When a dog bites," said Dr. Charles Naylor, director of Animal Studies at the Johns Hopkins Institute, "there is always a reason—he's being teased, frightened, stepped on or run into, he's being beaten, and so on. What would *you* do if a stranger manhandled you? Dogs don't dash around the streets looking for people to bite. Respect a dog's rights, and he'll respect yours." As for unleashed animals, DOG suggested that enforcement of existing statutes would curtail the problem. To avoid burdening the already overworked police, DOG proposed a corps under the auspices of the ASPCA, that would be empowered to give tickets to owners of unleashed dogs.

Medical arguments against dogs were attacked as specious at best, perhaps even deliberately misleading. Howard Grossinger, DVM and president of the Veterinary Medical Association of the United States, testified: "Common prophylactic measures have all but eliminated rabies as a disease of domestic animals in the United States. There hasn't been a single case in the New York area for thirty-five years. It would be more reasonable to fear a cholera epidemic than an outbreak of rabies." Abundant documentary evidence made clear that dog wastes, no matter how aesthetically objectionable, posed no special threat to health. Dismissing DIM's largest bugaboos, Dr. Grossinger commented: "A much larger incidence of ringworm and scabies is found among humans than dogs. If a dog contracts either, chances are that he got them from his owner. In any event, both diseases are easily treated. Leptospirosis can be contracted by swimming in water polluted with infected dog urine. However, since male dogs, as I'm sure you're aware, employ the classic three-legged stance while urinating, and females must squat, swimming dogs rarely release their urine into water. Someone would have to dump several gallons of the diseased stuff into a swimming area. And having read the results of the Mayor's Pure Water Survey, I assure you that persons daring most of the waters found in the Greater New York area would be felled by a variety of other diseases long before they could develop leptospirosis. This disease, as well as Toxocara canis, may also be contracted by prolonged handling or ingestion of earth moist with the excrement or urine of infected dogs. I see little possibility of infection by this means unless New Yorkers are devoted to what would certainly be a most peculiar fetish. Gentlemen, without resorting to boldface lies you are simply not going to be able to condemn the dog as a health hazard. If you want to talk about the four or five million rats in this city, fine; I'd be happy to testify on behalf of the 'anti' faction."

In four consecutive years DOG managed to roll back four proposed pieces of restrictive legislation sponsored by DIM. Among these were an exorbitant annual license fee and a 1% surcharge on city income tax. Both were defeated on the grounds that they would discriminate in favor of the well-to-do.

The ASPCA and the American Kennel Club worked indefatigably with DOG to persuade pet owners to police themselves and reduce the annoyance quotient of their animals. Training handbooks were distributed free of charge by the ASPCA. DOG installed and serviced 25 experimental "Canine Comfort Stations," public animal toilets. The stench from these was indescribable; many dogs refused to use them; most owners ignored them. Owners were urged to carry excrement retrieval equipment (cheap plastic tongs and plastic "Good Citizen" bags) but the clean-up process was rejected as embarrassing and/or inconvenient. Inconvenience (and protests from neighbors and landlords) also undermined a program in which corners of basements and roofs were to be designated "Relief areas."

The battle was waged with unflagging zeal and escalating hostility by both sides. Eventually most semblances of objectivity were lost and partisans went at each other with abandoned ferocity. It came down to the simple question: "You for 'em, or against 'em?" Buttons reading *Cities Are For Humans* appeared on hundreds and thousands of lapels. DOG countered with its own buttons, which bore a paw print. Cleveland Amory, social commentator and long an influential champion of animal welfare, was one of DOG's most eloquent and passionate spokesmen. At the public hearings late last year, he said in a tremulous voice: "Cities are indeed for humans, but to be human is to recognize one's place in the totality of the natural world, to realize that the phrase 'Man's Best Friend' was not the invention of a Madison Avenue copywriter, but the natural result of untold thousands of years of history in which man has shared his domicile with this most wondrous of creatures, in which the dog has worked for man, has loyally defended him, has been a boon and merry companion, and has solaced him through countless dark and lonely nights. Cities are for humans, yes, but the dog is inseparably bound to humans, and humans to it. The people who cry ban the dogs are those who would also have us build even higher skyscrapers, who would lay concrete over our parks, who would have us befoul what little remains of our once beautiful world, and who would trap and destroy our souls in an automated vacuum of technological marvels. To these people I say, Never! Never! Never!"

Pete Hamill followed Mr. Amory to the stand. Grown cynical and snappish during the years of his repeated work in behalf of DIM,

Hamill ended his testimony with his customary: "Put a bounty on the beasts; my rifle is ready."

Mr. Amory shouted, "Put a bounty on Hamill! *My* rifle is ready!" and rushed the stand, where he and Mr. Hamill grappled furiously. One bailiff was kicked in the groin and another bitten on the arm before the combatants could be separated.

DOG's efforts were valiant, but its cause foredoomed. Four elements were decisive in the passage of Section 161.05. (1) There were (and still are) so many dogs in the city that no one could escape them; there were, therefore, very few neutrals, and the majority were non-dog owners. (2) Severe or not, a bite remains a bite, and animals who puncture New Yorkers at the rate of 46,000 per year do not endear themselves to New Yorkers. (3) The 24-hour-per-day racket of these creatures shatters equilibrium and psyches. (4) The city, as Mr. Foster said, stinks, and, in the words of Mayor Spinelli, "We will just not, *just not,* put up with having to clean dogs—t off our shoes five and six times a day."

Passage of the bill in March of this year caused a massive protest march of 200,000 persons down Fifth Avenue and touched off numerous demonstrations. There were small riots in East Harlem, Bryant Park, Tompkins Square, Sheridan Square and the Chase Manhattan Plaza. Pete Hamill, Mayor Spinelli and several other city officials were burned in effigy.

Dog owners were given six months to find new homes for their pets beyond the city limits. Both sides used their influence to obtain quick legal rulings on the constitutionality of the law. The city was upheld throughout the United States District Court and the United States Court of Appeals. In July, the Supreme Court refused to hear the case. There was no further legal way to fight Section 161.05. New York's dogs had little more than two months' grace remaining.

Never in the history of the United States—including prohibition, the racial struggle, and the wars in Indochina and Latin America—has such a great percentage of the population reacted with such consummate bitterness and openly declared that a law could be damned. Hundreds of thousands of buttons, bumper stickers, decals, and door and window banners blossomed throughout the city. These bore one of two slogans: Cleveland Amory's *Never! Never! Never!* or State Senator John Gordon's reworking of an old radical cry, *Hell, No, Dogs Won't Go!* Mr. Gordon (Rep., Queens) once condemned William F. Buckley, Jr., as a "com-symp," was a screaming hawk on the Latin

American war very nearly before there was a Latin American war, and last year carried the standard of Law, Order & Morality to previously unimagined heights when he introduced in the state legislature, and fought in behalf of with the zeal of God's Soldier, a bill mandating the death penalty for any person convicted of desecrating the American flag. (The bill was defeated 55 to 2.) Accused by *Time* magazine, among others, of contradicting the stance of his last 40 years, Mr. Gordon, who is never seen without Fiji, his AKC champion Old English sheep dog, replied: "That's ridiculous. There is no inconsistency whatsoever in my positions. The relationship between man and dog was born in antiquity. We are inseparable, almost a single corporate entity. As man has neither the right nor the ability to legislate against his heartbeat, so has he neither the right nor the ability to legislate against his dogs."

Conservative Party strategist Terrence Campbell commented, "I think it is time to muzzle John Gordon."

"No gun control, no dog control," said Clarence Brown, Black Panther leader famed for the two attack-trained Dobermans always at his side.

Osai Adoko, national director of BAM! (Black Action, Man!), spat, "Cities for the People. Off Whitey's motherf——g mutts!"

"This is simply one more fascist bootheel jammed in the face of the American people," said Timothy O'Malley, S.J. Father O'Malley, the fugitive priest recently placed on the FBI's Ten Most Wanted List in connection with the bomb-destruction of the Army Chemical Warfare Computer Center at Fort Bellamy, made his remarks in a secret interview taped by an American Broadcasting Company crew. "By what right does any legislative body constituted by man presume to deprive human beings of those few comforts that remain in this death-worshiping, soul-shriveling society? The military-industrial complex is trying to lobotomize the citizenry and create a nation of mechanized automatons who will do their bidding without question. Defy them! Keep your dogs! Spit on their godless and thanatotic encroachments. Brothers and sisters, *venceremos!* We shall be victorious!"

Bugaboo Bob, thirty-four-year-old founder of the New Yippie Yassuh White Radical Bandersnatches, exhorted: "For the brotherhood of Man, for the cause of Peace, Freedom and Equality, get rid of the goddamn dogs. Take the cities! Kill the stinking animals and use the bloody meat to feed the poor and the starving. Death to dogs!"

There were scattered incidents of violence: several persons were beaten; a bomb was detonated in DIM's headquarters after hours, causing extensive damage but no personal injury; politicians, and officers and spokesmen of DIM received threatening letters; and East Side gynecologist Irving Siegel shotgunned his neighbor to death after the man taunted Siegel about the impending removal of Siegel's pet Airedale.

Roughly 3,000 persons did dispose of their animals during March through April. Cleveland Amory characterized them as "the kind of people who would press a loaded pistol to their temples, smile and pull the trigger while saluting the flag if the government told them to." More than 15,000 dog registrations were removed from ASPCA's files, which are the sole repository of the city's dog records. No formal charges were made, but three clerks were dismissed, and the ASPCA public relations director implied in an ambiguous press release that the men were zealous dog lovers who had undertaken a systematic destruction of as many records as possible. Only half of New York's dog owners have ever bothered to obtain the required license for their animals. This meant that of slightly more than 750,-000 dogs, records existed for only 360,000, a serious obstacle to the implementation of Section 161.05.

Ignoring outraged cries of *Police State!* the city opened an office to which "responsible citizens" could report the locations of their own or other persons' dogs by letter or telephone. Dog partisans crippled this agency by overloading it with false information. DIM stepped in again, rented an IBM computer and hired a clerical staff of 30 and a team of 100 field investigators. The system worked this way. Upon receipt of a lead, the computer checked the informant's name against the city telephone directories. If there was no listing, the report was rejected out of hand. If the name did appear, the informant was called to verify that it was indeed him who had made the report. Upon confirmation, a field investigator was dispatched. If existence of a dog at a given address was validated, that information was locked into the computer. If invalidated, the informant's name was listed as unreliable, and any additional intelligence he offered was dismissed. Two field verifications earned automatic acceptance of further notifications. Investigators often initiated their own reports, and a loose system of volunteer block captains was organized.

DOG fought the program hard, but DIM's computer, backed by its human adjuncts, was relentless and very nearly invulnerable. By shifting animals to the homes of sympathetic friends for a few days and then filing informant's reports, dog owners managed to salt a few thousand erroneous cases into the machine's memory cells, but these were of little consequence.

On September 6, DIM turned over to the city a print-out which pinpointed the locations of 617,359 dogs, all of whom would be declared contraband in one week.

The city became suddenly quiet. The furor of the last many years vanished in an afternoon. Alternatives exhausted, rhetoric useless, New York City prepared in grim silence to go to war against itself.

Newspapers and local television and radio stations reminded their audiences several times daily that as of 9:00 a.m. Tuesday, September 13, all dogs not sanctioned by Approval Form 758 from the Environmental Protection Administration would be subject to confiscation. Only 1,100 such documents had been issued. Many dog lovers, across the country and in other parts of the world as well as in New York, had believed that the ultimatum was a bluff. Several commentators alluded to the Berlin Wall crisis in which the Soviet Union had threatened the United States with war unless it withdrew from the Berlin Wall. Nothing happened. Large numbers assumed it would be the same with New York's dogs. Even English Prime Minister Douglas Pierce-Bryson called upon Americans to "end this nonsensical farce."

But New York was quite serious. Obviously, 750,000 dogs would require a lot of rounding up. City officials enlisted the help of strategists from the Pentagon and Sperry Rand in devising a game plan. They selected Manhattan, where the canine population was most concentrated, as the primary target, then further refined this to 6 of the borough's 22 precincts. It was estimated that 30,000 to 40,000 animals could be removed per week, and hoped that this number would rise as many dog owners, faced with the inevitability of confiscation, removed their pets from the city themselves. Planners predicted that Manhattan would be "sanitized" within six weeks. Manhattan-based police were ordered to work 12-hour shifts for the duration, and all leaves were canceled. The National Guard's 569th Transportation Battalion, the 669th Transportation Detachment, and the 102nd Engineer Battalion were mobilized for support of the program. A staging area with fenced perimeters and several hundreds of ground stakes and short bench-chains was constructed in the Central Park Sheep Meadow. Confiscated dogs were to be brought here first, registered, then dispatched to holding depots in Queens and the

Bronx. Ironically, the city hired handler and attack-dog teams from a private agency to protect the Sheep Meadow installation after it had been vandalized three successive nights by pro-dog forces. 500 ASPCA auxiliaries were also standing by, hastily trained volunteers who were to assist in taking troublesome dogs into custody, and to see that the animals were treated humanely.

Dogs for whom new homes could not be found would, as facilities became crowded, be "euthanized." While DOG's only response to Section 161.05 was militant antipathy and rejection, the ASPCA and the American Kennel Club organized a contingency adoption program. Appeals were broadcast for two months, specifically aimed at New Jersey, Connecticut, Massachusetts and Pennsylvania. Proximity of relocated dogs to the city was important, a psychological comfort to original owners, who would be able to visit their pets; and, since the city had no funds for the project, new "parents" had to pick up their dogs from the holding depots themselves. Offers of new homes were received from each of the 50 states, and totaled more than 1,500,000.

Studies by the federal government indicate that Tuesday is the least likely day for employees to absent themselves from their jobs. Accordingly, the campaign was to begin on a Tuesday morning; though some resistance was expected, the fewer heads of households who were home, planners reasoned, the more this resistance would be miminized. The six precincts had also been carefully selected. The 20th and 24th precincts cover the area from Central Park west to the Hudson River, and from 59th Street north to 110th Street. This contained the highest ratio of dogs to humans in the borough and it was hoped that by purging the "enemy's" stronghold, morale among dog owners in other precincts would be damaged and the job made easier. The 19th and 23rd precincts run from the east side of the park (Fifth Avenue) to the East River, and from 59th Street to 110th. This is Manhattan's wealthiest enclave. These educated, affluent and privileged citizens were expected to submit without much difficulty. The precincts were also logistically attractive; they bracketed the park and the staging area, and trucks bound for the holding depots could be routed with equal ease to the Triboro and 59th Street bridges, or the Midtown Tunnel. The 13th precinct runs from Fifth Avenue to the East River and from 14th Street to 38th Street, a rather nebulous and undefined area without any easily observed neighborhood characteristics. Authorities did not anticipate much trouble here. The 5th precinct encompasses New York's Chinatown and Little Italy. The

Chinese, traditionally, defer to the law without protest, and New York's Italian community has enthusiastically supported Law, Order & Morality for the last decade and a half. The city's strategy, then, was (1) flush the dogs from their biggest enclave, and (2) begin with areas in which the prominent sentiment was, if not strongly anti-dog, then at least supportive of the city's legislative and judicial authority.

In theory, the operation was meticulously planned, streamlined and highly effective.

In practice, it was a disaster of the first magnitude.

Integrated units of police, ASPCA auxiliaries and National Guardsmen were to be in position by 8:45 a.m. on Tuesday, September 13, and to begin confiscating animals promptly at 9:00. That of course was high optimism. It is remarkable that the program got under way as early as it did—11:55 a.m. At that moment a city policeman and an auxiliary were admitted to an apartment on Park Avenue and 76th Street, and there took into possession without difficulty a Welsh corgi.

At 11:58, two patrolmen armed with the blanket "premises of John Doe, harborer of an illegal canine" search warrant that had been issued to all participating police entered an apartment on Broome Street with the help of the building superintendent, who opened the door with his passkey. No human occupant was present. The police took custody of a black Labrador retriever, and left the required receipt on the kitchen table.

The first incident occurred at 12:00. Mrs. Ellen Puckett of West 87th Street refused entrance to two officers and an auxiliary. Patrolman Donald Summers attempted to reason with her through the door while Patrolman Michael Esposito summoned the superintendent. The superintendent opened the lock and admitted the officers. Mrs. Puckett's fox terrier was barking in a closet where she had attempted to conceal it. As Patrolman Esposito snapped a leash to the animal's collar, Mrs. Puckett struck him over the head with a plaster of Paris statue. Five stitches were required to close Esposito's wound, and Mrs. Puckett was charged with felonious assault.

Isolated, the episode possesses a certain low comedic value; akin, say, to second-rate Buster Keaton. But, far from humorous, it was the beginning of Bloody Tuesday, a day which has been referred to by respected social analysts as "the worst civil disorder since the Draft Riots of the 1860's"; and "the initial stumble of what will prove to be the total collapse of American society."

At first, most resistance took the form of individual defensive tactics: new locks to which superintendents had no keys; doors barricaded with furniture or even nailed shut; dogs hidden in basements or the apartments of friends; animals rushed to new buildings as police cars and National Guard trucks pulled to the curbs; pets removed to precincts not included in the pogrom. Dog owners and their sympathizers glared at law officers and frequently insulted and cursed them. DIM supporters walked up to police and National Guardsmen, shook their hands and clapped them on the back. A few fistfights were reported between the two factions.

At 12:30 a patrol car on Mulberry Street radioed that some 30 persons had barred the officers from a building and were now pelting them with eggs and garbage. Similiar occurrences were reported on East 61st and Prince streets. On Bayard Street stones were hurled, shattering a patrol car's windshield. These were Law, Order & Morality precincts. Officials felt the first tiny stirrings of doubt. On East 26th Street, three officers and two auxiliaries with half a dozen barking canines in tow were followed from a building by a handful of owners who were both irate and grieving. The policemen found two National Guardsmen tied and gagged at the curbside, and every tire on the patrol car and the Guard truck slashed. A small crowd stood grinning around the disabled vehicles. The police received hoots and jeers when they untied the Guardsmen. One dog owner snatched his pet's leash from an auxiliary's hand and dashed away. The crowd prevented the officers from giving chase.

Anti-dog elements were also active. They gave up-to-the-minute intelligence to the police, informing them, for example, that certain dogs had been moved a few flights up or down to another apartment, or taken to the building next door. They produced tools and happily assisted in forcing sealed doors. They stood voluntary guard over vehicles while officers were in buildings, and they clashed with dog supporters who harassed or attempted to interfere with police. On West 63rd a small gang cornered persons foolish enough to be out walking dogs, seized the animals and hauled them to police. "It was weird," one patrolman later remarked, "I'd look at those people who brought us dogs, and all I could think of was that they were like puppies who wanted to be petted. Hell, we needed help. So we'd thank 'em, and it was just like telling 'em, 'Go fetch me another one, boy!' And they'd run off again."

For the first hour, it was a little like a holiday—for everyone but dog owners. The police were determined, but somewhat embarrassed, and even they, like most other persons, couldn't quite believe that Section 161.05 was actually being implemented.

At 12:40 the first serious incident occurred when Patrolmen Gerald O'Malley and Walter Ensley were attacked and severely beaten in the apartment of Joseph D'Agostino.

Then, with frightening quickness, an empty patrol car was fire-bombed on First Avenue and 23rd Street, and Bloody Tuesday's first fatality was registered. Dorothy Birien, a sixty-seven-year-old widow and pensioner, fled with her pet mongrel to the basement of the building in which she lived on West 92nd Street. Four neighbors pursued her while a fifth went to summon police, who were knocking on her door on the sixth floor. The police descended to the basement in the elevator. As the car came to a stop its occupants were horrified to hear a piercing shriek, which ended abruptly. The officers leapt out when the door opened, and saw blood oozing from beneath the car. Mrs. Birien and her dog were both found crushed to death at the bottom of the shaft, where they had taken refuge.

Radio and television stations fed an uninterrupted stream of on-the-spot reports, half truths and rumor to New Yorkers, but no one had any clear picture of what was actually happening. Although there is still no agreement as to where the ultimate blame for Bloody Tuesday should be placed—if indeed it can be placed at all—there is a consensus on the inflammatory role played by the news media. The early broadcasts were singularly dramatic and sometimes embellished by eager reporters. They appear to have been responsible for many hundreds of persons leaving their jobs to return home. Some went to protect their pets, others to support the police and the confiscation, and still others to make sure their families were indoors and safe. This infusion of frightened, tense and angry persons only worsened the situation.

At 1:15 a sniper opened fire from a rooftop on 109th Street, killing one auxiliary and one policeman, wounding a second policeman and an innocent bystander. The sniper disappeared several minutes before police reinforcements arrived. He was never identified, nor did he strike again.

At Grand Central Station a burly man snatched up a Seeing Eye dog and hurled it into the path of an incoming train, where it was killed. Many persons screamed, but there were also several cheers. Scuffling broke out. The blind owner of the dog was himself assaulted, and suffered bruises and lacerations.

Policemen, ASPCA auxiliaries and National Guardsmen were set upon and beaten numerous times. Attacks against law officers spread from the target areas into other precincts.

By midafternoon bands of anti-dog people were roving the streets chanting "Ho! Ho! Ho! Dogs Must Go!" and waving American flags, and pennants which read: *Do It for Mama!* and *Cities for Humans.* Vigilante-like, they ran down dog walkers and appropriated the animals. These dogs were at first turned over to authorities, but before long this process was deemed unnecessarily time consuming. Arthur Feldman was jumped by such a band on Orchard Street. He was kicked and punched by several men when he tried to protect his Airedale. Then they pinned him to the sidewalk and, while he screamed, beat his dog to death with clubs. Similar incidents were reported with mounting frequency. A surprising number of dog owners were unaware of what was occurring, or simply didn't believe it, and, until well into the early evening, they took their pets out for their customary strolls . . . only to be overtaken by horror.

Led by building residents, anti-dog forces invaded apartments, killed pets, and in many cases, swept up by the passions of their acts, went on to vandalize the apartments and inflict injuries upon the occupants. On Bank Street, four men who had been drinking through the afternoon broke in the door of Melinda Flemming, a receptionist. They flung Miss Flemming's miniature poodle through the window, then gang-raped the girl. In the Pavilion, a luxury building on East 77th Street, a group of men forced entrance into the apartment of Aldous Merriwhether, an interior decorator who owned a brace of Afghans. They were greeted with a fusillade of shots from Merriwhether's .357 Magnum revolver. Two were killed and two more wounded before Merriwhether fell dead, his skull split open by a crowbar.

Dog supporters formed their own patrols. They "liberated" caged animals, escorted dog walkers back to their apartments, and established sentry units around many buildings. On several occasions they came into violent confrontation with anti-dog groups, and fought with fists, feet, empty bottles and clubs.

The ASPCA auxiliaries were supposed to have been men interested in seeing that dogs were taken into custody, and later treated, in a humane manner. Care had been taken to weed out volunteers whose motivation was to assist the city in ridding itself of dogs as quickly as possible. The auxiliary program failed utterly. As many as a third of the recruits were DIM supporters who had successfully masked their true sentiments. Dozens of auxiliaries abused and actually killed animals in their charge. Others were dog lovers who had planned from the start to sabotage the operation, and still more, essentially honest men, were horrified by the slaughter they saw and began releasing confiscated animals. Hundreds of dogs were set free on the streets, and they provided both factions with additional objects of contention.

Two false reports of catastrophic consequence were broadcast on most of the city's radio stations between 8:00 p.m. and 9:00 p.m. Announcers stressed that the information was unsubstantiated, but most New Yorkers, already inflamed and their critical faculties at a low, accepted them as fact. The first claimed that members of DOG had captured four policemen, lined them up against a wall and executed them. The second alleged that the Police Department, in retaliation, was moving its cars up and down the streets killing dogs and their owners with submachine gun and shotgun fire. There was no truth whatsoever to either report, but New Yorkers were spurred by them to actions that rocked the sensibilities of the nation.

On East 34th Street, John Hanck and his wife placed their collie in their car intending to drive the animal out of the city to safety. Hanck became hysterical when a large group of club-waving anti-dog people barred the intersection of 34th Street and 1st Avenue. He punched the accelerator to the floor and ran three persons down, one of whom was fatally injured. Police Sergeant Dennis Toombs killed Hanck with a single shot from his service revolver, and the car careened into a lamppost. The mob tore its doors open, stabbed the collie to death, and beat Mrs. Hanck severely before Sergeant Toombs could rescue her.

An unidentified woman who boarded the IND "F" train to Queens with her cocker spaniel was accosted by Transit Patrolman George Halina, who, according to witnesses, gently informed her that it was against the law to bring dogs onto public transportation vehicles. The woman sank a bread knife into Halina's heart. Although her dog was killed by incensed passengers, the woman escaped in the confusion.

Isman Silverberg, a tavern supplier from the Bronx, parked his delivery truck on Amsterdam Avenue near 96th Street and left his Doberman pinscher on guard in the vehicle while he wheeled cartons of potato chips into the Red Hook Bar & Grill. Hearing gunshots, Silver-

berg ran outside and found his dog dead in the front seat. Armed men
were marching up the streets shouting "Death to dogs!"

On Thompson Street, dog supporters dragged two Guardsmen from
the cab of their truck, then opened the hood and ripped loose the
distributor wires. They were driven off by a larger band of anti-dog
people, who decided that since the dogs in the disabled vehicle could
not be moved, it was better to destroy them rather than to risk having
them set loose. They fired the truck, and 27 animals were burned to
death in small wire cages.

Nine-year-old Magdalena Torres of Mott Street, the daughter of
a plumber, filled a saucepan with sulfuric acid she had taken from
her father's kit, and hurled it into the face of Patrolman Anthony
Corniel when the police attempted to remove the family's pet mongrel. Corniel was permanently blinded.

A mob attacked DIM's headquarters, seriously beat a watchman
and the 12 staff members who were on duty, then went on a rampage
causing an estimated $400,000 in damages to equipment and to the
building itself.

A gang of juveniles, spurred by adults, ran through several buildings on West 83rd Street, bursting into apartments and flushing dogs
into the halls. The frightened animals were driven up the stairs to the
roofs, where gang members cornered them one by one and threw them
over the parapets to their deaths on the concrete below. Fifteen-year-
old Thomas Simmons was killed when an 80-pound Weimaraner
sank its fangs into the boy's arm and dragged the youth off the roof
with it.

Helmuth Steinbraun, a psychoanalyst, nailed shut the doors and
barricaded the ground floor windows of his West 88th Street brownstone. He threw pots of boiling water from the upper windows at
policemen and civilians who tried to breach his defenses. After two
officers had been badly scalded, reinforcements were summoned. The
analyst and his family were finally driven from their home with tear
gas. Their pet schnauzer, who ran out with them, was shot by an unknown civilian, and the brownstone was set afire.

Jim Buck's Dogs, a kennel on Madison Avenue and 80th Street,
was stormed by a mob. Buck, a hefty six-footer who breeds and trains
dogs in addition to operating his kennel, met the invaders with a lead-
weighted baseball bat in his hands and two attack-trained Great
Danes at his side. The dogs bloodied half a dozen men before they
were killed by blasts from a 12-gauge shotgun. Buck laid several

more low and was then beaten unconscious. The group entered the kennels, and the man carrying the shotgun, aided by another with a Luger, walked slowly up and down the ranks of caged animals and systematically shot to death 31 of the helpless creatures.

Several dogs—some formally attack-trained, others simply large and vicious animals—fought for the lives of other canines as well as their own. Rick Faller of East 26th Street, a construction worker, attack-trained his German shepherd, Turk, during July and August with the aid of a military manual. The massive dog took to his lessons avidly and by September 13 had metamorphosed into a nightmare beast eager to destroy anyone who approached within 15 feet of his master. "I made damn sure nobody was going to take him without a fight," Faller said. Faller went out to see for himself what was happening on the streets the night of Bloody Tuesday. "It was sick! They were murderin' defenseless animals right on my own block!" He called a friend who owned an attack-trained bull mastiff, then the two men and their snarling dogs undertook to patrol their immediate neighborhood. "We rescued six dogs," Faller said proudly. "We drove off four bunches of them gutless bastards, maybe sixty guys all together. Turk chewed up a dozen by himself. He caught one guy in the leg and I heard the crunch when the guy's kneecap went to pieces. I tell you, that's one mother that'll never walk right again!"

Philip Brouton, stockbroker, spent most of the night sitting in a chair which faced the door of his penthouse apartment on Lexington Avenue and 69th Street. A small marble table with a pot of coffee stood nearby. Brouton's wife was in the bedroom moaning; not even the triple dose of Seconal she had taken was able to quiet her anguished mind. The Brouton's Yorkshire terrier whimpered on the pillow next to her, and occasionally licked her face. Brouton, who had never in his life committed an act more hostile than tongue-lashing a rude cabdriver, was holding a double-barreled sawed-off shotgun. In a choked voice he said: "I don't care if it's a Black Panther or the Commissioner of Police. I'll blow anybody's head off who comes to take away our Pericles!"

Patrolman David Ottley, twenty-one years old and a member of the force for less than six months, went berserk when he witnessed one member of a gang tear a dog from a woman's arms and begin swinging the animal by its hind legs against the pavement. The young officer emptied his revolver into the group, killing two and wounding another, then attacked them with his nightstick. He was subdued by other police, and rushed to Bellevue where he was put under restraint and held for observation.

Riot squads were summoned to the Sheep Meadows and four times had to lay down heavy barrages of tear gas and nausea gas to repulse large numbers of persons who rushed the staging compound attempting to free the dogs there.

More than 1,500 dogs actually were taken to the Bronx and Queens holding depots. Violence occurred there, too, as an estimated 2,000 persons from neighboring communities and states converged to "rescue" the abandoned canines. Many bereft owners also appeared, intent on reclaiming their pets before they could be placed with adoptive families or put to sleep. Traffic blocked several streets and thoroughfares for hours; nearly 200 dogs were loosed from their cages by saboteurs; and pro-dog and anti-dog forces battled each other, as did ex-owners and out-of-towners who had come to adopt animals.

Violence did not abate in Manhattan until the small hours of the morning. Occasional screams and gunshots were still being heard when dawn, as if in sympathy, broke in a crimson flood over the wounded and bleeding city.

Many officials, particularly Mayor Spinelli, were harshly criticized for not having ordered an immediate stay of Section 161.05 and clapping a curfew on Manhattan as soon as the direction of the day became evident. James Carlson, an aide to the mayor, testified that Spinelli had been urged to do so several times, but that he had refused, allegedly saying: "I don't give a damn if they destroy half the island. The law is the law, and they're going to comply if I have to send tanks down Fifth Avenue." Carlson was promptly dismissed. Spinelli denied the charge and accused the ex-aide of attempting a political smear. In an official release, the mayor stated: "Our fair city will bear the scars of this tragic day for generations to come. We must each of us look into our hearts to determine the extent of our own personal responsibility and guilt, and we must resolve to a man that nothing like this shall ever occur in this city again. The consequence of disobeying the mandates of legally constituted authority and taking the law into our own hands can only lead, inevitably, to catastrophe." A movement to impeach Spinelli flourished briefly, but it soon lost its momentum; the mayor's attorneys are still considering legal action against Carlson.

Whatever the case, the City Council finally did convene in emergency session at 9:00 a.m. on Wednesday morning. With few preliminary words, they voted unanimously to retire Section 161.05 for an indefinite period of time. Their action was immediately endorsed by the mayor. Every local television and radio station was broadcasting the news by 9:45.

Spinelli appointed a blue-ribbon committee to investigate and report on the occurrences of Bloody Tuesday. Chaired by Clayton J. Brodie III, president of the Chase Manhattan Bank, the committee has taken the testimony of more than 400 witnesses to date. One member, who wished to remain anonymous, told this reporter: "It is going to be a three-pound document not worth the paper it's printed on: a thousand people explaining in great detail the errors and crimes everyone else committed."

Sociologist Henry Wade Williams of Columbia University insists it was simply typical mass behavior. "Riots are as old as towns and cities," Williams said. "We've always had them, we always will. There was nothing unique about this one. Its basic patterns were entirely consistent with the classic examples of mob behavior."

Philosopher James R. Madden of the same university said: "New York is a seething hell of hate and despair. It is a knife that flays each of us daily, reducing us to raw, quivering nerve ends. Such a witch's caldron of agony, terror and rage can't help but to boil over sooner or later. I'm only surprised that it wasn't much worse."

Psychiatrist Elliot Frankel of the New York City Psychoanalytic Association said, "It was a projective response. Dogs are fawning, will-less creatures who are at the mercy of the whims of their masters. The average man in our society feels precisely the same way. By destroying dogs, these people were actually attempting to destroy those qualities they find so hateful in themselves."

The most unusual interpretation was offered by Dr. Karl Droter, director of the Institute for the Development of Human Potential: "As strange as it may sound, Bloody Tuesday was a positive rather than a negative event, vastly more constructive than destructive. In a sense, it was sacramental. For years we have been a divided people, isolated, singular, awesomely lonely creatures desperately needful of connecting with our fellows, of coming together in mutually succoring and enriching harmony. There were admittedly two 'sides' involved, but what is *important* is that within each of these 'sides' widely disparate groups such as the poor and the rich, the radical and the conservative, white and black, set aside their differences and bonded together for one glorious day in mutual love and camaraderie. Bloody Tuesday was in fact an *agape!*"

Dr. Paul Ehrlich, population biologist, explained: "Every experiment of record demonstrates conclusively that creatures forced to crowd too close together—even such docile examples as rabbits—will eventually disintegrate and turn in fury upon each other. American cities are intolerably overcrowded, and New York, especially Manhattan, is the worst. We simply must give ourselves more room if we are to have any hope of saving what remains of our sanity."

Committees and learned speculation are all well and good, but the dogs are still here, and so are the passions of those who love them and those who hate them.

A survey conducted by this magazine last week reveals that the city's locksmiths are working 16 and 17 hours per day installing steel doors, iron window-grills, and the heaviest dead bolts and bar locks that can be purchased. Construction firms are supplying citizens with sandbags at the rate of 350 per day. Sporting Goods stores and Army & Navy Surplus outlets report gun sales that have averaged triple to quadruple the normal rate for the last five weeks. Dog schools specializing in attack work are, for sheer lack of space and manpower, turning away large numbers of prospective customers each day. DIM boasts 75,000 new members. DOG's membership has doubled.

No one in New York wants to see a recurrence of Bloody Tuesday. Mention the idea, and people recoil from you in horror. But everyone is preparing for it.

Unfortunate Solutions
#2

Today World War 3 will begin as brought to you by the People of the Free Universe. From this day forward anyone and/or company of persons who misuses the natural environment or destroys same will suffer the penalty of death by the People of the Free Universe. I and my comrades from this day forth will fight until death or freedom, against anything or anyone who does not support natural life on this planet. Materialism must die or mankind will.

—A California murder note, quoted in *Newsweek*

THE DREADFUL HAS ALREADY HAPPENED
by Norman Kagan

After all, it's not that awful . . . in Italy for thirty years under the Borgias they had warfare, terror, murder, bloodshed—they produced Michelangelo, Leonardo da Vinci, and the Renaissance. In Switzerland they had brotherly love, five hundred years of democracy and peace, and what did that produce . . . ? The cuckoo clock.

—Graham Greene, *The Third Man*

I.

The drugs I'm sent to make me go crazy never match the drugs to go sane again, quite. About three years ago I lost an eye and burned away most of the skin in back, sprawled in my clearing for a week with only my long legs in the shade, frangipani and salt reef's smell mixing

with my char. Now I'm all translucent there, pasty and slick. Another
time I lost half of the Phylogeny Corps package somehow and smashed
my mouth up, even less how, laughing and screaming on the phone
until a Corps overcraft brought more. I've also got these puckered
ugly red radiation scars, which actually pay for my pension, and regular hereditary pattern baldness, which is the part I hate. I wanted a
hairpiece, but finally I let it grow long and red where it still would
grow at all: "half long hair, half bald, I bridge the Generation Gap"
somebody said twenty years ago, before we all fell in. The bald patch
is angry red, but the rest of the skin is brown to black, tanned and
tanned and tanned. I read a lot outside.

Once in a while, I go down to the village green where the smiling
brown men square off to Te Ano, the hard ball hurtling from one out-
flung hand and smacking or thudding into another, the tall handsome
men darting and jostling, hair flying, laughing, shrieking, their calves
bracing in the high summer grass, or surging as they leap. They stay
away from me: my fault. I made friends and used to play and jump
till one day I misjudged the drugs, or perhaps the "I" that—you know
that number. I woke up with blood on my hands and stiff, strong
smelling dark bodies all around me. No one spoke as I rolled to my
feet. I grinned and one of them murmured their words for "dreadful
people." Now my only friend is Funafala.

Since then I just stand and stare all evening while they shout and
shriek and lash their bodies about. At dusk, Funafala lowers the flag,
the old Stars and Stripes and Bloodstains, and all of them: old men,
players, children stand at attention. Power. Then the little native tears
the flag up, or grinds it into the grass, or throws it to someone and they
play on again until dark when the winners break into a wild comic
dance to cheer up the losers. I grin too, going along with it and sometimes they take me back. Why not. The dreadful has already
happened.

Noon is always hot and humid, but in the jungle it stays still and
cool except for a few blinding white chinks and chips of day. Grass
lizards scuttled among the leaves and enormous black velvet and violet
butterflies fluttered up as I stumbled past, looking over my shoulder
with the feeling of someone or something behind, as you get in the
jungle, till the bright silver aerodyne came down in a clearing and the
girl leaped free, bright-eyed.

She came towards me, her short hair bouncing, her long legs thrusting ahead like swords, enormous-eyed and intense. In the noonday

hush I held still, half expecting . . . suddenly: "Like you know any old way one or the other one is out there and into one's own thing and gee I tried to make it all together and you know all the varieties get in there and if your mind can follow you're pretty far in and pretty far out and you have no concept . . ."

"Are you tripping?" huskily, tightly controlled.

"No. It's the jungle." I let her cast her eyes on the tight thickets of bush and fern, then up at the great dark-winged birds she'd startled out of the trees, and now lazily flapping back into the highest branches, finally on the darkness between.

"Hey!" I called softly, then tossed a fallen nut at her. "Hey."

"It's quiet," she said, her fingers moving smoothly to the loop of worry beads around her neck while her eyes came back to me and saw the insignia on the heavy canvas backwards jacket that was all I wore.

She smiled lasciviously, innocently, and I acknowledge the same insignia on the enormous shimmering mercury blob of the aerodyne. "Phylogeny Corps."

"What's this?"

She was down on one knee, touching the worn leather box and the ampules, the attention getters; the rest I'd laid out.

"An old . . . reselfing kit," I gave the new name, putting my hand on hers, kidding, not kidding. "This is," I said, shrugging my shoulders so the clumsy arms of the jacket, with their one-way cuffs, flapped. Her eyes moved from kit to jacket to me and she stopped, studying the scars and the smashings.

I ignored them, kept to the kit and her legs, which quivered slightly and deliciously. "An old reselfing kit," I muttered. "Tranquilizers, soporifics, hypnotics, ups and downs and sidewayzers. Attention getters: mandalas and mirrors and keyed pictures. A phone. An emergency squealer. Pack of trauma tapes." I glanced up. "*You* know."

"I know," she said softly, studying, slim fingers wrapped around a knee. "But you shouldn't have it . . . you're too old." It was no reproach; her eyes were soft on the scars. It's good being a bit of a monster; the reading is all one way.

Behind her, a wary crab hustled out from under some rocks, paused, and then skittled suddenly back out of sight. A long way off, someone was dragging dried fronds through the sand, "bringing the spirit home." Sunlight dazzled in the clearing off the aerodyne.

"No . . . not for some of us, and what we did," I said slowly.

"Anyway, it's going to be a present for a kid." I began putting it back together again, so I didn't look up for a while.

Finally I rose; she was still staring with the curious drowning look of a Corpsman at ease. She had lovely clear skin and one of those beautiful heart-shaped faces, and came to her feet in a three-quarter French turn.

"A three-quarter French turn."

"I used to model, a while back."

"I've been places and seen things."

"I've been things and played scenes," she said, completing the Corps motto.

She paused. "Then you're really Iago Lewis." She touched my chest and smiled.

"That's what the beacon in the house is signaling," I told her.

"Well . . . yes," she said.

Abruptly I swung clumsily around so the skin of my waist and hips ached and stumbled towards my house. In the sunlight my stomach and legs stayed cool but I began to sweat ferociously inside the white canvas backwards jacket. The girl followed like an anxious panther, loping. "You're the one that . . . wiped out Whole Earth Park . . . and . . . and the California communes . . ."

The drugs soften the glue that stick the personality together, but it hardens again, the pieces shifting a bit more each time. It was twenty years since California but the pieces were still there, the pictures too, against all I'd done to fracture and smash them. The Phylogeny Corps, still there and now here, waging their terrifying, murderously transcendental war against all we knew, all we know: in a worldwide random series of napalming, machine-gunning commando raids, in the two hundred biggest most lushly financed research centers on earth, in twenty thousand counseling and therapy centers across the earth, in the spectacular cloud-seed mannas that have saved three continents from starvation, and in their hidden command post, where, each month, a beautiful child is tortured to death, his mutilation and murder relayed around the world in full-colored stereoscopic television.

"That's ri-ight," I told her merrily, bitterly over my slimy-looking shoulder.

"You live here alone? Aren't there any people . . . like us? But what can you do . . . ?"

"You're really just a kid, aren't you?"

"I'm seventeen!"

"I knew a sixteen-year-old in one of the California communes. Beautiful as you, only long blond hair. The first time I met her she said, 'I'm clean, white and twenty-one. Let's ball!'" My face stayed impassive with a touch of slyness.

She smiled slowy.

"Did you really think at all about what you were doing . . . coming here to . . ."

"I'm here with a mission." Her voice shrilled a little. "Bernie Luntz and the rest of the squadron are coming in at dusk. To Funafuti Airport. I'll be meeting them there." She looked over toward the aerodyne.

We were standing before my little house, which is almost all glass, and mostly underground. I felt tired and sweaty, and abruptly, lonely.

"What a funny-looking place!" She ran her fingers down the glass wall.

I licked my lips. "It's The House of the Future. It's mostly underground."

Her eyes narrowed and looked at the machine again.

"A project of mine. This is the way people in the nineteen thirties thought we'd be living today." I clumsily struck at the lightbeam across the doorway and the glass hissed back.

She laughed delightedly.

"You've got time. I'll show you. I'm writing a history of the future from the past."

I pointed to some pictures on the wall. "The transatlantic railroad bridge. Togas for clothes. The Council of Scientists."

She was inside the glass house preening on the thick carpet, sighing in the coolness. Out of the sun, she was handsome, darker, but a little coarse. I took a huge white spider lily and put it behind her ear.

"I've got some time. Could we have something to eat?"

I got grated and creamed coconut from the freezer, then went to the study downstairs and came up again with my notes and manuscripts and pictures. She moved around behind me, leaning over my bald head or on my shoulder, tensing me, though she didn't notice it, doing sports or military turns when her legs got tired.

She was the first I'd shown it to: the technology worship of the thirties merging into the super-organizations and societies of the forties and fifties, the ones that'd conquer space and make a new world of steel and glass and snow-white concrete. Laughter. Through the fifties and sixties a second thread, sometimes woven with the first, sometimes snarled with it: the psychology and sociology of the new worlds, the people who made them or destroyed them because they didn't fit. Most of the raw material was corporate handouts, year's-end pieces in the media, and science fiction. Then the seventies, with the social crises, mental breakdowns, and drug dependency leading to . . .

We laughed again and I made my pass.

II.

"See-lo, See-lo!"

"Ta' Aldfa, Iago," like a shrill pigeon's cry, the fawn-faced boy kicking up the sand as he ran to me, swift gray fans. The handsome faces of the other youths looked cool; some had black noodles or the crook-winged frigate birds on their slim dark wrists, fondling and admiring them. The air was cooler, the beach filling up with handsome men and plump, broadly smiling women. Under a coconut leaf thatch, one of the island's hereditary canoe builders brushed feather shavings from an outrigger boom. Salt reef smell dominated the air.

He was tobacco gold except for his sulu loincloth; I'd added Bermuda shorts to my canvas backwards jacket. Together we wandered through the village, children sweeping the sandy paths with brooms of dried twigs, bunches of green bananas and nuts hanging from the shacks.

"They're working," he nodded, swinging his arms loosely as we went on. "I found a nestling in the palms by the graveyard and tamed it without nets or food, in a single day."

"Are you doing anything yourself?"

The boy smiled around his flat nose.

"It's relaxing to swing your arms, but most people don't keep them parallel when they're doing it."

He snorted laughter, kicked up his feet, shivered, hugged himself. I touched the worn brown leather kit at my belt. "Got something for you."

He looked at me with the strange drowning expression that I'd already seen once that day: Joanne, tousled and sweating, had said the current slang for it was: "The other side look."

See-lo and I'd met when he volunteered to help build my house; gradually I'd let him build a friendship out of that, or "a friendship on this side" as Joanne might call it. He'd chosen to hustle for the Stars and Stripes and Bloodstains as a way into the Corps. "We pluck at the living present," he'd read me once, from one of their old poems:

> But we cannot reach it
> A wall comes before us
> And we flutter at it like moths . . .

See-lo believed the Corps was a way over that wall, and for all the popular media and analyses of what the academy is pleased to call transpsychological behavior, he may have been right.

I suppose I'd come out ahead: *kaka alas* with thirty kinds of fish and coconut, and ragged hysterical dances by matriarchs and virgins; *saka* dancing around the flames on shimmering hips and seizing, exploding hands; and twice, when the boy's tongue dervished, striking out across the sea breakers in an open canoe at dusk, an oil lamp slung from a forked stick shimmering over the phosphorescent sea, led only by the instinct of a humped, bright-eyed great-grandfather. All for a few rambling lecturers and worn books, and now a worn talisman of otherness.

"Here it is."

A hundred feet away, tapering rocks led down to the island's southmost point where ocean ripples and lagoon ripples lashed and fused in light and foam. I opened the worn old case and spread it out, pointing out the various appliances. The boy dropped into a tailor's squat before me, while I faced him on my knees, wiping and wiping at my broken mouth so all the words would be clear.

"Now I'm told they call it a reselfing kit."

See-lo blinked, memorizing the slang.

"In the old days it was called a sanity stash. Understand, See-lo, there are just the return gimmicks. The old prescriptions would've been inert by now anyway, and besides, you'll need a few thousand hours of conditioning before they'd do anything but drive you into a particularly rococo and inaccessible catatonic state."

His eyes shone on me.

I was abruptly angry. "There's nothing here you couldn't get from a druggist and a few friends." I stopped, shrugged. "But I'd like you to have it anyway, a birthday gift. If you hear from the Corps you can trade it for a complete one." I laughed nastily.

He smiled and held the old kit to him tightly, indenting his dark smooth sable skin, studying my face as if he couldn't own it until he saw it in my eyes. Finally, he relaxed, then pointed dubiously to the line scored across the top of the inside, near an old water stain: *Corruption empowers, and absolute corruption empowers absolutely.*

"Dirty pictures," I grunted.

"Yes?"

"Something you wouldn't understand. When the Phylogeny Corps was started, the first of us often found ourselves too socialized, too repressed to really use the, uh, Other Side. Best way around that was to view it all as rotten, a monstrous amoral inhumanity that'd let us do pretty much w—well, anything. It worked."

He gazed at me again and I thought sourly, as I'd been doing more and more, that the kid would never cut it, that he'd never understand what it was, never could. But of course no one could, not from this side, not even myself, and I'd been over several thousand hours. It'd been fifteen years. So I let him look, while beyond the surf line a solitary fisherman stood bent over his line on the glassy waters of the lagoon, and it got darker.

"A squadron, Luntz's group, are coming to Funafuti Airport at dusk," he burst out at me.

"Yeah, I know."

"They'll be here for a Sharffing," the boy went on slowly, doubtfully. "Do you know what that is?"

I nodded. Knots pulsed and chafed above, behind my eyes. A mixture of desire, contempt, fear, webbed my thoughts: parallel lines in that non-Euclidean psychology which had shifted and shaped the world. "That's the way they did . . . we did it to the Earth People's Park." I peered at him through shaggy, suddenly heavy brows.

The boy inhaled, fingers tightening on the sanity stash. "But that means they'll just total us . . ."

I shook my head and croaked, over a bottomless crevasse. "No, it's a Sharffing: that means they'll let you all through, all the way, and Bernie Luntz, my old boss, will see to it that you . . ." All the time the words shifted and slanted as the old pattern took over, the Dreadful Happening, and suddenly I threw myself at him, grabbing the worn old strap of the stash as we went over into damp sand, me gouging at his eyes while I kneed him till he stopped moving. Then I doped him up and started for the beach.

The dark children were frightened when they saw me.

The feverishness of the transition to otherness was on me. I hopped and stumbled through the village. In the darkening shadows buxom figures squatted pounding wild taro or root food. Chickens scratched and pecked away at the scraped-out coconut shells till I scattered them, rolling and squawking respectively, then swerved to knock down some children playing in a circle. Pattern makers! Two fell to their knees, their dark round faces dry-eyed and staring, but the three I had not touched all burst into tears.

I hated them and stumbled on, sweating now, panting. The drugs were on me now, the inevitable avalanche of hormone shifts and neurological revisions, the personality reshaping that would carry me to the Other Side. I reached into my pocket and dropped the crumpled box of last month's dope. A warning, a red herring, a talisman, a monument? I was halfway there.

At the airport, Luntz's group hadn't landed, of course. I stood looking at the stars and bars and bloodstains for an hour, high on its bamboo pole in the twilight.

Gradually the perimeter of the field filled up with the dark, fawn-faced people, mostly women. Somehow the news had gotten out. I supposed most of the men were still working away and sending money home from the phosphate islands.

I kept watching them, the passive faces, the calm expressions, the soft cheerful cooing of their greetings, all for the last time. Staring at their calmness, their quiet, their peace, my chest ached with an un-bearable longing, my teeth twisted together in hatred. I was over. Soon they would be over as well. The Dreadful was about to happen.

In another hour the bruised and bloody See-lo joined me numbly, the sanity stash open and hung unevenly from one umber hip, his lovely eyes glazed, his arms slack at his sides. I smirked bitterly and slapped him on the back so he rocked. "Call me Charon," I grunted, a good title. I put it into my permanent memory.

"Let's see if we can get some action," I told him at length, and led the boy around to the island's control bunker. I laughed. I knew exactly what he was feeling. *If I can't stay with my nice friend Iago who likes me I'll go mad. If I can't get to someplace quiet I'll go mad. If I can't keep up this front for the next few moments I'll go mad.* I grinned at the big insignia on the control bunker: United States of

America. *States* indeed! Yes, and those states didn't have anything to do with geography these days! I led See-lo to the command module.

It echoed, dimly.

The place was deserted, of course; the regular staff knew what a Sharffing entailed, even if they hadn't been ordered to evacuate. Safelights glittered on the equipment.

The wind from outside made the big room grow cooler as I led the boy clumsily to one of the traffic controller's modules and let him collapse, crying and shaking. I turned on the operations lights and the tracking equipment in two dozen swift automatic gestures. I could still understand the equipment fifteen years later. Technology doesn't beat the big drum any more in the States; the States beat it in the technology.

While the equipment warmed up I wandered into the lounge, and found the place had been hit by the Knot, one of the new artificial forces of nature, like the old artificial men that were called corporations. A strange mass of crystals that looked like lapis lazuli and hung and grew like moss covered the ceiling, and along one wall was a strange mutilated lamp sculpture, or something that glowed and grew and slumped and quivered, emitting small puffs of nitrous oxide. On a table was a tube of some of the new Knot family-planning spansules, some of which could extend the lives of you and your offspring almost two hundred years, others of which could cut them to weeks or days. Most people who used them took at least one a month. At random, of course.

I went back to the command module and watched the automatics track Luntz and his group in, an intense blue constellation of lights sliding across the pale screens, past the spangles of the traffic beacons, casting great dim shadows on the high ceilings. A dim glowing mass on the edge of the screen must have been their mother crafts with the educational modules, humped and dark in their cargo bays, waiting.

I tried the traffic commander module but it burned my shiny parts, so I stood and turned a switch so Luntz's face showed on one of the screens, his pupils wide, his lips drawn back, his pores open beneath thick dark dirty never-combed hair. He hasn't changed, I thought, and then, looking at his eyes: it's going to be some Sharffing. Beside him, tousled and sweating and smiling and sleeping, Joanne, also in a flight harness, but nothing else. Luntz called twice, and the image blanked.

I slammed my whole arm against the emergency alarm, so it screamed and clattered. See-lo moaned and I quickly doped him, staring at the screen. "Get it together," I mumbled, and regret anger and confusion jumbled once more. I stared down at See-lo, wondering what he'd thought when I turned on him on the beach, bruising my knuckles, ramming and scraping his eye sockets so he tumbled terrified over, splashing sand. "Just a bit of the Dreadful," I muttered, wiping his forehead with a tissue, for it was feverish. The air had a touch of ozone from the electronics, and now a little chill from the dusk outside. A bit of the Dreadful, and I recalled a chill dawn with a red sun peering moronically under the edge of the shabby tent of night, and Luntz giving the weapons slung under the wings a meaty slap. "A bit of the Dreadful," he wheezed.

On the base's control tower, half a mile away, several lights blinked.

"They can't help being what they are," I'd said.

"Sure can't," he laughed, head tilted, one eye high, one low.

"I mean the kids in those communes, and their Park."

"I meant them. They are what they are, and we are what we are, and also what we're not." He shivered in the wind down the runway, even in the beat-up old Air Force jacket with the insignia ripped off.

"Yeah."

Luntz rose on his toes a few times on the burned concrete, looking past the lead plane to the rest of the squadron of brilliant silver, Mach-8 fighter-bombers the Air Force had cringingly given him. "Life and death. What's the difference, I always say . . ."

I looked down at him from the narrow open hatch: humped professorial shoulders, long skinny arms, black mass of hair, a youthful face with eyes warm and hateful and terrified.

"You know," he said conversationally, "once you're up there, you could just as soon total us."

I grinned (I had a great sardonic grin in those days) but he knew me, with the dreadful clarity of the Other Side, knew so well the skittering murderous hurtling suicidal chaotic trajectories he'd plotted in the last days of the universities, when the oldest faculty members had called him the "Madman's Marcuse."

"Except the Dreadful's already happened to us," he cried suddenly, his face going blank. He knew, I knew, we knew: It. "It's just too much for less than everyone."

In a furiously jealous and endlessly agonized moment, the whole bottom of my face twisted into a fierce hideous determined grin and my lungs collapsed in sorrow. The thought filled me as I sealed the small tight vibrating blinking room and signaled, and spoke to slam the shimmering mercurial squadron ramming upward and outward into a bloody flaming helmet that grew and blazed and retreated as it expanded, so that it never protected anything at all.

III.

I followed Luntz and the girl past the fresh-smelling huts with their rosaries of knotted string swinging in the wind, down to the beach. A few of the natives stood at a distance, hulking and distrustful, with one languid-looking Phylogeny Corps girl with long dark hair and an oiled body laughing at them.

The crews had lighted a few fires and were setting out the sensualities and drugs and foods in the starlight. Several were already drifting off into uncommon or intimacy states, the fires and an understated yet mesmerizing light show illuminating their unfocused or agonized eyes in shadowed sockets. An Other Side party, on the site of a Sharffing!

I hunkered down in the dry sand, looking over the dope and the sensualities on a low oiled teak table that cast my twisted face at me. I recognized a few of them from the old days, more from my reading. Firelight beat against them, so they pulsed with a dark bloodbeat all their own.

The sea tossed its head, turned, tossed its head again, sleepily, giddily.

Joanne stood facing me, fire lighting her low body brightly, thighs like pythons. I looked up at her eagerly, let my face slide toward disgust, reversed and moved toward a grin, stopping short. I blinked.

She laughed, understanding all, her deep voice lifting, her eyes taunting, her hands behind her, arms rigid, cocking her head to stare at me so I shivered. Her good mouth went soft; her face turned to the sky, one arm came out; she smiled, then made one of her French turns into the darkness.

I shivered under the impact of the jammed together, multisided, piercing emotions of the Other Side from within and without. The hot amorous afternoon had not been merely a betrayal, but . . .

There was a massive figure behind me, swinging long arms. Luntz. I went up and around, opened my mouth to look uglier and make him nervous. His own mouth was tilted, interrogative.

"It's tonight," I grunted.

His mouth quirked. "You've been away a long time."

"I've been doing things. My history book. And there were a lot of people who didn't want me around when the reports got out on the Park and the communes. At the time, I was very much connected with them." I touched the big red puckered radiation scars.

Luntz kept looking at me hard, not apologetic. "Those camps were a seduction, a threat . . . stability, frozen deadness." Even on the Other Side we still need words to carry thoughts and ideas and abstractions.

"They were alive," I mumbled vaguely. "I lived among them for eight months, scouting them out for you. I think I was happy there, not daring to dream that—"

He threw the glass in his fist into the darkness, where it shattered against something, startling us both. "That's right," he cried, sighing grotesquely. "Not dreaming, not daring, always sticking to their context, always safe and sane; alive and dead, no difference."

"No difference," I told him woodenly, and then silence. In twenty years the argument hadn't gotten beyond that point, never could. If only there were some other way of looking at it, some Still Other Side . . .

The odors of sweet and pungent fish, foaming coconut milk, and the hot toddy syruplike molasses used for dipping, coursed around us, then were replaced by bitter smoke. Supersensitized, we both moved stumblingly away from the wind shift and when I stopped, I was alone in darkness. Overhead, the starfields blazed mightily, the way they never did when I lived in Los Angeles when I was small. I wondered what the Other Side had made of Los Angeles.

Down on the beach, near the surf line, a tall technician was talking quietly with one of the youngest pilots. Behind, the waves hissed and tumbled salt smell and moisture over them.

"The Orwell book seems true: 'A boot stomping on a human face, forever.' The governments grew more and more uh . . . repressive?"

The man ducked his head, then scraped at the glowing meat of a lobster. "Repressive is right."

"But with automation, there was really enough for all the dead-heads," the thin blond boy burst out in exasperation.

The man, who was big and dark and gnawed at the shiny shell, shrugged. "Their world view, their universe shape was competition: 'Stomping on a human face' didn't mean power for power's sake; it was really the ultimate competition. Like the Righters tight-fisting what they had, the Lefters wanting to pass it out their own way. Business was money competition, schools were brain competition, their common state, what they called love and sex, was getting the best."

"Everyone was always at everyone else," the boy laughed. "Did they have the Dreadful?"

The man massaged the boy's legs, digging in with hard fingers. The boy gasped, twisted. Up the beach someone screamed, the voice cracking. The waves smacked in, slid out, smoking. The scream rose unevenly, was cut off. Neither had stirred.

"The Dreadful was the other side of the Competition. Some believed they could live at peace"—both laughed grotesquely—"even tried, in Earth People's Park, other places. But competition, progress, measuring supersaturated everything. The lust, the fear to break the rules for doom power, uncertainty. It grew: each person seemed ready to smash and shatter into a million bits of what-I-am and what-I-am-not, of what-I'll-do and what-I-won't: the Dreadful."

The boy, whose eyes had never swerved, in spite of the pain as he listened, suddenly spurted: "And then . . ."

"One day the Dreadful did happen, and here we all are on the Other Side," the man told him coolly, then laughed darkly.

The boy grimaced, then let the man pull him into the sand. The man squatted clumsily behind him, kneading the other's back so he groaned and laughed in the darkness.

I pulled farther back from their surging mass, turned and rambled up the beach. So that was the way they told it now.

Between the teak tray and the fire, See-lo was fighting one of the Corpsmen, his body covered with slime, his face knotted. The man, in coveralls with his scalp shaved, laughed and giggled and then struck at him heavily. The Corpsman, in some private megalostate, complete with hysterical strength, slipped closer and lashed out with a foot, leaving a great blood bruise on See-lo's right calf, then shrugging.

The boy with the coppery face was good; he'd dance around his own copper fires, of course. His hips swung, his hands opened and closed and turned as he moved. Then the shaved man leaped at him, tumbled him over, rose, stumbled away, and turned.

The dark boy grunted and tossed his head. "What're you *doing?*" he gasped in a rush, raggedly seizing another breath. "Why"—gasp—"don't"—swipe at sweat in eyes—"you do something I understand?"

The man went to his knees and threw two handfuls of sand in his face.

After years on the island, I'd forgotten the ways of the Other Side. A few Corpsmen were slumped in states of their own, but most watched the fight vaguely, assigning meanings to it of their own moment. Down at the beach, a dozen stood enraptured by the shifting patterns of liquid brilliance, keening to each other in the Corps' special language. A few yards across the sand, Joanne danced to herself, smiling.

The boy caught sight of me and wailed: "Iago, what do I do? What does he want? Tell me!"

"He's on the Other Side," I told him bleakly, walking away. He didn't seem to hear me, but stunned and confused he did the same, trotting out of the circle of scuffed-up sand. But instead of turning to meet me, he scrambled up the bluff of boulders to where dark figures crouched and stared among the breadfruit trees.

The man in coveralls wandered away too and the party resumed its lackadaisical moon: light splashed like third-rate fireworks until you stared at it, fires gutting out from under the barbecue spits, dim classical music, the momentary lacy patterns of sea thrown on sand, Corpsmen wandering, or solitary with madly grinning or agonized faces. It would go on until dawn.

I took some heavy dope in one hand, a compatible sensuality in the other, and put them into the worn leather sanity stash I still had slung over my canvas backwards jacket and shuffled toward Luntz, who had seen the whole thing.

"We'll Sharff them at noon," he said softly, twitching his wrist at the land side of the beach.

I pointed to where See-lo had gone between two dark heavy trees. "He wanted to join up."

"Still might, afterward . . . if he makes it." He took a deep breath.

"Luntz," I asked in another voice, "did Sharff ever know that we called it Sharffing?"

"No, he died in the seventies. The techniques were obscure for a

long time, colossal information lag . . . oh, one of the university
riots, a black janitor and a blond cheerleader took him . . . He'd
never thought people capable of such things," Luntz went on in an
effeminate huff. His eyes were hooded.

"Well, now we know that everyone's capable of everything . . .
every minute."

We regarded each other silently. Then I went up the path and began crashing through the brush toward my glass house.

IV

I woke to humming, and sore muscles, then rolled over in the
knee-high grass and saw a highlight of my house. The humming was
getting louder. The sun said early afternoon.

The sound of bombs falling, but too slow, then three of the massive mother ships swept overhead, down.

I half rose, fell to one knee, made it, pawed at my face, grunting. I
kicked my way toward the house for, well—turned and started toward
the village.

From the rutted road, the village looked unchanged, but a handsome boy with pageboy hair was slumped by the road beside his
bicycle, his dark face smiling, eyes closed. He hadn't collapsed in the
dust; he'd pulled his machine into the grass and lay beside it: one of
the new aerosols that activated the yawn reflex a few minutes before
inevitable unconsciousness.

In the village the women sat dozing beside the baskets of green
coconut leaves, holding the morning meal, the men slumped around
the walls.

Overhead, the great smoldering gray mother ships hung in the
damp air. Corpsmen trotted around putting the graceful brown bodies
into the sturdy education modules, setting the needles of the elec-
trodes, strapping on the hypodermic sequences to their slim arms.

Like most ordinary Other Siders at simple tasks, the Corpsmen
seemed almost somnambulant, very quick, working with dreamlike
smoothness as if totally isolated. Competition zero. As they finished
with each umber slack shape, they put a bracelet with a familiarization
message on it.

"Haven't sweated like this since I was a kid in Tangier," Luntz
puffed, noticing me. His eyes were haunted.

I felt cold myself, my back chill. I watched a young mother going through her sequence in her module, her dark face plump, tousled black hair to her shoulders. But her cheerful features were curled and relaxed into an unreadable mask, over which emotions rippled and exploded as she learned, without myth, tradition or trauma to impact the shock, every ecstasy, monstrousness and limbo of which she, and everyone, is capable.

With a metallic creaking and a detonating roar, half a dozen bulbous mother craft swung out on racks and then soared free, quartering the island. I noticed a new Stars and Stripes and Bloodstains on a new pole, slack in the dampness, taller and bigger than the old.

I walked through the shabby little village remembering Earth People's Park and the sprawled bodies there: wild wiry tanned ones, a little gaunt from malnutrition, new pale soft ones from the cities, blistered and sunburned and sideburned, their trailers and army tents and tippy geodesic domes. Sand in their hair, sand in the food . . . and later, how they'd passionately trampled each other, loving it, for a place on the transports, hysterical for the richness, the hatreds, the lustings, the idealism, the humiliations, the bewilderments, hooked on the contradictory madness that'd lashed, seduced, and struck at them like snakes till they fled to the cool emptiness of nature and honest feelings—except that they hadn't quite forgotten slyness, as their booby-trapped little stockpile flared like a sun, protecting too late.

One blond young Corpsman jostled me with his reselfing kit as he hurried past, startling me. He turned swiftly, his eyes burning as my own, and we swung to confront each other, squatting, fists ready, assuming nothing, anticipating everything, capable of dealing with an outsider the way an old-fashioned neurotic smothered a compulsion.

The man barked a laugh, hurried away. With a cold shock I realized I had been about to, ready to throw back my shoulders, hump my torso so as to throw myself into my canvas backwards jacket, so the one-way cuffs closed and it would become a straitjacket, which in fact it was.

I wondered, in spite of all the tapes and films, what the mainland was like. The Phylogeny Corps, with all their training and talent, were capable of self-control and social behavior for only weeks at a stretch and I'd had a good look at them: people on the Other Side with no control.

* * *

Later I found See-lo on the other side of the island, hiding on the old white lime beacon, like a brown grasshopper on a wedding cake for the feebleminded. He had smashed some of the empty bottles that serve as an ornamental border for the beacon and had thrown them down at me shouting, so I called one of the bulbous mother craft which roared and thrummed and sprayed.

Luntz, moisture on his glasses, stared at me pityingly as they hauled the slack dark shape into the machine.

"Your technique is poor; you're not getting everyone," I croaked.

"The others will bring them in . . . or play games with them to learn how they've changed themselves. You'd better stay away—"

"I don't care that much," I smirked, baffled. "Just get out."

V

The air had begun to unstick and my house to fade into the shadows as I stomped back into the glade. One of the hovercraft had even tornadoed down at the far side and left my next batch of supplies. I stumbled up to it and began tearing the casing, hysterical, clumsy. Alone, unstimulated, I could feel myself sliding back to being furious, futile, normal.

"Iago."

She was sitting on the doorstep watching. "About the Sharffing . . ."

"It's not my island. Do what you please," I huffed. I could feel her coming up in back of me slowly. She put her hands on my hips. "It's something I haven't figured out yet," I whined into the quiet, turning clumsily. "What're you doing, still here?"

"Luntz is working down the chain. Nukulaelae the day after to-morrow."

"Yeah? Pulling us all down into the passion pit . . ."

She stepped back. "It's not like that and you know it. The Dreadful is total actualization: thinking, feeling, doing, living, all at once, all the way." Her eyes were wide, her voice shrill: probably the drugs still working on her.

"So you can read me in an hour or two for Luntz. Even before I left, people on the Other Side wouldn't stay together more than a month or two. Couldn't. Without secrecy, privacy, respect—I know you don't understand," I yelled at her raised eyebrows. "They'd tear each other apart, kill each other, couldn't help it."

She stood with her legs apart, looking at me narrow-eyed, grinning in a mischievous way, then an ugly way, remembering something. "It's like that now, isn't it? Isn't it?" She crossed her arms in front of her. "A week . . . sometimes . . . if you're lucky."

"See, we weren't built to be cranked that wide. People are too strange by themselves, but have too much in common too."

"But it's not important, really."

"And there were other things: friendships, something, teams, I don't know. But you can't be honest, and you couldn't lie; everything showed. Those people in Earth People's Park may really have had something, you know, even if they were bored or doing routines, or even nothing ninety percent of the time. Something . . ." I rubbed my eyes.

She was silent, lush, white trimmed with pink, in nothing but her flight harness amid the green and black ferns in the dimming light.

"You've got a radio or something . . . call Luntz. Go back to the Other Side."

She moved back toward the stoop, stopped. "But Iago, what about you? This island will be like the United States too . . ." I liked the new way they pronounced "United States."

"That's none of your business," I laughed at her, laughing and laughing. "None of your goddamned business."

"But you can't end it all that way. There's so much, all my feelings, things to be said, bed, betrayal, we've got to—" She moved toward me with that drowned look on her face, sunk in Otherness.

I squinted at her in the fading light and went in through the glass door alone. I turned. "No."

> At Manchester, in England,
> This blessed fire began,
> And like a flame in stubble,
> From house to house it ran;
> A few at first received it,
> And did their lusts forsake;
> And soon their inward power
> Brought on a mighty shake.

—Stanza 6 of "Mother," a Shaker hymn, said to have been written by Elder Richard McNemar of the Union Village community, circa 1813.

THE SHAKER REVIVAL
by Gerald Jonas

TO: Arthur Stock, Executive Editor, *Ideas Illustrated,* New York City, 14632008447
FROM: Raymond Senter, c/o Hudson Junction Rotel, Hudson Junction, N.Y. 28997601910
ENCLOSED: Tentative Lead for "The Shaker Revival." Pix tapes upcoming.

JERUSALEM WEST, N.Y., Thursday, June 28, 1995—The work of Salvation goes forward in this green and pleasant Hudson Valley hamlet to the high-pitched accompaniment of turbo-car exhausts and the amplified beat of the "world's loudest jag-rock band." Where worm-eaten apples fell untended in abandoned orchards less than a decade ago a new religious sect has burst into full bloom. In their fantastic four-year history the so-called New Shakers—or United Society of Believers (Revived), to give them their official title—have provoked the hottest controversy in Christendom since Martin Luther nailed his ninety-five theses to the door of All Saints Church in Wittenberg, Germany, on October Thirty-one, Fifteen-seventeen. Boasting a membership of more than a hundred thousand today, the New Shakers have been processing applications at the rate of nine hundred a week. Although a handful of these "recruits" are in their early and middle twenties—and last month a New Jersey man was accepted into the Shaker Family at Wildwood at the ripe old age of thirty-two—the average New Shaker has not yet reached his eighteenth birthday.

Richard F, one of the members of the "First Octave" who have been honored with "uncontaminated" Shaker surnames, explains it this way: "We've got nothing against feebies. They have a piece of the Gift inside just like anyone else. But it's hard for them to travel with the Family. Jag-rock hurts their ears, and they can't sync with the Four Noes, no matter how hard they try. So we say to them, 'Forget it, star. Your wheels are not our wheels. But we're all going somewhere, right? See you at the other end.'"

It is hardly surprising that so many "feebies"—people over thirty —have trouble with the basic Believers' Creed: "No hate, No war, No money, No sex." Evidently, in this final decade of the twentieth century, sainthood is only possible for the very young.

The "Roundhouse" at Jerusalem West is, in one sense, the Vatican of the nationwide movement. But in many ways it is typical of the New Shaker communities springing up from La Jolla, California, to Seal Harbor, Maine. At last count there were sixty-one separate "tribes," some containing as many as fifteen "families" of a hundred and twenty-eight members each. Each Shaker family is housed in an army-surplus pliodesic dome—covering some ten thousand square feet of bare but vinyl-hardened earth—which serves as bedroom, living room, workshop and holy tabernacle, all in one. There is a much smaller satellite dome forty feet from the main building which might be called the Outhouse, but isn't—the New Shakers themselves refer to it as Sin City. In keeping with their general attitude toward the bodily functions, Sin City is the only place in the Jerusalem West compound that is off-limits to visitors.

As difficult as it may be for most North Americans to accept, today's typical Shaker recruit comes from a background of unquestioned abundance and respectability. There is no taint of the Ghetto and no evidence of serious behavorial problems. In fact, Preliminary School records show that these young people often excelled in polymorphous play and responded quite normally to the usual spectrum of chemical and electrical euphorics. As underteens, their proficiency in programmed dating was consistently rated "superior" and they were often cited as leaders in organizing multiple-outlet experiences. Later, in Modular School, they scored in the fiftieth percentile or better on Brand-Differentiation tests. In short, according to all the available figures, they would have had no trouble gaining admission to the college of their choice or obtaining a commission in the Consumer Corps or qualifying for a Federal Travel Grant. Yet for some reason, on the very brink of maturity, they turned their backs on all the benefits their parents and grandparents fought so hard for in the Cultural Revolution—and plunged instead into a life of regimented sense-denial.

On a typical summer's afternoon at Jerusalem West, with the sun filtering through the translucent dome and bathing the entire area in a soft golden glow, the Roundhouse resembles nothing so much as a giant, queenless beehive. In the gleaming chrome-and-copper kitchen blenders whirr and huge pots bubble as a squad of white-smocked Food Deacons prepares the copious vegetable stew that forms the staple of the Shaker diet. In the soundproofed garage sector the Shop Deacons are busily transforming another hopeless-looking junkheap into the economical, turbine-powered "hotrod"—one already known to connoisseurs in this country and abroad as the Shakerbike—and the eight Administrative Deacons and their assistants are directing family business from a small fiber-walled cubicle known simply as The Office. And the sixteen-piece band is cutting a new liturgical tape for the Evening Service—a tape that may possibly end up as number one on the federal pop charts like the recent Shaker hit, *This Freeway's Plenty Wide Enough.* No matter where one turns beneath the big dome one finds young people humming, tapping their feet, breaking into snatches of song and generally living up to the New Shaker motto: "Work is Play." One of their most popular songs—a characteristic coupling of Old Shaker words to a modern jag-rock background—concludes with this no-nonsense summation of the Shaker life-style:

> *It's the Gift to be simple,*
> *The Gift to be free,*
> *The Gift to come down*
> *Where the Gift ought to be.*

MORE TO COME

XEROGRAM: June 28 (11:15 p.m.)
TO: The Dean, Skinner Free Institute, Ronkonoma, New Jersey
72441333965
FROM: Raymond Senter, c/o Hudson Junction Rotel, Hudson Junction, N.Y. 28997601910

Friend:
My son Bruce Senter, age 14, was enrolled in your institute for
a six-week seminar in Applied Physiology beginning May 10. According to the transcript received by his Modular School
(NYC118A), he successfully completed his course of studies on
June 21. Mrs. Senter and I have had no word from him since. He
had earlier talked with his Advisor about pursuing a Field-research
project in Intensive Orgasm. I would appreciate any further information you can give me as to his post-seminar whereabouts.
Thank you.

TO: Stock, Ex-Ed, *I.I.*
FROM: Senter
ENCLOSED: Background tape. Interview with Harry G (born
"Guardino"), member of First Octave. Edited Transcript, June
29.

Q: Suppose we begin by talking a little about your position here as
one of the—well, what shall I say? Founding Fathers of the Shaker
Revival?
A: First you better take a deep breath, star. That's all out of sync.
There's no Founding Fathers here. Or Founding Mothers or any
of that jag. There's only one Father and one Mother and they're
everywhere and nowhere, understand?
Q: What I meant was—as a member of the First Octave you have
certain duties and responsibilities—
A: Like I said, star, everyone's equal here.
Q: I was under the impression that your rules stress obedience to a
hierarchy?
A: Oh, there has to be order, sure, but it's nothing personal. If you
can punch a computer—you sync with The Office Deacons. If you

make it with wheels—you're in the Shop crew. Me—I fold my bed in the morning, push a juice-horn in the band and talk to reporters when they ask for me. That doesn't make me Pope.

Q: What about the honorary nomenclature?

A: What's that?

Q: The initials. Instead of last names.

A: Oh, yeah. They were given to us as a sign. You want to know what of?

Q: Please.

A: As a sign that no one's stuck with his birth kit. Sure, you may start with a Chevy Six chassis and I have to go with a Toyota. That's the luck of the DNA. But we all need a spark in the chamber to get it moving. That's the Gift. And if I burn clean and keep in tune I may leave you flat in my tracks. Right?

Q: What about the Ghetto?

A: Even the Blacks have a piece of the Gift. What they do with it is their trip.

Q: There's been a lot of controversy lately about whether your movement is really Christian—in a religious sense. Would you care to comment on that?

A: You mean like "Jesus Christ, the Son of God"? Sure, we believe that. And we believe in Harry G, the Son of God and Richard F, the Son of God and—what's your name, star?—Raymond Senter, the Son of God. That's the Gift. That's what it's all about. Jesus found the Gift inside. So did Buddha, Mother Ann, even Malcolm X—we don't worry too much about who said what first. First you find the Gift—then you live it. The Freeway's plenty wide enough.

Q: Then why all the emphasis on your Believers' Creed, and the Articles of Faith, and your clothes?

A: Look, star, every machine's got a set of specs. You travel with us, you learn our set. We keep the chrome shiny, the chambers clean. And we don't like accidents.

Q: Your prohibitions against money and sex—

A: "Prohibitions" is a feebie word. We're free from money and sex. The Four Noes are like a Declaration of Independence. See, everybody's really born free—but you have to know it. So we don't rob cradles. We say, let them grow up, learn what it's all about—the pill, the puffer, the feel-o-mat—all the perms and combos. Then, when they're fifteen or sixteen, if they still crave those chains, okay. If not, they know where to find us.

Q: What about the people who sign up and then change their minds?
A: We have no chains—if that's what you mean.
Q: You don't do anything to try to keep them?
A: Once you've really found the Gift inside there's no such thing as "changing your mind."
Q: What's your attitude toward the Old Shakers? They died out, didn't they, for lack of recruits?
A: Everything is born and dies and gets reborn again.
Q: Harry, what would happen if this time the whole world became Shakers?
A: Don't worry, star. You won't be around to see it.

MORE TO COME

XEROGRAM: June 29 (10:43 p.m.)
TO: Connie Fine, Director, Camp Encounter, Wentworth, Maine, 47119650023
FROM: Raymond Senter, Hudson Junction Rotel, Hudson Junction, N.Y., 28997601910

Connie:
    Has Bruce arrived yet? Arlene and I have lost contact with him in the last week, and it occurred to me that he may have biked up to camp early and simply forgotten to buzz us—he was so charged up about being a full counselor-leader of his own T-group this season. Anyway, would you please buzz me soonest at the above zip? You know how mothers tend to overload the worry-circuits until they know for sure that their little wriggler is safely plugged in somewhere. Joy to you and yours, Ray.

TO: Stock, Ex-Ed., *I.I.*
FROM: Senter
ENCLOSED: Fact sheet on Old Shakers

    Foundress—Mother Ann Lee, b. Feb. 29, 1736, Manchester, England.
    Antecedents—Early Puritan "seekers" (Quakers), French "Prophets" (Camisards).
    Origin—Following an unhappy marriage—four children, all dead

in infancy—Mother Ann begins to preach that "concupiscence" is the root of all evil. Persecutions and imprisonment.

1774—Mother Ann and seven early disciples sail to America aboard the ship *Mariah*. Group settles near Albany. Public preaching against concupiscence. More persecutions. More converts. Ecstatic, convulsive worship. Mother Ann's "miracles."

1784—Mother Ann dies.

1787—Mother Ann's successors, Father Joseph and Mother Lucy, organize followers into monastic communities and "separate" themselves from sinful world.

1787-1794—Expansion of sect through New York State and New England.

1806-1826—Expansion of sect across Western frontier—Ohio, Kentucky, Indiana.

1837-1845—Mass outbreak of spiritualism. Blessings, songs, spirit-drawings and business advice transmitted by deceased leaders through living "instruments."

1850's—Highpoint of Society. Six thousand members, 18 communities, fifty-eight "Families."

*Total recorded membership—from late 18th century to late 20th century—approximately seventeen thousand.

*Old Shakers noted for—mail-order seed business, handicrafts (brooms, baskets and boxes), furniture-manufacture.

*Credited with invention of—common clothespin, cut nails, circular saw, turbine waterwheel, steam-driven washing machine.

Worship—Emphasis on communal singing and dancing. Early "convulsive" phase gives way in nineteenth century to highly organized performances and processions—ring dances, square order shuffles.

Beliefs—Celibacy, Duality of Deity (Father and Mother God), Equality of the Sexes, Equality in Labor, Equality in Property. Society to be perpetuated by "admission of serious-minded persons and adoption of children."

Motto—"Hands to work and Hearts to God."

MORE TO COME

XEROGRAM: June 30 (8:15 a.m.)
TO: Mrs. Rosemary Collins, 133 Escorial Drive, Baywater, Florida
   92635776901
FROM: Raymond Senter, Hudson Junction Rotel, Hudson Junction,
   N.Y. 28997601910

Dear Rosie:
   Has that little wriggler of ours been down your way lately?
Bruce is off again on an unannounced sidetrip, and it struck me
that he might have hopped down south to visit his favorite aunt.
Not to mention his favorite cousin! How is that suntanned teaser
of yours? Still taking after you in the S-L-N department? Give
her a big kiss for me—you know where! And if Bruce does show
up please buzz me right away at the above zip. Much Brotherly
Love, Ray.

TO: Stock, Ex-Ed., *I.I.*
FROM: Senter
ENCLOSED: Caption tape for film segment on Worship Service.

JERUSALEM WEST, Saturday, June 30—I'm standing at the entrance to the inner sanctum of the huge Roundhouse here, the so-
called Meeting Center, which is used only for important ceremonial
functions—like the Saturday Night Dance scheduled to begin in exactly five minutes. In the Holy Corridor to my right the entire congregation has already assembled in two rows, one for boys and one for
girls, side by side but not touching. During the week the Meeting Center is separated from the work and living areas by curved translucent
partitions which fit together to make a little dome-within-a-dome.
But when the sun begins to set on Saturday night the partitions are
removed to reveal a circular dance floor, which is in fact the hub of
the building. From this slightly raised platform of gleaming fibercast,
I can look down each radial corridor—past the rows of neatly folded
beds in the dormitories, past the shrouded machines in the repair
shops, past the partly finished Shakerbikes in the garage, past the
scrubbed formica tables in the kitchen—to the dim horizon line where
the dome comes to rest on the sacred soil of Jerusalem West.

All artificial lights have been extinguished for the Sabbath cele-
bration. The only illumination comes from the last rays of the sun,
a dying torch that seems to have set the dome material itself ablaze.
It's a little like standing inside the fiery furnace of Nebuchadnezzar
with a hundred and twenty-eight unworried prophets of the Lord.
The silence is virtually complete—not a cough, not the faintest rustle
of fabric is heard. Even the air vents have been turned off—at least
for the moment. I become aware of the harsh sound of my own res-
piration.

At precisely eight o'clock the two lines of worshipers begin to move
forward out of the Holy Corridor. They circle the dance floor, the
boys moving to the right, the girls to the left. Actually, it's difficult to
tell them apart. The Shakers use no body ornaments at all—no paints,
no wigs, no gems, no bugs, no dildoes, no flashers. All wear their hair
cropped short, as if sheared with the aid of an overturned bowl. And
all are dressed in some variation of Shaker gear—a loosely fitting,
long-sleeved, buttonless and collarless shirt slit open at the neck for
two inches and hanging free at the waist over a pair of baggy trousers
pulled tight around each ankle by a hidden elastic band.

The garments look vaguely North African. They are made of soft
dynaleen and they come in a variety of pastel shades. One girl may be
wearing a pale pink top and a light blue bottom. The boy standing
opposite her may have on the same colors, reversed. Others in the
procession have chosen combinations of lilac and peach, ivory and
lemon or turquoise and butternut. The range of hues seems endless
but the intensity never varies, so that the entire spectacle presents a
living demonstration of one of the basic Articles of Faith of the Shaker
Revival—Diversity in Uniformity.

Now the procession has ended. The worshipers have formed two
matching arcs, sixty-four boys on one side, sixty-four girls on the
other, each standing precisely an arm's length from each neighbor.
All are barefoot. All are wearing the same expression—a smile so
modest as to be virtually undetectable if it were not mirrored and re-
mirrored a hundred and twenty-eight times around the circumference
of the ritual circle. The color of the dome has begun to change to a
darker, angrier crimson. Whether the natural twilight's being artifi-
cially augmented—either from inside or outside the building—is impossible to tell. All eyes are turned upward to a focus about twenty-five
feet above the center of the floor, where an eight-sided loudspeaker
hangs by a chrome-plated cable from the midpoint of the dome. The

air begins to fill with a pervasive vibration like the rumble of a distant monocar racing toward you in the night. And then the music explodes into the supercharged air. Instantly the floor is alive with jerking, writhing bodies—it's as if each chord were an electrical impulse applied directly to the nerve ends of the dancers—and the music is unbelievably loud.

The dome must act as an enormous soundbox. I can feel the vibrations in my feet and my teeth are chattering with the beat—but as wild as the dancing is, the circle is still intact. Each Shaker is "shaking" in his own place. Some are uttering incomprehensible cries, the holy gibberish that the Shakers call their Gift of Tongues—ecstatic prophesies symbolizing the Wordless Word of the Diety. One young girl with a gaunt but beautiful face is howling like a coyote. Another is grunting like a pig. A third is alternately spitting into the air and slapping her own cheeks viciously with both hands.

Across the floor a tall skinny boy has shaken loose from the rim of the circle. Pirouetting at high speed, his head thrown straight back so that his eyes are fixed on the crimson membrane of the dome, he seems to be propelling himself in an erratic path toward the center of the floor. And now the dome is changing color again, clotting to a deeper purple—like the color of a late evening sky but flecked with scarlet stars that seem to be darting about with a life of their own, colliding, coalescing, reforming.

A moment of relative calm has descended on the dancers. They are standing with their hands at their sides—only their heads are moving, lolling first to one side, then the other, in keeping with the new, subdued rhythm of the music. The tall boy in the center has begun to spin around and around in place, picking up speed with each rotation—now he's whirling like a top, his head still bent back, his eyes staring sightlessly. His right arm shoots out from the shoulder, the elbow locked, the fingers stiff, the palm flat—this is what the Shakers call the Arrow Sign, a manifestation of the Gift of Prophecy, directly inspired by the Dual Diety, Father Power and Mother Wisdom. The tall boy is the "instrument" and he is about to receive a message from on high.

His head tilts forward. His rotation slows. He comes to a halt with his right arm pointing at a short red-haired girl. The girl begins to shake all over as if struck by a high fever. The music rises to an ear-shattering crescendo and ends in mid-note.

"Everyone's a mirror," the tall boy shouts. "Clean, clean, clean—oh, let it shine! My dirt's not my own but it stains the earth. And the

earth's not my own—the Mother and Father are light above light but
the light can't shine alone. Only a mirror can shine, shine, shine. Let
the mirror be mine, be mine, be mine!"

The red-haired girl is shaking so hard her limbs are flailing like
whips. Her mouth has fallen open and she begins to moan, barely
audibly at first. What she utters might be a single-syllable word like
"clean" or "mine" or "shine" repeatedly, so rapidly that the conso-
nants break down and the vowels flow into one unending stream of
sound. But it keeps getting louder and louder and still louder, like
the wail of an air-raid siren, until all resemblance to speech disap-
pears and it seems impossible that such a sound can come from a human throat. You can almost hear the blood vessels straining, bursting.

Then the loudspeaker cuts in again in mid-note with the loudest,
wildest jag-rock riff I have ever heard, only it's no longer something
you can hear—it's inside you or you're inside it. And the dome has
burst into blooms of color! A stroboscopic fireworks display that ob-
literates all outlines and shatters perspective and you can't tell whether
the dancers are moving very, very slowly or very, very fast. The movement is so perfectly synchronized with the sound and the sound with
the color that there seems to be no fixed reference point anywhere.

All you can say is: "There is color, there is sound, there is
movement—"

This is the Gift of Seizure, which the New Shakers prize so highly—
and whether it is genuinely mystical, as they claim, or autohypnotic or
drug-induced, as some critics maintain, or a combination of all of
these or something else entirely, it is an undeniably real—and pro-
foundly disturbing—experience.

XEROGRAM: July 1 (7:27 a.m.)
TO: Frederick Rickover, Eastern Supervisor, Feel-O-Mat Corp.,
    Baltimore, Maryland 6503477502
FROM: Raymond Senter, Hudson Junction Rotel, Hudson Junction,
    N.Y. 28997601910
(*WARNING: PERSONALIZED ENVELOPE: CONTENTS WILL
POWDER IF OPENED IMPROPERLY*)

Fred:
I'm afraid it's back-scratching time again. I need a code-check on
DNA No. 75/62/HR/t1/4-9-06^5. I'm interested in whether the
codee has plugged into a feel-o-mat anywhere in the Federa-

tion during the past two weeks. This one's a family matter, not business, so buzz me only at the above zip. I won't forget it. Gratefully, Ray.

TO: Stock. Ex-Ed., *I.I.*
FROM: Senter
ENCLOSED: Three tapes. New Shaker "testimonies." Edited transcripts, July 1.

TAPE I (Shaker name, "Farmer Brown"): What kind of mike is this? No kidding. I didn't know they made a re-amper this small. Chinese? Oh. Right. Well, let's see—I was born April seventeenth, nineteen-seventy-four, in Ellsworth, Saskatchewan. My breath-father's a foremen at a big refinery there. My breath-mother was a consumer-housewife. She's gone over now. It's kind of hard to remember details. When I was real little, I think I saw the feds scratch a Bomb-thrower on the steps of City Hall. But maybe that was only something I saw on 2-D. School was—you know, the usual. Oh, once a bunch of us kids got hold of some fresh spores from the refinery—I guess we stole them somehow. Anyway, there was still a lot of open land around and we planted them and raised our own crop of puffers. I didn't come down for a week. That was my farming experience. (LAUGHTER) I applied for a bummer-grant on my fifteenth birthday, got a two-year contract and took off the next day for the sun. Let's see—Minneapolis, Kansas City, Mexico—what a jolt! There weren't so many feel-o-mats in the small towns down there and I was into all the hard stuff you could get in those days—speed, yellow, rock-juice, little-annie—I guess the only thing I never tried for a jolt was the Process and there were times when I was just about ready.

When the grant ran out, I just kept bumming on my own. At first you think it's going to be real easy. Half the people you know are still on contract and they share it around. Then your old friends start running out faster than you make new ones and there's a whole new generation on the road. And you start feeling more and more like a feebie and acting like one. I was lucky because I met this sweet little dove in Nashville—she had a master's in Audio-Visual but she was psycho for bummers, especially flat ones.

Anyway, she comes back to her coop one day with a new tape and puts it on and says, "This'll go right through you. It's a wild new group called the Shakers."

She didn't know two bobby's worth about the Shakers and I didn't either—the first Shaker tapes were just hitting the market about then. Well, I can tell you, that jagged sound gave me a jolt. I mean, it was bigger than yellow, bigger than juice, only it let you down on your feet instead of your back. I had this feeling I had to hear more. I got all the tapes that were out but they weren't enough. So I took off one night for Wildwood and before I knew it I was in a Prep Meeting and I was home free—you know, I've always kind of hoped that little dove makes it on her own—Oh, yeah, the band.

Well, I'm one of the Band Deacons, which is what's called a Sacrificial Gift because it means handling the accounts—and that's too close to the jacks and bobbys for comfort. But someone has to do it. You can't stay alive in an impure world without getting a little stained and if outsiders want to lay the Kennedys on us for bikes and tapes, that's a necessary evil. But we don't like to spread the risk in the Family. So the Deacons sign the checks and deal with the agents and the stain's on us alone. And everyone prays a little harder to square it with the Father and Mother.

TAPE II (Shaker name, "Mariah Moses"): I was born in Darien, Connecticut. I'm an Aquarius with Leo rising. Do you want my breathname? I don't mind—it's Cathy Ginsberg. My breath-parents are both full-time consumers. I didn't have a very interesting childhood, I guess. I went to Mid-Darien Modular School. I was a pretty good student—my best subject was World Culture. I consummated on my third date, which was about average, I've been told, for my class. Do you really want all this background stuff? I guess the biggest thing that happened to the old me was when I won a second prize in the Maxwell Puffer Civic Essay contest when I was fourteen. The subject was *The Joys of Spectatorism* and the prize was a Programmed Weekend in Hawaii for two. I don't remember who I went with. But Hawaii was really nice. All those brown-skinned boys—we went to a big luau on Saturday night. That's a native-style orgy. They taught me things we never even learned in school.

I remembering thinking, *Oh, star, this is the living end!*

But when it was all over I had another thought. If this was the living end—what came next? I don't know if it was the roast pig or what but I didn't feel so good for a few days. The night we got back home— Herbie! That was the name of my date, Herbie Alcott—he had short curly hair all over his back—anyway, the night I got home my breath-parents picked me up at the airport and on the way back to Darien they started asking me what I wanted to do with my life. They were trying to be so helpful, you know. I mean, you could see they would have been disappointed if I got involved in production of some kind but they weren't about to say that in so many words. They just asked me if I had decided how I wanted to plug into the Big Board. It was up to me to choose between college or the Consumer Corps or a Travel Grant—they even asked me if Herbie and I were getting serious and if we wanted to have a baby—because the waiting-list at the Marriage Bureau was already six months' long and getting longer. The trouble was I was still thinking about the luau and the roast pig and I felt all—burned out. Like a piece of charcoal that still looks solid but is really just white ash—and if you touch it it crumbles and blows away. So I said I'd think about it but what I was really thinking was *I'm not signing up for any more orgies just yet.*

And a few days later the miracle happened. A girl in our class was reported missing and a friend of mine heard someone say that she'd become a Shaker.

I said, "What's that?"

My friend said, "It's a religion that believes in No hate, No war, No money, No sex."

And I felt this thrill go right through me. And even though I didn't know what it meant at the time, that was the moment I discovered my Gift. It was such a warm feeling, like something soft and quiet curled up inside you, waiting. And the day I turned fifteen I hiked up to Jerusalem and I never went home. That was eleven months ago . . . oh, you can't describe what happens at Preparative Meeting. It's what happens inside you that counts. Like now, when I think of all my old friends from Darien, I say a little prayer.

Father Power, Mother Wisdom, though their Gifts, set them free . . .

TAPE III (Shaker name, "Earnest Truth"): I'm aware that I'm something of a rarity here. I assume that's why you asked me for a testimony. But I don't want you categorizing me as a Shaker intellectual or a Shaker theologian or anything like that. I serve as Legal Deacon because that's my Gift. But I'm also a member of the vacuum detail in Corridor Three and that's my Gift too. I'd be just as good a Shaker if I only cleaned the floor and nothing else. Is that clear? Good. Well then, as briefly as possible: (READS FROM PREPARED

TEXT) I'm twenty-four years old, from Berkeley, California. Breath-parents were on the faculty at the University; killed in an air crash when I was ten. I was raised by the state. Pacific Highland Modular School: First honors. Consumer Corps: Media-aide First-class. Entered the University at seventeen. Pre-law. Graduated *magna cum* in nineteen-ninety. Completed four-year Law School in three years. In my final year I became interested in the literature of religion—or, to be more precise, the literature of mysticism—possibly as a counterpoise to the increasing intensity of my formal studies. Purely as an intellectual diversion I began to read St. John of the Cross, George Fox, the Vedas, Tao, Zen, the Kabbala, the Sufis. But when I came across the early Shakers I was struck at once with the daring and clarity of this purely American variant. All mystics seek spiritual union with the Void, the Nameless, the Formless, the Ineffable. But the little band of Shaker pilgrims, confronted with a vast and apparently unbounded wilderness, took a marvelous quantum leap of faith and decided that the union had already been accomplished. The wilderness was the Void. For those who had eyes to see—this was God's Kingdom. And by practicing a total communism, a total abnegation, a total dedication, they made the wilderness flower for two hundred years. Then, unable to adjust to the methodologies of the Industrial Revolution, they quietly faded away; it was as if their gentle spirit had found a final resting place in the design of their utterly simple and utterly beautiful wooden furniture—each piece of which has since become a collector's item. When I began reading about the Old Shakers I had of course heard about the New Shakers—but I assumed that they were just another crackpot fundamentalist sect like the Holy Rollers or the Snake Handlers, an attempt to keep alive the pieties of a simpler day in the present age of abundance. But eventually my curiosity—or so I called it at the time—led me to investigate a Preparative Meeting that had been established in the Big Sur near Jefferstown. And I found my Gift. The experience varies from individual to individual. For me it was the revelation that the complex machine we refer to as the Abundant Society is the real anachronism. All the euphorics we feed ourselves cannot change the fact that the machinery of abundance has long since reached its limits as a vital force and is now choking on its own waste products—Pollution, Overpopulation, Dehumanization. Far from being a breakthrough, the so-called Cultural Revolution was merely the last gasp of the old order trying to maintain itself by programming man's most private senses into the machine. And the childish Bomb-throwers were nothing but retarded romantics, an anachronism within an anachronism. At this juncture in history, only the Shaker Revival offers a true alternative—in the utterly simple, and therefore utterly profound, Four Noes. The secular world usually praises us for our rejection of Hate and War and mocks us for our rejection of Money and Sex. But the Four Noes constitute a beautifully balanced ethical equation, in which each term is a function of the other three. There are no easy Utopias. Non-Shakers often ask: What would happen if everyone became a Shaker? Wouldn't that be the end of the human race? My personal answer is this: Society is suffering from the sickness unto death—a plague called despair. Shakerism is the only cure. As long as the plague rages more and more people will find the strength to take the medicine required, no matter how bitter it may seem. Perhaps at some future date, the very spread of Shakerism will restore Society to health, so that the need for Shakerism will again slacken. Perhaps the cycle will be repeated. Perhaps not. It is impossible to know what the Father and Mother have planned for their children. Only one thing is certain. The last of the Old Shaker prophetesses wrote in nineteen fifty-six: "The flame may flicker but the spark can never be allowed to die out until the salvation of the world is accomplished."

I don't think you'll find the flame flickering here.

MORE TO COME

XEROGRAM: July 1 (11:30 p.m.)
TO: Stock, Ex-Ed., *I.I.*
FROM: Raymond Senter, c/o Hudson Junction Rotel
(*WARNING: PERSONALIZED ENVELOPE: CONTENTS WILL POWDER IF OPENED IMPROPERLY*)

Art:
Cooperation unlimited here—until I mention "Preparative Meeting." Then they all get tongue-tied. Too holy for impure ears. No one will even say where or when. Working hypothesis: It's a compulsory withdrawal session. Recruits obviously must kick all wordly habits before taking final vows. Big question: how do they do it? Conscious or unconscious? Cold-turkey, hypno-suggestion, or re-conditioning? Legal or illegal? Even Control would like to

know. I'm taping the Reception Deacon tomorrow. If you approve, I'll start putting the pressure on. The groundwork's done. We may get a story yet. Ray.

XEROGRAM: July 2 (2:15 a.m.)
TO: Joseph Harger, Coordinator, N.Y. State Consumer Control, Albany, N.Y. 31118002311
FROM: Raymond Senter, c/o Hudson Junction Rotel, Hudson Junction, N.Y. 28997601910
(*WARNING: PERSONALIZED ENVELOPE: CONTENTS WILL POWDER IF OPENED IMPROPERLY*)

Joe:

I appreciate your taking a personal interest in this matter. My wife obviously gave the wrong impression to the controller she contacted. She tends to get hysterical. Despite what she may have said I assure you my son's attitude toward the Ghetto was a perfectly healthy blend of scorn and pity. Bruce went with me once to see the Harlem Wall—must have been six or seven—and Coordinator Bill Quaite let him sit in the Scanner's chair for a few minutes. He heard a muzzein call from the top of one of those rickety towers. He saw the wild rats prowling in the stench and garbage. He also watched naked children fighting with wooden knives over a piece of colored glass. I am told there are young people today stupid enough to think that sneaking over the Wall is an adventure and that the process is reversible—but my son is definitely not one of them. And he is certainly not a bomb-thrower. I know that you have always shared my publication's view that a selective exposure to the harsher realities makes for better consumers. (I'm thinking of that little snafu in data-traffic in the Albany Grid last summer.) I hope you'll see your way clear to trusting me again. I repeat: there's not the slightest indication that my son was going over to the Blacks. In fact, I have good reason to believe that he will turn up quite soon, with all discrepancies accounted for. But I need a little time. A Missing Persons Bulletin would only make things harder at the moment. I realize it was my wife who initiated the complaint. But I'd greatly appreciate it if she got misfiled for 48 hours. I'll handle any static on this side. Discreetly, Ray

TO: Stock, Ex-Ed., *I.I.*
FROM: Senter
ENCLOSED: Background tape; interview with Antonia Cross, age 19, Reception Deacon, Jerusalem West. Edited Transcript, July 2.

Q: (I waited silently for her to take the lead.)

A: Before we begin, I think we better get a few things straight. It'll save time and grief in the long run. First of all, despite what your magazine and others may have said in the past, we never proselytize. Never. So please don't use that word. We just try to live our Gift—and if other people are drawn to us, that's the work of the Father and Mother, not us. We don't have to preach. When someone's sitting in filth up to his neck he doesn't need a preacher to tell him he smells. All he needs to hear is that there's a cleaner place somewhere. Second, we don't prevent anyone from leaving, despite all rumors to the contrary. We've had exactly three apostates in the last four years. They found out their wheels were not our wheels and they left.

Q: Give me their names.

A: There's no law that says we have to disclose the names of backsliders. Find them yourself. That shouldn't be too hard, now that they're plugged back in to the Big Board.

Q: You overestimate the power of the press.

A: False modesty is not considered a virtue among Shakers.

Q: You mentioned three backsliders. How many applicants are turned away before taking final vows?

A: The exact percentage is immaterial. Some applicants are more serious than others. There is no great mystery about our reception procedure. You've heard the expression, "Weekend Shakers." Anybody can buy the gear and dance and sing and stay pure for a couple of days. It's even considered a "jolt," I'm told. We make sure that those who come to us know the difference between a weekend and a lifetime. We explain the Gift, the Creed, the Articles of Faith. Then we ask them why they've come to us. We press them pretty hard. In the end, if they're still serious, they are sent to Preparative Meeting for a while, until a Family is ready to accept them.

Q: How long is a while?

A: Preparative Meeting can take days or weeks. Or longer.

Q: Are they considered full-fledged Shakers during that time?

A: The moment of Induction is a spiritual, not a temporal, phenomenon.

Q: But you notify the authorities only after a recruit is accepted in a Family?

A: We comply with all the requirements of the Full Disclosure Law.

Q: What if the recruit is underage and lies about it? Do you run a routine DNA check?

A: We obey the law.

Q: But a recruit at a Prep Meeting isn't a Shaker and so you don't have to report his presence. Is that right?

A: We've had exactly nine complaints filed against us in four years. Not one has stuck.

Q: Then you do delay acceptance until you can trace a recruit's identity?

A: I didn't say that. We believe in each person's right to redefine his set, no matter what the Big Board may say about him. But such administrative details tend to work themselves out.

Q: How? I don't understand.

A: The ways of the Father and Mother sometimes passeth understanding.

Q: You say you don't proselytize, but isn't that what your tapes are— a form of preaching? Don't most of your recruits come to you because of the tapes? And don't most of them have to be brought down from whatever they're hooked on before you'll even let them in?

A: The world—your world—is filth. From top to bottom. We try to stay as far away as we can. But we have to eat. So we sell you our tapes and our Shakerbikes. There's a calculated risk of contamination. But it works the other way too. Filth can be contaminated by purity. That's known as Salvation. It's like a tug of war. We'll see who takes the greatest risk.

Q: That's what I'm here for—to see at first hand. Where is the Jerusalem West Preparative Meeting held?

A: Preparative Meetings are private. For the protection of all concerned.

Q: Don't you mean secret? Isn't there something going on at these meetings that you don't want the public to know?

A: If the public is ignorant of the life of the spirit, that is hardly our fault.

Q: Some people believe that your recruits are "prepared" with drugs or electro-conditioning.

A: Some people think that Shaker stew is full of saltpeter. Are you going to print that, too?

Q: You have been accused of brain-tampering. That's a serious charge. And unless I get a hell of a lot more cooperation from you than I've been getting I will have to assume that you have something serious to hide.

A: No one ever said you'd be free to see everything. You'll just have to accept our—guidance—in matters concerning religious propriety.

Q: Let me give you a little guidance, Miss Cross. You people already have so many enemies in that filthy world you despise that one unfriendly story from *I.I.* might just tip the scales.

A: The power of the press? We'll take our chances.

Q: What will you do if the police crack down?

A: We're not afraid to die. And the Control authorities have found that it's more trouble than it's worth to put us in jail. We seem to upset the other inmates.

Q: Miss Cross—

A: We use no titles here. My name is Antonia.

Q: You're obviously an intelligent, dedicated young woman. I would rather work with you than against you. Why don't we try to find some middle ground? As a journalist my primary concern is human nature—what happens to a young recruit in the process of becoming a full-fledged Shaker. You won't let me into a Prep Meeting to see for myself. All right, you have your reasons, and I respect them. But I ask you to respect mine. If I can look through your Reception files—just the last two or three weeks will do—I should be able to get some idea of what kind of raw material you draw on. You can remove the names, of course.

A: Perhaps we can provide a statistical breakdown for you.

Q: I don't want statistics. I want to look at their pictures, listen to their voices—you say you press them pretty hard in the first interview. That's what I need: their responses under pressure, the difference between those who stick it through and those who don't.

A: How do we know you're not looking for something of a personal nature—to embarrass us?

Q: For God's sakes, I'm one of the best-known tapemen in the Federation. Why not just give me the benefit of the doubt?

A: You invoke a Deity that means nothing to you.

Q: I'm sorry.
A: The only thing I can do is transmit your request to the Octave itself. Any decision on such a matter would have to come from a Full Business Meeting.
Q: How long will it take?
A: The Octave is meeting tomorrow, before Evening Service.
Q: All right. I can wait till then. I suppose I should apologize again for losing my temper. I'm afraid it's an occupational hazard.
A: We all have our Gift.

MORE TO COME

TO: Stock, Ex-Ed., *I.I.*
FROM: Senter
ENCLOSED: First add on Shaker Revival; July 3.

It is unclear whether the eight teenagers—six boys and two girls—who banded together one fateful evening in the spring of 1991 to form a jag-rock combo called The Shakers had any idea of the religious implications of the name. According to one early account in *Riff* magazine, the original eight were thinking only of a classic rock-and-roll number of the nineteen fifties *Shake, Rattle and Roll* (a title not without sexual as well as musicological overtones). On the other hand, there is evidence that Harry G was interested in astrology, palmistry, scientology and other forms of modern occultism even before he left home at the age of fifteen. (Harry G was born Harry Guardino, on December eighteen, nineteen seventy-four, in Schoodic, Maine, the son of a third-generation lobster fisherman.) Like many members of his generation he applied for a Federal Travel Grant on graduation from Modular School and received a standard two-year contract. But unlike most of his fellow-bummers, Harry did not immediately take off on an all-expenses-paid tour of the seamier side of life in the North American Federation. Instead, he hitched a ride to New York City, where he established a little basement coop on the lower west side that soon became a favorite way-station for other, more restless bummers passing through the city. No reliable account of this period is available. The rumors that he dabbled in a local Bomb-throwers cell appear to be unfounded. But it is known that sometime during the spring of nineteen ninety-one a group of bummers nearing the end of their grants gathered in Harry G's coop to discuss the future. By coincidence or design the eight young people who came together that night from the far corners of the Federation all played some instrument and shared a passion for jag-rock. And as they talked and argued among themselves about the best way possible to "plug into the Big Board," it slowly began to dawn on them that perhaps their destinies were linked—or, as Harry G himself has put it, "We felt we could make beautiful music together. Time has made us one."

Building a reputation in the jag-rock market has never been easy —not even with divine intervention. For the next two months, The Shakers scrambled for work, playing a succession of one-night stands in consumers' centers, schools, fraternal lodges—wherever someone wanted live entertainment and was willing to put the group up. The Shakers traveled in a second-hand Chevrolet van which was kept running only by the heroic efforts of the group's electric-oud player, Richard Fitzgerald (who later—as Richard F—helped to design the improved version of the turbo-adapter which forms the basis of to-day's Shakerbike.)

On the night of June the first the group arrived in Hancock, Massachusetts, where they were scheduled to play the next evening at the graduation dance of the Grady L. Parker Modular School. They had not worked for three days and their finances had reached a most precarious stage—they were now sharing only four bummer-grants between them, the other four contracts having expired in the previous weeks. From the very beginning of their relationship the eight had gone everywhere and done everything as a group—they even insisted on sleeping together in one room on the theory that the "bad vibrations" set up by an overnight absence from each other might adversely affect their music. As it turned out, there was no room large enough at the local Holiday Inn, so, after some lengthy negotiations, the Modular School principal arranged for them to camp out on the grounds of the local Shaker Museum, a painstaking restoration of an early New England Shaker community dating back to seventeen ninety. Amused but not unduly impressed by the coincidence in names, the eight Shakers bedded down for the night within sight of the Museum's most famous structure, the Round Stone Barn erected by the original Shakers in eighteen twenty-six. Exactly what happened between midnight and dawn on that fog-shrouded New England meadow may never be known—the validation of mystical experience being by its very nature a somewhat inexact science. Accord-

ing to Shaker testimony, however, the spirit of Mother Ann, sainted
foundress of the original sect, touched the Gifts of the eight where
they lay and in a vision of the future—which Amelia D later said was
"as clear and bright as a holograph"—revealed why they had been
chosen: The time had come for a mass revival of Shaker beliefs and
practices. The eight teenagers awoke at the same instant, compared
visions, found them to be identical and wept together for joy. They
spent the rest of the day praying for guidance and making plans. Their
first decision was to play as scheduled at the Grady L. Parker graduation dance.

"We decided to go on doing just what we had been doing—only
more so," Amelia D later explained. "Also, I guess, we needed the
jacks."

Whatever the reason, the group apparently played as never before.
Their music opened up doors to whole new ways of hearing and feeling—or so it seemed to the excited crowd of seniors who thronged
around the bandstand when the first set was over. Without any pre-
meditation, or so he later claimed, Harry Guardino stood up and
announced the new Shaker dispensation, including the Believers'
Creed (the Four Noes) and a somewhat truncated version of the
Articles of Faith of the United Society of Believers (Revived): "All
things must be kept decent and in good order," "Diversity in Uniformity," and "Work is Play." According to the Hancock newspaper,
seventeen members of the senior class left town that morning with
the Shakers—in three cars "borrowed" from parents and later returned. Drawn by a Gift of Travel, the little band of pilgrims made
their way to the quiet corner of New York State now known as Jerusalem West, bought some land—with funds obtained from anonymous
benefactors—and settled down to their strange experiment in monastic
and ascetic communism.

The actual historical connections between Old Shakers and New
Shakers remains a matter of conjecture. It is not clear, for instance,
whether Harry G and his associates had a chance to consult the documentary material on display at the Hancock Museum. There is no
doubt that the First Article of Faith of the Shaker Revival is a word-
for-word copy of the first part of an early Shaker motto. But it has
been given a subtly different meaning in present-day usage. And while
many of the New Shaker doctrines and practices can be traced to the
general tenor of traditional Shakerism, the adaptations are often quite

free and sometimes wildly capricious. All in all, the Shaker Revival seems to be very much a product of our own time. Some prominent evolutionists even see it as part of a natural process of weeding out those individuals incapable of becoming fully consuming members of the Abundant Society. They argue that Shakerism is a definite improvement, in this respect, over the youthful cult of Bomb-throwers which had to be suppressed in the early days of the Federation.

But there are other observers who see a more ominous trend at work. They point especially to the serious legal questions raised by the Shaker's efforts at large-scale proselytization. The twenty-seventh Amendment to the Federal Constitution guarantees the right of each white citizen over the age of fifteen to the free and unrestricted enjoyment of his own senses, provided that enjoyment does not interfere with the range or intensity of any other citizen's sensual enjoyment. Presumably this protection also extends to the right of any white citizen to deny himself the usual pleasures. But what is the status of corporate institutions that engage in such repression? How binding, for example, is the Shaker recruit's sworn allegiance to the Believers' Creed? How are the Four Noes enforced within the sect? Suppose two Shakers find themselves physically attracted to each other and decide to consummate—does the United Society of Believers have any right to place obstacles between them? These are vital questions that have yet to be answered by the Control authorities. But there are influential men in Washington who read the twenty-seventh amendment as an obligation on the government's part not merely to protect the individual's right to sensual pleasure but also to help him maximate it. And in the eyes of these broad constructionists the Shakers are on shaky ground.

TO: Stock, Ex-Ed., *I.I.*
FROM: Senter
(WARNING: CONFIDENTIAL UNEDITED TAPE: NOT FOR PUBLICATION: CONTENTS WILL POWDER IF OPENED IMPROPERLY)

FIRST VOICE: Bruce? Is that you?
SECOND VOICE: It's me.
FIRST: For God's sake, come in! Shut the door. My God, I thought you were locked up in that Prep Meeting. I thought—

SECOND: It's not a prison. When I heard you were prowling around town I knew I had to talk to you.

FIRST: You've changed your mind then?

SECOND: Don't believe it. I just wanted to make sure you didn't lie about everything.

FIRST: Do they know you're here?

SECOND: No one followed me, if that's what you mean. No one even knows who I am. I've redefined my set, as we say.

FIRST: But they check. They're not fools. They'll find out soon enough—if they haven't already.

SECOND: They don't check. That's another lie. And anyway, I'll tell them myself after Induction.

FIRST: Brucie—it's not too late. We want you to come home.

SECOND: You can tell Arlene that her little baby is safe and sound. How is she? Blubbering all over herself as usual?

FIRST: She's pretty broken up about your running away.

SECOND: Why? Is she worried they'll cut off her credit at the feel-o-mat? For letting another potential consumer get off the hook?

FIRST: You wouldn't have risked coming to me if you didn't have doubts. Don't make a terrible mistake.

SECOND: I came to see you because I know how you can twist other people's words. Are you recording this?

FIRST: Yes.

SECOND: Good. I'm asking you straight out—please leave us alone.

FIRST: Do you know they're tampering with your mind?

SECOND: Have you tasted your local drinking water lately?

FIRST: Come home with me.

SECOND: I am home.

FIRST: You haven't seen enough of the world to turn your back on it.

SECOND: I've seen you and Arlene.

FIRST: And is our life so awful?

SECOND: What you and Arlene have isn't life. It's the American Dream Come True. You're in despair and don't even know it. That's the worst kind.

FIRST: You repeat the slogans as if you believed them.

SECOND: What makes you think I don't?

FIRST: You're my flesh and blood. I know you.

SECOND: You don't. All you know is that your little pride and joy ran away to become a monk and took the family genes. And

Arlene is too old to go back to the Big Board and beg for seconds.

FIRST: Look—I know a little something about rebellion, too. I've had a taste of it in my time. It's healthy, it's natural—I'm all for it. But not an overdose. When the jolt wears off, you'll be stuck here. And you're too smart to get trapped in a hole like this.

SECOND: It's my life, isn't it? In exactly one hour and ten minutes I'll be free, white and fifteen—Independence Day, right? What a beautiful day to be born—it's the nicest thing you and Arlene did for me.

FIRST: Brucie, we want you back. Whatever you want—just name it and if it's in my power I'll try to get it. I have friends who will help.

SECOND: I don't want anything from you. We're quits—can't you understand? The only thing we have in common now is this: (SOUND OF HEAVY BREATHING). That's it. And if you want that back you can take it. Just hold your hand over my mouth and pinch my nose for about five minutes. That should do it.

FIRST: How can you joke about it?

SECOND: Why not? Haven't you heard? There're only two ways to go for my generation—The Shakers or the Ghetto. How do you think I'd look in black-face with bushy hair and a gorilla nose? Or do you prefer my first choice?

FIRST: I'm warning you, the country's not going to put up with either much longer. There's going to be trouble—and I want you out of here when it comes.

SECOND: What are the feebies going to do? Finish our job for us?

FIRST: Is that what you want then? To commit suicide?

SECOND: Not exactly. That's what the Bomb-throwers did. We want to commit your suicide.

FIRST: (Words unintelligible.)

SECOND: That really jolts you, doesn't it? You talk about rebellion as if you knew something about it because you wore beads once and ran around holding signs.

FIRST: We changed history.

SECOND: You didn't change anything. You were swallowed up, just like the Bomb-throwers. The only difference is, you were eaten alive.

FIRST: Bruce—

SECOND: Can you stretch the gray-stuff a little, and try to imagine

what real rebellion would be like? Not just another chorus of
"gimme, gimme, gimme—" But the absolute negation of what's
come before? The Four Noes all rolled up into One Big No!
FIRST: Brucie—I'll make a deal—
SECOND: No one's ever put it all together before. I don't expect
you to see it. Even around here, a lot of people don't know what's
happening. Expiation! That's what rebellion is all about. The
young living down the sins of the fathers and mothers! But the
young are always so hungry for life they get distracted before they
can finish the job. Look at all the poor, doomed rebels in history:
whenever they got too big to be crushed the feebies bought them
off with a piece of the action. The stick or the carrot and then—
business as usual. Your generation was the biggest sellout of all.
But the big laugh is, you really thought you won. So now you
don't have any carrot left to offer, because you've already shared
it all with us—before we got old. And we're strong enough to
laugh at your sticks. Which is why the world is going to find out
for the first time what total rebellion is.
FIRST: I thought you didn't believe in violence and hate?
SECOND: Oh, our strength is not of this world. You can forget all
the tapes and bikes and dances—that's the impure shell that must
be sloughed off. If you want to get the real picture, just imagine
us—all your precious little gene-machines—standing around in a
circle, our heads bowed in prayer, holding our breaths and click-
ing off one by one. Don't you think that's a beautiful way for your
world to end? Not with a bang or a whimper—but with one long
breathless Amen?

MORE TO COME

TO: Stock, Ex-Ed., *I.I.*
FROM: Senter
ENCLOSED: New first add on "Shaker Revival" (scratch earlier
transmission; new lead upcoming).

JERUSALEM WEST, N.Y., Wednesday, July 4—An early critic of
the Old Shakers, a robust pamphleteer who had actually been a member of the sect for ten months, wrote this prophetic appraisal of his
former cohorts in the year seventeen eighty-two: "When we consider
the infant state of civil power in America since the Revolution began,

every infringement on the natural rights of humanity, every effort to undermine our original constitution, either in civil or ecclesiastical order, saps the foundation of Independency."

That winter, the Shaker foundress, Mother Ann, was seized in Petersham, Massachusetts, by a band of vigilantes who, according to a contemporary account, wanted "to find out whether she was a woman or not." Various other Shaker leaders were horsewhipped, thrown in jail, tarred and feathered and driven out of one New England town after another by an aroused citizenry. These severe persecutions, which lasted through the turn of the century, were the almost inevitable outcome of a clash between the self-righteous, unnatural, uncompromising doctrines of the Shakers—and the pragmatic, democratic, forward-looking mentality of the struggling new nation, which would one day be summed up in that proud emblem: The American Way of Life.

This conflict is no less sharp today. So far the New Shakers have generally been given the benefit of the doubt as just another harmless fringe group. But there is evidence that the mood of the country is changing—and rapidly. Leading educators and political figures, respected clergymen and prominent consumer consultants have all become more outspoken in denouncing the disruptive effect of this new fanaticism on the country as a whole. Not since the heyday of the Bomb-throwers in the late Seventies has a single issue shown such potential for galvanizing informed public opinion. And a chorus of distraught parents has only just begun to make itself heard—like the lamentations of Rachel in the wilderness.

Faced with the continuing precariousness of the international situation, and the unresolved dilemma of the Ghettoes, some Control authorities have started talking about new restrictions on all monastic sects—not out of any desire to curtail religious freedom but in an effort to preserve the constitutional guarantees of free expression and consumption. Some feel that if swift, firm governmental action is not forthcoming it will get harder and harder to prevent angry parents—and others with legitimate grievances—from taking the law into their own hands.

MORE TO COME

Arnold Toynbee has pointed out that the decadence of a great culture is usually accompanied by the rise of a new World Church which extends hope to the domestic proletariat while serving the needs of a new warrior class. School seems eminently suited to be the World Church of our decaying culture. No institution could better veil from its participants the deep discrepancy between social principles and social reality in today's world. Secular, scientific, and death-denying, it is of a piece with the modern mood.

—Ivan Illich, in *The New York Review of Books*

AMERICA THE BEAUTIFUL
by Fritz Leiber

I am returning to England. I am shorthanding this, July 5, 2000, aboard the Dallas-London rocket as it arches silently out of the diffused violet daylight of the stratosphere into the eternally star-spangled purpling night of the ionosphere.

I have refused the semester instructorship in poetry at UTD, which would have munificently padded my honorarium for delivering the Lanier Lectures and made me for four months second only to the Poet in Residence.

And I am almost certain that I have lost Emily, although we plan to meet in London in a fortnight if she can wangle the stopover on her way to take up her Peace Corps command in Niger.

I am not leaving America because of the threat of a big war. I believe that this new threat, like all the rest, is only another move, even if a long and menacing queen's move, in the game of world politics, while the little wars go endlessly on in Chad, Czechoslovakia, Sumatra, Siam, Baluchistan, and Bolivia as America and the Communist League firm their power boundaries.

And I am certainly not leaving America because of any harassment as a satellitic neutral and possible spy. There may have been surveillance of my actions and lectures, but if so it was as impalpable as the checks they must have made on me in England before granting me visiting clearance. The U.S. intelligence agencies have become almost incredibly deft in handling such things. And I was entertained in America more than royally—I was made to feel at home by a family with a great talent for just that.

No, I am leaving because of the shadows. The shadows everywhere in America, but which I saw most clearly in Professor Grissim's serene and lovely home. The shadows which would irresistibly have gathered behind my instructor's lectern, precisely as I was learning to dress with an even trimmer and darker reserve while I was a guest at the Grissims' and even to shower more frequently. The shadows which revealed themselves to me deepest of all around Emily Grissim, and which I could do nothing to dispel.

I think that you, or at least I, can see the shadows in America more readily these days because of the very clean air there. Judging only from what I saw with my own eyes in Texas, the Americans have completely licked their smog problem. Their gently curving freeways purr with fast electric cars, like sleek and disciplined silver cats. Almost half the nation's power comes from atomic reactors, while the remaining coal-burning plants loose back into the air at most a slight shimmer of heat. Even the streams and rivers run blue and unsmirched again, while marine life is returning to the eastern Great Lakes. In brief, America is beautiful, for with the cleanliness, now greater than that of the Dutch, has come a refinement in taste, so that all buildings are gracefully shaped and disposed, while advertisements, though molding minds more surely than ever, are restrained and almost finically inoffensive.

The purity of the atmosphere was strikingly brought to my notice when I debarked at Dallas rocketport and found the Grissims waiting for me outdoors, downwind of the landing area. They made a striking group, all of them tall, as they stood poised yet familiarly together: the professor with his grizzled hair still close-trimmed in military fashion, for he had served almost as long as a line officer and in space services as he had now as a university physicist; his slim, white-haired wife; Emily, like her mother in the classic high-waisted, long-skirted

Directoire style currently fashionable; and her brother Jack, in his dress pale grays with sergeant's stripes, on furlough from Siam.

Their subdued dress and easy attitudes reminded me of a patrician Roman's toga dropping in precise though seemingly accidental folds. The outworn cliché about America being Rome to England's Greece came irritatingly to my mind.

Introductions were made by the professor, who had met my father at Oxford and later seen much of him during the occupation of Britain throughout the Three Years' Alert. I was surprised to find their diction almost the same as my own. We strolled to their electric station wagon, the doors of which opened silently at our approach.

I should have been pleased by the simple beauty of the Grissims, as by that of the suburban landscape through which we now sped, especially since my poetry is that of the Romantic Revival, which looks back to Keats and Shelley more even than to Shakespeare. Instead, it rubbed me the wrong way. I became uneasy and within ten minutes found myself beginning to talk bawdy and make nasty little digs at America.

They accepted my rudeness in such an unshocked, urbane fashion, demonstrating that they understood though did not always agree with me, and they went to such trouble to assure me that not all America was like this, there were still many ugly stretches, that I soon felt myself a fool and shut up. It was I who was the crass Roman, I told myself, or even barbarian.

Thereafter Emily and her mother kept the conversation going easily and soon coaxed me back into it, with the effect of smoothing the grumbling and owlish young British poet's ruffled feathers.

The modest one story, shaded by slow-shedding silvery eucalyptus and mutated chaparral, which was all that showed of the Grissim home, opened to receive our fumeless vehicle. I was accompanied to my bedroom-and-study, served refreshments, and left there to polish up my first lecture. The scene in the view window was so faithfully transmitted from the pickup above, the air fresher if possible than that outdoors, that I found it hard to keep in mind I was well underground.

It was at dinner that evening, when my hosts made such a nicely concerted effort to soothe my nervousness over my initial lecture, and largely succeeded, that I first began truly to like and even respect the Grissims.

It was at the same instant, in that pearly dining room, that I first became aware of the shadows around them.

Physical shadows? Hardly, though at times they really seemed that. I recall thinking, my mind still chiefly on my lecture, something like, *These good people are so wedded to the way of war, the perpetual little wars and the threat of the big one, and have been so successful in masking the signs of its strains in themselves, that they have almost forgotten that those strains are there. And they love their home and country, and the security of their taut way of life, so deeply that they have become unaware of the depth of that devotion.*

My lecture went off well that night. The audience was large, respectful, and seemingly even attentive. The number of African and Mexican faces gave the lie to what I'd been told about integration being a sham in America. I should have been pleased, and I temporarily was, at the long, mutedly drumming applause I was given and at the many intelligent, flattering comments I received afterward. And I should have stopped seeing the shadows then, but I didn't.

Next morning Emily toured me around city and countryside on a long silvery scooter, I riding pillion behind her. I remember the easy though faintly formal way in which she drew my arms around her waist and laid her hand for a moment on one of mine, meanwhile smiling cryptically over-shoulder. Besides that smile, I remember a charming Spanish-American graveyard in pastel stucco, the towering Kennedy shrine, the bubbling, iridescent tubes of algae farming converging toward the horizon, and rockets taking off in the distance with their bright, smokeless exhausts. Emily was almost as unaffected as a British girl and infinitely more competent, in a grand style. That one day the shadows vanished altogether.

They returned at evening when after dinner we gathered in the living room for our first wholly unhurried and relaxed conversation, my lectures being spaced out in a leisurely—to Americans, not to me— one day in two schedule.

We sat in a comfortable arc before the wide fireplace, where resinous woods burned yellow and orange. Occasionally Jack would put on another log. From time to time, a light shower of soot dropped back from the precipitron in the chimney, the tiny particles as they fell flaring into brief white points of light, like stars.

A little to my surprise, the Grissims drank as heavily as the English, though they carried their liquor very well. Emily was the exception to this family pattern, contenting herself with a little sherry and three long, slim reefers, which she drew from an elegant foil package covered with gold script and Lissajous curves, and which she inhaled sippingly, her lips rapidly shuddering with a very faint, low, trilling sound.

Professor Grissim set the pattern by deprecating the reasons for America's domestic achievements, which I had led off by admitting were far greater than I'd expected. They weren't due to any peculiar American drive, he said, and certainly not to any superior moral fiber, but simply to technology and computerized civilization given their full head and unstinting support. The powerful sweep of those two almost mathematical forces had automatically solved such problems as overpopulation, by effortless and aesthetic contraception, and stagnant or warped brain potential, by unlimited semiautomated education and psychiatry—just as on a smaller scale the drug problem had largely been resolved by the legalization of marijuana and peyote, following the simple principle of restricting only the sale of quickly addictive chemicals and those provably damaging to nervous tissue— "Control the poisons, but let each person learn to control his intoxicants, especially now that we have metabolic rectifiers for the congenitally alcoholic."

I was also told that American extremism, both of the right and left, which had seemed such a big thing in mid-century, had largely withered away or at least been muted by the great surge of the same forces which were making America ever more beautiful and prosperous. Cities were no longer warrens of discontent. Peace marches and Minutemen rallies alike, culminating in the late sixties, had thereafter steadily declined.

While impressed, I did not fall into line, but tried to point out some black holes in this glowing picture. Indeed, feeling at home with the Grissims now and having learned that nothing I could say would shock them into anger and confusion, I was able to be myself fully and to reveal frankly my anti-American ideas, though of course more politely and, I hoped, more tellingly than yesterday—it seemed an age ago—driving from the rocketport.

In particular, I argued that many or most Americans were motivated by a subtle, even sophisticated puritanism, which made them feel that the world was not safe unless they were its moral arbiters, and that this puritanism was ultimately based on the same swollen concern about property and money—industry, in its moral sense—

that one found in the Swiss and Scottish Presbyterians and most of
the early Protestants.

"You're puritans with a great deal of style and restraint and wide
vision," I said. "Yet you're puritans just the same, even though your
puritanism is light-years away from that of the Massachusetts theo-
crats and the harsh rule Calvin tried to impose on Geneva. In fact," I
added uncautiously, "your puritanism is not so much North European
as Roman."

Smiles crinkled briefly at that and I kicked myself for having myself introduced into the conversation that hackneyed comparison.

At this point Emily animatedly yet coolly took up the argument
for America, pointing out the nation's growing tolerance and aestheti-
cism, historically distinguishing Puritanism from Calvinism, and also
reminding me that the Chinese and Russians were far more puritani-
cal than any other peoples on the globe—and not in a sophisticated
or subtle way either.

I fought back, as by citing the different impression I'd got of the
Russians during my visits in the Soviet Union and by relaying the
reports of close colleagues who had spent time in China. But on
the whole Emily had the best of me. And this was only partly due to
the fact that the longer I sparred with her verbally, the less concerned
I became to win my argument, and the more to break her calm and
elicit some sharp emotional reaction from her, to see that pale skin
flush, to make those reefer-serene eyes blaze with anger. But I wasn't
successful there either.

At one point Jack came to her aid, mildly demonstrating for American broad-mindedness by describing to us some of the pleasure cities
of southern Asia he'd visited on R.&R.

"Bangkok's a dismal place now, of course," he began by admitting,
"with the Com-g'rillas raiding up to and even into it, and full of
fenced-off bombed and booby-trapped areas. Very much like the old
descriptions of Saigon in the sixties. As you walk down the potholed
streets, you listen for the insect hum of a wandering antipersonnel
missile seeking human heat, or the faint flap-flap of an infiltrator coming down on a whirligig parachute. You brace your thoughts against
the psychedelic strike of a mind-bomb. Out of the black alley ahead
there may charge a fifty-foot steel centipede, the remote-controlled
sort we use for jungle fighting, captured by the enemy and jiggered to
renegade.

"But most of old Bangkok's attractive features—and the entrepreneurs and girls and other entertainers that go with them—have been transferred en masse to Kandy and Trincomalee in Ceylon." And he went on to describe the gaily orgiastic lounges and bars, the fresh pastel colors, the spicy foods and subtly potent drinks, the clean little laughing harlots supporting their families well during the ten years of their working life between fifteen and twenty-five, the gilded temples, the slim dancers with movements stylized as their black eyebrows, the priests robed in orange and yellow.

I tried to fault him in my mind for being patronizing, but without much success.

"Buddhism's an attractive way of life," he finished, "except that it doesn't know how to wage war. But if you're looking only for nirvana, I guess you don't need to know that." For an instant his tough face grew bleak, as if he could do with a spot of nirvana himself, and the shadows gathered around him and the others more thickly.

During the following off-lecture evenings we kept up our fireplace talks and Emily and I returned more than once to our debate over puritanism, while the rest listened to us with faint, benevolent smiles, that at times seemed almost knowing. She regularly defeated me.

Then on the sixth night she delivered her crowning argument, or celebrated her victory, or perhaps merely followed an impulse. I had just settled myself in bed when the indirect lightning of my "doorbell" flooded the room with brief flashes, coming at three-second intervals, of a rather ghastly white light. Blinking, I fumbled on the bedside table for the remote control of the room's appliances, including tri-V and door, and thumbed the button for the latter.

The door moved aside and there, silhouetted against the faint glow of the hall, was the dark figure of Emily, like a living shadow. She kept her finger, however, on the button long enough for two more silent flashes to illuminate her briefly. She was wearing a narrow kimono—Jack's newest gift, she later told me—and her platinum hair, combed straight down like an unrippling waterfall, almost exactly matched the silvery, pale gray silk. Without quite overdoing it, she had made up her face somewhat like a temple dancer's—pale powder, almost white; narrow slanting brows, almost black; green eye shadow with a pinch of silvery glitter, and the not-quite-jarring sensual note of crimson lips.

She did not come into my room, but after a pause during which I sat up jerkily and she became again a shadow, she beckoned to me.

I snatched up my dressing gown and followed her as she moved noiselessly down the hall. My throat was dry and constricted, my heart was pounding a little, with apprehension as well as excitement. I realized that despite my near week with the Grissims, a part of my mind was still thinking of the professor and his wife as a strait-laced colonel and his lady from a century ago, when so many retired army officers lived in villas around San Antonio, as they do now too around the Dallas-Fort Worth metropolitan area.

Emily's bedroom was not the austere silver cell or self-shrine I had sometimes imagined, especially when she was scoring a point against me, but an almost cluttered museum-workshop of present interests and personal memorabilia. She'd even kept her kindergarten study-machine, her first CO_2 pistol, and a hockey stick, along with momentos from her college days and her Peace Corps tours.

But those I noticed much later. Now pale golden light from a rising full moon, coming through the great view window, brimmed the room. I had just enough of my wits left to recall that the real moon was new, so that this must be a tape of some past night. I never even thought of the Communist and American forts up there, with their bombs earmarked for Earth. Then, standing straight and tall and looking me full in the eyes, like some Amazonian athlete, or Phryne before her judges, Emily let her kimono glide down from her shoulders.

In the act of love she was energetic, but tender. No, the word is courteous, I think. I very happily shed a week of tensions and un-certainties and self-inflicted humiliations.

"You still think I'm a puritan, don't you?" she softly asked me afterward, smiling at me sideways with the smeared remains of her crimson mouth, her gray eyes enigmatic blurs of shadow.

"Yes, I do," I told her forthrightly. "The puritan playing the hetaera, but still the puritan."

She answered lazily, "I think you like to play the Hun raping the vestal virgin."

That made me talk dirty to her. She listened attentively—almost famishedly, I thought, for a bit—but her final comment was "You do that very well, dear," just before using her lips to stop mine, which would otherwise have sulphurously cursed her insufferable poise.

Next morning I started to write a poem about her but got lost in analysis and speculation. Tried too soon, I thought.

Although they were as gracious and friendly as ever, I got the impression that the other Grissims had quickly become aware of the change in Emily's and my relationship. Perhaps it was that they

M

showed a slight extra fondness toward me. I don't know how they guessed—Emily was as cool as always in front of them, while I kept trying to play myself, as before. Perhaps it was that the argument about puritanism was never resumed.

Two evenings afterward the talk came around to Jack's and Emily's elder brother Jeff, who had fallen during the Great Retreat from Jammu and Kashmir to Baluchistan. It was mentioned that during his last furlough they had been putting up an exchange instructor from Yugoslavia, a highly talented young sculptress. I gathered that she and Jeff had been quite close.

"I'm glad Jeff knew her love," Emily's mother said calmly, a tear behind her voice, though not on her cheeks. "I'm very glad he had that." The professor unobtrusively put his hand on hers.

I fancied that this remark was directed at me and was her way of giving her blessing to Emily's and my affair. I was touched and at the same time irritated—and also irritated at myself for feeling irritated. Her remark had brought back the shadows, which darkened further when Jack said a touch grimly and for once with a soldier's callousness, though grinning at me to remove any possible offense, "Remember not to board any more lady artists or professors, Mother, at least when I'm on leave. Bad luck."

By now I was distinctly bothered by my poetry block. The last lectures were going swimmingly and I ought to have been feeling creative, but I wasn't. Or rather, I was feeling creative but I couldn't create. I had also begun to notice the way I was fitting myself to the Grissim family—muting myself, despite all the easiness among us. I couldn't help wondering if there weren't a connection between the two things. I had received the instructorship offer, but was delaying my final answer.

After we made love together that night—under a sinking crescent moon, the real night this time, repeated from above—I told Emily about my first trouble only. She pressed my hand. "Never stop writing poetry, dear," she said. "America needs poetry. This family—"

That broken sentence was as close as we ever got to talking about marriage. Emily immediately recovered herself with an uncharacteristically ribald "Cheer up. I don't even charge a poem for admission."

Instead of responding to that cue, I worried my subject. "I should be able to write poetry here," I said. "America is beautiful, the great golden apple of the Hesperides, hanging in the west like the setting sun. But there's a worm in the core of that apple, a great scaly black dragon."

When Emily didn't ask a question, I went on, "I remember an advertisement. 'Join all your little debts into one big debt.' Of course, they didn't put it so baldly, they made it sound wonderful. But you Americans are like that. You've collected all your angers into one big anger. You've removed your angers from things at home—where you seem to have solved your problems very well, I must admit—and directed those angers at the Communist League. Or instead of angers, I could say fears. Same thing."

Emily still didn't comment, so I continued, "Take the basic neurotic. He sets up a program of perfection for himself—a thousand obligations, a thousand ambitions. As long as he works his program, fulfilling those obligations and ambitions, he does very well. In fact, he's apt to seem like a genius of achievement to those around him, as America does to me. But there's one big problem he always keeps out of his program and buries deep in his unconscious—the question of who he really is and what he really wants—and in the end it always throws him."

Then at last Emily said, speaking softly at first, "There's something I should tell you, dear. Although I talk a lot of it from the top of my mind, deep down I loathe discussing politics and international relations. As my old colonel used to tell me, 'It doesn't matter much which side you fight on, Emily, so long as you have the courage to stand up and be counted. You pledge your life, your fortune, and your sacred honor, and you live up to that pledge!' And now, dear, I want to sleep."

Crouching on the edge of her bed before returning to my room, and listening to her breathing regularize itself, I thought, "Yes, you're looking for nirvana too. Like Jack." But I didn't wake her to say it, or any of the other things that were boiling up in my brain.

Yet the things I left unsaid must have stayed and worked in my mind, for at our next fireside talk—four pleasant Americans, one Englishman with only one more lecture to go—I found myself launched into a rather long account of the academic Russian family I stayed with while delivering the Pushkin Lectures in Leningrad, where the smog and the minorities problems have been licked too. I stressed the Rosanovs' gentility, their friendliness, the tolerance and sophistication which had replaced the old rigid insistence on *kulturny* behavior, and also the faint melancholy underlying and somehow vitiating all they said. In short, I did everything I knew to underline their similarity to the Grissims. I ended by saying, "Professor Grissim, the first night we talked, you said America's achievement had been due almost entirely to the sweep of science, technology, and computerized civilization. The people of the Communist League believe that too—in fact, they made their declaration of faith earlier than America."

"It's very strange," he mused, nodding. "So like, yet so unlike. Almost as if the chemical atoms of the East were subtly different from those of the West. The very electrons—"

"Professor, you don't actually think—"

"Of course not. A metaphor only."

But whatever he thought, I don't believe he felt it only as a metaphor.

Emily said sharply to me, "You left out one more similarity, the most important. That they hate the Enemy with all their hearts and will never trust or understand him."

I couldn't find an honest and complete answer to that, though I tried.

The next day I made one more attempt to turn my feelings into poetry, dark poetry, and I failed. I made my refusal of the instructorship final, confirmed my reservation on the Dallas-London rocket for day after tomorrow, and delivered the last of the Lanier Lectures.

The Fourth of July was a quiet day. Emily took me on a repeat of our first scooter jaunt, but although I relished the wind on my face and our conversation was passably jolly and tender, the magic was gone. I could hardly see America's beauty for the shadows my mind projected on it.

Our fireside conversation that night was as brightly banal. Midway we all went outside to watch the fireworks. It was a starry night, very clear of course, and the fireworks seemed vastly remote—transitory extra starfields of pink and green and amber. Their faint cracks and booms sounded infinitely distant, and needless to say, there was not a ribbon or whiff of chemical smoke. I was reminded of my last night in Leningrad with the Rosanovs after the Pushkin Lectures. We'd all strolled down the Kirovskiy Prospekt to the Bolshaya Neva, and across its glimmering waters watched the Vladivostok mail rocket take off from the Field of Mars up its ringed electric catapult taller far than the Eiffel Tower. That had been on a May Day.

Later that night I went for the first time by myself to Emily's door and pressed its light-button. I was afraid she wouldn't stop by for me and I needed her. She was in a taut and high-strung mood, unwilling to talk in much more than monosyllables, yet unable to keep still, pacing like a restless feline. She wanted to play in the view window the tape of a real battle in Bolivia with the original sounds too, muted down. I vetoed that and we settled for an authentic forest fire recorded in Alaska.

Sex and catastrophe fit. With the wild red light pulsing and flaring in the bedroom, casting huge wild shadows, and with the fire's muted roar and hurricane crackle and explosions filling our ears, we made love with a fierce and desperate urgency that seemed almost—I am eternally grateful for the memory—as if it would last forever. Sex and a psychedelic trip also have their meeting point.

Afterward I slept like a sated tiger. Emily waited until dawn to wake me and shoo me back to my bedroom.

Next day all the Grissims saw me off. As we strolled from the silver station wagon to the landing area, Emily and I dropped a little behind. She stopped, hooked her arms around me, and kissed me with a devouring ferocity. The others walked on, too well bred ever to look back. The next moment she was her cool self again, sipping a reefer.

Now the rocketship is arching down. The stars are paling. There is a faint whistling as the air molecules of the stratosphere begin to carom off the titanium skin. We had only one flap, midway of freefall section of the trip, when we briefly accelerated and then decelerated to match, perhaps in order to miss a spy satellite or one of the atomic-headed watchdog rockets eternally circling the globe. The direction comes, "Secure seat harnesses."

"I just don't know. Maybe I should have gone to America drunk as Dylan Thomas, but purposefully, bellowing my beliefs like the word or the thunderbolts of God. Maybe then I could have fought the shadows. No. . . .

I hope Emily makes it to London. Perhaps there, against a very different background, with shadows of a different sort . . .

In a few more seconds the great jet will begin to brake, thrusting its hygienic, aseptic exhaust of helium down into the filthy cancerous London smog, and I will be home.